Sniper

A Detective Al Warner Suspense
by
George A Bernstein

Award-Winning Amazon Top 100 Author

GnD Publishing LLC

GnD Publishing LLC
Palm Beach Gardens, Florida 33418

Author's Note: This is a work of fiction. Names, characters, and incidents are a product of the author's imagination. Locales and public names are sometimes used for atmospheric purposes, but details about those locations may have been altered to meet the demands of the story. Any resemblance to actual people, living or dead, or to businesses, companies, events, institutions, or locales is completely coincidental.

Cover Design by Paradox Book Covers

Ordering Information: Quantity sales. Special discounts are available on quantity purchases by corporations, associations, bookstores, and others. For details, contact the publisher.

Sniper/George A Bernstein
1st edition

ISBN 978-0-9894681-8-3

Praise for Bernstein's Novels

White Death (5.0) Kindle Customer - **A must read book**
This was a great book you don't want to put down. I really enjoyed it can't wait until the next one.

The Prom Dress Killer **(4.5*)** Dr. Cynthia L Clark, Psy.D., Ph.D., Diplomat Homeland Security
Young auburn-haired women are killed and left in a frilly prom dress. There is no sign of trauma. Al Warner is the detective assigned to the case. With few clues, he must profile this killer. Why red heads? Why this age? Why pose them? Why put them in prom dresses? Working alongside the FBI, Al works hard to capture the serial killer who eventually messes up. But that leaves Al with a decision that will affect his entire life. What will he do? THE PROM DRESS KILLER is a look at how a serial killer is evaluated and then hunted. It is an intriguing and fascinating read. Enjoyable.

Death's Angel – Midwest Book Review, 12/16 magazine
A masterfully crafted suspense thriller from beginning to end, *Death's Angel* is a terrifically absorbing read and very highly recommended.

K. Lintncron (5*) 12/14 A "Keep You Up All Night" Read.
After reading Death's Angel, it is easy to see why George Bernstein is a top selling writer on Amazon. The story is ripe with suspense and action. All of the characters are excellently developed and bring the story to life with dialogue that feels natural and never forced. Death's Angel breaks out of the formulaic police procedural/serial killer genre and excels above

its peers. Al Warner could easily be the next Alex Cross. A thrilling murder mystery with a surprise ending no one will guess!

Born to Die **(5*)** Readers' Favorite Magazine, by Tracy Fischer.

Whoa! Just, whoa! That's exactly what I thought when I got to the end of the fantastic new book by George A. Bernstein. This book grabbed me from the very start and had me obsessively reading all the way through until the very end. I loved it. How's that for a review? Well, it's definitely how I felt about this book. Author George A Bernstein has done a fantastic job in creating realistic and interesting characters, a fascinating and sympathetic story line, and a simply great read in general! I highly recommend this book to any reader who loves mysteries or just loves great fiction.

Trapped - (5*) Angie F –Amazon review - Paperback

George Bernstein has done a wonderful job with his novel, "Trapped." Imagine if you went in for routine surgery and were trapped in a coma - seemingly unresponsive, but you're fully aware of what's going on around you. Imagine you find you also have "awoken" with a psychic ability to KNOW how others are feeling. Imagine if you determined that your "accident" was no accident! "Trapped" is a wonderful, gripping thriller that grabs the reader's attention from the first page and refuses to let go.

A 3rd Time to Die (5*) Dianne O'Keefe - A thrilling ride - don't miss it.

Bearing in mind that I like paranormal romance novels, I was pretty convinced that I would like this novel, especially since I also like horse riding. The big surprise was that I never expected it to be comparable to great writers of this genre such as Dean Koontz or Stephen King. "*A Third Time to Die*" really delivered, providing an intriguing storyline and very believable characters. As I reached midway in the book, I was turning pages almost as fast as I could read to find out what would happen next. I enjoyed it immensely and am glad I tried it out. I look forward to more, and am delighted the author already has another book out. Time to download it to my Kindle!

DEDICATION

To my wife, Dolores, and my two critique partners, Sharon and Fred, whose valuable input made this book the best it could be.

Sniper

~ 1 ~

The time had come for people to begin dying.

I cracked open the door and my eyes swept the roof. Deserted. No surprise, considering the already intensified South Florida morning sun, as it arced above the distant palm trees. Mirrored sunglasses donned, I tugged down the brim of a Marlins ball cap to shade my eyes from the glare.

There, I spied what was needed sitting near the eastern parapet . . . a three-foot high steel mechanical box. Perfect. It offered a clear view of Bayfront Park, just across Biscayne Boulevard. The roof's black-tarred surface was quickly traversed, staying low, my backpack and an oversized guitar case slung over my shoulder,.

Shrugging off both, I removed a bedroll and spread it across the green top of the metal case. Latex gloves assured I would leave no prints or DNA. I flipped open the case and removed the pieces, taking less than a minute to assemble the rifle. A moment later, sprawled atop the flannel blanket, facing east, I loaded a 12.7mm round into the weapon's breach, jacked four more into the magazine, and snapped it in place. More than needed.

I arched my neck and took a quick preview of the landscape, then shed the gloves and pocketed them. A compact wind gauge set on the coping would give me direction and speed of the currently mild breeze.

Sprawled atop the flannel blanket, I settled the weapon's bi-pod on the metal surface. A gentle exhale to quiet my heart before I made a preliminary adjustment to the telescopic sight. My right eye against the scope, I tweaked the focus and began a scan of the area.

There, the bus stop at NE 1ˢᵗ Street, and to the right, a path exiting the park. With a minor correction to the Leupold 5 x 25 scope, I swept the grounds, spotting the famous headless torso sculpture that bordered the winding path.

Three joggers bobbed along the paths: a fit, thirtyish woman coming toward me, a paunchy guy in his 50's going away, and a young jock—probably mid-twenties—on a crosswalk. Two kneeling Latino gardeners planted spring annuals along the trail. Drifting left, out along Biscayne Boulevard, I located morning foot traffic striding along the walk, all apparent business-types on their way to offices in Miami's Financial District—a myriad of opportunities.

I sighed again, spread my legs a bit wider, and steadied my base as I fitted the butt of the TAC-50 snug against my shoulder. My clenched jaw required a wiggle to relieve tension as I sucked in a measured breath. This begins the first act, spawned from hours of scouting, detailed research, and the endless target practice at a remote 'Glades savannah. Something very different from my usual contracts, and using a new tool I'd come to love.

Now to initiate a reign of terror that would obscure my real motive. While I wasn't the first at this scenario, mine was certainly the cleverest. No time for qualms, because as they say, the end justifies the means.

Been there, done that before, but this was the first time it was personal. Innocents sometimes perished to achieve a greater goal, but never before at my hand. That was about to change.

Starting now.

Who first? Ahh, the woman, just about to exit the park. I steadied her rhythmically loping body in the telescopic sight. Eleven hundred meters—an easy shot to baptize my deadly, new McMillan sniper rifle, acquired on the Dark Web. A soft breath eased from my lungs, and my lips tightened with resolve as I smoothly squeezed the trigger.

The sound-suppressed rifle emitted a quiet, high-pitched pop. The woman's blond hair billowed out in a red-stained cloud, tossing her peaked cap away, as the huge slug caught her left temple while in mid-stride. The impact slammed her to the ground as the exit wound blew away half of her face.

I blinked to moisten my eye and swung the scoped rifle left toward Biscayne Boulevard, searching for my next target. There, a guy hurrying along the walk, briefcase in hand, unaware of the mayhem just occurring behind him. I made a minor sight adjustment, exhaled, and squeezed off the next shot, catching him squarely between the shoulder blades. The big slug drove him across the walk, flattening him face down along the grassy border. Red spatter peppered the path in front of him. There was a loud yelp, and a third victim, fifty-feet in front, tumbled over, clutching his shoulder.

I grunted, then pivoted my attention back to the park. *Hmmm. Two with one shot.* Unexpected consequences, but of little concern now. One of the gardeners straightened up by the flowerbed. A hand shaded his eyes as he searched for the source of the sudden ruckus.

The rifle emitted a soft burp and my third shot pitched the kneeling man backward, arms flung wide, as he took the round on the breastbone.

No pause to examine the results. I knew all three shots were instantly fatal. The fourth, unplanned victim must have caught a ricochet of the super-sonic slug as it blew through my victim and bounced off the concrete walkway. Just some collateral damage. There'll be a lot more of that soon enough.

I slipped off the steel box and pulled the rifle and bedroll down. Scampering around in a squat, I collected and pocketed the three still-hot spent casings. Then, duck-walking away from the tile-topped parapet of the tall office building, I reached the exit door. Hunkering over in the shadows, I folded the rifle's bipod and removed the detachable scope and stock. I wondered, glancing up, if someone in the nearby taller apartment buildings had noticed my activity. Speed now was essential.

I secured the disassembled weapon inside my customized guitar case and shrugged on the backpack with the bedroll already fastened on top. With the cased weapon slung over a shoulder, I hurried through the door toward the staircase. It would be a long trip down on foot, but not a problem for someone as aerobically fit as me. An extra precaution, because a homeless musician might be remembered if spotted riding the elevator.

Reaching the ground floor, I eased open the door, and searched the building's lobby.

Empty.

Any possible onlookers would see an innocuous street guy taking a shortcut across the marble-floored foyer, headed for a rear door that exited to the parking lot. Hurrying between rows of cars and past the next building on NE 3rd Ave., I strode north toward my beige Honda CRV. It sat at the curb with eight minutes still on the meter. My backpack and gun case found the floor in front of the back seat, and a moment later, I'd slipped into the driver's side, started the engine, and hustled north on NW 2nd Ave., heading for Interstate 395.

It had begun.

The first move of many to come—Miami about to become the center of panic again, and it would stay that way until the completion of this mission.

Speculation would abound about my motive, but I doubted anyone would come close to my real goal. Not even the famed Detective Al Warner would likely make this connection.

I sighed. *Time was in short supply, but I had to get it done. No excuses. The next round of kills would be one that counts, but I couldn't stop there if I were to continue misdirecting the cops. This was different from anything I'd ever done for hire.*

I contemplated my next move as I sped north, now on I-95. Probably Hollywood, in south Broward County, after things cool for a few days. Its main library was one not yet visited. I took obsessive care not to leave any pattern or Internet trail for some clever detective to discover.

A blond wig and a pair of uncorrected tortoise-shell glasses were in a small bag on the passenger seat. Every library visit entailed the use of a different disguise.

Once this was over, life should return to my new normal. Had it only been six-months? I shook my head and breathed another gentle sigh.

Such unreasonable schedule restrictions. I grunted. Careful planning and sharp execution would triumph, as always. I've been on a tight wire more than once. Anyone getting in the way won't make it out alive.

They never did.

~ 2 ~

Detective Al Warner slipped his nearly new, coffee-colored custom coupe between two patrol cars that blocked off northbound Biscayne Blvd. He stepped out and ran a hand over the Kevlar-lined hood of his third Dodge Charger in less than two years. This one was fully bulletproofed. The previous ones were destroyed while aiding in apprehending two lunatics. He sighed, his eyes drawn to the hectic scene in the park.

What a mess. Way too many local cops on the site, but the magnitude of the event drew everyone who could find an excuse to be there. He spied two black CSU vans already on the scene, one at the entrance to the park, and the other stationed a half-block up the boulevard. At least they kept the site secure.

Humid, salt-laden air hung over him like a sodden blanket. Sweat already peppered his brow and trickled down his armpits. Only May, but summer had already started its annual onslaught. He pulled the blue MDPD cap's peak tighter against the top rim of his mirrored sunglasses. His dark eyes swept the area, and he spotted one of his lead detectives.

"Olvida," he called and waved.

He trotted to Warner's side. "Hi, Boss. What a fucked up scene."

"Yeah. Harris here yet?"

"En route. I was only a few blocks away when the 911 came in." He glanced toward the park, already encased by yellow crime-scene tape that spread from trees to signs to lampposts. "It's chaos."

"But it ain't a circus. Clear out all the unnecessary patrol teams and anybody else who doesn't belong here. Just keep the first two cars on the scene, and block off the boulevard in each direction at both ends."

"On it, Boss." He turned to leave.

"Olvida." Warner reached out and touched his sleeve. "Then organize whatever witnesses there are. Some place out of the sun. Maybe that gazebo in the park."

"Right."

"And when Harris arrives, have him get after CSU. See what they know about the shooter. Is the Hawk here yet?"

"Yeah. He's working the scene on the sidewalk." Olvida nodded toward a small gaggle of techs and uniformed cops, seventy-five yards north, close to the street.

"Okay, get to it. Clear the scene, and let's get to work," Warner said to the detective's back as he scurried off.

Warner lingered in the shade of a black olive tree, hands on his hips and scanned from the group on the street to the team working the park, and back again. He shrugged and strode toward the boulevard where Moe Gold crouched, assessing the mayhem. No one dug out the truth better than the legendary Hawk.

The scrawny, round-shouldered little man, no more than five-six, stood near the curb, arms folded, as he watched a red and white EMT ambulance start up the boulevard. A siren pulsed and red and blue lights flashed to announce its hurried departure. He turned at Warner's approach and ran a hand through thinned brown hair. Bushy eyebrows arched over a predominant, hooked Semitic beak and skinny moustache. He smiled.

"Ahh, the Hero has arrived." He extended his hand.

"Cut the crap, Moe," Warner said and took the hand. "That shit gets pretty jaded."

"But every year you manage to keep revitalizing the legend, Detective. How can we think less of the man who just took down ISIS here?"

"Yeah, but that's three months old. So, who's that en route to Jackson?" He gestured after the disappearing ambulance.

"The fourth vic. Probably an unintended consequence."

"Huh?"

"The second vic took a through-and-through that ricocheted off the concrete walk and hit a probably accidental target in the right shoulder."

"So, he's alive?"

"Yep. That was he on the way to the hospital. Quite a bit of blood loss, but looks like he'll make it okay."

"The bullet?" Warner asked.

"Still lodged in his scapula. They'll remove it at Jackson and get it to me."

"Any idea on the weapon?" Warner pivoted and peered back into the park. "This looks like long-range shots."

"I agree," Gold said and rubbed the nose that had earned

him his Hawk nickname. "A high velocity, big bore slug, from the trauma it created. Blew right through all three intended vics, and caused extensive exit-wound damage."

"Like that Barrett .50 sniper rifle Agent Yeager used against those terrorist thugs?" They had moved to the body sprawled face down, angled across the concrete walk. His arms and legs were flung wide, looking like a frog that had been flattened by some giant's foot.

"I suppose, but those military sniper rifles aren't readily available to civilians." Gold squatted next to the body. His eyes swept a path across the street to the towering buildings on the other side.

"From a preliminary estimate of the angle of penetration on this poor soul, and the subsequent ricochet, I suspect your shooter was on top of one of those three buildings. When I finish with the two vics in the park, I should have a better idea of which one."

Warner knelt next to the little man and followed his gaze. "I think you're right. Probably the roof, not a window. Gotta be at least a thousand yards. Not the work of some casual marksman who—"

"You two praying for a clue, or something?"

They turned and found the medical examiner poised over them, hands in his pockets.

"Whatever works, Doc," Warner said as he lumbered up.

"Well, I hope you find this guy before he starts filling up my morgue. This seems like motiveless carnage."

"There's always motive, Doc," Warner said, as he offered Gold a hand up. "Sometimes it's damned elusive, but it's always there." He glanced at the group in the park.

"Finished with those two?"

"Yep. They're all yours, Detective. Just this last one to process, and you can have him too. Messy business. The woman is especially disturbing."

"You didn't move the bodies at all, did you?" The Hawk watched two pairs of his techs work the crime scene. "We need entry and exit angles to triangulate the shooter's position."

"C'mon, Moe." The doctor chuckled. "You know me better than that." He knelt beside the man's body and opened his black bag. "I've got two vehicles ready for you to finish your work so we can get them to my table for their autopsies. COD is obvious. The rest may be just routine."

"Okay." Warner gripped Gold's shoulder. "Olvida's got teams lookin' for the spent slugs. If can we locate them, it should help get a line on the shooter's perch."

"Right. I'll get the site processed ASAP. Once we calculate the angles you can move the bodies and look for IDs.

"Good. Whether this is random lunacy or calculated evil, it smacks of just the beginnin' of worse to come." He pivoted and scanned the two entire scenes.

"Where the hell is Jack Harris?" his voice strained with impatience.

"Just arrived, Boss." Raphael Olvida joined Warner and pointed to the tan Chevy Camaro as it passed under the crime scene tape.

"About damned time," Warner grumbled. "Let's find those spent slugs. We've got a cold-hearted bastard to catch."

He spun and strode into the park, headed for the first casualty, stretched across some freshly planted red begonias at the side of the path. The impact of the shot had blown her out of one of her sneakers.

Just a few months since that crazy gun battle, and here we are again. His thoughts drifted to the clever serial lunatic, The Prom Dress Killer, he took down earlier last year. *My gut says this one ain't gonna be any easier.*

Al Warner's gut was seldom wrong.

~ 3 ~

"There it is, Dad," Hunter pointed to the sign at the entrance of the Sunset Harbor Yacht Club on the Miami Beach shore of the Intracoastal Waterway.

"Good job, son," Brian Fiore swung his aging Dodge Caravan onto the access road. A moment later, they entered the parking lot. A few pick-ups and SUVs sporting empty boat trailers lined one side, partly shaded by towering Queen Palms. He found a vacant slot between a black Ford Expedition and a Lexus 570 SUV.

"That's Uncle Charlie's car." The nineteen-year-old nodded at a silver Lexus.

"Yeah. No surprise he beat us here. Probably already on the boat." Brian popped the rear hatch where they gathered a small cooler and a duffle bag filled with changes of clothes and yellow slickers. Better to be prepared. Although only the first week in May, the summer rainy season had arrived early.

A cool dousing might feel refreshing during a sun-baked day on the water, but Hunter's immune system needed protection at all costs. The seven AM air clung to them in a thick, salty blanket, tinged by a hint of fish, but somehow it was not oppressive.

Hunter slung the duffle bag over a shoulder while his father toted the Styrofoam case, as they started toward the small boat moorings. Charlie Seagrave's twenty-four foot Mako center-console sport-fisherman was small only in comparison to the many larger yachts that lined the extensive docks in the marina.

"That way." The elder Fiore gestured toward the finger

docks. "As I remember, his boat is out near the end."

They started down the planked main dock walk, and Hunter's emerald eyes scanned through beige polarized lenses a myriad of bobbing crafts. Lots of open fishermen and small cruisers with cuddy cabins.

"There he is," he said and pointed at a waving man, clad in long khaki pants and a long-sleeve shirt. A peaked cap with ear and neck flaps sat atop his cacao-brown hair. His uncle was scrupulous about sun protection.

They hurried along to the finger-dock where Charlie Seagrave's boat, *Valkyrie,* bobbed to the wake of a small yacht cruising by on the canal's rippled green water.

"Hi, kiddo," Seagrave said as he pulled in the boy for a gentle hug. "How are you feeling?"

"Pretty good, Unc, and ready to go. We gonna catch some fish today?"

"That's the idea," he said, and stepped into the boat. He took the boy's hand to steady him as he came aboard. "They've been catching some dolphin and a few sails. Plenty of feisty bonito and a few of their relatives, blackfin tuna, to keep us busy until something better comes along."

"Always the optimist, Bro," Brian said as he jumped onto the deck. "Need any help getting set up?"

"Nope. Rods are ready. I got some fresh ballyhoo already rigged for the flat lines, and some really nice seven-inch finger mullet set up for the 'riggers."

"Nothing I can do to help?" Hunter asked.

"Just cast off that stern line and take a seat. Brian, you get the bow line, and we're ready to go."

Everyone's' tasks completed, they were soon idling along the no-wake zone, headed for Government Cut, the Miami inlet leading to the cobalt blue of the Gulfstream.

~~~

Thirty minutes later, Seagrave eased the twin one-hundred-fifty horse Yamaha outboard engines to trolling speed, lowered the outrigger poles, and began setting out lines.

"Whooeee," the boy yelled, "this baby can fly!"

"Yeah. When we've got a pretty calm day like this, she can do nearly forty knots." He dropped a bait in the water and spooled off about fifty feet of line from the aft rod, sitting in a rod holder. The chrome-plated, lead head lure skimmed along just below the surface, causing a rippled wake.

"You stay in that fighting chair and get ready," Seagrave told Hunter. "This starboard flat line with the feather and strip might get hit pretty quick. Lots of hungry bonito around." A swimming ballyhoo—a long, flat-bodied silvery fish— trailed from a similar rod on the port side.

Seagrave ran third and fourth lines up on the two outriggers and studied their split-tail mullet skipping across the surface, seventy feet astern.

"Nice job, Charlie," Brian said. "The baits look great."

"Yeah, I learned a lot working as mate on weekends on Moe's charter boat during high school."

"He was a hell of a good captain, wasn't he?"

"No one caught more fish than Moe Yates," Seagrave said, then gestured for Brian to come closer.

"Any news on the kid," he whispered as he grasped his brother-in-law's arm.

Brian shook his head. "Not many donors for his rare blood-type, and there are two on the list in front of him."

"Shit! Liver disease is for drunkards, not kids."

"Yeah, you'd think so. Not much we can do about it."

"You look into black market suppliers?" He glanced at his nephew, perched on the edge of the fighting chair, awaiting action. He'd lost weight in his battle with terminal liver disease. Seagrave intended to change that.

"That's pissing in the wind, Charlie. We don't have the cash for something like that. You know your sister and I . . ."

"I'd pay, Brian." He turned back to the man. "You know I love that kid as if he were mine, and I don't have anybody else, other than Kim, to spend my money on."

"We appreciate that, Bro, but there's nothing out there for him right now. Not as far as we know, anyhow."

"How long? The docs give you a timeline?"

"Maybe a year." Brian sighed, dropping his eyes. "If we're lucky. The meds help him feel okay, but nothing's slowing the deterioration." Droplets trickled across his suntanned cheeks.

"I don't see any signs of jaundice. That's good, isn't it?"

"Yeah, I guess. It isn't fucking . . ."

A whoop from Hunter interrupted Fiore.

"Fish! Fish on!" He snatched the starboard flat line from its holder and dropped back on the chair, securing the rod butt in the seat's gimbal socket. The light trolling rod arched, and the reel squealed as monofilament line streaked off, slicing the water with an audible hiss.

"Hang on, kid," Seagrave said as he idled the engine and moved to the boy's side.

"Looks like a good one. Just let him run. You've got plenty of line."

~ **4** ~

"Warner?" The Hawk rose, swiveling his head, searching for the detective.

Warner came up from a crouch where he'd been aiding in the search for the spent slug that had torn half the face off the woman jogger. What a grisly mess. He joined Moe Gold as he adjusted two long, yellow plastic rods stuck in the soil, angling upward.

What's up?" he asked.

"Best we can calculate the shot trajectory, everything seems to point to that office building—probably the roof."

They turned to gaze at a structure about twenty-five stories high on the opposite side of Biscayne Blvd., probably fronting on NE 3rd Ave.

"Gotta be at least a thousand yards," Warner said, rubbing his stubbled jaw. "Not a shot made by some everyday hunter."

"No, this guy was—"

"Moe. Detective. Over here." One of the CSU techs was pushing to his feet, something clutched in his vinyl-gloved hand.

Warner and Gold hurried to his side. "Whatcha got, Art," Gold asked.

"A bullet. *The* bullet, I suspect. Not your everyday caliber." He opened his palm.

The Hawk plucked it off his hand and held it up, turning it slowly. ".50-cal rifle," he muttered. "Pretty well intact, so we should be able to get what we need to see if there's a match on file anywhere."

"That's from a typical 12.7mm sniper rifle, Moe. Those are military weapons. This smacks of a trained government or Special Forces shooter." Warner gazed at the forensic chief. "You got access to military data bases?"

"Not usually, but I'll see if I can pull a string or two." He slipped the slug into a small plastic bag, marked an ID number on it, and scribbled a note in his log. A numbered yellow cone was placed to mark its location.

"Okay," Warner said, flexing his interlocked fingers. "Harris and I'll check out the roof of that building and see what we can find."

He pivoted, scanning the park. "Harris," he called.

"Here, Boss." He stepped out of the gazebo. "Just

interviewing a few witnesses."

"Gettin' anything?" Warner strode over to his old partner and peeked inside the open structure where three men and a woman fidgeted on benches.

"Not much. No one heard shots or anything. The Latino guy got sprayed with blood spatter when his partner got hit." He glanced at his tablet. "The suit in there said he heard what was probably the round ricocheting off the concrete and saw the guy who took it in the shoulder go down."

He looked back into the shadowy confines of the shelter and shrugged. "So far, that's about it." He gazed up at his taller friend. "You?"

"Moe thinks he's IDd the shooter's position." He nodded toward the boulevard. "That office building."

"Wow, that's a helluva long shot."

"Yeah. Smacks of a professional. I was gonna bring you up there with me to case it out, but you stay and finish your interviews." Warner patted him on the shoulder. "I'll take Olvida. Doubt we're gonna find much, if the guy *is* a pro."

~ ~ ~

Warner and Olvida pushed through the rooftop door and onto the roof. Dark sunglasses were quickly donned in defense against the reflected sun, shimmering over the tarred surface.

Warner scanned the area and pointed to the eastern parapet. "That'd be it, if this is the right place. Let's see what we can find."

Their eyes swept the area as they advanced, looking for any signs of activity.

"That mechanical box looks like an ideal perch, Boss."

"Yeah. Gives an unobstructed view over the edge. Looks freshly painted. See if you can find any shell casings."

"Not likely, if this guy's a pro," Olvida muttered, as he

wandered back and forth, eyes cast down.

Warner began investigating the top of the green metal box. "There's a couple of small scrapes here, just about the width of a bi-pod support." His vinyl-gloved hand swept lightly over the surface. "And another one about three feet back, maybe from a belt buckle. You got anything?"

"No casings, but maybe a singe-mark on the coping here that could have been from muzzle blast. I bet those big .50-cals emit a pretty good tongue of flame."

"Good work. I think we got the shooter's perch." Warner retrieved his cell phone and hit auto dial.

"You were right on the shooter's location, Moe," he said when the Hawk answered. "The top of the office building. Get a team up here and do a full sweep." He listened for a moment, then said, "Olvida'll stay on site to show your guys what we've found so far. I'm comin' down to work vic IDs, if your done processin' them." He disconnected.

"I'm gonna take the stairs, Olvida. This guy may not have wanted to be seen on the elevator. Be sure CSU processes the lift, though. Bound to be loads of prints there, but maybe we'll get catch a break."

"Got it, Boss, but I'm betting we won't be so lucky."

"Yeah," Warner paused, his dark eyes sweeping the rooftop. "I'm worried this is just the beginning of a spree. If I'm right, we're gonna need some luck somewhere to end this before it gets any more outta hand."

He shook his head and rolled his shoulders to relieve building tension as he strode toward the exit.

He hated murderers, but apparent senseless random killing was worse than anything.

~ 5 ~

Hunter hunched over the throbbing rod and whistled. "Look at this baby take line. What d'ya think it is?"

"I was expecting a bonito, which is a small type of tuna," Seagrave said, laying a hand on the boy's shoulder, "but this may be a blackfin tuna. They've been catching a few up to twenty pounds recently."

The fish swept hard to starboard. The line hissed through the water, sounding like the release of steam from a kettle.

"Reel in that line fast, Hunter. He's doubled back toward the boat. I'm gonna clear the other flat line. Brian, knock down the starboard outrigger line and bring it in."

"Got it." A brief flurry of activity as lines were retrieved, and they settled in for the fight.

After ten minutes of give and take, the fish came reluctantly to the gunnel.

"Tough fight, kid. How're you doing?" Brian laid a hand on his son's shoulder.

"I'm good, Dad." Hunter panted and ran a sleeve across his sweaty brow. "I love this!"

"There he is." Seagrave snatched the end of the monofilament leader. "Wow. A skipjack! I shoulda known."

"Skipjack?"

"Yeah, skipjack tuna. Also called Arctic bonito, and looks like a beauty, too. They're terrific fighters."

"Tell me about it." The boy chuckled and flexed his left arm, relaxing as his uncle took control of the leader. "Can we release it?"

"I'll try." Hauling on the leader, he flipped the silvery

twenty-pound fish aboard. It slid across the deck, its sickle-like tail beating a rapid tattoo on the floorboards. Seagrave pounced on the flopping tuna and removed the hook.

Brian perched on the captain's chair, his iPad poised for a photo. "Hold him up, guys. Your mom's gonna love this."

Seagrave cradled the fish and crouched next to his nephew, still sitting in the fighting chair.

Hunter cracked a grin that could have eclipsed the sun and grabbed a fin of the torpedo-shaped, silver-sided beauty. Several pics were snapped, and it was ready to go back into the water to live and fight another day.

"You want to do the honors?" Seagrave asked and handed the quivering fish to Hunter. "Hold him by the tail and drop him in, head first. He should be okay."

The small tuna hit the water and sped off like a shiny torpedo. "Wow, that was fun. I love it out here."

"Me, too, kiddo. Hopefully, that's only the first of many, if you're not too tired."

"Best I've felt in weeks, Uncle Charlie. Let's see what else we can catch."

He rose and along with his dad, began putting out the other two lines.

Seagrave rerigged the flat line, glad he'd brought some joy into the unhappy future of his nephew. He had to find a way to change that dire outcome.

He had a plan.

~ 6 ~

Warner balanced on one knee on the grass and studied the woman's body. He took her shoulder with a gloved hand and rolled her over. As hardened to mayhem as he was, she was still disquieting to look at.

The right side of her face, which may have once been attractive, had been annihilated—the eye and cheek gone, and the corner of the mouth a jagged gash. The corn-silk hair was matted with blood and gore. Her right foot was still encased in a black Nike jogging shoe, while its partner lay upside down at the edge of the path. No pockets in her lilac jogging tights or her coral-colored cotton tee.

He chased off an early gathering of flies and unzipped a small fanny pack that had worked around to her side. There were a few dollar bills, a VISA card, and driver's license, both proclaiming her to be one Amy Howard, thirty-three, residing in a nearby Brickell Avenue condo. He'd have Harris follow up her information. See if there was an obvious reason for her murder.

Based on the eclectic variety of victims, he doubted they would find anything concrete. This smacked of a senseless, random shooting, but he knew no killing was without some purpose, no matter how obscure. Two serial killers in the past thirty months were more than enough.

Grunting, he pushed to his feet, flexed his neck, and swiveled his head, gazing into the park. Might as well do the gardener next. His partner had IDd him as Alonso Miranda, a forty-four-year-old, green-carded Guatemalan worker who'd been employed by the city for the past four years as a maintenance worker. Warner didn't expect to find much there, either.

The apparent exec that lay sprawled and unmoved off the sidewalk might provide more possibilities. It wouldn't be the first time someone killed innocents to mask his real target. Those kinds of investigations took time to uncover the real motive, and in the meantime, more people were likely to die.

He intended to keep that carnage to a minimum.

~~~

Forty minutes later, Warner sat on the tan leather bucket seat of his Charger, reviewing his notes. The engine idled, and the a/c battled the steamy grasp of the rising mid-morning temperature. Old Sol reigned proudly over a clear, robin-egg blue sky, already firing up heat waves that shimmered off the pavement.

Warner flipped through pages of his spiral-bound notebook, reviewing his entries. He was old school, and while he owned an Android pad, forced upon him by the department, he preferred pen and paper. Raphael Olvida would send everything they had to his Samsung at the end of the day, but Warner mainly used the device as a camera whenever he needed one.

He glanced back at the yellow-bordered crime scene. Three CSU techs still patrolled the grounds, searching for some unlikely scrap of evidence. The videographer had finished after the last witness had been questioned, and he was now on the roof with the Hawk and two of his crew, searching for anything damning the shooter may have left behind.

He grunted, shaking his head. Good luck with that. This was no careless perp. He withdrew his cell phone and tapped an auto dial code. It was answered on the third ring.

"Nag, nag, nag," Maurice Gold said with a chuckle. "Always in such a hurry, Detective. Science takes time."

"That's something I suspect is gonna be in short supply here, Moe. Ya got anything probative?"

"Well, we've verified this *was* the shooter's site. Your guess that he lay atop that mechanical box is right. It was freshly painted, so the markings from his belt buckle and rifle's bi-pod are clear."

"Makes sense," Warner said. "It made a perfect sniper's nest."

"I agree," Gold said, "but no prints as of yet. No casings, either, but the rim of the parapet test positive for gunshot residue. We've scoured the surface of the box and the path he probably took from the entrance to his perch but haven't found a single piece of trace—no hair, no fiber—nothing. There's been a pretty stiff breeze up here which may have blown away any residue from his perch, and this was one very careful dude, Al."

"I didn't expect him to be any less, Moe." Warner sighed. "Send me whatever ya got. Meanwhile, I'm gonna get some boys to hit the upper stories of those two tall apartment buildings. See if anyone noticed anything."

"You'd think they'd call it in, Detective, if they had."

"Yeah." He pocketed his notebook. "But sometimes they don't realize what they saw until someone asks 'em about it."

"Right. Well, we'll keep at it up here for a while until we're sure we didn't miss anything. It's too damned hot out here for this aging Jew. I'd rather be in the lab."

"Yeah. Seems summer's in a hurry this year. Talk to ya later." Warner disconnected and dialed another number.

"Olvida," he answered.

"Olvida, I need four guys to interview possible witnesses on the high floors of those two adjacent taller buildings. Maybe someone was havin' breakfast on a terrace and saw something. You and Harris pitch in and supervise. I'm gonna check the workplace of Eric Boxer, the third vic."

"On it, Boss."

"Keep in touch if ya come up with anything. We gotta get in front of this thing before a new bunch of vics show up. Whoever this is, I'm bettin' he's just gettin' started."

Warner pocketed the phone and eased back in the seat, his fingers absently finding the crosshatch scars hidden under the thick thatch of dark, curly hair on the right side of his thankfully hard head. Reminders of his near-visits from the Grim Reaper during the bloody climaxes of the *Baby Butcher* and *The Angel of Death* serial-killer cases.

He sat up, flexed his neck, and engaged his seatbelt. He'd seen enough death in the last three years to last a lifetime. He blinked, shaking away the memories.

Just a short drive to an office building where Eric Boxer had worked. Warner wasn't very hopeful of learning anything of value, but none of the proverbial stones were going to remain unturned.

He sighed.

I got a really bad feeling about this one.

~ 7 ~

They'd had an entertaining morning, with three speedy bonito taken on the feathered jig flat-line, and a colorful, high-jumping twelve-pound dolphin that hit the swimming ballyhoo. Nothing exceptional since the big skipjack had started the action, but good fights and Hunter was having a ball. He shared the action with his father, conserving energy.

Seagrave and his brother-in-law stood under the small canvas sunshade, while the boy—a young man now, but Seagrave always thought of him as a kid—slouched on the fighting chair, watching the skipping outrigger baits. A sailfish would be icing on the cake, and a few still lingered in the area after the usual winter/spring run.

"The kid's looking a bit worn, Brian. You think this is getting to be too much for him?"

"Maybe," Fiore mused, rubbing his chin. "He's fought all but two fish so far, and loved it. He's not ready to quit."

"Well, we've still got two or three hours to fish." Seagrave glanced over the bow and initiated a slow, sweeping turn to the starboard, heading south. The powerful Gulfstream had carried them offshore of Hollywood. They'd probably need three hours at fast trolling speed to reach Government Cut.

"I love seeing him so happy," he said, "but I'm worried about wearing him out."

"I know," Fiore answered, "but if we don't get a viable transplant soon—well, I want to get as much pleasure as I can into what little may be left to his life. He really loves spending time out here with you."

"Me, too. But, you get ready to take over the rod if we get into something like a sail, in case a longer fight's too much for him."

Fiore nodded, then plucked a bottle of water from the cooler and brought it to his son. He sat on the transom, facing Hunter, and they talked.

Seagrave gave them some time alone, lost in his own thoughts.

This stinks! Somehow, we've gotta come up with a liver for this kid. Kim's checking her contacts, but that's just pissing in the wind.

"Hey, Unc."

His head came up, shedding morose thoughts. "What's up, kid?"

"A fin. I think I saw a fin behind the port 'rigger."

Seagrave jumped up on the gunnel and shaded his eyes, studying the skipping mullet, seventy feet behind the boat. There it was, a dorsal fin, shadowing the bait. *Holy shit!*

"It's a white marlin, guys! Jesus, I've never taken one on this boat. Get ready."

"Wow! How do you know it's a white marlin?"

"The top of the dorsal is rounded, instead of pointed." He dropped back onto the deck and inched up the throttle a knot or two.

"Hand Hunter the rod, take the reel outta gear, and let's

hook up the shoulder harness. I don't know how big this baby is, but if he takes, we're gonna be in for one helluva fight." He took two steps and laid a hand on the boy's shoulder.

That barely said when two feet of black bill slashed through the water, striking the silvery little bait, knocking the line out of the 'rigger. With a flash of iridescent blue, the marlin rolled, gulping in the mullet.

"Christ, what a beauty! He's already eaten it, Hunter. You flip the drag lever up to the STRIKE mark when I tell you, and brace yourselves, 'cause I'm gonna hit the throttles to help with the hook up."

"Wowee! I'm gonna catch a marlin. Whenever you're ready. He's taking line."

"Okay, *now*. Hang on, Brian."

Seagrave revved up to half-throttle, the boat surging ahead as Hunter engaged the drag, braced his feet, and hauled back. The graphite rod arched in a deep curve and thirty-pound monofilament line raced off the Penn International reel, concurrent with Hunter's scream of ecstasy.

"Hit him again," Seagrave yelled as he throttled back the engines, "and watch for the first jumps."

As if taking instructions, the eight-foot long, silver and blue-barred beauty blasted above the surface, skittering upright across fifty feet of the cobalt blue of the Gulfstream— tail-walking. Plunging back, he quickly reappeared, executing three bounding leaps, each clearing twenty-feet.

"Yow-eee," Hunter yelled. Line sped off the singing reel.

"I'm coming around to port." He slowed the boat as the boy began to gain line.

"Wow, look at that!" Fiore yelled, as the marlin erupted in a lengthy tail-walk, not fifty feet away.

"That's a hulluva big white," Seagrave shouted. "Could be a hundred pounds. No record, but a rare catch." He glanced at his nephew, braced in the seat, leaning against the deeply arched rod, as the big fish raced off.

"How're you doing, Hunter?" he asked.

"I got 'em, Unc. This baby's gonna be mine."

"Yeah, if we're lucky. That's a lot of fish on that light rod. You start getting tired, you let us know. Your dad can take over for a while, if you need a rest."

"No, I can do it. This is a fish of a lifetime, isn't it?"

"You bet, kiddo. Brian, stay on the back of his chair and keep him pointed down the line."

He looked at Hunter, shook his head, and sighed. *Might be too damn short a lifetime if we can't find him that liver.*

He watched the boy haul back on the rod, then reel the tip down; haul back and reel down—pumping back line. He glanced at his watch. With such a big fish, this was going to take a while. He hoped the kid had it in him.

It would be a memory he wished Hunter could have for a full lifetime, and he would do whatever he could to see that happen.

~ 8 ~

Jack Harris paused at the door of 28B and studied his Samsung Galaxy. This was his eighth and last stop in this thirty-four story condo, the southern of the two buildings that towered over the shooter's twenty-fourth floor perch.

Two other detectives were working the floors above and below him. So far, no witnesses had been found, although three apartment owners hadn't been home. He'd get a list from the building manager and call them in the evening, presuming they were off to work by now.

He pressed the buzzer, and in a moment, noticed a

darkening at the door's peephole.

"Who's there?" The weak, raspy voice of an older man.

"Detective Harris, Miami PD." He displayed his shield. "I've got a few questions for you, if you've got a moment."

"Regarding what, officer?" Being properly cautious before opening the door to a stranger, badge or no badge.

"To see if you noticed anything from your balcony this morning. May I come in?"

"Just a moment." There was the click of a deadbolt being released, and the door swung in to a darkened room. A frail, five-foot-six man with watery eyes and thinning gray hair regarded the not-much-taller detective.

"Come in, come in." He made a sweeping gesture. "I don't get many visitors. What can I do for you?"

Harris strode in, his eyes sweeping the room, noticing the sliding glass door to an expansive patio. These were two and three-bedroom condos, just six to a floor—two on each side and one at each end. All had large, shaded and screened patios, but just two on each level facing east had the view they were looking for.

"There was an incident in the park this morning, and I hoped—"

"Yes, I heard the sirens. Was that man on the roof shooting a gun?"

"You saw someone on the roof of that office building?" Harris took the elderly man by the bicep and walked him toward the glass doors.

"Yes. I was having breakfast on the patio, watching the sunrise, and I noticed him lying on that thing on the roof. First, I thought he, too, was awaiting the arrival of the sun. But then he had what I thought was a tool, doing some kind of work."

"What else did you see?" Harris took notes on his Galaxy.

"Well, I lost interest until I heard someone scream. When I looked back, he was at the door to the roof. Looked like he was carrying a guitar or something. Then he was gone."

"It was a man?"

"Looked that way to me." He pulled at his ear. "Yes, it certainly looked like a man."

"Can you describe him at all, Mr. . . .?"

"Moody. Arlo Moody." He ran a hand over his scalp. "He seemed slim and—athletic, I'd say, but the clothes were kind of baggy and loose-fitting. Couldn't see his face, of course, and he was wearing some sort of ball cap, but maybe dark hair.

"I was sitting right here, having my orange juice, rye toast, and coffee." They gazed together at the roof below.

"Got any idea how tall he was? What he was wearing?"

"How tall?" Moody rubbed his eyes. "Is that the usual size door?" he asked, gesturing toward the distant roof.

"Yeah, I think so." Harris glancing at it over his shoulder.

"Then I'd say—maybe six feet, or maybe a bit less."

"His clothing?" Harris watched the man eyes roll up, searching his memory.

"Long khaki pants and a long-sleeve shirt, as I remember. Like I said, kind of baggy. Looked like a street performer. You know, someone who plays music for tips by the bus or train station. Didn't give it much thought until I heard all the hubbub. Was he shooting at people?"

"I'm afraid so. Killed three people in the park, and so far, you're our only witness."

"My goodness, how terrible. Well, I didn't see many details, but I hope I've been some help."

"You have, sir." Harris handed him his card. "Call me if you think of anything else." He paused. "Any chance you might pick him out from a mug shot book?"

"Oh, no." He shook his head. "Never had even a glimpse of his face, and my eyes aren't that good, anyhow. Dry eye syndrome. Sorry I can't be more help."

"You gave us more than we had, sir." Harris pocketed his

Galaxy. "Someone will contact you later for a written statement, just for the record. Thanks for your time."

He escorted Harris to the door, and they shook hands.

As it turned out, Arlo Moody was their only eyewitness, and that wasn't going to do them much good.

~ 9 ~

The magnificent silver, blue-striped warrior battled for an hour, making twenty-six spectacular jumps, as white marlin are known to do, before coming reluctantly to the boat.

Brian Fiore had taken over for his exhausted son, who suffered cramps and threw up fifteen minutes into the fight. Hunter crawled onto a cuddy cabin bunk to recover and was ready to take the rod back during the last few minutes, so he could be the ultimate conqueror.

Seagrave grasped the fifteen-foot heavy mono leader and drew the fish alongside the boat. Leaning over the gunnel, his canvas-gloved hand snatched the long, rough spear of the upper jaw. After a moment of thrashing, he drew the beautiful creature up, balancing it across the boat's transom.

"Wow, gorgeous," the exhausted, pallid-faced boy extolled. "How heavy do you think?"

"Hundred, maybe a hundred-ten pounds. May be the biggest white taken off Miami in years. This is a Bimini fish." He nodded at Brian. "There's a tape measure on the console. Let's get a length and girth, and then get this baby back in the water."

"You're going to release him?" Fiore asked, returning with the tape.

"Yeah. A fish like this is too rare to kill."

"Cool," Hunter said, giving a wan grin. He ran a hand over the fish's head before grabbing the end of the tape as he and Seagrave completed the measurements. Fiore snapped photos and took a video of the measuring.

"Eight-foot-four inches, and a thirty-seven inch girth. Surely over a hundred pounds." He withdrew pliers from his rear pocket and removed the circle hook from the corner of the fish's jaw. He slid the marlin to side and eased it into the water.

"Put her in gear, Brian, and move us up to a fast idle so I can resuscitate this guy." With the boat making way, Seagrave held the warrior by the bill keeping him upright. After thirty seconds, the fish began to swim. Seagrave released his grip, and the marlin shook his head, rolled slightly to one side and seemed to look at them before swimming slowly away.

"Geez, that was strange," Hunter said, waving at his disappearing foe.

"Looked almost like he was saying good-bye, and thanks for the fun," Seagrave said, and grinned.

"You think?" the boy asked, eyebrows arched.

"No," his uncle laughed, "not really. So, how are you feeling now, kid? That was a pretty good workout."

"Tired. I'm embarrassed I puked all over your boat."

"Already washed it down." He patted the boy's back. "Throwing up on an offshore boat's not so uncommon."

"We calling it a day?" Hunter's father asked.

"Yeah. I think we've had enough for now, and that was a great finale. The sea's up a bit, so it's gonna be at least an hour's run to make it back to the Cut. You guys relax in the chairs and have a drink."

~ ~ ~

Two hours later, they tied up at *Valkyrie's* dock. Fiore toted their gear back to his car, while Hunter lingered on the fighting chair. Seagrave perched on the fish box, hands on his knees.

"So how are you feeling—really? You managing things okay?" He respected his nephew too much to avoid reality.

"I guess. I just tire more easily. That's the first time I've puked." He sighed. "It's really stressful in the house, with everyone focused on trying to find a donor."

"They love you, kid. We'd really like to keep you around, you know." He patted the young man on the knee.

"Yeah, I know. I'm not eager to go—you know—that way either. I can't picture myself going to sleep and not waking up. No memories; no dreams; nothing. I—I . . . ." He stammered to a stop, his green eyes wet pools.

"I know." They rose, and Seagrave pulled him into a bear hug. "I'm not gonna let that happen. We're gonna find that liver for you. I promise. Somehow . . . ."

"Thanks." They eased apart, and the man squeezed the boy's shoulder and nodded.

"I can't express how much your involvement in this means to me. And all you do for me—this fishing and everything. It's great." They stepped onto the dock and started wending their way toward the parking lot.

"It seems unfair that O-Negatives can donate to anyone but can only receive tissue from another O-Negative, and we're just six percent of the population. I hate the idea of sorta hoping for the right person to die so I can live."

"I understand, but that's life. Accidents and other bad things occur." They paused at the entrance to the parking lot as Brian Fiore pulled up in his tan Dodge Caravan.

"We just gotta be ready when that happens," Seagrave continued, and gave the boy another hug before he entered the minivan. "I've got feelers out to every possible agency, so I'll know as soon as the right liver comes available. Kim's working her angle, too."

Hunter closed the van's door and opened the window. "You got lucky when you landed *that* beauty, Unc." The boy grinned. "She's a better catch than my white marlin."

"You aren't kidding. Never thought that after so many years of bouncing around, I'd finally find love. She's one amazing babe."

"She's as lucky as you are, Charlie," Brian called from the driver seat. "You're a pretty great catch, yourself."

"Thanks, Bro. We're a team united for Hunter's cause. Be sure of that. She's as passionate about this as I am." He stepped back as Fiore shifted into gear.

"And don't think we don't appreciate it," Fiore said. "We'd be lost in the weeds without you guys support." He waved as they drove off.

Hands in his pockets, Seagrave watched their departure. He'd call Kim once he started home. She said she was spending the day on some more research, looking for a way to get that terrific young man a new lease on life.

Something better happen quick. He had his own strategy to speed this along, but everything took time, something they were running out of too quickly. Maybe a lot less than a year.

He'd made the first move yesterday on a new plan to find the boy a donor. It would take a while to see if it bore fruit.

~ 10 ~

The red and white ambulance, lights flashing and siren echoing off the walls, skidded to a halt at the Emergency entrance of Miami's Doctor's Hospital. The rear doors flew open and two EMTs leaped out drawing a stretcher after them.

"What do you have?" a doctor in blue scrubs asked, taking the patient's wrist.

"Fifty-two-year-old man in cardiac arrest and un-responsive. Continuous CPR for . . . ." he glanced at his watch "eleven minutes." They rushed through the pneumatic doors, heading for an ER. "We hit him with paddles three times en route with no response."

"He'd be better off at Jackson," the doctor said.

"We know, but it's at least eight minutes farther away, and this man had no heart beat for five or six minutes before we got to him."

"Okay," the doctor said as they transferred the figure to an ER bed. "Not much chance for him at this point, but we'll give it a go." He signaled a nurse to take over the oxygen mask pump, still being administered by the ambulance tech. He peeled back an eyelid and flashed a pen light at the pupil. No response.

"You get anything from the family as to what happened?" he asked.

"Not much," the taller EMT said, "but it looks like he's had a recent transplant—kidney, I think. They were reluctant to talk about it."

They stood back as another doctor applied defibrillator paddles and yelled, "Clear!" The patient arced up slightly at the surge of electrical current. No response on the EKG monitor.

"Turn it up and try it again," the first doc said, shaking his head. "Not likely to help at this point," he mumbled.

The second try never changed the flat line on the green electronic screen, which exuded a soft, steady hum.

"That's it," he said. "He's gone." He glanced at a big wall clock. "TOD, ten-eighteen AM. Strip him down. I want to see if we can verify why he's dead."

"You want to do an autopsy here, doctor?" a male nurse asked, his eyebrows raised.

"No, just a quick exam to slake my curiosity. Any family here?"

"Yes," the Latin member of the EMT team said. "I noticed his wife outside just now." He stroked a thin moustache. "You want me to tell 'em, Doc?"

"No, not my favorite thing, but I'll do it. Meanwhile, get him ready. I want to examine that apparent recent transplant." He turned and strode from the room, glancing at the EMT who followed. "You got a name for him?"

"Yes, sir. Oberlin. Philip Oberlin." He cast his eyes down and shook his head.

The doctor paused, gripped his shoulder, and squeezed. "This the first one you've lost?"

"Yeah. I've had some close ones before, but we were always able to save 'em. It's tough . . . ."

"Nothing you could do any better. From what you've said, he was already gone by the time you arrived." The doctor patted him on the back as the medic turned to hurry back to his vehicle.

The trauma surgeon ran a hand through his hair, sighed, and stepped into the waiting room. Not busy today, and the tearful fiftyish woman pacing the floor seemed to stand out. He took two steps and paused.

"Mrs. Oberlin?"

She jerked to a stop and looked up, her eyes wildly sweeping the small, sterile white room before settling on his.

"Yes. My husband . . .?"

"I'm Doctor Mikos." He shifted from foot to foot. This was never easy.

"My husband . . .?" she repeated.

"I'm sorry. There was nothing we could do."

He reached out, but she spun away with a small wail and collapsed into one of the armchairs. Tears were in full flood, punctuated with heaving gasps that shook her core.

"I knew we should have found some other way," she hissed through hiccupped breaths.

"Other way? I don't understand?" He settled in the next chair, taking her limp hand.

"That damned transplant! That's what killed him, isn't it?" She looked up, her dark eyes squinting, her brow creased.

"We don't know that yet. Why do you suspect the transplant? Wasn't he taking his anti-rejection meds?"

"Of course, it's just how . . ." She sputtered to a halt and shook her head, emitting a soft, soulful wail.

"I've . . . I've said too much. I gotta get home. Tell the kids. Make arrangement. When . . . will you release the body?"

Dr. Mikos heaved to his feet. "Not immediately. We may have to do a preliminary autopsy."

"Oh, shit!" She struggled to stand.

"Sorry, but it's protocol. We need to find out why he died. The county medical examiner may want to take it further, depending on what we find. With unexplained—"

"Shit," she repeated, snatching up her purse. She brushed away tears, her eyes the proverbial deer in headlights.

"We were just trying to save his life." She threw her sweater over her arm, shouldered her black leather bag, and rushed toward the doors, glancing back.

"He's dead," her voice hoarse and cracked. "Can't you leave us alone? We didn't know what else to do." Head down she charged the double doors. "We just didn't know what else to do," came back in soft lament. She headed toward the restrooms, a tsunami of tears cascading down her cheeks.

What the hell is she talking about? Hopefully, the autopsy should tell us something. He spun on his heel and returned to the ER, where Philip Oberlin was being stripped and prepared for a quick exam. An actual autopsy would have to await his arrival in the morgue

Doctor Nick Mikos' curiosity was in full flood.

~ 11 ~

Warner slouched back in his black leather chair, a gift from Eva. He grinned. Hard to say 'no' to that beautiful woman. He was happily back together with her after that deadly bastard, Batchler, had put a crimp in their relationship.

He sighed and brought his thoughts back to the present. Ankles crossed, his feet draped across a corner of his scared oak desk, he flipped through pages of his notebook, reviewing his observations from his meeting with Eric Boxer's boss.

The young attorney seemed well liked and was moving up the ladder at the firm. He specialized in real estate contract law, and dealt mostly with buying and selling commercial properties—office buildings, apartments, and high-end single-family homes. It was primarily large deals, often with complex partnerships and financing.

Warner couldn't find any initial reason for his murder, other than a random act of violence, but he'd long ago learned motives for some killings were often far from obvious. And there *was* a specific purpose behind these three deaths, even if it were no more than being in the wrong place at the wrong time when some lunatic decided to vent his anger.

He shifted forward, shuffling though scattered papers on his desk. He plucked up Jack Harris' background report on the first victim, Amy Howard, and scanned it.

Hummm. Ms. Howard was a real estate broker. His eyes swept over the two-page document. She specialized in commercial property—condos and office buildings. Just like Mr. Boxer.

"That's a possible connection," he muttered. *But to what*

end? Were they involved together, knowingly or not, in some endeavor that made them a mutual enemy?

"Harris, you out there?" he called.

"Yeah, Boss. Coming." A moment later, the diminutive detective appeared in the doorway. "What's up?"

"Looks like two of the shootin' vics—Boxer and Howard—were both involved in commercial real estate." He handed Harris both files. "Check it out and see if there's any connection."

"On it, Boss. Don't seem too likely, though. You know, them being in the same place at the same time. Mighty convenient."

"Unless they were meetin' for some nefarious caper. Probably nothin' there, but we ain't gonna let anything go without checkin' every angle." He planted his hands on the oak desktop and jacked himself to his feet. "Not gonna repeat the missed connection like we did with the Angel of Death."

Harris glanced up from scanning the files, eyebrows knitted together, and nodded. "Right, Boss. No stone left unturned." He hurried off to begin further digging into both lives.

Warner circled his desk and approached the Murder Board, recently erected in his office. They hadn't used it much since the Prom Dress Killer. Currently, it only displayed photos of the three victims, but Warner's gut told him more were coming—and sooner rather than later. He sat back against the edge of his desk, hands on hips and scanned what little they had.

A soft rap on the door pulled him from his thoughts.

"Got a minute, Boss?" His newest detective, Ciro Salinas, stood with a file in hand.

"Sure. What d'ya need?"

"An opinion on this murder-suicide I'm working." He stepped in and handed Warner the folder.

"What's botherin' ya, Salinas?" Warner skimmed the two-page report, then looked at his detective. "Ya don't think the husband did it, do ya?"

"It just doesn't feel right, but I'm wondering if I'm over thinking it?"

"Follow your instincts, Detective. When it comes to murder, we can't afford to be too quick to accept what appears to be obvious." Warner handed him the file. "I'd dig deep into the wife's activities. Could be a jilted lover in there somewhere."

"You mean the husband offed her because she was having an affair?"

Warner glanced at the murder board, than back at Salinas.

"Could be, but that," pointing to the file, "paints him as a straight-arrow. Maybe a jilted illicit girlfriend was lookin' for revenge. Might get a heads-up by tracin' the origin of the gun."

"Yeah. Thanks, Boss. The guys were right."

"About what?" Warner's thought drifted back to his three sniper vics.

"That no one has better instincts about murder than our Chief of Detectives." He snapped off a casual salute and left.

Warner chuckled as he returned to the task at hand. He studied the mostly blank white board, then repositioned the photos so Boxer's was next to Amy Howard's, and using an erasable marker, drew an arcing line, joining them. He printed "REAL ESTATE?" below the line and stood back.

On the right side of the board, Harris had printed:

Male shooter, 5'9" – 6'-2"
slim, dark hair, guitar case
Looked like street musician

Warner ran a hand through his thick hair, and shrugged. *Not much to go on yet.*

He sighed at what he realized was inevitable—they probably weren't going to have any real direction unless this loony killed again—if then. It took four strangled beauties before they finally clicked on a possible motive for the Angel of Death, and they never really figured what drove the Prom Dress Killer until the very end.

He detested waiting for more victims, like they had with both The Angel of Death and Batchler, The Prom Dress Killer, before they discovered why a psychopath plied his deadly trade.

He hated that worse than anything.

~ 12 ~

Doctor Nick Mikos pushed through the swinging doors and tugged down his facemask. He shook his head, his mouth twisted into thin scowl as he tossed his surgical gloves and gauze mask into the medical trash.

"Unbelievable," he muttered and glanced at his watch: only ten-fifty, but he'd seen enough to know there was a problem. He exited the ER wing and strode with restrained determination toward the waiting room. *What the hell do I tell this woman, if she's returned from the restroom? Her husband's dead, and she may be guilty of abetting a felony?* He sighed and paused, gathering himself before entering the room. He saw her, red-eyed and haggard, hanging off the edge of an armchair.

"Mrs. Oberlin?"

Her head swiveled toward him, and she rose on shaky legs, one hand braced on the pale green wall behind her.

"Doctor Mikos?" Her voice scratchy, barely more than a whisper.

He nodded and took her hand. "I'm sorry for your loss, but

I need to talk to you. I've just finished a preliminary examination of your husband."

Sara Oberlin dropped back onto the chair, delivering small, high-pitched wail.

"May I ask, how long ago did he have the kidney transplant?" He settled on the seat beside her.

"Three weeks." She thumbed away tears. "Three weeks ago, this coming Tuesday." She managed to hold his eyes with hers, lips trembling. "Was it the kidney that—that . . .?"

"I believe so. Where . . .?"

"He took his anti-rejection medicine religiously." Her hand shook as she wrapped her arms around herself, rocking back and forth.

"While organ rejection, as such, may have contributed to his death," He placed a hand on her shoulder, "the early indications are the kidney may have been riddled with infection. There'll have to be an autopsy, but I believe he died from massive septic shock."

"Oh, god, Oh, god!" Her voice a shrill wail. "I told him we shouldn't trust those people, but he was so desperate . . ." Her words trailed away, usurped by racking sobs. Her head dropped into her hands, and she continued to cry.

"The transplant?" Mikos said and squeezed her shoulder, trying to break through her grief. "Where did he get it?"

"I—I can't . . . He's *dead*. Can't you just . . .?"

"Mrs. Oberlin, if you bought an organ . . ." He paused. "If someone directly donated the kidney, that's okay. But if it was an anonymous source, it had to come from a registered organ donation bank like the Florida Organ Bank. Otherwise, it's illegal. Possibly even a felony." He rose, arms folded.

"So, you have to tell me where . . .?"

"I—I can't. He's gone. Isn't that enough? Oh, god, what am I going to do?" She struggled out of the chair and gathered up her purse. Her eyes were wild as she swept the room, then she staggered toward the exit.

Mikos snatched at her sleeve. "You must tell me, where did you . . .?"

"No. Just leave me alone." She jerked free. "Leave me alone." She started down the hall, shaken by heaving sobs.

Doctor Mikos watched her unsteady departure, and shook his head.

I can't do that, lady. What he could do was check the various donor registries to see if Mr. Philip Oberlin received a kidney from an authorized source, and if so, where the transplant was performed.

He was pretty sure he knew the answers to both those questions, which was no answer at all. Then he'd have to talk to the hospital administrator. That poor woman had enough problems, but he had no other ethical choice. Some black market organ profiteers weren't as concerned as they should be with the quality of their product.

Meanwhile, they'd run some blood tests on Oberlin's body to verify his suspicion of septic shock. From there, it would be up to the county medical examiner to do an autopsy.

And eventually, he guessed, it would go to the police.

~ 13 ~

Warner bounded up the steps to the entrance to his townhouse, then paused. He glanced at the door of his left-hand neighbor, shrugged, and stepped over to ring her bell.

"Who's there?" The voice over the intercom was strong and musical, not something expected from a soon-to-be-ninety-year-old.

"It's Al, Adele. Just thought I'd say 'hi' on the way home."

"How nice. Just a moment, Detective."

A few seconds passed before he heard the click of the deadbolt, and the door opened. Adele Gerber stood in the doorway, adorned in a flowered apron and drying her hands on a green-striped dishtowel.

"Well, don't just stand there, Detective." Her pale blue eyes twinkled as she patted her gray hair into place. "Come in." She stepped back and gestured. At five-foot-three, she was still slim, the picture of elegance. Savory wafts of cinnamon drifted out. "I'm baking apple pie, but it won't be ready for another twenty minutes."

"Smells super, Adele, but I can't stay. Just checkin' that you're okay."

"No need for you to rescue me again, Al." She grinned and winked. "I'm doing fine. I saw Ms. Guttenberg's Jaguar in your drive. She's preparing dinner, I suppose?"

"Yep, and I don't want to keep her waitin'." He took her hands. "I'm already late."

"Of course. Why don't the two of you stop by after you eat, and I'll serve some pie for dessert." Her smile was soft. "I'd love the company."

"It'd be our pleasure. Probably in about an hour or so, if that's okay?" He turned to leave.

"Whenever you're ready. I always make time of my newly adopted son and daughter. You both make my life special."

Warner's cheeks tinged pink as he turned back and planted a soft kiss on her forehead. "Mine, too, Adele. You're the mom I never knew."

Her eyes brimmed, and she patted his cheek. "I'll be expecting you, then."

He nodded. "You bet. See ya soon." He stepped over to his own porch, unlocked the door, and hurried inside. He strode toward the kitchen and smells of garlic and oregano. His Jewish princess loved to cook Italian.

The clatter of paws previewed a golden flash of fur. Buff, Warner's big retriever skidded to a sitting halt at his feet and offered a paw in greeting. He dropped to one knee, scratching the dog behind the ears, and received a tongue-slathering kiss as a reward.

He chuckled. "Hey, honey. I'm home." Poking fun at the domestic relationship he never quite believed he deserved.

"You nut," the auburn-haired beauty stepped out of the kitchen to meet him. "Buff and I heard you pull up five-minutes ago. Visiting with Adele?" Her gray eyes sparkled as she slid into his arms for a kiss, gentle but still heated by passion.

"Yeah." They disengaged, his heart doing back-flips. He cradled her face in his hands, his thumbs caressing her cheeks.

"She's bakin' apple pie and invited us over for dessert. I kinda hoped we'd have our special appetizers first, though." He swept her up and his lips brushed her eyes, her mouth, and her throat as he headed for the bedroom.

"Darling." She whispered, her voice husky. She wrapped her arms around his neck. "I've got a Bolognaise pasta sauce on the stove. It'll burn."

He detoured into the kitchen, and supporting her with one arm, turned off the burner. He had a flash of memory of not pausing to do that once, two years ago, with near-disastrous results.

"Good," she murmured, her face buried in the crook of his neck. "It's about done, anyhow."

"Maybe, but we're only gettin' started." He chuckled as he entered the bedroom, settling on the bed with Eva sprawled across his lap. Amorous kisses morphed into a slow dual strip. He restrained his rush of desire as he teased over her face and body with busy lips and tantalizing fingers. They were soon joined in the ancient dance of love, relishing the very essence of their passions.

~ ~ ~

They exited the bedroom fifty minutes later, freshly showered, he wearing boxers and a tee shirt and she clad in one of his red-checkered flannel shirts. He retrieved an already prepared salad from the fridge along with a cold bottle of pinot grigio.

Settling at the dinette, he watched her fussing at the cook-top and sink as she strained angel hair pasta, plated it, and slathered on the thick red sauce. His tongue danced across his narrow lips, savoring her elegant grace far more than the coming meal, which he knew would also be delicious. He had never known such love was possible, and to have it returned by this incredible woman was beyond his grasp.

The food served, she perched on the seat across from him, her twinkling gray eyes fastened on his. Eva reached across the table and took his hand in hers, the corners of her lips tweaking gently upwards.

"I love you, you know." Her grin broadened. "Just saying, so you don't think I'm an easy woman."

He chuckled and squeezed her hand. "That the feelin's mutual goes without sayin', but it's gotta be the mystery of the century, Eva."

"What?"

"That someone like you could actually love a hard-case like me. I haven't been too lucky in love in the past."

"I know who you *really* are, Al, and that's who I love. So, let's eat before this sauce gets cold." She tucked a napkin into the open collar of the shirt and took a sip of the cold, white wine. "Adele's apple pie is waiting."

They dug in, both ravenous, and made quick work of the meal. She settled back, dabbing the corners of her mouth and studied his face.

Warner glanced up after mopping up the last of the sauce

with a sourdough biscuit. "What?" His eyebrows arched as he noticed her serious face.

"Where are we going from here, Al?" Her russet eyebrows arched.

"To Adele's for pie." Seeing a small shake of her head, he sighed. "What else did ya have in mind, Eva?"

"I mean *us*, Al. I know you've wanted to protect me after what happened with Ron Bachelor . . ."

"Eva, our engagement almost . . ."

"I know. I know, but we can't live in fear of that. I'm almost thirty-nine. I'm not afraid to be the Hero of Miami's wife. It's no secret we're back together again, and . . ." she trailed off, studying her hands, folded on the table.

"And . . .?"

"I've stopped taking the pill, Al. I want to get pregnant again. Have your—our—baby." She glanced up, a single tear wandering over her cheek. "Time's running out on that."

"Wow! You're sure? I mean, last time . . ."

"That was then, this is now." She sat up, taking both his hands in hers. "I want to live together again. Plan to *marry* again, and the hell with it being dangerous for me."

They rose, and Warner circled the table, folding her into his arms and tilted back her chin, as his lips found hers.

"Nothin' would make me happier, if you're sure . . . ." His voice choked, the words trailed off.

"Never been surer of anything," she said, giving him a fierce hug. She chuckled. "Now, we'd better get over to Adele's for her delicious apple pie. She's going to wonder what happened to us."

"I've got a hunch she's got a pretty good idea. You know, she's turnin' ninety soon."

"Yes. It's amazing how youthful she is." They walked toward the bedroom to change.

"We're the only thing like family she's got," he said, as he pulled on a pair of tan chinos and a beige knit shirt. "I'd like to arrange a small surprise party. It'll be mostly our people, but I think there are three women she plays bridge with on Wednesdays we could probably ask."

"I'll see what I can find out." She slipped into a flowered spring dress, turning for him to zip her. "Ready?" she asked.

"Yeah, let's go." He kissed her at the base of her neck. "I got a lot to think about, and I'm really ready for some pie."

They exited, arm in arm, each deep in thought, wondering what the future would bring.

~ 14 ~

Charlie Seagrave settled at his English mahogany desk and moved the mouse to activate his desktop computer. The large flat-screen monitor lit up, displaying his last search: The South Florida Organ Bank in West Palm Beach.

He clicked through several options until he got to the donor wait-list. He found Hunter's name but was frustrated after a half-dozen attempts to accurately learn his position in the queue. There were no notations as to how many O-Negative patients awaiting livers were ahead of him.

Seagrave slouched back on his black leather chair and swiveled back and forth while stroking his chin. *This is getting me nowhere.* He leaned forward and began clicking on the site's tool bar, searching for inspiration. He turned at a creak from the Brazilian cherry floor and found Kim quietly sidling into the room.

"Sorry, hon." Her hands settled on his shoulders, and her marauding thumbs gently bore into knots at the base of his neck, easing away his tension. "Didn't mean to disturb you."

He sighed, almost a purr. "Feels great, babe. Just what I needed." He rotated the chair, hooked an arm around his five-foot-ten lover's slim waist, and drew her onto his lap.

Kim draped her arms around his neck, her chocolate-brown hair creating a tent around their faces as she planted a gentle kiss on his lips, the tip of her tongue teasing his.

"Having any luck?" she asked after they drew apart.

He pecked her on the tip of her straight, narrow nose and shrugged. "Not much. I guess he's still third on the list of O-Neg candidates for a liver." He sighed. "There hasn't been a single useful donor in almost three months."

Kim slipped off his lap as he rose, her arms still hooked around his neck. They hugged, more friendly than passionate, then he led her by the hand into the den. She draped herself over a beige loveseat while he went to the wall-bar to pour two tumblers of Scotch, neat. Even carelessly slouched across the leather sofa, her slim, taut body was the picture of athletic grace.

Seagrave handed her the glass and perched next to her. "I have a new angle I'm gonna pursue."

Kim sat up and took one of his hands, as her hazel eyes caught his. "Tell me about it. Anything I can do?"

"Did a little digging and learned the name of the South Florida Organ Bank's administrator: Corbin Carthwright." He lifted her hand to his lips for a gentle kiss. "I'm gonna find a way to meet him. See if I can convince him to move Hunt up on the list."

"A bribe?" A tiny smile tickled the corners of her lips.

"If I thought cash might work, yeah, but I doubt it. I did some Web surfing. He comes from old money, so I don't think that'll move him." He leaned into the leather backrest. "But I also learned he's a member of the NRA and loves to hunt."

"Aha!" Her wide mouth split into a sparkling grin. "A shooter. Now, there's some common ground to work with."

"Yeah. According to his Facebook page, he's taken several nice bucks but had a very disappointing trip last fall out west for elk."

"You got all that off the Web?" She sipped the warm Scotch.

"He's one of these obsessive types who post something almost daily. I friended him, and I'm gonna start posting comments about the Exotics Game Ranch. It's every big game hunters dream, but we haven't taken a new member in ten years."

"I've hear about that place." She finished her drink and set the glass on a coaster on a mahogany side-table. "It's near Atlanta, isn't it?"

"In the hill country, near Perry. Over a thousand acres, where a guy can hunt exotics like red stag, Indian blackbuck antelope, and even Russian Boar." He tossed down the rest of his drink and rose. "What makes it more unique than most other ranches is, you're on foot, chasing big game in natural-looking environs, not shooting baited animals from a blind."

"You're a member there?" She tucked a leg under her, studying him. "You never mentioned it."

"Oh? I'm one of the founders, but I haven't hunted there in three or four years. Not since I met you." He started to pace.

"Sounds like you're planning on baiting this Cartwright guy." She left the loveseat, trailing after him.

"That's what I'm thinking." A grin tickled at his lips. "Once I get his attention with some posts, I'll mention I've scheduled a three-day trip, but my usual hunting pal had to cancel." His grin widened. "Very disappointing."

"So, you hope he'll contact you?"

"I'm betting on it." He settled at his desk. "Especially when I mention I'll be trying out my new Weatherby 300."

"The Mark V you just got at auction? That's a beauty." She moved behind him, her hands lightly draping across his shoulders.

"Yeah." He awakened the computer and opened his Facebook page. "Once I post a pic of the rifle, showing the carved stock with a gold lion inlay, and the Leupold sight, I'm guessing he'll be salivating."

"It's a great idea, if you think it'll work." She hunkered behind him, her face next to his, watching him write the first post. "But time isn't your friend here."

"I know," he said as he searched his files for photos of his classic and very elegant custom rifle. "I'll be on Facebook more this week than I've been all month. Money won't move this guy, but a trip to an otherwise unavailable hunt for exotic trophies, and maybe a chance to shoot that gun, just might."

"I hope you're right." She pecked him on the ear and ruffled his hair. "Hunter's a great kid, and I know how much he means to you. That makes him very important to me, too, so be sure to keep me in the loop." She straightened up. "I'll do anything I can to help."

"You're the best, gorgeous," he said as he uploaded his first post, mentioning he was a founding member of the ranch and was planning a three-day trip. "I don't know how I got so lucky to find you, after all those years of bachelorhood."

"I'm the fortunate one." She eased against his back with an embrace and a soft kiss on his neck. "You're the first self-made guy I've met not totally consumed with himself. It's the proverbial breath of fresh air."

Seagrave chuckled, reaching back to stroke her cheek. "I got lucky that some rich dopes thought my little dot-com company was worth fifteen million bucks." He pushed out of his chair.

"I can't begin to spend all the investment income on myself, no matter how hard I try, and I get more of a rush helping others." He came out of the chair and turned to her. "Seeing the joy that bubbled out of Hunt when he caught that marlin—that was priceless. I'm damn well committed to insure he has a lot more years doing that."

"I know. That's priority one for both of us. I've got an algorithm running at the hospital that picks up any accident victims on life support and searches records for their blood types."

"Aren't those medical files private, Kim?"

"Supposedly." She chuckled, her eyes sparkling pools, "but because I'm a trauma nurse at Jackson, I was able to get to their mainframe and install a gadget a hacker friend gave me." She perched on the rim of a side chair. "Sends me alerts and opens their records to my phone."

Seagrave dropped to a crouch beside her, taking her hand. "That's incredible. Gives us a chance to be the first to talk to their guardian and offer something to ease their pain at their coming loss."

"That's the idea. You keep trying to get the boy to the top of the list, and meanwhile, I've got several irons in the fire. Something's bound to work."

"Soon, I hope." He pushed to his feet. "That's not the only angle I'm working, either."

"Good. We're a team with plans. Now, are you going to buy me dinner, or are you grilling steaks?"

"Let's change. I made a res at that new Italian bistro that got raves in the Herald last week."

"Yum. I'm famished. Let's eat, and then we've got some serious work to do."

They headed for the bedroom, but her closet full of clothes waited forty minutes. When he saw Kim bra-less and in panties, Seagrave decided they'd have a special appetizer at home first.

Kim needed no coaxing.

~ 15 ~

I leaned away from the table, thrusting both arms toward the ceiling, fingers locked together in a protracted stretch. This drew lecherous glances from the two boys poised at nearby computers. My pair of considerable breast held their immediate attention.

I adjusted the black driving cap, set jauntily on my curly, blond hair and pushed tinted glasses back up the bridge of my nose. My notebook, pens, and pocket calculator in hand, I slipped from the seat and leaned over to return the library's computer to Home Page.

I smiled at the two entranced boys, and with a swirl of a plaid midi-skirt, I twirled around and did a hip-swinging saunter across the library's tiled floor toward the exit. My grin widened. If the cops ever traced any searches back to this facility, all anyone might remember was a buxom blond, one of many users of their open-to-the-public desktop computers. No way they'd tie that woman to a silver-haired man, a dowdy brunette woman, or the shaggy street musician, all who'd visited other libraries.

To succeed as an assassin, one needed many convincing personas so no one victim or cop—saw you coming.

Pushing through the swinging glass door into the blazing Florida afternoon, I replaced my prop specs with a pair of silver-lens sunglasses. Skeins of cottony cumulus clouds invaded the cerulean morning sky, playing peek-a-boo with the molten disk, edging toward the afternoon horizon.

I beeped the alarm on my CRV and slid into the driver's seat, quickly cranking the engine and boosting the a/c to max. I lingered for a moment, scanning notes from my computer searches. Not complete, but should be enough for now.

I reached under the back of my cashmere blouse, unsnapped the bra, and freed my arms from the shoulder straps. No longer necessary to play a buxom floozy. I checked the parking lot through my heavily tinted windows, and seeing no one around, stripped off the blouse and slid on a striped, v-neck cotton sport shirt.

Ahh, better.

Shimmying out of the long skirt exposed a pair of khaki cargo shorts. I rolled up the skirt and blouse and stowed them, along with the blond wig and driving cap, in a gym bag on the passenger seat.

Back to normal. I hated that damned bra, but it was a necessary discomfort to hide my identity. I glanced again at my notes, already mentally constructing my next attack. It was a convenient coincidence that two of my first vics were connected to real estate. I may be able to use that next time to create a solid red herring for the cops.

My second hit would be . . . The warble of my burner "work" cell phone, nestled in a side pocket of the gym bag, cut off my thoughts. I frowned and ground my teeth.

Shit! Why now? I glanced at the caller ID and swore.

"Yeah, what?" Impatience colored my words, my voice altered by a built-in cloaking device. *Get control. You're a professional.*

"Wow! Very testy, Ace. Is that a way to talk to the jefe?" Latin nuances confirmed his identity

"Maybe not, if I had one. I'm freelance, remember?"

"Okay, but I *do* got you on retainer, so . . ."

"Right, but just for one last contract, and now's not a good time." I twisted the a/c knob, dropping the fan speed. The high setting was noisy, and the car was already cooling.

"You working for someone else, Ace? Without telling me?"

"Like I said, I'm freelance. You don't own me. No one does." I sighed, glanced at the phone, and shrugged. If he needed a job done, there was no way I could duck it.

Damn! I didn't have time for this. "What d'ya need. Maybe I can work it in."

"This other job you're on—?"

"Is none of your business. What I do for you is between you and me. Other client is between me and them. Got it?"

"Yeah. Okay. So one more job for me, and then what?"

"Maybe I'll retire. So . . .?" I flexed my jaw, easing tension.

"Retire? You? You got rich enough to afford that?" He chuckled.

"Not with what you pay me. So get to it. What's the job?" I plucked a paper pad and a pen from the glove box. Nothing from this business was ever electronically recorded.

"Okay, so this upstart hotshot, he thinks he can muscle into my Little Havana territory. I need him erased and his pals scattered—and I don't want it to look like no accident."

"You want me to send a message, huh?" My fingers pinched the bridge of my nose. Maybe I can work this into my personal crusade. Broaden the scope of what I was doing, and add some more confusion. Just might work.

"Yeah. It don't pay to fuck with me."

"Right. So send the details to the usual drop, and I'll pick them up later in the day. With luck, it'll be done by the end of next week—maybe sooner."

I was already constructing how I was going to tie it into my current project.

"This is going to cost you an extra fifty Gs," I said.

"What?" There was pain in his voice.

"I got other things cooking, and this is taking me off target. Wire half to my offshore account today. Once I see it there, I'll get to it."

"Fifty more Gs? *Dios mio*, Ace, . . ."

"Don't fuck with me, pal. Wire the cash, and I'll get on it. You want it done right. That's why you called me."

"Okay, okay. Don't get nasty. The money'll go in the next hour. Keep me posted."

"Roger that. Now I gotta run. You'll know when it's done." I disconnected, not awaiting a reply.

My fingers rested lightly on the steering wheel while I considered the next move. My preferred hit was an engineered accident, where it was harder for the cops to assign blame. But this pain-in-the-ass Cuban don wanted everyone to know who was behind it—just as long as no one could prove anything.

Well, I've never left anything for the cops, or I wouldn't have survived nearly twenty years at this game.

I glanced at my watch, shrugged, and shifted the Honda into reverse and backed out of the parking slot. Better get this baby into hiding, retrieve my regular wheels, and get back to my other life.

And I had to digest my notes from the library and set up some surveillance schedules to work out final details—for two jobs now, damn it. I needed to get both done by the end of next week, before I run out of time.

I pulled onto the street, melding with traffic, my mind sorting information, dropping items into various queues for action. It was all coming together.

This is what I did, and no one knew I was doing it.

Or did it better.

~ 16 ~

Doctor Nick Mikos charged into his office, scrambling for his desk phone before the caller hung up. He snatched it up in the middle of the fifth ring.

"Doctor Mikos." He panted softly as he circled his mica-topped desk and dropping onto his leather chair.

"Hi, Doc. This is Moe Gold from the crime lab."

"Yes?" The famous Hawk. Was this about Oberlin's death?

"I got results for you on the Oberlin kidney transplant. I can e-mail it to you, if you'd like."

"Sure, but I was expecting to hear from the medical examiner."

"Yeah, well they kick it up to me if it smells bad, and something is definitely off, so . . ."

"So, I was right." Mikos dragged over a pad of paper and drew a pen from his breast pocket. "Can you give me a quick recap? Something was wrong with that organ?"

"In spades," Gold said. "The kidney was at least twenty-four to thirty-six hours past viability when they implanted it, and it didn't appear to be a good tissue match, either. I thought you'd want to know."

"I knew it! Thanks for the update, Mr. Gold."

"Everyone calls me Moe, Doc. Even people I don't know."

"Or the Hawk, I believe."

"That, too," Gold chuckled. "Anyhow, I'm sending the results up to homicide. It's in their ballpark now."

"Homicide? Wow, I never thought . . ."

"This wasn't an accident, Doctor. Whoever transplanted that organ *knew* it wasn't viable. They're facing at least manslaughter charges."

"If you catch them," Mikos said, easing back in the chair.

"Yeah, if we catch them. We've got some pretty good cops up there, you know."

"So I've heard. Anyhow, thanks for letting me know—Moe. 'Bye." He replaced the receiver, rubbing his jaw.

Poor Mrs. Oberlin. Her husband's gone, and now here come the cops. Life can be pretty unfair sometimes.

He leaned forward, sorting through reports on his desk. He had three major surgeries scheduled for tomorrow.

He'd better get a good night's sleep.

~ 17 ~

Warner noticed it the moment he entered his office—a red binder, nestled atop the scattering of papers that usually obscured his desktop. He chuckled, appreciating that the Hawk catered to his preference for printed data. He knew it would also be on his Samsung note pad, but he was still old school. He didn't like e-books either.

He read the label as he slipped onto the chair behind his battered oak desk: *Forensic Findings - Bayfront Park Shootings.* He leafed through the opening pages to get to the technical details. 12.7mm rounds, which he knew, but the rifling patterns indicated the weapon was probably a McMillan TAC-50 sniper rifle. That was a high-tech, military gun, not readily available to the general public.

Warner slouched back in his scuffed leather chair, stroking his chin. The weapon and expert, long-range marksmanship smacked of a military-trained shooter, but how could he obtain that weapon? Warner didn't think a retired special-ops guy could bring his rifle home with him. He'd expected it to be a Barrett .50, like the one FBI agent Ina Yeager had used to save his life in that Opa-locka Airport shootout last year. Either rifle, in the hands of an expert, were effective from as far as two thousand meters.

Hmmm. Trained snipers and over-watch shooters, like Army special-ops, usually worked with spotters who'd feed the marksman distance, wind, and weather data. He wasn't sure if

Navy SEALs worked with a team or alone. So, was their culprit a single shooter, or a two-man team? He shook his head, glancing back at the report. Could be either, but Yeager had calculated all that data alone and on the fly that scary day, and had done an outstanding job. *Thank God!*

No evidence from the shooter's perch that there was more than one assailant, and Harris's single witness saw only one guy leave the roof. The uniqueness of the weapon gave them something to chase down. Not many legit places a civilian could buy one without leaving a record.

Warner lurched out of his chair and started prowling around his desk, hands thrust into his pockets.

Of course, there's the infamous Dark Web. I suppose one of our tech guys could penetrate it, but would anything exist there to point them to their guy? Probably not. The whole idea of an illegal Internet, where felons could buy all sorts of bad stuff, boggled his mind.

He dropped back on his chair, hands slapping flat on the desktop. This shooting had all the earmarks of a spree-killer, and if that was what he was, things were going to heat up again very soon. Those kinds of nuts were seldom patient.

He'd already reviewed the victims' reports, and the one thing that bore investigation was that Amy Howard and Eric Boxer both had ties to commercial real estate. There were no apparent evidence they knew each other or were in any way connected through an active project, but he'd have Olvida dig deeper there.

Warner's stream of thought was broken by a rap on his doorjamb. He looked up and spied Detective Salinas, lingering in the doorway.

"How's your investigation comin', Detective?" He eased back in his chair and waved the man in.

"In the hands of the DA. Just wanted you to know we were right."

"So, not a murder/suicide?"

"No. When I started tracing the woman's activities, I discovered she'd had an affair with some guy she met in Publix." He perched on the edge of a chair. "Told a friend sex life at home was too mechanical. Apparently the boyfriend was hot and skilled, but she got cold feet after three months and called it off."

"I'm guessing Don Juan didn't like that." Warner chuckled.

"Right. The wife told her friend the guy was openly stalking her, but she was afraid to go to the cops."

"Yeah." Warner nodded. "She'd have to admit to the affair."

"Deadly mistake, unfortunately. We got CCTV footage from a neighbor's doorbell cam of the guy coming and going right at the time of the shooting." Salinas push out of the chair. "Got a warrant and CSU found GSR residue and a bit of blood spatter on one of his shirts. DNA matched the blood to the husband."

"So, sounds pretty open and shut." Warner rose and offered the man his hand. "Good job."

"Thanks, Boss. The ME was ready to call it murder/suicide, but you steered me right, and we caught the perp. Just wanted you to know."

Warner nodded, the detective turned, and left just as Captain Santiago entered, carrying a small file.

"What's up, Bob?" Warner asked.

"I know you're in deep with the Bayfront Park shooting, Al, but I have something else that needs you, too." He handed the stapled sheath of papers to Warner.

"What's this?" The detective glanced at the cover sheet. "An ME report? On what, Cap?"

"A guy died two days ago at Doctor's Hospital, and the COD was kidney failure from an illegal transplant."

"And this comes to Homicide why?" He began leafing through the report.

"According to Moe, the transplanted kidney was at least twenty-four hours past viability, and apparently not properly tissue-typed. The black market surgeon *knew* he was probably killing his patient, who eventually died of rejection and septic shock." Santiago perched on the edge of an armless side chair. "There's been a growing spate of these illegal transplants, and this was the second death linked to bad organs."

"Really?" Warner pushed back from his desk. "So it's the beginnin' of a pattern." He looked at his captain, who pushed out of his chair.

"Yeah, and the commissioner wants this network broken up, the sales stopped, and one or more people charged with First Degree Murder."

"So, it's gonna be up to Homicide, huh?" He stood and leaned over his desk, fisted hands braced on its surface. "Like I ain't got enough on my plate, with a probable spree-killer gettin' ready to take off."

"There's no one better to do this than you and your team, Al. You're going to have to multi-task."

"Yeah, I know." He groaned and plucked the report off his desk, glancing at the second page. "We'll get on it, Cap."

Santiago nodded, clapped the detective on his shoulder, and left the room.

"Harris," Warner yelled through the open door.

"Coming, Boss." Fifteen seconds later the wiry little detective was in the doorway. "What's up?"

"We got another case." Warner gestured with the file. "Set up an interview with this . . ." glancing at the paper, "Mrs. Oberlin. Black Market kidney transplant gone bad."

"This is for Homicide? Shouldn't it–?"

"The butcher used a knowingly corrupted kidney. Commish wants 'em found, stopped, and charged with Murder One. Take Beck with you. Olvida's workin' the shooter."

"Got it, Boss." He hurried back into the bullpen.

Warner settled back at his desk and started reviewing the Hawk's report on the mass shooting, looking for some tiny crack he could dig into. Something to expand the investigation. He hated waiting for another massacre to look for new evidence.

But there was nothing there but the haunting knowledge more people were going to die—and sooner than later.

~ 18 ~

"There it is, I think." Kim twisted in the Lexus' passenger seat and pointed toward Seagrave's side window. "That's the address, and . . . oh, there's the sign."

SOUTH FLORIDA ORGAN BANK

"Got it," Seagrave said, "and here's an open spot at the curb. Maybe a good omen." He stopped alongside the car in front and activated the silver 570's auto-parking feature. The car backed smoothly into the opening, perfectly positioned next to the curb.

"That's amazing," Diana, his sister, offered from the back seat.

"I sorta feel like it's cheating," he said, chuckling. "Let's go. We're right on time."

"Who are we meeting?" Diana asked as she exited the rear door and joined Seagrave and Kim at the curb.

"Dr. Corbin Carthwright," Kim said, grabbing Diana's hand as they darted through continual traffic on Evernia Street. "He's the top honcho there." The three of them paused when they reached the sidewalk in front of the unimposing two-story. Its walls were precast concrete slabs, pale blue, and nearly windowless on the first floor.

"You really think this will work, Charlie?" Diana asked.

"We'll see. A personal connection always helps, and I've got a plan."

"Charlie's got something we hope is more alluring than money in Carthwright's eyes."

"Yeah." He guided the women toward the glass entry door. "But I'm just planning on teasing him with it today. I'll let him play with the bait for a day or two before I set the hook." He smirked. "Just the way Hunt nailed that marlin."

Diana sighed, taking her brother's hand. "I wish I'd been there. Catching that fish was all he talked about for two days." The smile drained from her face, and tears bloomed in the corners of her eyes. "This has to work, Charlie. If Hunt doesn't get a liver soon, it's . . . it's . . ." Her words dwindled away.

"I know, sis. I know." He reached over and thumbed away the trickling tears.

Kim squeezed her hand. "Hang in there, Di. You've got two dedicated warriors fighting this battle. We're going to come out on top. Somehow, on top. You'll see."

They pushed through the doorway, entering a tiled foyer. A dark-haired, Hispanic woman, sitting behind a weathered-teak desk, glanced up and smiled as they approached.

"May I help you?" she asked.

"I'm Charles Seagrave, and this is my sister, Diana, and my friend," patting Kim's shoulder. "We have an appointment with Mr. Carthwright."

She glanced at her monitor, "Yes, and you're right on time. I'll let the Director know you're here. Have a seat." She gestured toward a row of gray armchairs. "He's up stairs, and it may take a few moments for him to come fetch you."

Seagrave nodded, and ushered the women to the seats where they settled, awaiting the arrival of the man who, in a sense, held Hunter's fate in his hands.

Diana's fingers were busy in a nervous flutter, picking at

the hem of her black skirt and tugging at the collar of her white blouse. A total contrast to Kim, who had slouched back, her fingers interlaced across her belly, the planes of her tanned face and slitted eyes still, in quiet introspection.

Seagrave perched on the edge of the chair, checking his android phone for messages. His eyes swiveled at the entry of a tallish man, black-haired with graying temples. His ramrod posture smacked of a military background.

"Mister Seagrave?" He started toward the sitting threesome.

"That's me," Seagrave said, rising, "and this is my sister, Diana Fiore," He drew Diana up by the forearm, "and my friend, Kim Tate." Kim rose with nimble grace.

"Ah, yes," Carthwright said, taking Diana's hand. "Your brother told me of your son, Hunter I believe, who is on our waitlist. "A liver, isn't it?"

"Yes." Her voice cracked and her eyes flooded. "He doesn't have long . . ."

Seagrave, still holding her arm, gave a gentle squeeze, cutting off her words. "Can we move to your office, sir, where we can have some privacy?"

"Of course, of course." He pivoted, heading for the door he'd just come through. "Right this way. We'll take the stairs, if that's okay with you."

All muttered their agreement, with Seagrave offering his sister his arm. They entered a hallway, intermittently lined with heavy, insulated doors, the portals to the cold storage rooms housing a variety of less perishable donations, like bone marrow, eye corneas, and even skin. Organs requiring blood circulation, like kidneys, livers, and hearts, had viability measured in only hours.

Stopping at a door, the director swiped a keycard, opening an entry into a stairwell, ascending to the second floor office area. They followed him in silence, exiting into another hallway which led to an open bullpen, filled with a dozen desks. All but two were occupied, mostly by men, busily plying large-screen computers—the business of organ acquisition and placement hard at work.

Carthwright signaled for them to follow him toward a small bank of private offices at the rear of the room until they reached a door marked DIRECTOR. The smallish room contained a gray steel office desk circled by four armchairs. A large, four-pane window brightly lit the cream-colored walls, which were adorned by photos of the man posed with his hunting trophies—two with large rack mule deer, and one with an antelope.

"Please pardon the—uh—utilitarian office." He made a dismissive wave. "We're not into glitz here. Too busy trying to help save lives." He settled onto his desk chair, gesturing for them to take seats.

"So, what can I do for you? We don't see many visitors." He steepled his fingers under his chin.

"As I said, my nephew, Hunter Fiore, is on your waitlist for a liver. Diana," Seagrave nodded toward his sister, "is desperate to find a compatible organ before it's too late."

"I see." Carthwright swiveled toward his computer and started tapping keys. "F-I-O-R-E? Yes, here he is. Oh, dear!" His fingers stroked a slim, graying moustache. "O-Negative. And only nineteen. So young to need a liver, and such a rare blood-type." He glanced at Diana. "No one else in the family O-Neg? A living donor of a partial transplant is often more successful, long-term."

"No." She knuckled away a tear. "Hunter was adopted as a newborn. He was an anonymous drop-off, so we have no genetic history of his family."

"So sad." The director eased back in his chair. "I see he's number three on the list. Unfortunately, that can—"

"We understand the problem." Seagrave leaned forward,

placing his hands on the desk. "We were hoping you may have some idea how we can accelerate his opportunities."

The men's eyes locked for an interminable moment. "Well, there's protocol, and no way to jump the list," Carthwright broke the tension, glancing away, "unless someone in front waives their position. Sometimes that can happen if the need is critical."

"Can you check who they are? Maybe give me some names to talk to?" Seagrave peeked at Kim who had gently squeezed his thigh and gave him a tiny head shake.

"I'm sorry. Those records are privileged." The director rose. "I wish I could be more help, but there's little I can do."

Seagrave and the women also stood. "I understand. We thought it was worth asking, but I wouldn't want to cause you any trouble." He drew a business card from his pocket. "Here's my contact info, should anything change."

Seagrave glanced at the photos on the wall. "I see you're a hunter, as am I. Those are nice bucks. So we have something else in common."

The man's eyes followed Seagraves, and he nodded, smiling. "Yes, I usually take two or three trips a year. Tried for elk last fall, but only saw cows. You?"

"I took an eighteen-point red stag at the Exotic Game Ranch last fall. We probably have the biggest exotics in the world at the ranch. I'm a director there. Maybe we'll have a chance to discuss our trophies, once Hunter's situation is, hopefully, safely resolved."

Carthwright's eyes brightened, and his handshake with Seagrave lingered before leading the trio from the office and returning them to the building's lobby. The director wished them good luck, and lamented that he was helpless to do anything to improve Hunter's chances for an organ.

As they exited onto the glare of the sun-bathed sidewalk, Kim took his arm, leaned in and whispered, "I can find the names of the two people in front of Hunter. No need to make waves with this guy."

"Okay, good." He glanced at his sister, "but don't tell Diana. Can you learn how urgently they need their transplants?"

"Maybe." She hooked her arm through his as they started toward his Lexus sedan. "You hoping to make it worth their while to wait one round, and move Hunter up?"

"It's a possibility. Depends on how desperate they are for cash." He waited at the curb for Diana to catch up, then hurried them across the street to his waiting sedan.

"Well, that would certainly simplify things." Kim slid into the back seat, leaving the front for Diana. "Maybe we'll finally catch a break. The boy sure could use one."

"Damned right," Seagrave muttered. "We keep all our irons in the fire, something's gotta turn up."

He fired up the engine and peeled away from the curb. His pent up anger drove a heavy foot onto the accelerator.

Nineteen was too damned young for a great kid to cash in his chips. Plan B was risky, but it may be the only way to get what they needed.

Regardless, he was going through with everything.

~ 19 ~

I cruised through the parking lot of the Atlantis Shoppes Mall and noted CCTV camera locations and the lack of security guards. Nothing seemed changed from my last visit, ten days ago, when I managed to collect the discarded foam coffee cup. I steered my nondescript Honda CRV onto North Miami Avenue, and then made an immediate left onto a side street. Three blocks later, I slid the SUV to a curbside stop under a sprawling eucalyptus tree.

DNA samples taken from the cup had been rushed through a private, very discreet lab, finally confirming a probable match. This was the fourth O-Negative subject I'd surveilled, seeking an unwitting volunteer. The two-day wait for preliminary DNA results from each potential "donor" was time I couldn't spare, but unlike TV crime dramas, real lab answers didn't happen in a few hours. Even this one was only a likely match, requiring further tissue-type comparisons for positive results. I shrugged, knowing that was the best I could do.

I exited the car, retrieved my guitar case from the back seat and slung it over my shoulder, then locked the Honda and donned silvered sunglasses. The brim of a black Stetson tugged down, I started back toward the mini-mall. Just a shaggy, blond-haired street musician off to ply his trade.

I glanced at my digital Casio: Twelve-fifty. No need to rush. Previous scouting indicated my main objective wouldn't finish lunch for at least thirty minutes. If I were lucky, the perfect secondary target would be there about the same time. Someone who would help muddy the waters for the cops. Her car was in the valet lot, but not the congressman's, so hers wouldn't be an extended meal today.

Ten minutes later, I was about to access the stairwell of a twelve-story office building, one block from the mall, when the elevator opened, spewing six women into the lobby. Apparently clerical types on a late lunch break.

I paused pretending to read the directory, waiting for them to disperse, but three lingered in animated discussion. Then one began a search on her cell phone. Only able to stall for so long before being noticed, I exited the front door, and finding no onlookers, hurried into the passageway between buildings.

"Damn!" I checked my watch: one-ten. Time was getting short. Can't make it to another building quick enough, and none have been scouted as alternates. Not a mistake I'd make again, if this op failed today. I scampered to the back of the building and slipped through a rear door. A peek into the lobby showed the three women just ambling out the front.

I darted into the stairwell and raced up the stairs, taking them two-at-a-time. Untypically reckless, but speed was paramount if I were to set up in time.

I paused at the top, panting for breath. Bounding up twelve stories spiked my heart rate a lot more than I liked. I cracked the door open, and surveyed the rooftop. Unoccupied, as expected. It offered an unrestricted view of the restaurant's entrance, and the usual a/c mechanical box provided another perfect shooting platform.

I'd scoped it out during my scouting visit and pegged the shot at eleven-hundred-forty meters. Not normally that difficult with the super accurate TAC-50, but this was a much greater challenge, requiring an extremely precise shot. Two hours of practice at my improvised 'Glades target range had provided confidence I could put the bullet exactly where I wanted.

I strode quickly across the softening tar surface, unconcerned by the tracks my oversized shoes were leaving. Everything was carefully scripted misdirection.

I shrugged off the guitar case and backpack, and unrolled the flannel sleeping bag, positioning it atop the green metal case. *Temper the need for speed not to impact precision. I've got time to do this right.*

The skin-tight pair of vinyl surgical gloves I'd donned while climbing the stairs were a slight inconvenience as I assembled the rifle's stock, bi-pod, scope, and sound-suppressor. The five-shot magazine snapped into place, I inserted a metal-jacketed sixth shell into the breach. It was important the first bullet was clean penetration, not mushrooming.

I placed elastic bands around my long-sleeve wrist and

ankles cuffs, sealing the openings. No inadvertent skin cells would be left behind for a possible DNA match, although I was confident no one had mine on file anywhere. Any hair fibers would be from the real hair blond wig and would lead nowhere.

Slipping into a prone position on top of the green metal box, I positioned the rifle, assuring the bi-pod was firmly footed, and waited for my heart rate to settle to a normal pace. The powerful scope focused, I swept the lot, searching for possible problems. I'd made it in time, and found nothing to concern me. I settled in and locked my sights on the valet kiosk in front of Restaurante Il Medici.

Now was the time for patient waiting.

~ 20 ~

Twelve minutes slipped by as I rested easily but unmoving, reclaiming calmness and a slowing heart rate. All was in order as I focused on the restaurant's entrance. One nervous moment when a patrol car swept through the lot and the driver paused to visit with one of the valet staff. After he moved on, I released breath I hadn't realized I'd been holding.

Now I was settled back into a normal pattern of waiting. Successful people in my line of work have learned patience. Suddenly, a pod of people swarm through the door, and two were waving stubs at the valets.

Perfect! How lucky that both of my preferred subjects were there at the same time, using the free valet parking.

I glanced at the portable wind gauge mounted atop the tile parapet: four mph, from the north-northeast. After dialing that modest adjustment into the sight, I focused my attention on the first car arriving from valet parking. Hers. Everything was falling into place, with even the right carhop delivering her Ford.

Cesar Perez exited the Taurus and remained, as expected, holding the door for Ms. Betje DeVries, chief bank teller at First City Bank of North Miami. As I'd hoped, he stood motionless, awaiting the driver.

I released an even, steadying breath and squeezed the trigger. The 12.7mm slug pierced the right edge of his skull, taking off his ear and liquefying his eye in a bloody mass. He folded up, slumping to the ground, like a marionette whose strings were cut.

Her face showered by blood spatter and gore, Ms. DeVries' screams were quickly extinguished as the second round blasted through her open mouth.

Manny Glick, frozen in shock next to the valet podium, was the third to go down, his face turned into a gory pulp from the exit wound.

I was hoping my execution was as precise as it looked as I slid off the box, disassembling the weapon, before the third victim had hit the ground. The TAC-50 was quickly stowed inside the guitar case, and the bedroll bundled and strapped atop the backpack. I found and pocketed the still hot, expended shell casings.

Fifty seconds after the last shot echoed, I had packed up and fled across the roof, heading for my exit. My heart pummeled my chest as I sped down the stairs. No matter how often I'd done this, it always produced an adrenalin rush. Today, money wasn't the objective. This was for something much more important. And it looked like everything had gone off perfectly.

I reached the ground floor and edged open the door, hoping lobby was clear. My sound-suppressed Glock was ready to eliminate any unlucky witnesses.

Shit! The three bimbos were loitering by the elevator, all peering at a phone, giggling. They apparently knew nothing of the mayhem occurring a block away. I fingered my pistol and sighed. I'd just sacrificed one life for another, if everything worked out as planned. I didn't have it in me to take three more without reason. A minute could be spared if they'd...*Damn!*

The warble of fast-approaching sirens indicated I was running out of time to make an unobserved getaway. They had fifteen seconds to move . . . or die. Three more victims would tell the cops where I'd shot from, but they'll figure that out on their own.

I checked the Glock's breech, assuring it was ready to fire. Could I slip away unnoticed? Not likely, but so what? They'd have an APB out on a six-foot cowboy musician, and that disguise would be gone as soon as I was in my Honda. I replace my pistol and decided to chance it. Five innocents had already died, and I couldn't stomach taking three more just then. Somehow, this project had given me a new moral compass.

I slipped out and headed for the exit. A quick glance over my shoulder showed the three women entering the elevator. I didn't know if they'd spotted me or not, but I was out the door and headed for my SUV. I'd done what I could to achieve my goal, but there still was a lot to do.

And the clock was ticking.

Tick-tock, tick-tock.

~ 21 ~

Al Warner lingered on the walk outside the restaurant, hands jammed in his pockets, scanning the still chaotic area. Jack Harris had finished a brief canvas of the few witnesses and had supervised taping off the crime scene.

Warner sighed. While this apparently senseless massacre was not unexpected, since they were obviously dealing with a blossoming spree-killer, it still knotted his gut. The "little voice" in his head whispered these deaths were not as random as they had first seemed.

Three killed in a matter of seconds, each by a large caliber weapon, fired from a long way off. No one heard the shots. Not surprising, since the Hawk's ballistic report for the slugs recovered from Bayfront Park showed minute sound-suppressor markings. Whoever did this was a trained marksman, using a hi-tech military weapon. Probably special ops training.

Warner's eyes swept west, searching the buildings outside the boundaries of the mall. Two office structures, one about six floors, and the other maybe twelve. The shorter one didn't offer sufficient line of sight, so he suspected the sniper had positioned himself on the roof of the taller one.

He spotted his detective, Raphael Olvida, talking with one of the valet staff. Warner started toward them, calling out his name.

"Yeah, Boss?" He looked at Warner and pocketed his Android tablet.

"Take one of Moe's CSU techs and check out the roof of that taller buildin'." He nodded in that direction. "Be sure he brings evidence cones and yellow tape, 'cause I'm bettin' that was the shooter's perch."

Olvida followed Warner's gaze. "On it, Boss." He hurried toward Jack Harris and a small gaggle of techs, finishing up with the victims' bodies before they were bagged and sent to the morgue for autopsies.

Warner trailed behind, studying the area, seeking something not obvious at first look, but found nothing. He arrived at Harris' side just as Olvida and a CSU tech took off in

Raphael's blue Caprice.

"So, whatcha got?"

His ex-partner turned and shrugged. "Not much yet, Boss. Looks like the slug was a through-and-through for the valet and ended in that key rack. The Hawk's retrieving it now."

"Fifty cal?"

"Looks like it. Usually blows up whatever it hits, that one was different. Probably metal-jacketed for penetration, not fragmentation." Harris tapped on his Android.

"That's strange. Got IDs on the vics?" Warner asked.

"First hit was Cesar Perez. Took one on the right side of his skull. Surprisingly, he's still alive because the slug didn't appear to mushroom, but he's got serious brain damage, according to the EMT. He's on life support, on the way to the hospital."

"Humph." Warner scratched his day-old stubble. "Not like this guy to miss a kill shot."

"He was apparently holding the car door for the second vic, Betje DeVries, so maybe he moved."

"Possible. And the third vic?"

"Mister Manny Glick, local real estate tycoon. Apparently, he ate lunch here regularly."

"Interestin'. Real estate, huh? Two from the Bayfront Park shooting were connected to real estate. May be a pattern there. See if there's any connection when you get back to HQ."

"Got it, Boss." Harris typed on his notepad.

"And do a deep dive on the other two. I got a gut feelin' these killin's aren't as random as the shooter wants us to believe."

The little detective nodded and continues to make notes.

"Hero."

Warner pivoted, finding Moe Gold behind him, lips tilted into a whimsical grin. "Cut the Hero crap, Moe. It's gettin' old."

"Probably," the almost dwarfed chief of Miami-Dade CSU

said, "but I like the sound. Anyway, we got the slug out of the valet stand. 12.7mm, just like Bayfront Park." He rotated the bullet in his fingers. "It's sufficiently intact to compare markings with the earlier ones."

"Good. I'm expectin' it'll be a match."

"Me, too," the Hawk said.

"So, if that's all you got for me, I'm gonna join Olvida and your tech on that rooftop. Try to figure out what this nut's up to—besides killin' people."

"Don't think it's a classic spree killer, Al?"

"Nope. I got a sense there's somethin' else going on. I intend to figure that out before we get any more body bags."

He headed for his Dodge, edgy, knowing more bodies were coming, and angry he knew too little to prevent that.

~ 22 ~

Kim's blue-nailed finger did a tap-dance on the keyboard, searching for Cesar Perez's history. The details of the shooting had popped up on her computer, compliments of the research app she'd installed, interrupting her quest for the names of the two other O-Negative candidates for a liver who preceded Hunter on the Transplant List. Perez had survived the attack, but was on life-support, suffering traumatic brain injury.

It hadn't required much hacking for her to wiggle into his medical file. A sheen of perspiration sprouted on her forehead, and her fingers developed uncharacteristic tremors as she retrieved the fact that he was O-Neg. She leaned back, icy mice feet tripping down her spine, as she scanned his records.

"It'll be worth a try," she muttered as she printed out the two pages. A quick Google search failed to reveal details of his unfortunate—for him—auto misadventure.

Kim sighed and returned to her quest for the identities of the hopeful recipients in front of Hunter. It was Seagrave's Grail, and no less important to her. No little stone, no matter how mossy, would be left unturned.

Hmmm. Better check to see if Perez is listed as a donor. She returned to his medical file, scrolling through several pages, hunting for a living will. Not likely for a twenty-six-year-old guy. The young never consider dying, but they may opt for donating their organs. A ten-minute search produced nothing, which for Hunter, was good news.

If the car-jockey wasn't registered to donate, they could approach his parents, seeking a direct donation. The man was surely brain-dead, but his organs were viable until they pulled the plug. Seagrave was willing to pay plenty, so this was a real shot at saving Hunter.

Kim rose and retrieved the pages from the printer, scanning for address and contact numbers. All there. She picked up her cell phone and hit an auto-dial number, answered on the second ring.

"Charlie, we've got to move." She collected her purse. "One of the victims from that sniper attack yesterday is O-Negative."

"Is he alive? I thought . . . ."

"Yeah, barely. The poor guy's apparently brain-dead. Intubated for breathing." She was out the apartment's door and hurrying down the stairs to the under-building parking lot. "We need to get to his parents before someone beats us to it."

"Wow! Did you check to see if he opted in as a donor if he died?"

"Not on the list and I can't find a recorded living will," she said as she reached her green Jeep Cherokee. "I'll text you his folk's address and meet you at their house. If you get there first, wait for me outside." She was already backing out of her parking slot.

"Roger." Seagrave's voice was charged with excitement. "I'm on the way."

Jesus, I hope this works. She peeled away, leaving two black tracks on the pavement. *We'd still have to check tissue-type matches to see if he's compatible, but it's a step in the right direction.*

~ 23 ~

Warner stood behind his cluttered desk, flipping through his three newest files. He grunted. Usually, he had to scratch to find leads to follow, but this last spree shooting offered a carload of opportunities.

Top of this list ought to be Manny Glick, real estate developer. Jack Harris' preliminary research indicated Glick had made a slew of enemies over the years, especially among tree huggers. He'd received questionable rezoning throughout Dade and Broward counties that smacked of payoffs that no one was able to prove. But if he were the main target, why was he the last one shot? Warner didn't put it past this obviously clever perp to create misdirection in choosing his victims' order to foster confusion of purpose.

Warner sensed a shadow in his doorway, and glancing up, saw Detective Olvida leaning against the jamb, a thin file in his hand.

"Hope you got something good." He gestured toward a chair.

Settling down, Olvida handed his boss the folder.

"Maybe, maybe not," he said. "The first vic shot, Cesar Perez, a twenty-six-year-old parking valet, appeared like a guy in the wrong place at an unlucky time—until I dove into his background. Seems he'd recently taken a short joyride in a customer's two-hundred-grand red Maserati Gran Turismo, lost control, and skidded out, putting a major crimp in the right rear bumper."

"So? That musta generated an angry customer and an insurance claim against the restaurant that coulda cost him his job, but not his life." Warner flipped open the file, scanning the contents.

"Yeah, you'd think." Olvida leaned forward, directing Warner to the second page. "Turns out, the owner of that pricy sportscar was Diego Cepeda."

"Wow! One of the Cuban Cartel dons who'd survived last year's gang war shootout. Not a good guy to piss off."

"Right." Olvida eased back in the chair. "And are you aware that two of Cepeda's *soldados* are ex-SEAL and ex-DELTA force? Both trained snipers who'd served overwatch assignments in Afghanistan."

"So you think the don may have been hot enough to extract lethal revenge for his banged-up Maserati?"

"I don't know, Boss. It seems kinda iffy, considering the Bayfront Park incident. If ballistics confirms it's the same shooter, it makes the real estate connection more likely. Still, it's something."

"Yeah. So follow it up. Right now, nothin's off the table. We've got two possible motives that are far from iron-clad."

"Make it three." Detective Beck strode into the room.

"Terrific." Warner plopped onto his chair. "Something about the woman with the funny name?"

"Betji DeVries. It's Dutch, I think."

"So? What's with her?" Warner leaned back and knuckled his eyes.

"Looks like she was having a not so clandestine affair with Congressman Anthony Copello."

"The chairman of the House Judiciary Committee?"

Warner's eyebrows arched.

"The same. He's also on the board of her bank. Rumor is she was threatening to go public if he wouldn't get a divorce."

"Isn't he married to that sugar cane heiress?" Olvida asked. "That's big bucks to walk away from."

"How'd you get this so fast, Beck?" Warner asked.

"Talked to her sister, Boss. She's devastated, and made a case for Copello arranging the hit to save his marriage—and his ritzy lifestyle. He's known to be pretty ruthless."

"Well, this is a switch." Warner heaved out of his chair and began pacing. "We're usually scramblin' to find a single lead, and here we got three." He paused and stared at his three detectives. "Something tells me we're gonna be barkin' up a bunch of empty trees, but get after 'em anyhow. That proverbial stone isn't gonna be left unturned.

"On it, Boss," their voices chorused as one, and the three men hurried from the room.

Warner returned to his desk, slumped into his chair, and sighed. He was still awaiting a ballistic match from the lab to confirm it was the same shooter in both events. Or at least, the same weapon.

If it was, the only one of their so-called leads that made any sense was the real estate angle, but his gut told him there was something else at work.

Well, time would tell, hopefully before more innocents died. If this was a spree killer with no motives other than dead bodies, things would get worse before they got better.

He ground his teeth, and turned to the papers on his desk. There were other cases to assign.

~ 24 ~

"Your destination is five hundred feet ahead, on the right," the female voice of the Lexus' GPS announced. Seagrave slowed, scanning for a vacant space at the curb. Kim's green Jeep Cherokee was there, perched in the middle of two spots, clearly saving one for him.

His tall, slim, lover stood by her SUV, dressed in a short denim skirt and a baby-blue cotton blouse. She grinned and waved, then slid into the Jeep and pulled forward, making room for his sedan. They scrambled from their vehicles and met on the walkway. The brunette grabbed his arm, her face flushed with excitement.

"I just rechecked with the hospital." She was steering him toward the left side of a large, yellow CBS duplex. "Perez is still on life-support, and there's no record of a Living Will."

"This is the parents' house?"

"His mother's," she said. "No father around. She's had sole legal custody since he was twelve."

"So, no one else can nix her decision?" He paused at the steps, taking Kim's hands. "I'm kinda uncomfortable with this. Seems predatory."

"I know, but Hunt's life is what's important here." She squeezed his hands. "If we can get her to give us a direct donation, he doesn't have to wait to come up on the National Donor List. Perez is O-Negative, and that's what counts."

"Yeah, okay, but how do we know it's also a tissue match?"

"I drew some blood from Hunter and asked a buddy in the Hospitals lab to check the lymphocytes with Perez. The HLA results were promising, but it'll take a while to be sure. If that's good, there are other tests needed to guarantee a match."

"Okay! So let's get to it." They mounted the steps and he rang the bell. "You think she's home?"

"She's supposed to work at home—a day care for local women." Kim leaned against him, her arms folded across her chest, trying to quell his nervous fidgeting. His feet were shuffling as if dancing barefooted on hot sand.

There was the click of a releasing deadbolt and the door opened, restrained by a safety-chain.

"*Si?*" A honey-colored face and dark brown eye peered at them through the crack.

"Mrs. Perez? I'm Kim Tate, a nurse from Cesar's hospital, and this is my friend, Charles Seagrave."

"You were my son's nurse?"

"I work at the hospital—a trauma nurse. May we come in? We'd like to talk to you about Cesar." She flashed her ID.

"What is there to talk?" A plaintive whimper, followed by a sigh. The door closed and then opened again, unhampered by the safety-chain. A middle-age brunette woman stood in a white flowered dress with billowed sleeves. Her dark, broad face spoke to her Latina-Indian heritage.

"He lives only by a machine that breathes for him." Her English was lightly accented. "The doctors say his brain is—is dead. They want me to disconnect him—let the rest of him die." A thick brown finger brushed away a tear.

"Is that why you are here? To convince me?" She sighed, and gestured them toward a small den, sparsely decorated with a brown leatherette sofa, two armchairs, and a small TV. "I cling to hope, praying for a miracle."

"I understand the prayer of hope." Kim settled on the sofa and took one of the woman's hands in both of hers. "And that, in a sense, is why we're here. We are also looking for a miracle."

Kim swiveled toward Seagrave, perched beside her, grasping his forearm. "Mister Seagrave's son, Hunter, is gravely ill. He's in desperate need of a new liver, but he's a very rare blood-type—O-Negative." Characterizing Hunter as a son rather than a nephew seemed more convincing. Seagrave glanced at Kim and nodded.

"My Cesar is O-Negative, too. He . . ." Her eyes widened, sweeping between their faces, her mouth forming a silent *oh*. "You know this? And you are wishing *my* son to die to save yours." A whimper slipped past her lips, and she covered her eyes.

Seagrave leaned forward, touching her knee. "As his nurse, Ms. Tate has this information." He sighed. "I know it seems cruel—heartless, even—but Cesar can *never* recover. Never live even a barely alert life." He leaned back, crossing his arms over his chest.

"But this way, part of Cesar would live on in my son. Hunter is a fine boy." Seagraves words were choked by tears. "A boy you would be proud to have saved. You can meet him—know him—even be part of his life, since he would be partly *your* son too, if you agree."

"But, if you take Cesar's liver, he will be dead." She glanced at Seagrave, then Kim, wringing her hands. "Now, at least maybe . . . ." Her words trickled to a stop.

"But he *is* dead. His mind is gone." Kim rose and knelt in front of her, taking a hand. "His *soul* is gone—gone to God." She snatched a look at Seagrave, whose face was creased by a frown.

"You can create a legacy for Cesar," he said. "Cesar, the giver of life. And I will pay for everything. I'm prepared to give you fifty thousand dollars to help pay expenses—pay for a proper funeral for your brave son."

"Fifty thousand dollars?" Her head rose, eyes widened, glistening with tears.

"Yes, to help you get back on your feet. Help you honor your son in any way you wish. And maybe give life to others who are in urgent need of rare blood-type organs, like kidneys, hearts, lungs, even bones." He crouched in front of the now sobbing woman.

"Cesar can live on, not only in Hunter, but in so many other desperate people. Think of it. Cesar's legacy of life."

"Fifty thousand dollars." She shuddered, her face twisted in anguish. "So you can cut my son to pieces. My beautiful baby boy!" She slouched back, racked by tears, her hands shielding her eyes.

"Don't picture that, Mrs. Perez," Kim said, rising. "Think instead of the happy faces of people Cesar can bring new hope of life. Wouldn't he be proud of doing so much good?"

"I—I can't think right now. Please, leave me alone."

Seagrave plucked a card from his wallet and pressed it into her hand. "I know this is difficult. You've lost a son, and believe me, I understand that, because I'm about to lose mine." He again gathered one if her hands in his.

"I realize the money won't buy back your son's life, but at least it will help you with expenses. Please consider—"

"I will, but this is too much to think about right now. Please leave." She struggled to her feet.

"Of course. I'm sorry we infringed on your grief, but time is of the essence here." He turned to Kim and shrugged.

"You'll call me—soon, I hope. Once Cesar passes, it won't be many hours before his organs are no longer viable for transplant." He touched her arm. "With your permission, we'd like to have the hospital check to see if Cesar is a match for my Hunter." Covering their butt for Kim's unauthorized lab tests. "I'll give you five-thousand-dollars to allow the tests, and they won't harm your son."

She nodded as she ushered them to the entrance hall, little rivulets still trailing from her eyes. "Yes, but I can't promise it will help you."

"Of course. We understand." The door eased quietly shut behind them as they started for their cars.

"What d'ya think, Kim? Should I offer her more?"

"What? Like a hundred grand? I don't get a sense that'd make a difference. Fifty thou is probably two years income for her." Kim nestled against him, wrapping her arms around his waist. "She's gotta get past the inevitable, and believe helping people trumps the image of dissecting her son for parts."

"Yeah, damn it." He brushed his lips across her forehead. "I've got an uncomfortable feeling the latter is gonna win out over being a Good Samaritan."

"Me, too. Did fate drop this chance in our laps just to tease us?" She sighed, kissed him on the neck and pulled away. "I'll call her tomorrow. Maybe better if it comes from the nurse, rather than the father."

"Right. That was clever of you to peg me as his dad, instead of his uncle. Makes it more personal."

"That's what I thought." She retrieved her car keys from her shoulder bag. "So, we keep hoping but keep chasing other avenues. You pursuing Carthwright?"

"Sure. We're lunching at the Governor's Club tomorrow.

"That oughta wow him. Full court press, Charlie?"

"I want to see what might interest him enough to juggle the recipient list. Meanwhile, I got something else I'm working on. Somehow, I'm gonna get that kid a new liver."

He pulled her in for a brief but heated kiss, and then they were in their cars, headed in different directions, each on their own private missions.

~ 25 ~

Warner spotted Eva's gray Jag convertible sitting in the drive of his townhouse. She's parked far enough to one side to allow him access to his garage. He waited for the door, ascending at the command of his remote, and smiled as his heart did a merry tap-dance.

Despite their nearly two years mostly together, it was still a struggle to wrap his mind around the idea that this terrific gal loved him. A small shake of his head, and he pulled his Charger into the garage and killed the engine.

With the file off the passenger seat in hand, he exited the coupe, triggered the switch to close the rollup door, and entered the house. The smell of Downey lingered in the laundry room, so Eva had done his laundry—again. Warner was fiercely self-sufficient, but he had to admit it was nice to be spoiled by that beautiful redhead.

"Hi honey, I'm home." He chuckled at his reprised play for normalcy and strode into the kitchen, finding her poised over a large stainless steel pot, stirring with a wooden spoon.

"Hi, yourself, handsome." Her head swiveled with a swirl of auburn hair. She continued churning the contents, a saucy smile tweaking pink lips.

"What'cha brewin'?" He dropped onto a chair, the sheaf of papers landing on the table with a soft splat. Buff trotted over and nuzzled a hand, looking for affection. Warner ruffled the dog's ears.

Eva stepped away from the stove. "Chicken thighs and veggies in a Marinara sauce. Made enough for two dinners, so you can freeze half for another night." She eased up behind him, her surprisingly strong thumbs boring into persistent knots in his shoulders and back of the neck.

"Ummm." He slumped forward, giving her better access. "You know the spots, Eva." Eyes closed, he continued to purr.

"UCT." She chuckled and kissed him on the ear. "Unsolved Case Tension. Only seems to happen when you run into something like this spree killer."

He reached back and pulled her around to spill onto his lap. Her arms draped over his shoulders, wrists crossed behind his head, their faces inches apart.

"You're my lifeboat, babe. The tension of this job can swamp a guy," he whispered. One hand circled her waist as the other slid into her hair, drawing her face to his. They hovered, inches apart, and then with a soft sigh, her lips brushed his. His arms tightened, molding her against him, their mouths fusing with molten heat. Tongues teased and danced in a growing carnal frenzy as he gathered her up, lurching to his feet.

She managed a breathless chuckle, her arms still locked around his neck. "Luckily, I turned the stove down to simmer when you arrived."

"Yeah." He was panting. "Seems like something's always on the burner when *we* get cookin'." He started for the bedroom.

"My favorite welcome home . . . ."

He smothered her last words with a fierce kiss as he stumbled toward the queen-size bed. They spilled across the pleated spread, their clothes already coming off.

Moans, squeals, and breathless grunts filled the air, telling the story, line by line, of their journey into ecstasy.

~ **26** ~

Warner eased back in his chair and dabbed at the vestiges of marinara sauce lingering on his lips. His coal-black eyes feasted on her as she leaned over, refilling his goblet with a rich Chianti.

"What?" Said with a soft chuckle, her gray eyes twinkling, filled with humor.

"Just thinkin' how much I love you. The look of you. The smell. The touch. The taste." He grinned. "*Especially* the taste."

Eva giggled, and her face bloomed a pale pink. "Ditto.

Especially the tasting part. Gives a grown woman too many indecent thoughts."

"That's the idea. I want you eager to come back for more."

They laughed, and then she gestured at the small stack of papers resting at the edge of the table. "Homework, Detective?"

"The file on our newest nutcase. Not much there, but I thought maybe my psychologist girlfriend might come up with some sorta insight."

"No leads, Al?"

"Too many. That's the problem. Could be a real estate graft connection, or a too-pushy mistress, or an angry mob boss—or just a loony killin' people for the thrill of it."

"Really? That's a lot of options." She reached out a slender arm and drew the slim stack in front of her, scanning the first page.

"Yeah, but they're all pretty thin. My gut tells me there's something else goin' on here." He nodded at the folder she had picked up and was leafing through.

"That's a photocopy of the file, so you keep it and take a look when you've got some time. See if anything speaks to you. Maybe something not so obvious as those other three connections."

"Of course, darling. First quiet moment I get, but I'm not sure I can be much help." She laid the file aside.

"I know, but it's a shot. Maybe you'll see something we missed."

He pushed out of his chair and began gathering the dishes. He carried them to the counter where he swept chicken bones and a few uneaten veggies into his trashcan, before depositing the tomato sauce covered plates in the sink.

"I'll do the dishes while you put away the leftovers," he said, wrapping a short apron around his waist.

"You look so domesticated." She chuckled, filled more with warmth than humor, as she tied the straps in a bow at his back.

Warner grinned and shrugged, then squirted a dash of soap into a salad bowl with some warm water. He dipped in a sponge and began washing the plates, bowls, and silver. Everything rinsed, they were stacked in a dish drain on the adjacent counter.

Eva emptied the rest of the pots' contents into a rectangular Pyrex container and snapped its lid in place, ready for the freezer. The balance of the leftovers were covered with plastic wrap and deposited in Warner's fridge. Teamwork had everything cleaned and stored in less than ten minutes.

Tasks completed, they strolled into his den, carrying their still half-full glasses of red wine. Both goblets were set on the coffee table as Warner settled on the sofa. He pulled Eva onto his lap, brushing russet hair from her right eye and planted a gentle kiss on her long, smooth neck. Buff curled at their feet, the retriever's head resting on Warner's shoes.

Warner sighed. "I've never been able to really relax like this durin' a tough case until I fell in love with you, Eva."

She swiveled her body and took his head between her hands, caressing his lips with a gentle kiss. "It's been transformative for me, too. You have *no* idea how special you are to me, do you?"

"Still hard to fathom." He chuckled. "But I ain't complainin'. I keep thinkin' of that afternoon, almost three years ago, when I was seeing you after the violent aftermath from The Angel of Death case. You said you were referring me to another therapist—'cause you'd fallen in *love* with me. Wow!"

"It was something of a shock to me, too." She ran a thumb over his lips and pecked him on the nose. "Especially since you were hooked on that sweet, blond nurse, Casey."

"Yeah." He drew her closer, resting his cheek on her breasts. "But nothin' was ever gonna happen there, with her history with the little boy's father. You caught me on the rebound," he drew back, grinning, "and fielded me like the pro you are. How lucky am I?"

They hung together in the warmth of the other's arms before, almost reluctantly, they separated, Eva sliding onto the sofa beside him, still holding hands. The golden retriever rose and padded to his bed in the corner of the den.

Warner hitched around and grinned. "So, all the arrangements made for Adele's party tomorrow?"

"Yes." She started ticking off fingers on her left hand. "The cake's coming around noon. I've arranged for a helper to serve, tend bar, and clean up. He's bringing the bubbly and soft drinks in the afternoon. Chris, from my office. He has some folding chairs and two tables he'll set up in the den, too."

"You'll be here to let 'em all in? I'm really tied up on this case . . . ."

"No worries, darling. I've arranged a free day." She laid a hand on his knee. "You've taken care of the invitations?"

"Yep. Still couldn't find any family. Guess she's outlived 'em all." He sighed, shaking his head. "Harris and Captain Santiago and their wives, and Olvida and his plus-one, are all comin'. I've located the three gals she plays bridge with: Clara, Belle, and Iris. They're all pumped and are pitchin' in for a gift." He rose and shoved his hands into his pockets.

"It'll only be twelve of us," he said, "but at least, with the exception of Olvida, they're people who know and care for her. Someone like Adele shouldn't pass her ninetieth year without friends there to help celebrate it."

"It's a lovely thing you're doing, Al. She's become really special to you."

"More like a mom to me than I've ever had, Eva. And I fill the hole left when her son died in combat. That was a forty year ache, before we met each other."

"Okay. So everything's on track. Now what do you have in mind? Something on TV?"

"Yeah, but let's do it on the bedroom set. All snuggled up, nice and warm."

"Uh-huh." Her lips tweaked into a wry grin. "What are we going to be watching?"

"How about a love story?"

"Got one in mind, Al?"

"Yeah, a blank screen. And we're the main characters." He drew her up and into his arms.

"That's what I thought." Her chuckle was breathless. "You're so *wicked*, taking advantage of this poor, weak girl."

"I don't think she really minds." He lifted her into his arms, heading for the bedroom.

"Only if you stop, darling." Panting softly, she gathered the lobe of his ear between her lips, teasing it with her tongue. "Only if you stop."

Thoughts of surprise parties and spree killers were swept away by surging rivers of passion.

It would be a respite not shared again for some time.

~ 27 ~

I pulled out of the Aventura Library's parking lot and onto Country Club Road, my brain filled with a swarm of conflicted thoughts. I shook my head and blinked, not used to a lack of a straightforward purpose.

I was usually tasked with a single objective, unemotionally involved with the target or its consequences. A client needed someone to die, and I carried out the contract. Long-range or close-up—"naturally" or violently. That never mattered to me. It was strictly business, with no personal involvement. Something I'd done for almost two decades while leading an otherwise normal everyday life.

But this was a totally different scenario, and I had a stake in its outcome—Hunter's life. I'd orchestrated two events to create a donor for him. The first was merely a smokescreen to obfuscate the motive for these shootings. The second, perfectly executed, provided a living but brain-dead candidate with the right blood type who was also a likely tissue match. In the process, I'd created other plausible connections that would keep the cops chasing their tails with fruitless investigations.

The problem was, the target's mother wouldn't cooperate, and sand was inexorably seeping through the hourglass. I had, at most, six-months to create a donor. I'd gladly offer up part of my liver, but there wasn't a sufficient match to make it a reliable alternative.

So, on to the next event. I'd used the library's computers to find my new batch of potential victims. DNA samples weren't always easily acquired, and this time it wasn't until the fifth that I'd discovered an O-Negative who was a possible tissue match and would also be a viable target.

This research was a lot more time-consuming than if I'd accessed the machines readily available to me, but that could create a trail connecting me to these killings. My work was drawing me farther and farther afield, since I never used the same library twice, and I was running out of disparate disguises. No review of any surveillance would uncover the same person—sometimes male and sometimes female—twice at any facility I'd used.

Now on I-95, heading south, I mentally sketched out the next attack. The day after tomorrow should have everyone in place. I'd drive by that afternoon to scout out the location, and after studying it on Google Earth, there seemed no obstacles to my success.

Meanwhile, other avenues were still being pursued, and I'd be pleased if something occurred to cancel the need for more innocent deaths. I sighed. No strangers' lives were as valuable as Hunter's, so if they must donate theirs, albeit unwillingly, it was a price they would pay. I wiggled my surprisingly clenched jaw and groaned. Who made me God?

I brush aside this spate of conscience with a headshake and concentrated on the road and unpredictable South Florida drivers. The new plan had already coalesced in my mind. Two days to prepare and set it up. Maybe a bit more target shooting tomorrow morning at my secret 'Glades range to polish my accuracy. This was a lot more delicate than just putting one in the head from a thousand meters.

Luckily, I was damned good at this.

Who could have guessed?

~ 28 ~

"Your guest is here, Mr. Seagrave," the elegantly uniformed black man said. He stood at the entry of the lounge, awaiting a reply, his hands folded in front of him.

"Show him in, Zeke." Seagrave rose and gathered some papers he was reviewing. "I'll meet him at the bar."

"As you wish, sir." He pivoted and headed back toward the hospitality desk.

Seagrave wove his way through the heavily upholstered armchairs and sofas that adorned the Governors' Club lounge and entered the dimly-lit bar. He dropped his files on one of the high-top tables and edged toward the front entrance, awaiting the arrival of his guest.

A moment later, Ezekiel appeared at the doorway, and with a sweeping gesture, directed the trailing man into the room.

"Mr. Corbin Carthwright, sir," he announced.

Seagrave strode forward, taking the man's hand. "Mr. Carthwright. Welcome to my club. I have a table." He led them to the high-top, near the rear of the barroom.

"My pleasure, and thank you for inviting me. And please call me Corbin."

"Of course. And I'm Charlie." They settled on comfortable, high-back stools, and Seagrave signaled for a waitress. "What are you having?"

"Scotch, neat, would be fine," Carthwright responded as the server arrived.

"Two Chivas, one neat and one on the rocks. And ice waters and bar treats, please." He swiveled on his stool and shoved his files toward the table's far edge. He glanced at his visitor.

"Any problems finding us here?"

"Rarely a problem finding anyplace nowadays, with GPS. But of course, I knew where the Governor's Club was. Doesn't everybody?"

Seagrave chuckled and nodded. "Mostly."

Carthwright's eyes swept the room. "I've never been inside before. Very—Old South décor, isn't it?"

He nodded. "The board wanted the plantation look. All the help used to wear typical uniforms and dresses from that era, but in this climate of political correctness, that's been abandoned. Still, they're rigorously schooled in the southern niceties and genteel manners of the mid-nineteenth century."

"Avoiding backlash from today's unforgiving culture?" Carthwright's eyebrows arched. Their drinks arrived, and he took a sip.

"Still get some." Seagrave sampled his Scotch. "But the pay's good and the help are treated well and with respect. No one complains, and the members seem to like it." They sat in silence, sipping their twelve-year-old Scotch.

"So, you mentioned you're a member of the Exotic Game

Ranch in Georgia?" Carthwright said. "Tell me about it."

"I'm a director and one of the founders, actually." Seagrave took another taste of his drink. "We have two hundred carefully vetted members and about a thousand acres of lush Georgia forest and broad meadows. All encircled by very high fences."

"To keep the animals from straying?"

"Sure—and the poachers out." Seagrave chuckled. "There's really no other place quite like it, so we're selective on who can shoot there. Even guests. We've got strict annual limits and close control on the animal population."

"All exotics?" Carthwright leaned back, his tongue brushing his lips. "Trophy-size red stags, I've heard."

"True. One of our members scored a twenty-two pointer last fall." Seagrave swirled the ice in his drink. "We've also got some of the biggest blackbuck in the world."

"The Indian antelope? I heard they're nearly extinct."

"They are, in India. We got our breeding stock from Argentina, though, where the world record was shot many years ago. Same with the European Axis and Chital deer—and there's Russian boar to four-hundred pounds." He grinned at his guest. "A hunter's delight, huh?"

"Certainly." Carthwright finished his drink. "I've dreamed of an Argentine safari for red stag, but the price is outlandish, and there's no guarantee of a trophy."

"I know." Seagrave nodded. "No guarantee at our ranch, either. This isn't baited shooting from a platform. We stalk through natural terrain, tracking the deer on foot. No dogs, either, except for the boar." He patted the man's arm. "It takes a real sportsman who's an accurate shot, to have any success. It's not for an amateur who wants something to boast about. Every member of the club is a crack shot and an experienced hunter."

"Sounds exciting, and it's the kind of hunt I've fantasized about, but you didn't invite me here to talk about shooting."

"Well, not directly." Seagrave chuckled and sat back.

"Your nephew's liver, I presume." He sighed and shook his head. "Sorry to say, there's been no movement on the transplant list. O-Negative organs are tough to come by." He stared at his host for a moment and shrugged. "There *is* a possible candidate on life-support at Jackson right now, but he isn't on any donor list, so . . ."

"I know. We've already visited his mother, hoping she'd make a direct donation, but she's unwilling to let him go. Still hoping for a miracle, I guess."

Seagrave leaned closer and lowered his voice. "I was hoping I could convince you to move Hunter up, in case something happens. You know, based on the urgency of his need. A couple of dedicated outdoorsmen, coming together to save a truly worthy young man."

Carthwright studied his interlocked fingers, resting on the table. "I don't know. There is some precedent for that," he whispered, "but there's an Oversight Committee . . ."

"I understand, but think how wonderful it would feel, celebrating Hunter's recovery as my guest, during our hunt at the Exotic Game Ranch. Taking a trophy red stag, shooting the classic Weatherby 300 Mark V I just acquired. A memory of a lifetime."

Carthwright stared at Seagrave's eyes and swallowed. "I'll—I'll see what I can do. Maybe there's a way . . ."

"I really hope so, Corbin. Think of our excitement during our semi-annual hunts together. Two sportsmen, sharing the successes, both in the field and at home."

"You—you mean, more than one hunt at the Ranch?" His eyes flared.

"Sure. We'd have something to share, wouldn't we? Provided, of course, Hunter got a liver off the list." He glanced sidewise at Carthwright. "So, let's order lunch."

They studied the menus, each lost in their own thoughts.

~ 29 ~

Warner tossed the file onto his already cluttered desk, slouched back, and rubbed his eyes.

He had Detectives Olvida and Beck chasing down any possible real estate connection. He'd be surprised if they found anything probative, but it had to be done. Ever since he missed the obvious *Playboy* connection with the *Angel of Death*, he wasn't going to skip over any possible lead, no matter how unlikely.

Jack Harris and he were about to pursue Congressman Copello's possible involvement with his dead mistress. He rated that only slightly more likely than the real estate angle, but they had to cover all the bases.

Then there was the Cuban crime boss, Diego Cepeda, and his banged up Maserati. That one was on hold, since the Don was in South America. Of the three, Warner rated this one the most likely, but something nagged at him that it wasn't any of them.

He leaned forward and shuffled through the mess on his desk, finding the other file he wanted. Warner flipped it open, and as he began reading, his brow wrinkled. Two more people, a fifty-five-year-old man and a forty-year-old woman, had died of septic shock resulting from implanted black-market kidneys from illegal surgeries. That made at least three that he knew of, and that was three too many.

Warner had run some searches, and it was clear that there were way more people awaiting new organs than there were donors—at least through authorized channels.

He'd learned there was nothing illegal about directly

bestowed organs from people not registered as donors. These were often family members who shared blood-type compatibility and were likely tissue matches, but those surgeries were performed by registered surgeons and done at hospitals, with rigorous safety measures in place.

He leafed through the file and shook his head, lips pressed into a knife-thin slit.

"Harris," he shouted. "You out there?"

"Coming, Boss." A moment later, the detective appeared in the doorway. "What's up?" His eyebrows arched.

"You find anything about these black market organs?"

"No leads yet." He slipped into an armchair. "What I do know is demand is much greater than supply, so illegal organs are a lucrative business." He hunched forward in the chair. "Olvida and I are trying to hunt down sources, but with this spree killer on the loose, our time is limited."

"Get a few guys from Detectives to do some of the legwork," Warner said, handing Harris the file. "Funeral homes may be a likely source from corpses received immediately after death. They could be passin' off kidneys and stuff that look viable, despite actually bein' too old."

"Okay. I got Dean Beck canvassing the homeless gathering areas for guys who may have suddenly disappeared." Harris rose to leave.

"Yeah." Warner leaned back, rubbing his neck. "Offer a mark a meal and shelter, then put 'em to sleep and harvest their organs. Who'd miss Joe Homeless? Task some patrol units to poke around the usual hangouts. See if anyone noticed anything suspicious." He pushed out of his chair and came around the desk.

"Get Tech to dig into the dark web. See if they can locate anyone peddlin' organs. Meanwhile, you and I gotta make an appointment to visit Congressman Copello to eliminate him from our shooter suspect list."

"Don't think it's him, Boss?" They exited Warner's office.

"No, but we gotta do our due diligence. My vote's for the Cuban Don, Cepeda."

"You got Olvida and Beck set to visit him, huh?"

"Right, but frankly, my nagging gut doesn't like any of the three. I feel something else is goin' on here. Anyhow, let's get to it."

"On it, Boss." Harris turned toward his desk.

"And, Harris," Warner called after him, "don't forget, tomorrow's Adel's party. You and Doris are comin', ain't ya?"

"Wouldn't miss it. That's a special old lady."

"You got that right." Warner chuckled. "One in a million."

The detectives went their own ways, smiles fading as their thoughts returned to the two pressing puzzles that filled their plates.

They had killers to catch.

~ 30 ~

My plastic drop cloth covered the tarred surface with a flannel bedroll spread on top. Skintight nitrite gloves insured no prints would be left behind, and the plastic sheet assured no trace fibers would embed in the soft surface. Forensics labs can do miracles if you give them half a chance.

Stretching out, I wiggled my body into a comfortable posture and positioned the McMillan TAC-50 to peek through the roof's parapet opening. Right eye against my scope, the entrance to the theater and its surroundings were clearly visible. A quick sweep of the area assured me of limited traffic. The midday sun warming my back played peek-a-boo with scattered puffs of cotton, drifting eastward across a cerulean sky.

I glanced at my watch. The awards ceremony wouldn't end for another twenty minutes. A small notebook retrieved from my rear pocket, I scanned my notes and flipped to a photo of my prime mark. The image of the Colombian teenager was indelibly etched in my near-photographic memory, but I wanted to re-study his facial contours.

His DNA came from a gym towel I'd collected, and it wasn't as clean as the lab liked, but results indicated a probably match seemed likely. The shot must again be perfectly placed to assure organ viability.

His drug cartel uncle would be there to help fete the kid's trophy, which through a rare stroke of luck, give me two for the price of one: my last contract for the Cuban don, and providing a potential donor for Hunter. Serendipity that both were connected by family. The hit would totally disguise the real purpose of today's melee. How perfect!

A commotion below drew my attention. I glanced across the street. *Shit! The affair must have ended early.* A stream of people spilled out of the theater. I shouldered the rifle and scanned the growing crowd through my telescopic sight.

There they were—the feted high school football Player of the Year and his doting *tio*. Every college in the country was chasing the young quarterback, but unfortunately for him, that was about to cease. What would end his career wasn't some blitzing linebacker. It was his O-Negative blood type. And it would seem like collateral damage from a mob hit.

A quick glance at my wind gauge, perched atop the tiled coping, brought a small sight adjustment. Returning my attention to the swelling crows across the street, I blinked and zeroed in on the seventeen-year-old who held the promise of life for Hunter. I sighed, stiffening my resolution. It was a steep price, a payment for a debt he hadn't knowingly contracted.

Young Mister Blake Rivera—a name with an unusual

mixture of ethnicities, was posing for a photo with his uncle.

You're mine now, kid. Both of you.

Perfect. He was motionless, arm over his uncle's shoulder during a flurry of photos. I steadied my breathing, taking a moment to line up the exact spot on his . . . .

What the hell . . .? What's with that fucking truck?

A thirty-foot, six-wheel food service monster had materialized and parked directly in my line of fire. Both targets were effectively shielded.

I fidgeted and shifted my position, trying to acquire them through the cab's windows. The driver had descended and opened the rear doors, apparently preparing to make a delivery. Lying on that five-story rooftop created too sharp an angle for success. I could try to wait this out—or abort.

Damn! When will I get another crack at this kid? Probably never. I gritted my teeth, face flushed with anger.

Don't do anything rash. I can get the aspiring drug lord anytime. I'd survived nearly two decades at this job by staying careful and unemotional. Errors were made in anger and those got you caught, but for the first time in my career I had a personal stake in my actions, and it was getting to me.

The driver was unloading boxes of soft drinks and vending machine snacks—carton after carton. I groaned. This was never going to happen. The young quarterback would be gone before this bastard moved that fucking truck.

All my time planning, practicing, preparing—wasted because of this stupid son-of-a-bitch and his damned van.

You've ruined everything! Suddenly out of control, I found him in my scope and squeezed off a round. Never pausing to see his head explode, I spotted an old guy, hobbling along on a cane. He flew ten feet as the 12.7mm slug caught him in the chest. Who cared? He was on his last legs, anyhow.

Sweeping right I spotted a patrol cop running toward the truck, yelling into his collar radio. Lucid enough to avoid killing law enforcement, I spied a tall guy in his thirties, videoing on his phone. My third round caught the phone and then his face, which disappeared in a gore-filled cloud.

I was panting hard, finally gaining restraint. I'd never lost it like that before . . . and I'd better not do it again. Time to boogie. I glanced down at a scene of panic, people running everywhere. And there was the fucking truck that blew up my entire operation. Without thinking, my fourth shot blasted through the hood's cowling and exploded the engine's block.

A headshake brought a wry chuckle at my first ever loss of discipline. I swept up all my items, gathered the spent shell casings, and fled for the stairs. Sometimes battles were lost, only to be fought another day.

Shit! Now I've gotta find another time to complete the Cuban don's hit. His fifty Gs were in my Cayman Isle account, and the balance wouldn't arrive until this Colombian upstart was gone. This would have been ideal, but the chance was gone

A tool other than the McMillan should be used for that job, because it could not be connected it to my little crusade. My .375 Winchester Magnum would be the perfect weapon to send the message the Cuban don wanted everyone to see.

Three days left to complete the job, plenty of time to plan it. Way too much going on at once, but I couldn't let current pressures infringe on a carefully executed operation.

I never let even the smallest detail slide. That was the measure of my success. Time constraints never pushed me out of my comfort zone.

In the Honda now and headed for the freeway, my current disguise was shed and stowed in a duffle bag on the rear seat floorboards, along with my guitar case. I sighed and gave a small shrug. The don's hit would be my last professional contract. Once I'd completed my efforts to save Hunter, I'd retire. Money was no longer a problem, so I could sit back and enjoy a stress-free life.

Chuckling, I wondered, could I *really* do that? I wasn't sure.

~ 31 ~

Unable to find a spot on the street amid all the black-and-whites crowding the area, Warner pulled his Dodge coupe onto a walkway. Hurrying through the kaleidoscope of strobing blue and red lights, he ducked under yellow crime scene tape and strode toward a gaggle of detectives and patrol officers already on the scene.

He spotted the back of Raphael Olvida, whose head was tucked under the hood of a large truck. Jack Harris was on the walk amid an edgy group of civilians, probably interviewing witnesses. Warner paused next to Olvida, clearing his throat so as not to startle the clearly engrossed detective.

"What're you lookin' at?"

"Oh, hi, Boss." He pulled back, turned, and pointed inside. "A blown up engine block. According to Harris's preliminary questioning, our shooter put his fourth round into the motor. Blew the hell out of it."

"Well, presumin' it's our sniper, those big fifty-cals aren't just anti-personnel. But this ain't a war. Destroyin' this truck doesn't make sense. What's the purpose of that?" Warner pivoted, his gaze sweeping the area.

"Three vics again?"

"Yeah." Olvida joined him as they walked toward Harris. "But at first glance, anyway, none of them fit with the two previous shootings. We got a truck driver, a geriatric guy on a cane, and a middle-aged man who was videoing the commotion."

"And the truck," Warner mused. "Interestin'. Dalwin and his team's just gettin' organized back at HQ. I wonder what the FBI's take on this is gonna be."

"Same BAU team as the last three, huh, Boss?"

"I requested them," Warner said. "They're good to work with. Don't try to take over the investigation like some."

"Yeah." Olvida chuckled. "And that blond Amazon, Yeager, *did* save your life last year."

"That, too." Warner grinned. "I contacted Special Agent Dalwin, and they're on the way here now."

They'd arrived where Harris was taking interviews.

"What'cha got?" Warner asked.

"Not much, Boss. The shooting started after that truck arrived. The driver was the first vic, as he was unloading his delivery." Harris gestured toward the rear of the truck where two CSU techs were hovered over a body. "That big slug almost decapitated him."

"Yeah." Warner ran his fingers through his dark, curly locks. "What about the other vics?"

"A seventy-three year-old man on a cane. CSU gave his wallet to Beck to check his ID. The third was a thirty-something white male who was using his phone to video the action. The slug took out the phone before pulverizing his face. Haven't seen his ID yet."

"Something doesn't make sense . . ." Warner's attention was drawn to a black Chevy Suburban arriving outside the yellow tape. "Looks like the BAU's arrived. C'mon, Harris." He strode off to meet the three Special Agents exiting the vehicle.

A tall, lean, sandy-haired man was followed by a towering, athletic blond woman and a short, stocky guy. Warner shook the leader's hand.

"Special Agent in Charge Dalwin. Glad to see you—again."

"Wish it were under better circumstances, Detective, but it seems it's only death that brings us back together."

"Unfortunately true, Ed," Warner said, then looking up. He grinned at the tall blonde. "Agent Yeager, my overwatch angel."

"Glad I was able to help, Detective. Looks like you've got someone else shooting a 50-cal sniper rifle besides me. You remember Harry Ashkin?" She gestured to the other agent.

"Sure. Hi, Harry. You're the crime scene guru, so maybe you can help our CSU team come up with something."

"Happy to, Detective," he said, shaking hands, "but as I remember, Moe Gold doesn't miss much."

"True." Warner pivoted, glancing back at the scene of mayhem, "but this bastard hasn't left much to work with."

"We do have a couple of things for you, though," Dalwin said. "Our lab checked the rifling on the slugs your team forwarded to us. Based on the groove pattern, we believe the weapon is a McMillan TAC-50."

"That's military," Warner said. "Any way to trace it?"

"We're trying." Agent Ina Yeager was looking at her tablet. "It's one of the few sniper rifles with the range of my Barrett .50. The weapon probably came off the dark web. Lots of arms dealers there, so finding the seller is the proverbial needle."

"The other thing," Agent Ashkin pitched in, "is, we think we know the shooter. No actual ID, but someone whose work we've seen before."

"Really?" Jack Harris had joined them.

"Yes," Dalwin said. "We believe he's an assassin we've dubbed The Shadow."

"Like, 'Who knows what evil lurks in the hearts of men?'" Warner's eyebrows knitted together. "That Shadow?"

"In name only," Dalwin chuckled mirthlessly. "This guy's been virtually invisible while he's been a contract killer for nearly twenty years. Very versatile, very deadly, and he leaves zero trace."

"Well, the bastard's offed nine people here in less than two weeks," Harris grumbled, "and showed all the signs of a spree killer, not a hit man."

"If it is the Shadow, there's nothing haphazard about this. He's got a purpose," Ashkin said.

"Yeah." Warner's fingers unconsciously traced the x-shaped scars on the right side of his skull. "He's given us three persons of interest: a US Congressman, a Cuban don, and a real estate magnate, but I'm guessin' they're all red herrings."

They had wandered over to where the truck lingered.

"What d'ya think of this, Ed? He pops the driver as he's unloadin' his truck, then caps and old guy on a cane, and a younger man, taking video of the scene. *Then* he puts one in the engine block." Warner stared at the agent in charge.

"Hmmm." Dalwin stroked his chin. "Not what we'd expect from this killer. Seems angry and frustrated."

"That's what I thought." Warner turned to Harris. "This truck coulda blocked his line of sight to his real target." He glanced across the street. "Might be something to do with that theater." He turned to Harris. "See what was goin' on there at the time of the shootin'."

"On it, Boss." The detective hurried off.

"Well, Ed, we got lots to follow up, but somehow, I don't expect to get much from it. My gut tells me we're still missin' the real motive here."

They strolled over to where Moe Gold watched the coroner's team bag the last of the bodies.

"Anything, Moe?" the detective asked.

"About the same as the last scene, Detective." The little man turned and ran a finger over his thin mustache.

"So, ya mean nothin', huh?" Warner jammed his hands into his pockets.

"Pretty much. We've recovered two of the slugs so far and are searching for the rest. I have a team on that roof," gesturing to a five-story office building across the street, "which was his shooting stand, but the only thing they've found so far is a couple of small depressions in the tar, probably from hot shell casings."

"Well, keep at it. We gotta get something before this guy moves onto another batch of vics." Warner glanced around then started toward his vehicle. "I'm headin' back to HQ. Keep me in the loop."

~ 32 ~

Warner stuck his head out of his doorway. "Harris?"

"Here, Boss." He rolled his chair out from behind the column that shielded him from Warner's view.

"My office," Warner said, pivoting to return to his desk.

A moment later the wiry little detective appeared in his doorway.

"What's up?"

"We gotta get goin' on our due diligence on the leads this sniper's given us." Warner settled behind his desk. "I want to start with Congressman Copello."

"You really think he's involved with this?" Harris dropped into an armchair.

"Could he have a motive? Yeah. Do I think he hired a hit man to take out a blackmailin' mistress? No." He eased back in his chair and ran his hands over his eyes. "I don't think *any* of the three are involved, but we gotta eliminate 'em before we can move on. We aren't gonna leave any stone unturned."

"So, what do you want me to do, Boss?"

"Contact the congressman's office and set up an interview." He slid closer to the desk, shuffling papers. "Tomorrow, or the next day, latest. If he gives ya any static, hint at lettin' the press know he's a person of interest. But be diplomatic."

"Olvida's better at sweet-talking, Al." Harris eased forward on the chair, resting his hand on the desk's edge.

"Yeah, but I'm taskin' him to chase down the Cuban don, Cepeda. Of the three, he'd be the most likely perp." Warner rose, a silent dismissal. "And send Beck in, willya? I got a new case for him."

"On it, Boss." The detective stood. "I'll let you know what I arrange with Copello."

Warner nodded and drew a report from the scattered files on his desk, scanning it. He grunted and shrugged. *Two more dead South Americans. I hope this ain't the beginnin' of another turf war.* He glanced up at a rap on his door.

"You wanted to see me, Boss?" Detective Dean Beck stepped into the room. "Some news on our sniper?"

"Nothin' yet," He handed Beck the file. "But we got other murders to solve. Two hits—a Colombian drug lord and his lieutenant. CSU's on the scene. May have nothin' to do with our bad boy. Preliminaries show a different weapon, but they *were* long-range shots." Warner returned to his desk.

"Take one of the new guys with you. This smacks more of a local boss nixin' some competition. See if this guy was tryin' to horn in on one of the Cuban dons. After that big shootout last fall wiped out most of both sides, they're just gettin' started again."

"Okay, Boss, but I've been working with Olvida. Shouldn't he . . .?"

"Normally, yeah," Warner leaned back, "but our spree killer is takin' up a lot of assets. Work it out."

"On it, Boss." He hurried off.

Warner shuffled through a stack of files teetering on his desk and found what he wanted—preliminary background checks on the three previous vics. He flipped open the cover and began reading about real estate mogul, Manny Glick. He was half-way down the page when his eyes swiveled toward a rap on his door.

"Got a minute, Boss?" Jack Harris leaned against the jamb.

"Sure. What's up?" He tipped back and signaled the detective to come in.

"I called Congressman Copello's office but got stonewalled." Harris dropped into a side chair. "Said he was busy working on some new law or some such shit. His aide seemed kinda nervous."

"Yeah. Murder investigations do that to some people." Warner chuckled. "You tell 'em we can get a subpoena?"

"May not be necessary, Boss. He's doing a fundraiser in Coral Gables tomorrow afternoon." Harris leaned forward, glancing at his Android tablet. "We show up, he can't dodge us without causing a fuss."

"Good. Get me the time, and we'll go together. We'll see how he feels about his girlfriend's murder."

"Right. I'll check the schedule and get back to you." He rose and pocketed his tablet. "We can catch him right after he speaks." He started to leave, paused, and turned back.

"That was a nice thing you're planning, Al."

"Huh? What?" He glanced up from the file he'd returned to.

"The party. Celebrating the old lady's birthday."

"Adele?" Warner chuckled. "Don't let her hear you call her an old lady. She's ninety-years young."

"Yeah, she's got plenty of vinegar. She's special to you, huh?"

"She's more of a mom to me than mine ever was. For Eva, too. And we're like an adopted family for her. She lost her only son in Vietnam. Besides her three weekly bridge buddies, we're all she's got."

"Yeah, well, I'm guessing she'll be really touched that you guys throw her a surprise party. Doris and I'll be there."

"Countin' on it. Credit Eva for doin' the heavy liftin'." He stretched, arms over his head. "She got the cake, made the hors d'oeuvres, and arranged for the snacks and drinks. But you and the captain comin' with your wives, and Olvida with his sexy new girlfriend—that'll be what makes it a party."

"Glad to do it." Harris turned toward the door. "Besides, why turn down good eats and drinks?" He looked back, grinning, as he exited. "I'll get us a time for the congressman's fund raiser."

As Warner watched Harris leave, his thoughts drifted to Eva. He'd never loved anyone like this before. His relationship three years ago with Sharon had been contentious passion. They *did* love each other, but were constantly at bitter odds over justice and punishment. Her nearly perishing at the hands of the Angel of Death was all the reason she needed to split back to Buffalo.

Now, love for the redhead dominated his soul, but their plan last year to marry was fractured by that loony serial-killer, Bachelor, and Warner almost lost her as well. Being in love with Al Warner seemed to be a dangerous thing, and that's why he had called off the marriage.

The thing was, he'd made a unilateral decision that Eva hadn't supported. Maybe it was time to . . . He blinked, his eyes returning to the file he was studying on the background check of Manny Glick.

He shook his head, and began skimming the report. The real estate mogul had been embroiled in a fight over development rights in Northwest Dade County. His death ended that controversy, but Warner could find nothing in the file indicating it was worth killing him over.

He leaned back, plopped the sheath of papers on his desk, and rubbed his tired eyes. Eric Boxer, the lawyer killed in the first attack, worked for a firm that had tenuous connections to the plaintiffs in that case. Amy Howard was a realtor that represented several properties in the area, but Olvida couldn't find any direct connection there, either.

Hard to believe three of the six vics, all with real estate interests, were linked to each other in a fight over land rights. But, rule number one was, there was no such thing as a coincidence, especially when it came to murder, so they'd have to chase down every wisp of possible connections.

He pushed out of his chair, snatched the file, and strode into the office bullpen. He'd have Olvida follow it to the end, whatever waste of time that might entail. Of the other two, he felt Congressman Copello may be a likely candidate, with a potential scandal that could ruin his career, but even that looked thin to him.

In a case like this, though, no dark corner left unexplored.

~ 33 ~

Hunter struggled awake, yawned, and stretched. He'd slept for over two hours in his Uncle Charlie's guest room after an abbreviated morning of fishing. Two-and-a-half hours of catching bonito and one king mackerel and he was pooped.

He rolled his feet to the floor and winced at the stabbing ache in his abdomen. A sudden tsunami of nausea propelled him into the bathroom where he emptied his hamburger lunch into the commode. The boy hung over the basin, caught his breath and spit out the last sour remnants of his meal.

Hunter pushed erect and ran fingers through his dark locks. He glanced at his hands, then arms, and shook his head. Had the lemony tinge darkened? Growing signs of jaundice, and more signals the end was nearing.

He groaned and knuckled away a tear. Nineteen and about to die, and nothing to stop it unless they found a liver donor.

He was so *helpless.*

Dad and Mom can only sit by and worry. Unc has pulled out all the stops, and Kim is constantly trolling every database. Charlie really lucked out with that woman. She'd made Hunter's case her own, all because it was priority one for the guy she loved.

He couldn't wrap his mind around the coming reality. What was it like to just—cease? No thoughts, no memories, just nothing. He'd read some books about past lives theory, and that had given him something to hold onto. They posited the soul didn't die. It lingered somewhere—the Well of Souls, or something—to be reborn again, maybe a hundred years later, usually along with the souls of the people in his current life.

He sighed and turned to the sink to wash his face and rinse the bile from his mouth. Then he went looking for Uncle Charlie and Kim.

He found the woman perched behind his uncle's home office desk, scanning the desktop computer. Seeing him at the door, her eyes crinkled, a sly grin tilting her lips.

"There's the sleepyhead. Feeling any better?"

"Not much." He dropped onto a chair. "Woke up with pain and nausea. Lunch ended up in the toilet." The back of a hand swiped across his lips. "Tasty!" He grimaced.

"Sorry about that, sweetie." Kim sat back, her arms folded across her chest.

"What'cha doing?" He nodded toward the flat screen.

"Surfing. Always surfing, looking for a donor. You're priority one, kiddo."

"I appreciate all the effort, Kim." He swiped away a tiny rivulet leaking across his cheeks. "We're—we're running out of time, aren't we?" His fingers trickled across the yellowing skin of his arm.

"I know it feels that way, Hunter, but we *are* going to get you that liver. Your uncle thinks we're really close to finding a donor."

"I hope you're right." He edged forward on the seat. "Where is he, anyhow?"

"He went to the rifle range to test fire his new Weatherby. He's taking Carthwright up to the game ranch next week for a three-day hunt."

"He's the donor guy?"

"Yeah. Charlie's working hard to get you to the top of the list." She rose and circled the desk, settling next to him. "If we can get the mother of the guy on life-support to let him go, we won't need the donor bank. Your uncle's covering all the bases." She took one of his hands in hers, rubbing it. "If there's something there, we're going to get it."

Hunter sighed and nodded. "Thanks. I know you guys are pulling out all the stops. Uncle Charlie and I are really lucky to have you on our team. You're—you're—"

"No need to say anything. He loves you like a son, so I love you too."

He struggled to his feet, swaying slightly. "It's more than I can put into words, anyhow." He weaved unsteadily toward the door. "I'd better be getting home. Mom will be worried."

"Hang on. You're moving like a drunken sailor. Listen, I'll drive you. You're looking too wobbly to go it alone."

"Yeah, I feel hazy, but I don't want to put you out. How'll you get back?"

"Charlie will come for me." She grasped his elbow to offer support. "He should be done shooting soon. I'm not gonna chance loosing you to an accident."

"Okay. Gotta admit, I'm still a bit groggy after that nap. You've become my beautiful guardian angel, Kim."

"Yeah? Well, I wish this angel had a better hotline to God, so He can make this right."

With a hand on her arm for balance, he headed for his car, hopeful something good would turn up.

~ 34 ~

"You ready?" Raphael Olvida asked Detective Beck.

"Yeah." He rose, gathering his shield and Glock from his desk drawer. "What's the schedule?"

"I figure we should visit the Perez home first." Olvida scrolled through his electronic tablet. "See if she was aware of any threat to her son after he dinged Cepeda's Maserati."

"Sounds like a plan," Beck said as they exited the squad room, en route to the garage.

"I'll drive," Olvida said, heading for his blue Caprice.

Olvida pulled into the gravel driveway of a small, yellow concrete block ranch house on the eastern side of Hialeah.

"Think she's home?"

"Should be. She runs a mini day-care for some of her neighbors. Licensed and everything. Upstanding Cuban immigrant."

"That's a switch nowadays." Beck chuckled as he rang the bell.

A moment later, they were facing an amber-skin, mid-fortyish brunette woman. Dark rings around her eyes were evidence of the strain she bore.

"Señora Perez?" Olvida asked.

"Sí. Que etsá?" Her eyes swung from one man to the other.

"I'm Detective Olvida, and this is Detective Beck." They flashed their shields. "Do you speak English?"

She nodded.

"Good. We'd like to talk to you about your son. May we come in?"

She sighed and stepped aside, holding the door open for

them, then led the way to her living room. The detectives settled on a faux leather sofa next to a low, glass-top coffee table, and she on an adjacent armchair.

"My poor Cesar. You have found the man who did this?"

"We're working on it," Olvida said. "Do you know of anyone who mighta wanted to harm him?"

"No." Her eyes glistened with unshed tears. "He's a good boy. Works hard at two jobs and stays out of trouble."

"He has another job besides parking cars at the resturant?" Olvida jotted a note on his tablet.

"*Sí*. He does the drywall for a builder. Houses." She dabbed her eyes with a tissue. "So he has money to marry his Carlita."

"Carlita?" Beck glanced at his notebook. "His girlfriend?"

She nodded. "Fiancée."

"Okay. But he *did* get in trouble when he dinged up the Cuban don's fancy Ferrari." Olvida leaned back and studied her face.

"Maybe." She shrugged. "Just a foolish boy, showing off for his girl. A quick ride in a car could never have—"

"Yeah, but Cepeda had to be really upset," Beck said, "and the resturant owner wouldn't be happy with the insurance claim against him. I'm surprised Cesar wasn't fired after that."

"And those might be reasons to try to kill him?" She shook her head. "Can people be so crazy?"

"Sometimes." Olvida shrugged. "It's just something to follow up. Can you give me the house builder's name? We'll want to talk to him, too."

"So, is there anything else you can think of, señora?" The men rose. "Even the smallest thing might be important." Olvida offered her his hand, helping her out of the chair.

"Nothing." She sighed. "My brain, it is still numb. The doctor's say Cesar will never recover. Those people, they want me to—how you say it—disconnect? *Sí*, disconnect him."

"People?" Olvida, who had started for the entrance, turned back. "What people?"

"A man and a woman. His son needs a liver, I think, and Cesar is the same blood type."

"Your son's a rare blood type?" Beck had his notebook out again.

"*Sí*, O-Negative, I think. This is important?"

"Don't know, but I wonder how they knew your son's blood type? If they left their name, we'll check it out." Olvida walked back into the room.

"I will get the card, but she was his nurse, I think. Can you leave the card with me? In case—in case Cesar . . . I would hope to help save their son."

"Sure," Olvida said. "Let me see it and I'll just copy the info."

She nodded and went into the kitchen, returning a moment later with the card: *Charles Seagrave, retired.* Flipping it over, he saw *Kim Tate* printed on the back.

Olvida typed the data on his tablet and thanked the woman as they left. Might be worth checking out, but if the Tate woman was the kid's nurse, she'd probably know his blood-type. Might be unethical to use it that way, but nothing really suspicious. Who could blame them?

Back in his car, Olvida checked his tablet. Next on their schedule was a visit with Diego Cepeda, Cuban crime boss. He'd see if the Boss wanted him to follow up on this Seagrave guy and the nurse too, but that seemed thinner than any of their other low probability leads.

Still, with a case like this, nothing would be left to chance.

~ 35 ~

"Your destination is one hundred feet ahead on your right."

Warner smiled. The *Waze* GPS on his Android phone made finding any place a snap. He slipped his Dodge into an open space, exited, and locked the coupe. He spotted Harris' Chevy parked four cars in front, and as he approached, the wiry detective stepped out, tossing a quick salute.

"Hey, Boss. Perfect timing."

"That the place?" Warner nodded toward the long, two-story stucco building. A sign above a red brick façade said:

Veterans of Foreign Wars

"Yeah. Copello's doing a fund-raising luncheon there. Should be done with his speech any time now."

"Okay. Let's go. I want to get him, soon as he's finished talkin'." He strode off toward the glass double entry doors with Harris trailing close behind. They paused in the small lobby. Hallways ran off in opposite directions, but a burst of applause from his left was the guidance they needed to find the speaker.

Warner waved Harris to follow as he hurried up the hall. Twin oak doors were the apparent entrance to the auditorium. They slipped inside and were in time to see Congressman Copello on the dais, shaking hands with two companions. He turned and made a victory sign to the crowd, firing up a new round of clapping.

His admirers began to rise, some working their way toward the stage, seeking recognition from the politician.

"C'mon, Harris." Warner weaved his way through the sea of bodies. "I want to catch him before he leaves." In a moment, both detectives stood at the foot of the platform's stairs, just as Copello began his descent.

"Congressman?" Warner touched his forearm, drawing his attention.

"Yes?" His forehead wrinkled, not finding an expected autograph seeker. "Can I help you?"

"I'm Detective Al Warner, Miami PD, and my partner," nodding at his companion, "Jack Harris." He flashed his shield. "We need a few minutes of your time. Somewhere we can go for some privacy?"

"What's this about?" He glanced at a small group of staff. "I've got a reception to attend."

"Ms. DeVries' murder." Warner's eyes bored into his. "We can talk about this now—or at the precinct. Your choice."

"Of course." He seemed to sag. "Anything I can do to help. There's a conference room in the back. Please, follow me." He waved away three men who began to approach, and took off at a brisk pace.

Warner and Harris trailed behind, and they were soon in a modest room with a long table surrounded by ten chairs. They settled at one end, and the congressman tilted back, his hands folded across his belly. He sighed.

"What can I do for you, Detectives? Betji's death was a devastating blow."

"Or a convenient one," Harris said, positioning his Android tablet on the table. "Mind if I record our conversation?"

"What? I'm a suspect? Jesus!" He rolled forward, slapping both hands on the table. He took a deep breath and sighed again. "Go ahead. I've got nothing to hide."

The little detective tapped a button, and looked up. "You say you got nothing to hide, Congressman? What about your secret affair with Ms. DeVries?" Harris studied the man's face. "We heard she was going to expose it. What would that do to your campaign?"

"You got it wrong, Detective." He eased back again, giving a small head shake. "*She* wasn't going to expose it. *We* were, together."

"What?" Warner leaned forward, taking over. "We learned—"

"Yeah," he interrupted, "I know the rumors. Truth is, we were going public right after the election." Copello's eyes shimmered with unshed tears. "We were in love. I was going to file for divorce in November. We were—"

"Your wife knew about this?" Warner glanced at Harris.

"That you'd found love somewhere else?"

"Of course. Ours was a political marriage of convenience. There was *never* any love involved." He ran fingers through his graying brown hair. "Both our families benefited from the union, but it was time to go our own ways."

"She was okay with that?" Warner sat back, stroking his stubbled jaw. "Losing access to your family fortune?"

"Happy? No. Ecstatic? *Yeah!*" He chuckled softly, then sighed. "She's got a terrific pre-nup and a hot young stud to spend it on. Maybe more than one, in fact. Wanda loves sex, just not with me. And the feeling's mutual." He pushed out of the chair and fished inside his jacket pocket, withdrawing a business card.

"Here's my attorney's card. I'll call him and authorize your full access to the divorce proceedings." He started for the door. "Feel free to interview my wife or any of my staff. You'll find I had every reason to want Betji DeVries alive."

He looked back as he exited. "I hope you find the sonofabitch who killed the first woman I ever really loved. I presume you can find your way out." And he was gone.

Warner and Harris exchanged looks. They'd follow this up and talk to the attorney. Maybe even the wife. But it looked like their suspect list had just gotten a bit smaller.

Harris gathered his Android and they headed for Warner's Dodge. The day was still young, and there was much more to do. They had a killer to catch.

~ 36 ~

"Anything new from the interviews, Al?" Captain Santiago leaned against the doorjamb, arms folded.

"Just goin' over the notes, Cap." He dropped a folder he'd been scanning onto his desk. "Nothin' promisin', unfortunately. Harris and I quizzed the congressman earlier this afternoon." He massaged his eyes. "We don't make him for a suspect." He rose and approached the murder board, scanning it for anything new.

"What clears the congressman for you, Detective?"

"Looks like he and DeVries were in love, and he was planning on a divorce after the comin' election." He paused to scrawl a notation on the white board. "His attorney verified it was in the works, mutually accepted. The wife's got a huge pre-nup, so there's nothin' there, Boss."

"Okay." Captain Santiago stood legs spread, hands on hips, watching Warner work. "So, what about the Cuban don? You liked him the best of what you had."

"Yeah, but I'm softenin' on him too. Olvida and Beck are followin' up on Diego Cepeda, but it's hard to believe even a turd like him woulda contracted a hit on that kid because he dinged up his fancy car." Warner returned to his desk and plopped down on the leather chair. "We'll see how that interview goes." He slid closer to his desk.

"Our guys quizzed that vic's mom. He's brain dead and on life-support, but she's holdin' out for a miracle." He sorted through some papers sprawled across his overcrowded desk and stripped one out of the pile, waving it.

"Here's a printout of their report that I was just gettin' to. We got a few more interviews to run, but I ain't expectin' much."

"What about the other case?" Santiago shoved aside a pile of reports and perched on the edge of the detective's desk.

"The murder in Little Havana looks like a spat over a woman." He leaned back and flexed interlocked fingers. "The fourteen-year-old killed in Overtown was a drive-by, motive, if any, still unknown. I've assigned some of our newer guys to those. Then there's—"

"What about the black market organ transplants?" Santiago pushed off the desk and jammed his hands into his pockets. "There a pattern there?"

'Don't know, Cap.' Warner shook his head. "Harris and I got some free time until this Shadow bastard kills again. We're gonna case some homeless hangouts. See if regulars are suddenly missin'."

"You're figuring somebody's snatching people off the street that no one would miss and harvesting their organs."

"Seems most likely. I got a couple guys interviewin' funeral homes, but they usually get the stiffs too late for organs to be useful. But we're gonna cover all the bases."

"Sounds like a plan," Santiago said. "Any leads on where they're doing the surgeries? We shut those down and the whole program may founder."

"Nothing yet, Cap, but we're diggin'. So far, the few recipients we've found to talk to seem too nervous to commit. They know they've broken the law, but they were desperate people. The national demand is like five times greater than the official supply." Warner stood and stretched. "We'll keep at it, and something will turn up. It always does."

"Okay, Detective." Santiago edged toward the doorway. "I got faith in you. Keep me posted."

"Copy that, Cap." He watched his boss depart, and began rearranging the stacks on his desk. His thoughts drifted to their current lunatic.

He's gonna kill again, and soon. The magic number seems to be three—if ya don't count a truck. A smile tweaked his lips at his internal humor. *There's a whole different motive behind this senseless killin' than the obvious leads. Are those clues an accident, or is this shadowy bastard intentionally leadin' us in a circle?*

He shook his head, then gathered his Glock, shield, and jacket.

He had work to do, and the afternoon was still young. He wanted to get home early. Tonight they were doing the surprise party for his ninety-year-old surrogate mom, and he didn't want to leave *everything* to Eva, despite how competent she was.

Then tomorrow was lunch with his guys to schedule their next teen camp weekend, if they could fit one in, with all these cases pending.

All some much needed distraction from murder and mayhem.

~ 37 ~

Warner's eyes were drawn to sounds from the door, and there were two of his buddies weaving between tables en route to his.

"Hey, Hector, Jorge. Grab a seat. Darnell and Ben texted they'd be a few minutes late."

The detectives dropped into chairs on either side of Warner, and Hector Carrera studied his friend. "You look bushed, Al. The sniper case talking a toll?"

"I guess, but I was also up late last night. We had a surprise party for my ninety-year-old neighbor, Adele Gerber, and with the cleanup, it was nearly midnight before Eva and I hit the hay."

"She's like your surrogate mom, huh?" Jorge Ignaccio said.

"Adele? Better. A very special lady." Warner stretched and yawned. "The whole thing was kinda touching, with the little gifts and all the huggin'. Not a dry eye in the room."

Jorge chuckled. "Never figured you for a softy, Al."

"A man with many sides, huh?" Carrera looked up from a menu "So, what's good here, Al? Never been to Abe's Deli before."

"What you'd expect." Warner chuckled. "Corned beef, pastrami, hotdogs, ham. Ya know . . . sandwiches. Great coleslaw." He looked up. "Here comes Ben."

"Yeah, and I just saw Darnell's Chevy pickup go by," Jorge said, gesturing at the plate-glass window.

Ten minutes later the five detectives had convened and ordered lunch.

"I know we're here to set up the next Dade County Boot Camp." Warner slumped back in his chair. "The judge's got a list of twenty-seven teens he hopes we can straighten out, "but I'm not sure I'll have the time, with our spree killer probably ready to take his next victims."

"You got any leads, Al?" Ben Ellison took a sip of iced tea.

"Yeah, Ben. Lots of 'em, but they all look like red herrings." Conversation paused as the waitress appeared with their sandwiches.

"We're followin' 'em up, but I'm pretty sure it'll be a waste of time. My department's also been tasked to look into a black market organ problem." He took a bite of his corned-beef-on-rye. "We've had three deaths in the last month from illegally implanted, unviable kidneys."

"They didn't die from botched surgeries?" Darnell Franklin asked.

"Nope." Warner paused to finish a mouthful of food. "Actually, the ME said the surgeries were pretty well done. It was unhealthy kidneys that did 'em in, and maybe faulty tissue-typing too. Just bad enough to fail, get rejected, or both, after a month or so. Septic shock was the most obvious villain."

"Hmm." Ellison pulled on an ear. "We haven't been unlucky enough to be visited by your sniper in North Miami—yet, but we just had a woman die from a failed liver transplant." He looked at Warner. "Sounds like you think this is an organized operation."

"Looks that way to me, Darnell. We're sweepin' the

homeless gatherin' spots to see if anyone noticed any regulars gone missin'."

"You think they're snatching people no one would miss to harvest their organs, huh?" Franklin asked. "We've got a three-block homeless city in Overtown, Al. I'll have some of our guys canvas that area too."

"Good idea, Darnell." He turned to the three other detectives. "You guys should probably do the same. Let me know what you find out, and we can coordinate our investigations. This is a nasty business."

After a chorus of agreements, Hector Carrera sat back, finished his coffee, burped, and glanced at Warner.

"So, what's the decision about the DCBC, Al. It's your ballpark."

"I hate to put it off, guys. The last three camps we managed to turn around eighteen kids—boys who never expected to live through high school, much less think about college."

"Yeah," Ignacio shoved back his empty plate. "Eighteen out of eighty-two. Kids we won't have to bust again. Your project is becoming a success, Al. I hear the Florida Police Association wants to give you an award."

"Yeah, but it's *our* project, Jorge. It wouldn't have happened without the four of you." He sat back. "They *did* contact me, though. Wanna do a big shindig—a fund-raiser—so they can start chapters all over the state. They wanna highlight our success. I just wish we could win over a larger percent of our candidates."

"So, . . .?" Ellison looked at Warner, eyebrows arched. "What about our next session? We going to do it?"

"Let's meet again in two weeks," Warner rose and picked up his tab. "I'm expectin' three more bodies any day now. That seems to be our sniper's number." He withdrew bills from his wallet. "I hope this careful bastard fucks up next time."

"You still got no idea of his motive?" Carrera also stood,

credit card in hand.

"Not a clue at this point. My fear is, he'll complete whatever he intends and disappear. That happens, we may never catch him. And his victims' families never get closure."

"You think he'll just quit, Al?" Ellison asked. "Don't these nuts–?"

"He's not a typical serial psychopath, Ben. And he's not really a spree-killer, either. The BAU's havin' a hard time puttin' a label on this, but we *know* this *Shadow* is a hired hit man. I think he has a specific agenda, and when that's done, he'll be gone. We gotta figure out what that is, and snag him before it's over."

"Somehow, you seem to get more than your fair share of these loonies, Al," Carrera said, shoving away from their table. "Anything I can do to help, let me know."

"Thanks, Hector. Little Havana isn't outta his target area, so you might be fieldin' the next batch of vics. I'm expectin' him to hit again, and soon."

Everyone stood, gathering up their chits. The five detectives headed for the cashier. Time to get back on the Job, catching bad guys, and four of them had new avenues to pursue—black market organ transplants. And maybe three sniper victims dropping in their laps any day now.

Not something to look forward to.

~ 38 ~

I slouched back in the chair, sighed, and removed my glasses, massaging tired eyes. I replaced the specs, uncorrected but lightly tinted blue to ease computer use, and scanned my notes.

This may be my last chance to get it right. Hunter was

running out of time. Unfortunately, even if perfectly executed, there was no guarantee a liver would be offered for donation. I'd learned that unpleasant lesson when the Perez woman still hung on to a ridiculous hope her son, Cesar, might somehow recover.

A yellow-lined pad was filled with the details for my next victim: Robert McClure, financial planner. I repressed a chuckle. Of all my victims, he was the first who really had it coming. Paroled after three years of a fifteen-year sentence for Ponzi scheme fraud, he was clearly back at it. I was amazed that after all his notoriety, foolish, rich people still lined up to buy non-existent mortgages from this thief. He was one hell of a salesman.

The con man was hosting a promotional luncheon tomorrow at a fancy Coral Gables eatery. He was the fourth potential candidate I'd collected sample from before my DNA lab found a probably tissue match.

So here I was, again needing to make the perfect shot to render him brain-dead but able to survive on a respirator. Seemed likely his estranged second wife would donate his liver if, like Perez, she was offered fifty-K. According to Google, the couple's separation was as acrimonious as they come, and court records revealed she had a pre-nup that blocked her from most of his remaining wealth in their coming divorce.

I had almost run out of candidates when I decided to hack prison records for recently released cons. The feds had full medical details on every inmate, and McClure was the only one who was O-Negative. Luckily, through a third party, I was able to gain access to blood from his prison physical. All this research was chewing up my time. Now I finally had target who was a probable match.

Lucky him. Or more accurately, lucky Carol McClure, who I suspected would be happy to be rid of her husband—and for a profit. With her modestly funded pre-nup, maybe she should pay *me*. I chuckled as I started packing up.

Hopefully, the Hialeah Public Library would be the last one I'd have to visit. If things fell through tomorrow, the kid might not have enough time for me to reboot and find another candidate.

A quick headshake as I rose, appearing to struggle under the weight of my backpack—a skinny, geriatric, balding guy, limping away. The last disguise needed if I succeeded tomorrow. Out the library door, I plowed into a wall of moist heat, a full onset of South Florida's summer. The Sun, uninhibited by a sparse layer of stratus clouds, climbed across the indigo sky.

En route to my CRV, I glanced up and sniffed fir-laden air. Bright light and gentle winds, almost perfect shooting weather. Just had to consider the dense humidity when adjusting my sights.

My nondescript Honda squatted at the far end of the parking lot. I slid inside, tossed my bag onto the passenger seat, and cranked her up, lolling for a moment as the a/c began wringing moisture from the air. Since no one seemed about, I yanked off the uncomfortable bald head disguise, slipped out of the tattered sport jacket, and pocketed my tortoise-shell glasses.

A brief stretch as I pondered my next move. I glanced at my watch, then backed the SUV out of its parking spot and drove off. Better hit my target range in the 'Glades for a last minute tune-up. Had to make the perfect shot again tomorrow to get that kid his liver. Enough time to do it all, with over three hours before needing to get home for dinner.

~~~

Sprawled atop the green mechanical box housing, I wiggled around, trying to hitch my body into a secure position. Of all the sniper nests I'd used, this was the least comfortable. My bulked up disguise made it that much more difficult.

I'd considered setting up to make the shot normally dressed and then slipping on the fat-suit for my exfil, but this was the most exposed I'd been during this whole venture. Taller apartment buildings loomed in every direction. Places where some casual onlooker might spot me. Maybe become suspicious enough to call the cops. A chubby, homeless female musician would attract less attention.

Little time was available for me to prepare today, so necessary to avoid as much exposure as possible. I was barely settled, adjusting my sight for wind and temp, when McClure's attendees began piling out of the resturant. They milled about in front of the entrance, awaiting the appearance of their host. With some luck, he'd be waylaid by investors with questions, giving me a stationary target for my shot.

With the entrance zeroed in through my telescopic sight, less than a minute passed before McClure appeared. He paused, surrounded by a small crowd of admirers who sought handshakes and answers to their questions. Soon to be moot advice.

Thankfully, the con man was six-six, an easy target when he paused, responding to what seemed to be a verbal barrage.

A quick glance at my wind gauge to verify nothing had changed, and I centered on my objective. With his hand on another's shoulder, he was momentarily motionless as they talked. A perfect setup for the precise shot required.

A smooth exhale, a short pause, and I squeezed off my first round. I hesitated just long enough to see the right edge of his skull and ear disappear, then picked out two random targets—a fiftyish man and a gray-haired woman—bringing both down in less than ten seconds.

I dropped to my knees, collected my casings, broke down and stowed the rifle, and secured my bedroll. The nylon hose

I'd donned as part of my disguise assured no trace or DNA would be left where I'd knelt, but I knew law enforcement didn't have any of my identifiers in its data bases. I intended to keep it that way.

After nearly two decades at this job, I was about to retire.

On my feet, I duck-walked, keeping a low profile, to the roof's exit and hurried down the stairs as quickly as my bulky fat-suit allowed. Out the rear door, I waddled more appropriately down the alley to my Honda, eager to learn if my shot was as perfect as it looked. A vagrant, rummaging in a trash bin, glanced up and gave me a vacant stare, before returning to his quest. Doubtful he would remember much if eventually questioned by the cops.

My thoughts centered on what I hoped was a brain-dead Robert McClure. If all went well, he could provide Hunter with the liver he desperately needed. From everything I'd learned, the oily crook's wife would eagerly give him up, especially for the wad of dough she'd probably be offered.

No love lost in that fractured marriage.

Lucky for Hunter.

~ 39 ~

Al Warner leaned against a squad car and watched as his detectives continued to quiz witnesses. The crime scene from the Shadow's latest assault swarmed with patrol officers, detectives, and CSU techs. Special Agents Ed Dalwin, Harry Askin, and Lon Pauletti were there to help access the scene and question and evaluate possible witnesses.

Warner shook his head, pushed away from the car, and

scanned his notes. He'd spoken to a tearful Joseph Tipco and the devastated Amy Bono, each spouses of two of the victims. Carole McClure, who hadn't attended her husband's promotional luncheon, was on the way to the hospital. The seemingly pure randomness of the attack had everyone stymied, and not a single witness could pose a motive for the killings.

But Warner *knew* there was one, hiding in the shadows of the Shadow. He grimaced, clenching his teeth.

Why the fuck does a contract hit man go on this kind of killin' spree? Elusive for nearly twenty years, why risk exposure with these blatant attacks. The more he's out there, the more likely to be caught. It made no sense, so there *must* be an underlying goal—something tying together just one victim in each attack.

One connection we haven't found yet.

He was drawn from his thoughts by the approach of Special Agent Dalwin and Jack Harris.

"So, any brilliant insight, guys?" Warner asked.

"Well, there's the obvious." Harris scanned his Android pad. "Someone wanting Bob McClure dead would be no surprise. The other two could be random vics, to muddy up the waters."

"But McClure *isn't* dead," Dalwin said, "and it's not like this lethal bastard to miss that shot. CSU found his perch, and it laser-measured just over eight hundred yards." He stuffed his hands in his pockets and surveyed the crime scene. "Easy pickings for a crack shot using that TAC-50 rifle."

"Interestin' thought." Warner ran fingers through his thick, curly locks. "Maybe because he moved just as the bastard fired? But that's the second vic left alive—more or less."

"Yeah," Harris said, "the EMTs suspect this guy's brain-dead, just like the Perez kid. They got him on life-support, but don't think he's got any shot of ever recovering."

Warner looked at Agent Dalwin. "You got anything to add?"

"We've done a preliminary run of the three names through our data base." The BAU Agent in Charge shrugged. "Nothing to indicate any link to your previous victims."

"No real estate connection?" Harris asked. "Nothing with the Cuban Cartel don or the congressman?"

"Not so far," said Agent Pauletti, who just joined them. "We've kicked it up to Quantico, and they're doing a deeper dive. We'll see if that turns up anything."

"Keep at it, willya?" Warner clasped Dalwin on the shoulder. "There's *something* there. We just gotta find it."

"I'm going to suggest they look into the two brain-dead victims." Special Agent Harry Ashkin punched auto-dial on his cell phone. "That's a bit thin. Like you said, the Shadow might have missed the kill because the vic moved a little. But it *is* another possible connection."

"I was thinkin' the same thing, Harry." Warner pocketed his notebook. "I'm heading back to the precinct to check that out from this end, too."

He turned and grasped Harris by the shoulder. "You check with the Hawk? We get lucky this time?"

"Naw. His CSU team really scrubbed his sniper nest. No casings, no fibers, nothing with DNA on it." He shrugged. "Some prints in the A/C housing, but he doubts they're from the perp. Nothing fresh. I got three detectives canvassing the upper floors of those apartment buildings," nodding at the tall condos surrounding the area. "Maybe they'll find someone who noticed the shooter from above, like the guy from Bayfront."

"And no one saw anything on the ground?" Warner stood, arms akimbo. "Nothing suspicious? No one sneaking away? Is this bastard really invisible?"

"Two people noticed a shabbily dressed, chubby woman walking up the street." Agent Pauletti glanced at his notes. "It registered with both of them because she seemed totally disinterested in the hubbub from the shooting."

"And . . .?" Warner's eyebrows arched.

"Looked like a homeless street musician to them." He closed and pocketed his notebook. "She was wearing a backpack with a bedroll, and carrying a guitar case."

"Not unusual for a homeless person to avoid contact with cops," Harris said.

"Hmm." Warner pulled an earlobe, then looked at Harris. "Didn't your witness at the first shooting see a homeless-type musician with a backpack on the shooter's roof?"

"Yeah, you're right, Boss. But that was a skinny guy." Harris looked at Agent Pauletti. "You said today's sighting was a chubby dame, right?"

The special agent nodded.

"Both had backpacks and guitar cases?" Warner flipped back through his notebook. "Yeah, here. A bedroll on the first perp's backpack too. A sleepin' bag would make an ideal prone shootin' pad, and its waterproof shell ain't likely to leave any trace fibers for CSU."

"So?" Harris shrugged. "They're totally different people. Sex and everything. What's the connection?"

"What d'ya think, Ed?" Warner looked at the FBI agent. "Isn't it likely someone as proficient at lurkin' below the radar, like this Shadow, uses disguises?"

"Without a doubt. We've had a half-dozen different descriptions of him over the years. It's his methodology that ties him to all his victims." He paused, a hand massaging the back of his neck. "And that guitar case. It could easily be modified to stow a disassembled TAC-50."

"I think we're ready to deliver a profile, Ed," Agent Ashkin said. "At least there's something to work with for a change."

"You're right, Harry. Let's get the team together at the precinct and draw it up." He laid a hand on Warner's bicep.

"You organize the troops, Al. Probably should include people from all the county's law enforcement units."

"Right. First thing during the morning briefin'. I wanna nail this shifty bastard before we fill any more body bags."

He pointed at Harris. "Meanwhile, we're still gonna follow up our previous leads. Olvida and Beck gotta talk with the Cuban don, and I want you diggin' into our newest vics. No stones left unturned."

"On it, Boss." He hurried off.

"Okay," Warner said, starting toward the yellow-taped crime scene. "Let's finish up here and get to it. This bastard's been plaguing us long enough."

The four men disbursed, each on his own mission, seeking justice for nine victims . . . so far.

Warner feared if they didn't nab this killer soon, they'd have another three bodies to deal with. An even greater worry was if the Shadow completed his mission and disappeared into the ether.

He wiggled his clenched jaw, trying to ease tension. If that happened, they'd probably never catch him unless he surfaced again.

That was a totally unacceptable scenario, so they'd better snag him now.

~ 40 ~

Charlie Seagrave entered his house through the garage, walked through the kitchen, and looked for Kim in the family room. Her Jeep Cherokee was parked in the drive, but she wasn't in the family room.

"Kim? Where are you?" He started toward the bedrooms.

"In your office. I'm on the 'Net."

He headed for his third bedroom, which he'd converted to his in-house office after he sold his dot.com business. Kim preferred using his equipment when she surfed the Web, since it was state of the art.

He found his lover at his computer station, hunched over the keyboard, fingers flicking across the keys. She glanced up and smiled.

"Got anything new, babe?" He circled behind her chair and studied the monitor.

"Yeah. You heard about the latest shooting?" She leaned back to receive a quick kiss.

"Yep. Really gruesome. Three more victims yesterday. This makes nine, doesn't it? What a nasty bastard, killing people at random like that." He pulled up a chair and settled down, one arm around her slim waist.

"I know, but there's no figuring a psychopath. However, as ugly as that is, there's some possibly good news for us. This time there's a second one on life-support." She looked at the screen. "I was just checking with Jackson Memorial, and it appears one of the victims is brain-dead but alive, at least for the moment."

"Jesus, what hell that is. Like the Perez kid, huh? Who's this guy?"

"Robert McClure. Remember him?" She swiveled in her chair and ran fingers across his cheek.

"Mmm." He caught her hand in his and brushed his lips across its back as he glanced at the screen. "The con man? Isn't he in prison?"

"Released on parole two months ago, and apparently back at swindling gullible investors." She chuckled. "This is the shooter's first victim who may have deserved it." She turned back to the screen. "According to Google, his estranged wife and he are in a bitter divorce battle. She may not be reluctant to pull the plug and might happily donate his liver if you make the same offer you did to Mrs. Perez. Most of McClure's assets were seized by the government, and she's stuck with a modest prenup."

"Wow! And you're suggesting he's O-Negative?"

"As luck would have it." She smiled and rose, taking his hands. "It's almost like this sniper is trying to provide us with possible donors."

"Yeah, what a lucky coincidence. If you got what we need, let's go." He towed her toward the exit. "Where to? The hospital or his house? We gotta find the wife first."

"Couldn't reach her with the phone number I found, so I left a voice-mail." Kim gathered up her shoulder bag. "Let's try Jackson first. See if she's there, or at least leave a notice of our interest."

"Sounds good to me. I'll drive," Seagrave said as they hurried from the room.

~ ~ ~

Fifty minutes later, Seagrave had parked in a staff slot, with Kim's nurses' ID displayed on the dash. They hurried into reception and headed for the third floor. Using her phone, Kim had located the room McClure was assigned to: 353, at the end of a long hall.

As they strode along, Seagrave touched Kim's arm. "You should probably do the talking at first. You know, the concerned nurse and all. Then I'll make the pitch. Try to see if the money will sway her, if she's reluctant."

"Okay." She glanced at him and grinned. "But from what I've learned from searching the Web, I don't think that's going to be a problem. She distanced herself from him right after he was charged. Sounded like it wasn't a surprise to her that he was a grifter."

"I hope you're right. We're running outta time." He pointed to an open-doored room to their right. "There it is—353."

They hesitated and surveyed the hallway, which was momentarily empty, and then slipped inside. They checked up when they saw an orderly making the bed.

The white-clad black man glanced over his shoulder at the man and woman, and returned to his task, ignoring them.

"Is this Robert McClure's room?" Kim asked, touching his shoulder to gain his attention.

The man shrugged as he rearranged the pillow.

"Where is he? Mr. McClure." She glanced at Seagrave and frowned.

"Don't know, ma'am. Not here though. Check with the nurses' station. I'm just an orderly."

"It's not like a guy on life-support would be out walking around." Seagrave frowned. "Something's wrong."

"C'mon." Kim grabbed his sleeve. "Let's find a nurse."

They retraced their steps, aiming for the cubicle that acted as a nurses' station. Two women in blue scrubs were behind the counter, one sipping from a paper cup, the other flipping through a logbook. Kim paused and cleared her throat.

The coffee-drinker looked up. "May I help you?"

"I'm Kim Tate from ICU." She flashed her ID badge. "I'm here to check on Robert McClure, room 353, but he's not there."

"Mr. McClure?" The other nurse glanced up from the log. "Oh, he's gone."

"Gone?" Seagrave couldn't restrain himself. "Gone where? He just got here yesterday, and he's on life-support."

"Not any more. He had a zero chance for recovery, so his wife disconnected him this morning and shipped him to a mortuary." She shrugged. "Clearly no love lost there."

"Sonofabitch!" Seagrave slammed his fist on the counter. "How long ago, and what funeral home?" His face screwed into angry planes, his eyes pooling.

The nurse's eyebrow arched quizzically as she paged through her log, mumbling. "What's the fuss? Now or later, he was already dead. Why should the living suffer, waiting for the inevitable?"

"You're right, of course," Kim said, gently kneeing Seagrave's leg, "but Mr. McClure was O-Negative, and Mr. Seagrave's son is also O-Neg and in desperate need of a liver. We were hoping to arrange a private transplant donation." She glanced at her watch. "There may still be enough time for the organ to be viable."

"Oh, I see. Well, you'd better hurry. The body went to Zlotnikov Funeral Home in Miami Springs four hours ago, and I believe they were planning an immediate cremation." She passed Kim a sticky-note with the facility's address.

"Let's go." Seagrave grabbed Kim's arm as she dialed the wife's phone. She answered this time, as they raced down the hallway.

"Mrs. McClure?" Kim briefly introduced herself as they ran. "You gotta call that funeral home and stop the cremation. We have a teenage boy who desperately needs Robert's liver. Get your husband's body on ice, and tell them we need to get it back to the hospital. His viable liver is worth fifty grand to you." She peeked at Seagrave as they burst from the entry doors. "Tell 'em we're on the way, but they gotta preserve that organ if you want to see that money. A boy's life depends on it."

A scream echoed over the phone line. "About time that bastard did something positive for me." And she disconnected.

They sped out of the lot as Kim made another call, trying to set up medically safe transport and staging for a possible kidney transplant later that day.

If they got there in time, and the organ was still viable.

~ 41 ~

Warner stood on the dais, watching the room fill with Miami patrol supervisors and detectives from the tri-counties. The BAU offering their perp profile had become an all too familiar scene over the past three-plus years as he'd hunted three serial killers and an ISIS cell that was intent on terrorizing the entire nation.

Special Agent in Charge, Ed Dalwin, and his team crowded the stage, waiting for the room to settle down. Scanning the crowd, Warner decided it was time to begin.

"I want to thank all the tri-county's detectives for comin', even though the subject of this profile hasn't yet ventured outta Miami-Dade. You guys surely remember Special Agent in Charge, Ed Dalwin," Warner nodded toward the tall, sharp-faced man, "and his BAU team from his other all-to-recent visits. He's gonna tell you what we know about this perp." He stepped back and gestured toward the podium. "Agent Dalwin."

Six FBI agents circled the lectern. Dalwin's eyes swept the gathering before he spoke. "I wish I could say we've got to stop meeting like this, guys, but unfortunately these are the very conditions that bring us together again today." His forehead wrinkled as he gathered his thoughts.

"We've IDd this perp through his MO as possibly the most elusive contract killer we've ever encountered. Prior to his recent activities here, we suspect he's been the force behind at least thirty-seven homicides over the past nearly twenty years. We've dubbed him The Shadow because he's been totally invisible. He's careful and methodical and has never left a single shred of evidence."

"He's also versatile," Agent Anita Solto injected. "Knives, garrotes, arrows, and once a bear-trap. Guns *have* been primary, but this is the first time he's used a long-range sniper rifle."

"You know the weapon?" A detective called out.

"According to ballistics, it's a McMillan TAC-50," Amazonian, blond Agent Ina Yeager, replied. "I've test fired one but prefer the Barrett .50 –"

"With which she saved my ass last year." Warner interjected, drawing chuckles from the crowd. All were familiar with the messy shootout at Hialeah's Opa-loca Airport the previous year.

"Anyway," Yeager grinned at Warner, then turned to the gathering. "It's a military weapon, not easily attained by civilians, and an expert can take down a target from two thousand meters. This guy *is* an expert in all ways to kill."

"Our problem is," Agent Ansel Whitehead stepped forward, "none of this makes sense with this perp. He's not a serial-killer by definition. Those target a specific victimology, selected through psychotic reasoning. He's certainly not a mass murderer, or his kills wouldn't have stopped at three each time."

"Nor is he technically a spree killer," said Agent Harry Ashkin. "Those rarely pause for days between killings. Still, had we not known this perp was The Shadow, that would be the closet similarity for all these senseless deaths." He grimaced.

"But we have a ninety-five percent confidence this perp *is* The Shadow, so none of the above makes any sense for him. This is *not* someone we'd expect to begin random slaughter— unless he'd had a psychotic break. Somewhere, there's a still undiscovered motive behind all these killings."

"Like the Beltway Sniper?" Detective Ben Ellison called out.

"Exactly," Agent Lon Pauletti nodded. "Many deaths to hide a specific target. We just don't know who or what that is yet."

"All we know, from one possible sightin'," Warner rejoined the group at the podium, "is that he's a slim guy, five-ten to six feet, and probably in his forties, from his history. And he *is* on an agenda. If we don't nab him before that's achieved, we'll probably never catch him. Just like that fictional Shadow, he'll disappear." He paused.

"The one thing we *do* have is twice there were sightin's of a street musician, wearin' a backpack with a bedroll and totin' a large guitar case. Once a skinny guy, and the last time, a chubby female." He glanced back at the six BAU special agents. "But this guy is apparently good with disguises, so it's a possible connection." He stepped back.

"The FBI is stayin' to help however they can. We don't have much to work with, so stay alert to anything even slightly suspicious. He's been on an acceleratin' schedule, so we suspect whatever he's doin' is connected to a time table that's gettin' ready to expire." He gestured to the milling crowd.

"So, let's get out there and catch this bastard. Too many seemingly innocent people are dyin'."

He turned away from the dispersing throng. "Thanks for the help, Ed."

"That's our job, Detective. Not sure how much we've aided this time. You always seem to come up with tough nuts to crack."

"Yeah, lucky me. And I got another case I'm workin' I gotta get to while there's a lull in sniper vics."

Warner headed for his office, hoping for an update from Harris on the illegal transplants they'd been chasing.

~ 42 ~

Seagrave's Lexus sedan slid into a guest-parking slot next to a silver F-Type Jag convertible in front of Zlotnikov Funeral Home. Kim had just disconnected from a call to Jackson Memorial, prepping them for the hopefully coming transplant. Hunter wouldn't be told until they were assured the organ was available, still viable, and a confirmed tissue match.

They burst from the car and hurried toward the front door. He shaded his eyes from the glare of the afternoon sun and grabbed her wrist as they ran.

"How do you think we should handle this? You, as the nurse, or me as the concerned parent? And is the widow going to be there?"

"I don't know about Carol McClure, but it sounded like your 50K offer put her on our team. I'll start it off with the funeral director. Let him know arrangements are made to facilitate the transplant. You jump in if we need pressure or money. These guys are Russian, so maybe part of their mob."

"Great. All we need is to be fucking with the Russian mafia!" He threw open the door and followed Kim into a dimly lit lobby, sparsely decorated with overstuffed, dark corduroy sofas and chairs. Little attempt there at trying to cheer the bereaved.

They skidded to a stop and glanced around the gloomy room. No attendant present. Just a woman perched on one of the chairs, head in her hands, sobbing softly. Spying the reception desk, Seagrave strode over and twice tapped a small bell's button. The musical "ding, ding" pierced the leaden silence. Lilies in two earthen vases lightly perfumed the air.

The woman on the chair glanced up, red-rimmed eyes welling with tears and shook her head before dropping it back into her hands with a groan. Kim looked at Seagrave and shrugged. A moment later an inner door opened, emitting a tall, angular man whose pasty countenance suggested maybe he belonged in one of the coffins probably stored in back.

"May I help you?" His voice thick with a Slovak accent.

"You the director?" Kim's eyes swept over him. "Mr. Zlotnikov?"

"There is no longer a Mr. Zlotnikov." His razor-thin smile bore no humor. "Passed on he has, over six years now. I am Gregor, at your service."

"I'm Kim Tate, a trauma nurse from Jackson. You received instructions to preserve Robert McClure's body for organ donations. We have a patient waiting for his liver, and I have air transport on the way."

A soft, protracted wail emanated from the woman on the chair. She raised her head, her face twisted into an agonized mask.

"Too late," she moaned. "Too late." Her head dropped back into her hands, her body racked by shudders and gasping sobs.

"Huh? What?" Seagrave's glance swung from her to Gregor and back again. "What do you mean, 'too late?' You were ordered to preserve the body."

The mortician sighed. "Unfortunately, I received that request after we had already begun the cremation. Mrs. McClure," nodding toward the weeping woman, "wanted 'that bastard fried ASAP,' to quote her demand." A grim smile twitched at his lips. "We always aspire to meet our clients' demands as promptly as possible." He shrugged.

"So, he's in the crematorium now?" Kim's eyebrows arched as she glanced at Seagrave. "May we see it?"

"Oh, so sorry." He held up his hands. "Only authorized personnel allowed."

"Can't you make an exception?" Seagrave stepped close to the man, his eyes raking him. "It's a matter of life and death for a young boy."

"I understand, but no." He edged back. "It is against regulations. There is nothing to be gained. Whatever organ you need is gone." He forced a smile. "I'm sorry for your young man, but we got the message too late."

"Bastard!" Carol McClure hissed from her perch, stealing the explosion about to erupt from Seagrave.

"Shit," was all he could muster. Kim snatched his arm with an iron grip to stall a physical attack.

McClure lurched to her feet, gathered her purse, and glared at Gregor. "Bobby's still screwing up my life, even as he turns to ashes." She started for the exit, and looking over her shoulder, threw a parting barb.

"Don't bother sending a bill. You just incinerated fifty thousand dollars. I got nothing left to pay you with." She blew through the door, which boomed closed behind her.

Seagrave's and Kim's eyes locked, then swung to the man, whose mouth hung open.

"Well, I never . . . ." he muttered, spun on his heels, and left them without another word.

~~~

They drove in silence for five minutes before Seagrave finally vented his anger.

"Fuck! This sniper guy hands us a liver for Hunter on a silver platter, and Murphy's Law sticks its nose in it."

"Yeah." Kim shook her head. "Whatever could go wrong *has* been going wrong, right from the start. We're teased twice by lucky coincidences provided by that psycho sniper, and both fall through." She squeezed his thigh. "It's been a heartbreak for the Perez and McClure families, and all his other victims, but it's a tragedy that the only good that may have come from it—a liver for Hunter—has been wasted."

Seagrave nodded, his cheeks knotted by a clenched jaw.

"Our only other shot now is Carthwright." He glanced at Kim. "I'm taking him hunting at the Exotic Game Ranch this weekend. I'll press him on getting Hunt the next available liver, if one shows up in time. It seems unlikely another one will fall into our laps again."

Kim shrugged. "It's desperate times, Charlie. Somehow, we gotta come up with that organ." She paused, pulling at an ear, and hitched around in her seat.

"What?" he asked.

"I'm just thinking, that cremation happened damned fast, even for a rush job." She paused. "I bet McClure never ended up in an oven."

"What do you mean?"

"These guys are Russians—maybe even mafia. Could be those organs were harvested for the black market. Then the remains got toasted."

"You think his liver might be available?"

"For the right price, yeah, maybe, but between McClure getting shot and his corpse ending up on Zlotnikov's table, and then him trying to market it, I doubt it's still a viable organ."

"Is it worth the risk? You're the trauma nurse."

"I don't think I'd chance it for Hunter. I've heard there's been a spate of people dying after black market transplants due to unviable organs being used. It's a deadly con game."

"Good to know. Damn, I was just thinking about searching the black market, but I'll can that idea for now. Somehow, we've got to come up with a good liver for that sweet kid before it's too late." He braked the Lexus for a red light.

"And that time's too damned near," Kim grunted. "You notice he's beginning to show early signs of jaundice?"

Seagrave nodded and sighed, grateful to have such a committed partner in this urgent endeavor. The light changed, and as he accelerated, his mind whirled over the few options left. He would do whatever was necessary, and she'd back him up. He had one or two more chances to make this work.

They continued in silence, lost in their own plans. Just a few months remained if they were going to save that boy.

He had to do something more, and soon.

~ 43 ~

Raphael Olvida strode to Detective Beck's desk, who was laboriously pounding out an action report. A paper cup of cold coffee and a half-eaten donut perched on a corner of his desk.

"C'mon, Beck, saddle up. I finally got a fix on Cepeda." He glanced at computer's monitor. "That the fatal domestic squabble you got sucked into?"

"Yeah. Writing it up is the worst part of the case." He rose, gathering his Glock and shield from his desk drawer. "Where's the Cuban drug lord holed up?"

"He's attending his daughter's grammar school graduation in Little Havana at two this afternoon."

"He's got a twelve-year-old daughter?" They headed for the door. "Jeeze, he's gotta be in his sixties."

"Yeah, but he's got a young, trophy wife who apparently wanted a family." Olvida chuckled. "Guy in his early fifties is still shooting live ammo."

"I guess." Beck slipped into the passenger seat of Olvida's Caprice and fastened his seatbelt. "Smart woman, having kids won't stop him from cheating, but it might keep him tethered."

"Sure," Olvida said, sliding into the driver seat, "and family is major with Cubans, even drug lords. I think he's got a younger son with her too." He fired up the engine and dialed the A/C to max. Summer heat was unrelenting.

"It a perfect place to tag him, too," Olvida said as they

exited the police lot. "He's not gonna make a fuss in front of his kids and wife."

~~~

The detectives lingered by Olvida's Chevy in the shade of a sprawling live oak and scanned the crowd spilling from the school's front doors. They'd marked a black Lincoln limo, hovering nearby, surely awaiting the crime boss.

"There he is." Olvida pushed away from the car and strode across the lawn with Beck at his side. "Show your shield as we approach so we don't spook him."

Don Diego Cepeda knelt on one knee, hugging a young girl. Their smiles turned somber at the detectives' approach. Car doors slammed from the direction of the Lincoln, but when he saw the cops' badges, he grimaced, shook his head, and waved off his fast approaching muscle.

He rose, arms folded and spoke in a harsh whisper. "You gotta ruin this happy day for me and my family?" He was a short, stocky man with a full head of salt-and-pepper hair, and he wore a navy blue suit.

"If you hadn't kept ducking me all week, this wouldn't be necessary." Olvida pocketed his shield. "We'll try to make this quick and quiet, if you just answer a few questions." He nodded toward the cooler protection of the big tree.

"Do I have a choice?" He followed the detective, both trailed by Dean Beck. "This is about the Maserati, I suppose."

"Yeah, and the kid who racked it up and lies on death's doorstep," Beck said. "You couldn't have been very happy with him, messing up your fancy toy."

"You think I'd have all those other people killed over one little mistake?" He shook his head. "I got better things to do."

"You got a rep for not playing nice. Nothing's stuck, but—"

"Look, I had no bone to pick with the kid. The cafe's insurance paid for the repairs." He fingered his goatee.

"Actually, I kinda admired the punk for trying to show off for his girlfriend. It took balls. Kinda thing I mighta done at his age." A frown drew down his lips and wrinkled his forehead.

"Hell of a thing to happen to him and all those other people. Gotta be a real strain on his mom, deciding to pull the plug or not." Cepeda shoved his hands into his pockets.

"You've followed him?" Olvida made notes on his Samsung.

"Occasionally." Cepeda glanced at his limo and his two bodyguards, leaning against the hood. "We done here? I got a party to go to."

"Yeah, for now." Olvida pocketed his tablet. "But don't be so scarce next time, in case we got a few more questions."

The don nodded and strode toward his ride, where his wife and two children had already gathered.

The detectives watched him go for a moment, then headed for Olvida's Chevy, parked next to the big tree.

"What d'ya think?" Beck asked as they walked.

"I don't make him for this. Seemed like an unlikely connection at best."

"Me, either. No inkling of any tension in his answers."

"Okay, you write it up, willya? I'll talk to the boss. Doesn't look like we're getting any closer."

Moments later, they were heading toward HQ, no nearer to finding the elusive Shadow. They wondered if anyone else was making any headway?

~ 44 ~

Al Warner slumped back from his desk, yawned, and stretched, fingers interlocked over his head. He rubbed tired, dry eyes, and glanced at the files strewn across his desk.

Nine vics with no apparent connection. Random killin' ain't what I'd expect from this assassin.

He pulled at an earlobe, studying the papers, and reached out for two of the folders.

Seven dead and two critically wounded and on life support. No, McClure died two days ago when his wife pulled the plug. *Little love lost over that con man, I guess.* The detective flipped through both reports, searching for commonality other than both lived after their attacks and ended up on life-support. From what he'd learned about the Shadow from Agent Dalwin's team, survivors were inconsistent with the skill levels of this killer.

Warner dropped the files atop the others and started to rise, but then paused and cocked his head, glancing back at the oaken surface of his desk. He flopped back into his chair and snatched up the two reports, flipping to their second pages, his eyes sweeping from one to the other.

Hmmm. Both O-Negative.

He set them aside and dug into the seven other background reports. McClure and the Perez kid from the second attack were the only O-Negatives . . . and the only ones who weren't killed outright. *Hmmm.*

He rechecked both the Perez and McClure's file and reaffirmed what he suspected. Each was the first ones shot, a necessity if you needed absolute precision. After the first vic went down, everyone would be moving—a tougher target if you weren't planning outright death. McClure's wife had quickly pulled the plug on her crooked husband and had him cremated. That eliminated him for organ donation, but had the Shadow expected that? Maybe not?

Well, they had nothing else to follow up on, and this was the first thing that even smelled like a lead.

He reached for his phone. He wanted to pick the BAU

agents' brains.

They were the experts on perp motivation.

~ 45 ~

Charlie Seagrave and Corbin Carthwright exited rear doors of the old safari model Land Rover and headed for the clubhouse. The late afternoon sun had ducked behind a ridge of cottony cumulus clouds.

"Helluva day," Seagrave said, clapping the older man on the shoulder.

"One that will be well etched in my memory forever, Charlie." He grinned at his host as he brushed trail dust from his sleeves.

"I bet." Seagrave held the door for him as they entered the lounge. "Your twenty-four point red stag is the second best ever taken here. That was a heck of a shot."

"Thanks to your Weatherby Mark V." They slipped onto stools at the polished mahogany bar. "That's a sweet weapon, and I appreciate you allowing me to try it out."

"My pleasure. It's great in the hands of an expert like you for long-range shooting. That kill-shot had to be close to eight hundred yards." He signaled for a waiter. "Other than me, there are very few here who can handle that distance with any success." He ordered drinks—a single malt Scotch for him and a vodka martini for his guest. "Those big stag are damned wary and hard to get close to."

"I couldn't have scripted it more perfectly," Carthwright said. "Hunting those royal beasts was a dream I never expected to fulfill, and to have a chance to make that kill from the ground in wild terrain . . . well, that was incredible."

"Yeah, definitely worth a toast." They clinked glasses. "To a trophy of a lifetime." They sipped drinks, momentarily lost in thought.

"I can't thank you enough for this opportunity." Carthwright set down his martini and swiveled toward his host. "I know you're hoping for a quid pro quo here."

"Just wishing you can do something you can live with, Corbin. My nephew is beginning to fade, and the doctors are only giving him months to live if he doesn't get a new liver. Any way to move him up—"

"I'll do what I can. He's third on the list, but one candidate has withdrawn. Apparently he was able to secure a private donation."

Seagrave grunted. He suspected he knew where *that* came from.

"The second candidate's need is much less dire than Hunter's, so I'll try to move your nephew to the top of the list." He sighed. "Unfortunately, there is nothing on the horizon for him. Your best hope may still be finding a direct donation, but frankly, I don't know from where."

"I appreciate whatever you can do." Seagrave squeezed his forearm. "We haven't given up." He finished his drink and slid off the stool. "Meanwhile, let's see how they're coming with prepping your trophy for the taxidermist. That'll make a great centerpiece on you wall."

They strode off, heading for the processing room, with Carthwright constructing in his head the perfect place to display this greatest of all his trophies.

Charlie Seagrave's head surged with thoughts of a hunt for a different prize—one bringing life, even if it required death. It was always a tragedy for the loss of a loved one, but the right person's passing could bring renewed life for Hunter, and that trumped any pain for others.

But time was not on his side. Something positive had to happen soon. So far, every opportunity had fallen short.

~ 46 ~

Warner arched back, stretched, and yawned. His gaze swept the six people scattered around the conference table as he leaned forward and glanced at the files in front of him.

"So, hit me with your best shot, guys. Ya think there's somethin' there?"

"It's an unusual coincidence," Agent Dalwin was paging through one of the victim's files, "and we all agree about coincidences."

"Yeah," Jack Harris said, "there isn't any such thing."

"Right." Agent Pauletti folded his hands together on the table. "The Shadow is too good at what he does to have missed two kill shots. He intentionally wounded those two victims badly enough to render them brain dead, but alive. Both with the same rare blood type."

"Sounds like he was trying to create an organ donor, doesn't it?" Psychology was Agent Whitehead's forte.

"That's what I wondered," Warner said. "We've had a spate of illegal transplant surgeries, many with corrupted black market organs. Could these shootin's be tied to that?"

"Maybe." Agent Ina Yeager mused. She was the last of the BAU agents able to attend this session. "But it just doesn't hang with the profile we developed for the Shadow. He's an assassin-for-hire, and not—"

"Could be someone hired him to create a donor," Jack Harris interjected. "Someone in need of an O-Negative organ who can't wait for his or her turn in line."

"That's my thinkin' too." Warner gathered his files. "We gotta revisit the two vics' families. See if anyone came to them about donatin' an organ." He rose and scanned the faces of the four BAU agents and his two detectives. "Anything else, before we get started?"

"Hang on." Olvida flipping through screens on his Android. "I just remembered . . . Yeah, here it is. The Cepeda woman said she'd been visited by a guy and a nurse right after her son was shot. They were looking for a donated liver for his son." He glanced at Warner. "Sorry, Boss. Never followed it up."

"Okay, we're on it now." Warner turned to Dalwin. "This help for your profile, Ed?"

"You bet. We'll prepare an updated version and have it ready to deliver this afternoon. Can you reconvene the troops, Al?"

"I'll see what I can do, Ed. They're pretty scattered, so you may have to text those who can't get back here." He caught Harris' arm.

"Meanwhile, Harris, you set up for us to meet with the Cepeda woman." He turned and looked at Detective Olvida. "You and Beck visit the wife of the other vic. Let's see if anyone else has been after an organ donation."

"On it, Boss," his two detectives responded in unison.

The seven exited the conference room, charged with purpose and an actual possible lead, for a change. Maybe they were finally getting somewhere.

~ 47 ~

Desperate now, I had hacked into the records of six Palm Beach County hospitals with no success. Fort Lauderdale was also a bust, so I had cast a wider net. The next forty minutes were spent scanning private patient files of twelve endocrinologists, seeking O-Negative candidates. Just one I could hunt down and turn into a possible liver donor.

Unfortunately, Hunter's blood type lived up to its reputation for being rare. No joy there. I hissed and swore softly under my breath, then glanced around the well-occupied computer banks at the library. No one seemed to have noticed my quiet outburst.

I slouched back on the rickety swivel chair and stretched, racking my brain for any other avenue to search for a likely donor. None came to mind, and too much time had been squandered at these too slow computers. Some libraries had modern equipment, but not this one.

I exited the program and withdrew my thumb-drive with its sophisticated hacking app. A quick scrubbing of the hard drive's cache, and I pushed somewhat unsteadily to my feet. Four-inch lifts caused a wobbly gait, a perfect performance for the tall, chunky, aged Latino guy I'd mimicked on that day. My tattered shoulder bag slung cross-body and a Panama hat pulled over my silver hair, I made a slow, shaky exit.

Dark glasses donned, I pushed through the doorway and into the cauldron of summer heat. Not difficult to maintain my role as I staggered toward my Honda, impeded by the weight of my current disguise and clumsy shoes. Once inside, shielded by heavily tinted windows, I slipped off the lift-shoes, and discarded the hat and gray wig. A moment later, with the engine running and the a/c wringing the inside air dry, I'd wiped the mahogany tint from my face and shed the stuffy body suit. It, along with the shoes and hat, were jammed into a canvas duffel bag.

Tilted back on my seat, I closed my eyes and contemplated my next move. The problem was, I couldn't think of one. There was no new candidate for a liver. McClure had been perfect . . . until his widow rushed his cremation.

The Perez kid was still out there, alive and on a respirator, but his mom hadn't given up on him.

Hmmm, wonder if I could make the decision for her. If he died . . . .

Bringing the seat up, I drove from the parking lot as I constructed a new plan. That may be the only viable option left, if I couldn't create a new donor. The boy needed a liver within thirty days or it'd be too late to save him.

Cesar Perez may be his last hope. Keeping Hunter alive and vibrant was my only job for now.

Somehow, I had to see to that.

~ 48 ~

Detective Olvida rapped on Warner's open door.

"Got a minute, Boss?"

"Sure. What's up?"

"Got an update on the black market transplants that needs some follow up." He slipped into a chair and dropped a thin file on the oaken desktop.

"Okay, whatcha got?" Warner drew the folder over and opened it.

"Beck, me, and two other teams have been canvassing the homeless conclaves in Hialeah, West Miami, and Sweetwater. Two things stand out in all three."

"Which is . . .?" Warner glanced up from his reading and leaned forward.

"Some of the street folks have mysteriously disappeared," Olvida reached over and flipped to the third page of the file, "and about the time their absence was noticed, several people remembered a tan or brown Ford SUV, probably an Explorer, cruising, the street."

"Every time?" Warner looked up, eyebrows arched.

"Yeah, pretty much. What's more, all of the missing people were relatively young and healthy. *Every* one, Boss."

"Huh." Warner grunted. "So, souls no one but locals would miss, all with potentially viable organs to sell. Sure sounds like a harvestin' organization." He leafed through the balance of the file. "You workin' on IDing the vehicle?"

"Got tech reviewing traffic cam footage, and Agent Dalwin has tasked his people to help. We've spotted the SUV three times so far, but the plate's mostly obscured with mud."

"The FBI's got a sophisticated vehicle recognition program that might be able to find that Ford and maybe follow it home." The Chief of Detectives rose and circled his desk, heading for the bullpen, with Olvida trailing.

"That's what's in the works, Boss. My team's teed up and ready to move if we can nail down their location."

"Great. At least we got a probable lead in one of our two cases. I want you to spearhead this one, Olvida." His eyes swept the busy desks of his Homicide Department. "Harris and I are goin' to meet Mrs. Perez, the mother of the first vic not killed. Seekin' an organ for a rare blood type might be motive there, too. Keep me posted."

"On it, Boss." The detective strode toward the conference room housing the BAU team.

"Harris," Warner called. "Update on Perez."

"Coming, Boss." The little detective popped up from his cubicle, pocketing his shield and holstering his Beretta.

"You got an appointment for us to talk to the mom, Harris?"

"Never reached her, so I left a voice mail. But I was just talking to Agent Dalwin, and they've worked up a list of eight locals who died from black market organ transplants."

"Wow. So many, right here?" They paused at the squad-room door.

"Yeah." Harris scrolled through his tablet. "All but one in Dade County. The other was in Lauderdale Lakes. Looks like this may be a bigger operation than we suspected."

"So, this has got federal racketeerin' implications. They gonna do family interviews?"

"Dalwin's team is setting it up as we speak. He wants us to join him, since we made the first connection."

"Okay. You can't reach the Perez woman anyhow, and I got a feelin' there's an overlap somewhere with the sniper." His eyes swung to the conference room housing the BAU team's acting HQ. "They ready to go?"

"Should be."

As if in answer, Special Agent Dalwin and three of his agents emerged from the room and headed toward the two detectives.

"Harris brought you up to speed, Al?"

"Yeah. I didn't realize we had so many vics." They headed for the exit.

"They didn't show up as victims of organized crime until you pieced it together. It's not what we were called in for—"

"But it may all be pieces of the same cloth," Warner interjected. "How d'ya want to handle the interviews?"

"We'll break up into three teams. I'll go with Harris, you with Agent Yeager, and Agent Pauletti with Agent Whitehead. Let's find who's running this operation and shut them down. Too many desperate people dying from false hope." He distributed the files to each pair as they reached the parking lot.

And the hunt was on. Warner hoped it would also bring him closer to their deadly Shadow. He'd had enough of wanton death on his watch.

~ 49 ~

Seagrave lounged at the mahogany desk of his home office, leafing absently through his monthly investment report, but his mind wasn't on finances. His eyes raised as Kim slipped in through the wood paneled door. He grinned, despites his earlier anxiety, and marveled at the quiet grace of this beautiful woman.

"Any news?" She sat on a corner of his desk.

"Nothing good. Just got back from visiting my sister." He eased back in his leather swivel chair and interlocked his fingers. "Hunter was in bed, not feeling well." He closed his eyes and shook his head. "We talked for a while. He's surprisingly calm . . . resigned, really." He heaved out of his chair and began pacing.

"His skin yellowing is worse, and it's dry and flaky." Hands jammed in his pockets, he spun to face her.

"Jaundice, Charlie." Kim moved against his body, wrapping herself around him, her head nestled in the crook of his neck. "It's the final sign of him fading. God, why can't we find a damned liver?" Tears seeped across her cheeks, moistening his skin. "He's such a sweet boy—"

She was cut off by the trill of Seagrave's cellphone. They slid apart as he fished it from his pocket, glancing at the screen.

"Carthwright. God, let's hope . . . ." He answered, switching to speaker so Kim could hear.

"Corbin. Good news, I hope."

"Yes and no. I've done some fancy dancing and got Hunter to the top of the list. That's the good news."

Seagrave sighed. "So I suppose the bad news is, there's no donor in the wings, huh?" One arm pulled Kim close for a supportive hug.

"Sadly true. I've put out a plea to all the organ banks,

nation-wide, emphasizing the urgency of your nephew's need, so maybe something will turn up. It's unfortunate his parents aren't compatible."

"He's adopted, remember, so no direct genetic ties." They settled on the office's leather loveseat. Kim leaned against him and dabbed at still trickling tears.

"Ah, yes. But even natural parents aren't always a match for an O-Negative child. The unfortunate vagaries of life."

"Well, I appreciate what you've done and are continuing to pursue, Corbin." He glanced at Kim. "Unfortunately, the boy is fading. We need something very soon or it may be too late."

"I'll keep hunting for you. Maybe something will turn up." He paused for a beat. "I do strongly advise against searching for a non-authorized organ, however."

"You mean black market?" Seagrave released his girlfriend and sat up, cradling the phone in his hands.

"Yes, I suppose that's the term. Those physicians are mostly unlicensed and often unskilled, and there's no guarantee the organ has been properly harvested and cared for, and careful tissue-typing isn't done. Livers have a short viability once removed, and there's been a spate of fatalities recently for that very reason."

"Thanks for the warning. We've seen the news and aren't going to take that risk. Kim and I are scrubbing every possible venue, seeking a viable kidney." He began pacing.

"The sniper who's been terrorizing South Florida has actually provided two possible candidates, but neither panned out." He paused his prowling and ran a hand through Kim's hair, drawing her head to him.

"Kim's using her hospital connection, trolling every venue she can think of, hoping to find a candidate, but so far that's been a dud too." She settled on the sofa and he perched next to her, kissing her forehead. "We'll let you know if there's anything promising, and you do the same. Again, thanks for your help." Farewells made, he disconnected.

Kim pushed to her feet and withdrew tissue from the pockets of her tan shorts to blow her nose and dry her eyes.

"I'm going to head to the hospital to do more research. I just thought of a few things I haven't tried yet."

"Anything I should know?" He took her hand as he pocketed his phone.

She shook her head. "Not yet."

"Okay. I've got a few errands to run, and have to get to the boat to arrange a hull cleaning." He checked his watch. "Maybe four hours. That good for you?"

"Fine." She took his face in her hands and planted a gentle kiss. "We *are* going to do this. That kid's too precious to lose."

"I hope so." He gathered his keys. "Going to give it our best shot. That's all we can do."

A quick hug and kiss, and they were off on their missions of mercy, hope still stubbornly glowing in their hearts.

~ 50 ~

Al Warner loped up then the narrow staircase, taking the wood steps two at a time. He burst through the metal door of the top floor of HQ and ran into an odorous wall of burnt coffee and stale pizza. He spotted Jack Harris outside the doorway to Miami-Dade's Tech Department. The detective waved at Warner, urging him to hurry.

"You gotta see this, Boss." He disappeared inside, and when Warner entered he found Harris looming over the back of Special Agent Anita Solto as she plied the keys of a large desktop computer. Images from a traffic camera scrolled across the monitor.

"Run it back, Anita," Harris said.

"You guys picked up the van?" Warner hovered over her other shoulder, studying the screen.

"Yeah, better than that, Boss. Watch."

"Here it is." The BAU agent pointed at the left side of the monitor.

"Got it." Warner leaned closer. "A brown Ford Explorer. You sure that's it?"

"No doubt, Detective. Keep an eye on it."

The SUV edged slowly along a street, apparently cruising through a homeless district in Overtown, north of Miami International Airport. Ragged men and women sprawled across the sidewalk, some in makeshift tents, others in open cardboard boxes or on soiled blankets. Most were tattered, scrawny, and dirty, and many lolled in what seemed a drugged haze.

"What am I looking for?" Warner asked.

"See that guy, a half block ahead?" Solto pointed to a black man in front of a small tent. He was unloading items he'd apparently collected for his use from a rickety shopping cart.

Warner nodded.

"Watch what happens," Harris said.

The van slowed, then stopped, blocking their view of the subject. The vehicle seemed to rock slightly on its wheels, and then accelerated, speeding off. The man was gone, his cart pitched on its side, spilling its contents across the walk. None of the three nearby vagrants seemed to have noticed his disappearance.

"What the hell!" Warner jerked up. "They snatched him in plain daylight?"

"Looks that way." The BAU agent sat back. "No one seemed to notice until later when one of your patrol officers questioned them."

"When did this happen, and were you able to follow the van?"

"Twenty minutes ago. Lost it three blocks away," Harris said. "A bunch of traffic cams were inop. We got a plate number, but when we ran it, it was for a Toyota sedan located in North Miami."

"You got people on the scene, Harris?" Warner stepped away from the computer while the FBI agent continued to pull up traffic cams, trying to reacquire the SUV.

"Yes. I sent two patrol cars right over, and Olvida and Beck should be there by now. I figured I should stay with Tech, in case the van shows up again."

"Good thinkin'. The guy they snatched looked relatively healthy, so it's likely this is our illegal organ gang." Warner shook his head, his lips pressed tight with anger. "We got any idea how many vics they've taken off the streets for this?"

"Olvida and Beck canvassed three homeless conclaves two days ago." Harris whipped out his Android. "So far, we're pretty sure of eleven, and . . ." swiping through pages on his screen, ". . . six more that need to be followed up."

"These people seem to keep pretty good tabs on each other, huh?" Warner glanced back at Agent Solto and two of his techs, busily accessing street cameras in search of the Explorer.

"Yeah. They're like a big, loosely knit family. When someone's been gone for a while with no known reason, they take notice. No one else seems to care."

"Damned shame," Warner grumbled. "Lot of these people are vets with PTSD and older teens who've timed outta foster care. The fuckin' politicians don't give a shit."

"Got him," one of the department's techs yelled. "A traffic cam on the corner of 59th Street and 28th Avenue, heading west."

Agent Solto's finger began flying as she started accessing nearby cameras. "There it is, heading southwest, crossing 30th Avenue."

"I got it passing 61st and 30th," another tech shouted a few moments later.

"Route some unmarked cars out there, Harris, and let's go." Warner headed for the door. "Tell 'em to keep tabs but not to interdict. We need to follow them to their facility."

They skidded to a halt as Solto called, "You're not going to find them there now, Detective."

"What d'ya mean, Anita?"

"These are recorded feeds, about twelve to fifteen minutes old." She swiveled on her chair as Warner and Harris reentered the room. "We'll follow them on the street cameras and try to see where they went. Then you can get a warrant to take them down."

"Yeah, okay. Just don't lose 'em." The two detectives hung over the FBI agent's shoulders, eyes glued to the monitor's display of six different traffic cams and two CCTVs.

"How'd ya get access to those private security cams, Agent? Aren't they closed circuit, and don't ya need permission or a warrant?"

"It's called hacking, Detective." She chuckled. "Some CCTVs are projected to the Cloud for remote viewing. We'd be hours behind if we waited for legal niceties, and none of this will cause problems in a trial. It's not evidence. Just investigative procedure."

"Wow. A Fibbie willin' to skate on thin ice. I knew I liked you, Anita." He gently squeezed her shoulder.

"Yeah." She chuckled as new images began filling the screen. "I know who I'm working with. You're a guy who'll do what it takes to get results. It brings out the beast in me."

"There, that's the Ford." Warner's finger tapped the glass surface of the monitor. "It's movin' outta range from that cam. Anyone pickin' it up on another one?"

A leaden shroud of silence draped the room for thirty seconds, then a minute, then . . . .

"Gotcha," Agent Solto's fingers flashed over the keyboard

as two cameras picked up different views of the Explorer.

"They're past the race track and are crossin' the north end of Miami Springs." Warner's brow creased as he studied the image.

"Where the hell are they going?" Jack Harris pulled an earlobe and glanced at his boss.

"That big, mostly deserted industrial district west of the Palmetto Expressway would be my guess. Loads of empty warehouses and small factories there. A great place to set up shop, and no more traffic cams or CCTVs to track 'em. They'll just disappear into the maze."

"Fuck," Harris grumbled, as he watched the SUV slip off the screen. "Is that the last operational camera?"

"Afraid so." The BAU agent pushed away from the desk and stretched, arms intertwined over her head. "It vanished into a wilderness of empty buildings about—" glancing at the time stamp on the screen "—twelve minutes ago. Gone without a trace."

"Maybe not." Warner had his cellphone out.

"Whatcha got in mind, Boss?" Harris perched on a corner of the desk.

"They gotta have A/C to keep the operating room cold. Recovery rooms, too. And power for lights and equipment."

"Of course!" Solto pushed her short, stocky frame out of her chair. "There must be a record of power usage not expected from a so-called vacant building."

"Right. And Captain Santiago's got a good contact at FPL who can probably bypass the red tape to see where it's bein' used." Warner hit autodial. "We got a judge available for a quick warrant on the week-end, Harris?"

"Yeah, Boss. ADA Sloan's on tap, and he's got two friendlies who'll issue warrants, once we show him the videos of the snatch."

Warner nodded as he began talking on the phone. "Cap, it's

Al. I need you to call your guy at FPL . . . ."

And the wheels were in motion. They had to hurry if they were going to save the latest victim.

~ 51 ~

I closed the file I'd been searching, eased back on the chair, rolled my shoulders, and stretched my neck. I glanced at the mostly manned computer stations lined atop a long table in the library. A soft sigh, then returning to stare blankly at the screen and search my mind for something else to try. If I didn't come up with a plan in the next few days I'd be out of time. Hunter was failing fast.

Searches of Jackson Memorial, Baptist, and Mount Sinai hospitals had been fruitless. So what was left? South Miami and Coral Gables were the only ones that offered any promise. I glanced around again. No one seemed interested in a bushy mustached, working-class guy in overalls surfing the web. Six others were plying keys and scooting mouses at the bank of public access computers at the Miami Shores Library.

I slid forward, again on the attack. Moments later, I'd hacked my way into the Coral Gables Hospital's database. I was always amazed at how paltry the security firewalls were for most hospitals. Charged with the task to protect patients' privacy, they did a shitty job of it.

My thumb-drive activated the program I'd developed to search their records for O-Negative patients. Forty seconds later, I had a short list of four names. I opened a Google search page and began digging into their backgrounds, using a publicly available app that revealed an amazing amount of detail about almost anyone's life.

The first was a seventy-eight-year-old man who had hepatitis C . . . certainly not a liver candidate. The second was a middle-age housewife, which made her an unlikely target. The third was a retired Air Force pilot who had a reoccurring heroin addiction. Not an organ I'd want for Hunter.

Shit. This is getting me nowhere. Maybe this last one . . . .

I plugged in the fourth, Celia VanMartin, and as her data filled the screen, a small shiver skipped down my spine.

Ms. VanMartin was thirty-three and a councilwoman for the Village of Coral Springs. According to the hospital's medical files, she was the picture of health, having just completed extensive tests for a life insurance policy. O-Negative, with a prime liver to offer, if I can find a way to get at her.

Switching screens, I located her Facebook and Twitter feeds. How lucky! The city was staging an open-air debate forum for Coral Springs' three mayoral candidates, of which VanMartin was one. It would be held in the park across from city hall in three days. Barely soon enough, but too quick to have a chance to verify a tissue match. I'd have to rely on Fate and good luck this time, something I'd enjoyed most of my adult life.

Two screen shots of her face recorded on my phone—a wholesome soccer mom from next door—I switched to Google Earth to scan the area for the meeting. As suspected, enough tall buildings to establish a shooting perch. Better visit the spot to pick my best vantage point, and I needed a new disguise.

I cleared the screen and emptied the cache, extracted my thumb drive, and packed up my supplies. I'd been in one place too long for comfort.

Five minutes later, I reclined in my Honda, its A/C battling the shroud of clammy heat that sucked away my breath. South Florida doing its usual summer dance a little early. I found VanMartin's Facebook page on my Android phone, and idly scrolled through her posts.

I groaned softly and gnashed my teeth. She *was*, literally, a soccer mom, a moderately attractive woman with three cute kids—two boys, ages six and ten—and a girl, eight. She was a middle-class woman, struggling to make ends meet and make a difference in her community. She didn't deserve to die because she had a rare blood type, and hers was the type of family that would likely make the donation.

A shudder shook me. I snatched off the tousled wig and bushy mustache and slammed them onto the seat. *What's wrong with me? I'm the consummate professional, never allowing even a tinge of emotion to creep into my work.* VanMartin wouldn't be the first seemingly innocent mark whose life I'd ended. It had never been personal.

But this time, it *was* personal, and I wasn't going to let unaccustomed sympathy growing in me interfere with what needed to be done.

Celia VanMartin must die to give Hunter a chance at life, and nothing—absolutely *nothing*—would get in my way. Two days to scout the ambush site and prepare, but it was Fate's job to provide a tissue match.

Teeth clenched, almost cramping my jaw, I drove off, discarding doubts as I constructed the event in my mind.

Celia VanMartin would be mine in three days. Whether that provided an acceptable liver was in the hands of the gods. I wondered if her life insurance policy was already in effect?

~ 52 ~

Special agent Dalwin joined Warner and Detective Harris in the squad's conference room. Each agent's body armor lay atop the long wood table, along with a half-empty box of mandatory donuts and an urn of strong coffee. Warner munched on his favorite chocolate-covered snack as checked his Glock and pocketed three extra magazines of .40-caliber rounds. Detectives Olvida hurried in, already decked out in Kevlar, tension hardening the planes of his face.

"Any news, Boss?" Olvida bounced from one foot to the other.

"Just about to go up to Tech. Beck's monitoring the search. Major Conklin's got SWAT teed up as soon as we get a location." He strode toward the stairway, leading to the Tech Department. "We got a sixteen-block grid that's the likely location. They're workin' with FPL, lookin' for a so-called abandoned building that's drawin' a lot of juice."

The two detectives trailed their boss as he hurried up the stairs, followed by Agents Dalwin and Yeager.

"I hope they nail down the spot soon." Harris elbowed Olvida. "This fucking waiting's the worst."

"You're the psych guys." Olvida tapped Dalwin's arm. "You think there'll be gunplay with this kind of perp?"

"Not normally," Dalwin said, glancing at the detective as they reached the doorway to Tech. "They'll be mostly medical types, but you never know who might panic. And they may have hired muscle for security."

They charged into the room, fanning out behind three computer stations where tech-savvy detectives plied the keyboards. Detective Beck hunkered over the shoulder of the middle operator, pointing to the monitor. An aerial map of the area and the buildings filled the screen.

"They've got it narrowed down to this section, Boss. Still some businesses and a few warehouses operating there."

"We're hopin' to find a supposedly empty unit usin' a lot of power. Any luck with that?" Warner stared at the screen.

"We're scanning FPL meters now," the guy at the keyboard said. "Luckily, everything has been converted to digital, or we'd be out of luck."

"We got a judge teed up for a warrant, Harris?" Warner glanced at his partner.

"Got an ADA sitting by his chambers. Just has to fill in an address, and he'll text it to us enroute, once it's signed."

"Okay. Hope we get on this before that new vic becomes an unwillin' donor." Warner glared at the monitor. "Why the fuck is this takin' so—"

"I think I got it!" The tech at the first screen's voice rasped with tension. "Let me check . . ." He scanned an addresses printout. "Bingo." He swiveled on his stool, facing the gaggle of anxious cops.

"A small, abandoned warehouse and offices, just off the rail tracks, drawing tons of power." He scribbled on a Post-it. "Here's the address."

Warner snatched the yellow slip and headed for the exit.

"Let's mount up, guys. This is it."

The detectives and FBI agents bolted from the room. Olvida called Major Kincaid to get his SWAT team moving. The adrenalin surge triggered by action quelled inactive nervousness.

This is what they lived for.

~ 53 ~

The Sun arced in descent from its peak in a cloudless sky as I loitered in my Honda SUV, nestled in a parking slot at the far end of the eight-store strip mall.

I scanned my surroundings and snapped a dozen photos with my Canon Eos . . . the street, City Hall, the park across from it, and the surrounding commercial buildings. Where will

I park in three days to facilitate a quick exit without drawing undue attention? A six-story office building on the next street to the south seemed most likely to offer the best shooter's perch.

An opening between buildings directly across from City Hall allowed a clear view of the royal-palm-lined park where the rally would be held. The extra thousand-foot distance didn't complicate the shot, and provided an easier escape, while the crowd focused on the victims.

Celia VanMartin was to debate two other candidates for mayor, but when I had finished, there'd be none left standing. It only seemed appropriate to eliminate all competition, rather than simplify the race for the other two. I chuckled softly at the irony and then shrugged, casting off a lingering sense of guilt. So many dying to save just one boy. I gritted my teeth. *I'm a merciless professional, killing without regret those who must die.* I sighed, strangely unconvinced.

I exited my vehicle, wearing the same disguise I'd used at the library, beeped the electronic door lock, and sauntered across the lot. The thick, moist air reeked with the odor of grilled hotdogs, courtesy of a deli, two doors away. A palm-lined street bordering the west end of the mall led me toward my prospective sniper's nest. I was already perspiring from the early afternoon kiss of old Sol.

When I returned on D-day, I would be a stocky, gray-haired, female guitarist, the last of my disguises. Not a homeless wreck. Just a middle-aged woman trying to make some spending money. Someone who fit in, but even if noticed, my face would be so drastically altered, even the FBI's facial rec program wouldn't recognize me. That's how I stayed free and earned my nickname . . . The Shadow . . . by being exceptionally careful and never careless.

A brick façade office building stood in the middle of the block on Valencia Avenue. Upon circling to the back, I found a half-empty parking lot . . . perfect so far. By hugging the wall, I evaded the view of the CCTV camera mounted above the rear door. It was unlocked, allowing easy entry to a short hall leading to the lobby. A door to the stairway stood beside the elevator, again out of view of two security cameras, which focused on the front entrance and elevator doors. Couldn't be better.

Unconcerned in my current disguise, I rode the Otis to the top floor, entered the stairwell, and found an access door to the roof. As expected, no one was about. Glancing around, I was pleased to see no towering condos nearby, so there'd be nobody likely to observe my activity.

A brief survey of the heat-softening tar surface found all I needed: the usual A/C mechanical box, perfectly located for my shooter's nest. Its green surface was hot from unshaded exposure to the sun, but I would bring an air mattress with a quick-inflation compressed-air canister. Easy to conceal in a large shoulder tote. My oft-used backpack and bedroll would be inappropriate for my character of the day.

I found the expected perfect line of sight to the park and an already erected dais for the rally. My handheld laser scope measured the distance: only eight-hundred-sixty-two yards. An easy shot, if I had a stationary target. VanMartin standing at a lectern would likely insure that.

A second sweep of the roof found nothing to complicate my mission, so I headed back toward the doorway. I noticed faint footprints in the soft, black surface but was unconcerned. I wore oversized short boots with weights in the toes, which would leave even footprints. When I returned for the main event, I'd don two-inch heeled shoes for the roof, and loafers for a fast escape.

The stairway provided my exit from the building, and I found nothing there to worry me. This could be my easiest task of the entire operation . . . the fourth and, hopefully, final act.

I sighed and shrugged. If this didn't work . . .

I shook my head, my jaw clenched, as I entered my SUV. It was Custer's Last Stand. Hunter wouldn't survive long enough for me to arrange a fifth gambit . . . even if I could find another candidate.

It required me to make the perfect shot, and the family must agree to allow their loved one to die so a brave young boy could live.

I damned well intended to see that happen.

~ 54 ~

"No lights or sirens," Warner said into his comm, as the six-vehicle squadron raced the rising sun westward across Miami's avenues. Detective Olvida sat with him as his Dodge followed two black SWAT vans. His other two detectives and the BAU team trailed close behind.

They sped across the Palmetto Expressway, then the turnpike and the East Coast Railroad tracks, and into the mostly deserted commercial district. The lead van followed GPS coordinates and bore right on NW 112th Avenue toward several large blocks of warehouses and small industrial buildings.

"Target structure is on the next block," came over the radio.

Warner responded, "Copy that. All vehicles pull up."

The streets ahead bristled with one and two-story CBS and metal-wall buildings, mostly warehouses and a few connected to taller office structures. Nothing surpassed three floors. Few cars peppered the mostly empty parking areas, but the brown Explorer sat in the lot of their suspected location, along with three cars, and two minivans.

He glanced back at Harris' Chevy.

"Harris, did the warrant come through?"

"Yeah, Boss. Got it on my Android. Authority for a complete search."

"Okay. SWAT, you ready to rumble?" Tension-inspired perspiration damped his armpits.

"Teed up and eager, Detective," Major Conklin responded. "B Team, take the rear and be ready to breach on my signal. Five minutes and counting."

Warner and Olvida slipped into their Kevlar vests and checked weapons. "Olvida and I will follow the front breach. Harris and Beck take the rear. Everyone in vests. I don't want a lot of shot-up detectives, like the last time."

Nervous chuckles came over the radio. "Copy that, Boss," Beck said.

Olvida tapped Warner's arm. "Just got a message from Tech that power usage just amped up, Boss."

"Damn! They're probably settin' up for another surgery. We gotta move!"

The two SWAT vans had taken off, bearing down on their target. Warner raced after the first, followed by a Chevy Suburban carrying half the BAU team. Harris' Camaro and the other half of the FBI agents sped toward the rear of the concrete block and metal-sided two-story building, trailing SWAT Team B.

Moments later, everyone was assembled by the front and rear doors, anxiously looking at their watches. The covered windows of the building made it unlikely their arrival was noticed.

One of Conklin's sergeants slipped a skinny fiber-optic camera under the door. "Dark. No visible activity, Major." He maneuvered the device and swept the area.

"I got a stairway with lights at the top," he said.

"Must be where their OR is." Warner gripped the SWAT commander's arm. "Maybe a silent entry so they don't have a chance to bolt. What d'ya think, Jim?"

"Good idea. Could catch them in the act." He keyed his helmet comm. "B Team, we're going silent. Entry achieved in thirty, and stand by for go."

"Copy that," came the reply. "We'll be inside in thirty."

The deadbolt and passage locks proved no competition for their automatic lock-pick guns. The door produced a bare squeal on opening. Dim light from the rear showed that the second team had also entered.

"B Team, maintain the perimeter. A Team will make the assault. Let's try to avoid gunfire unless fired upon." He glanced back at Warner, Olvida, and the three FBI agents. "I know you're eager, Al, but hang back and let my SWAT team do its job. That's what we're paid for."

"Not a problem, Jim." He gave a mirthless chuckle. "Despite what the media dubbed me, I ain't a hero. You do the fightin', if any, and we'll do the cleanup."

Major Conklin nodded, looked at his team, twirled his finger above his head, and pointed up the stairs. The five SWAT cops began the accent with surprising stealth, considering their heavy body armor and bulky equipment. Warner patted Olvida on the shoulder, and his team of five followed close behind.

Conklin signaled a halt at the top, and the fiber-optic camera peeked around the corner as the cop studied the small LED screen.

"Looks like the OR, Major," he murmured. "They may be beginning a surgery."

"Let's go" He triggered his mic. "B Team, we're initiating." He looked around the corner of the wall, saw an open door fifteen feet away, and a room with men and women dressed in white surgical gowns. He waved his hand, and the ten officers scurried silently across the floor, weapons at the ready.

"Miami-Dade Police," he bellowed as he burst through the doorway, followed by his team. They fanned out along the walls, M4 assault rifles raised, ready to fire. "Don't move. Stop what you're doing, and no one will get hurt."

~ 55 ~

Diana Fiore peeked through the door's sidelight panel and saw her brother on the stoop. Her fingers swiped across her eyelids, brushing away tears before she opened the door.

"Charlie. Good of you to come." She stepped aside, allowing Seagrave to enter. "Hunter's been asking for you."

"I was on my way up here anyhow, Sis." His eyes swept over her. "You look a little ragged, Diana. Looks like you lost some weight, and those red eyes . . . you've been crying."

"What do you expect?" She knuckled more moisture accumulating in her brown eyes. "He's not doing well." She grasped his bicep. "So, are you coming with news? Maybe the good kind?" She twirled the ends of her ash-blond hair, her eyes holding his.

"Potentially good, but maybe not soon enough." He took her hand and drew her down next to him on a worn, plush loveseat. "I *have* managed to get him to the top of the national transplant list."

"That's terrific, Charlie." She wrapped her arms around him and laid her head on his shoulder. "Your dedication to this would rival any father's. But if we don't have a liver within a week—ten days at most—it'll be too late."

"I know, Sis." He stroked her head. "Unfortunately, there's no donor in sight. Kim and I are pulling out all the stops, but short of going to the organ black market, we've got nothing."

She looked up. "You've said that isn't a safe option. We couldn't afford it anyhow, but—"

"You know cost isn't the problem, Diana. I'm ready to pay anything to save Hunter. It's just that we can't trust the organ will be viable." They separated, and he held her hands. "I'd hate to give him false hope . . . going through the surgery, then recovery, only to die if the organ failed." Seagrave rose, pulling her to her feet. "We're still searching for a better option." He turned, gazing at the bedroom hallway. "Is he up?"

"He was." She straightened her skirt and ran a hand through her short hair. "Looking forward to seeing you."

He nodded, patted her on the shoulder, and then strode toward the boy's bedroom. He rapped on the doorframe and stuck his head through the ajar doorway.

"Hey, Hunter. May I come in?"

"Uncle Charlie. Sure, you're always welcome." His voice soft, charged with a tired rasp. "Kim with you?"

"No." Seagrave slipped into the room and perched on the edge of the bed. Wall shelves sported baseball and basketball trophies from high school, and next to them, a large, framed photo of the two of them with his trophy white marlin.

"She's at the hospital, I think, scrounging data bases, searching for that elusive liver. She sends her love, though."

"She's really special. So, any . . . any good news?" His green eyes glistened with restrained tears. "This waiting is literally killing me." He gave a hoarse, wry chuckle.

Seagrave squeezed the boy's hand and brushed a lock of dark hair from his forehead. "Well, I've managed to get you to the top of the national list. You'll get the first O-Negative liver that comes available anywhere in the USA or Canada."

'You guys are the best." Hunter smiled softly and patted the back of Seagrave's hand, which was still holding his. "But there's nothing out there right now, is there?"

"No. Well, there *is* the Perez boy, but his mom won't give

up hope he'll recover somehow." He shrugged. "I know it's kinda gruesome, hoping someone dies so you can live, but that *could* happen at any time. Kim and I are on top of every avenue that might turn up that liver."

"You ought to marry that beauty. You're never gonna find another woman like her."

"I know. I'm planning to propose on my birthday. Like self-gifting myself the best possible present."

"That's next month, isn't it?" Hunter pushed up higher in the bed. "I wish I could be there when—"

"Don't quit on me now, kid." He ruffled his nephew's hair. "You being there would really be the best present. I don't think Kim would mind my proposal becoming second place." He chuckled.

"Yeah, maybe that's what she was taking out there . . . a birthday present for you."

"Taking out . . . where? What are you talking about?"

"To her storage locker."

"Storage locker?" Seagrave's eyebrows arched. "What storage locker?"

"The one off Collins Avenue, where she stores her files and stuff, I guess." He searched his uncle's face. "You didn't know she had one?"

"Nope." Seagrave stroked his chin. "She never mentioned it. How do you know about it?"

"Jeez." He frowned. "I hope I didn't ruin a secret for her. I was meeting some buddies for lunch a couple of weeks ago, and I saw her turn into the StoreIt lot. I followed to say "hi,' but when she started carrying some boxes into a large storage unit, I thought maybe she wanted privacy, so I left."

"Hmmm." Seagrave wrinkled his brow. *I wonder why she's keeping it a secret.* "It was a big locker?"

"More like a garage, with a rollup door."

"I hope she didn't buy that bike for my birthday." He rose,

shoving hands in his pockets. "She can't afford that."

"A bike?"

"Yeah. We'd discussed me getting a Harley CVO Touring bike. Thought it might be fun for a road trip. But, they're over forty grand. Maybe that's why she needed a secret garage. Damn that sweet woman." He started to pace the room.

"So, what are you going to do?" Hunter swung his legs out of the bed and put his feet into his slippers.

"I gotta think about it. Right now, our priority is your new liver. Where is this StoreIt joint, anyhow?"

"Seventy-First Street, just west of Collins."

"Thanks. Maybe I'll run up there tomorrow and check it out. See what she's up to."

"Can I come along?" He heaved to his feet. "I gotta get out of here for a bit while I still can."

Seagrave studied the boy, then nodded. "If it's okay with your mom, I'll pick you up after lunch."

"Great. A little adventure with my favorite uncle."

"It's a date." *Never seen her with keys except the house and car. I'll check her desk.* He turned to leave. "If she bought that Harley, I'll pay the dealer, and he'll refund her."

"Will that make her angry?" Hunter followed his uncle to the door and gave him a parting hug.

"I'll deal with it." He sighed. "She can't afford forty Gs."

He hurried down the step and headed home.

~ 56 ~

Warner, his detectives, and the BAU agents followed the SWAT team into the glare of the brightly lit room. Eight unarmed people in surgical whites, arms raised, shuffled away from two surgical tables, babbling in senseless concert. The air reeked of antiseptics.

"Knock it off." Warner holstered his Glock. "You've been caught in the act of committin' several felonies, and no blubberin' is gonna change that." He shivered at the cold as he strode toward two side-by-side surgical tables, each supporting an anesthetized man, draped in surgical cloths.

He glanced at a pair of men adorned in surgical gloves and masks, apparently the surgeons, and then back at the first table. A large, naked black man lay strapped atop one, surely the homeless guy just kidnapped. He oozed blood from what appeared a preliminary incision, probably opening a way to his kidney.

Warner growled and shook his head, then pointed at one of the doctors. "You better close him up, and be happy we got here before you committed murder."

The shorter man edged forward, signaling a woman to join him. Her hand shaking hard enough to rattle the instruments, she laid a stainless-steel tray on the table and offered the man sutures. He glanced at Warner.

"We weren't going to kill—"

"Miranda, Detective." Agent Dalwin laid a hand on Warner's shoulder. "Don't let him make a statement that will later be held inadmissible."

"Thanks, Ed." He held up his hand, slipped the card from his wallet, and read everyone present their rights. The SWAT team and his detectives were handcuffing the other perpetrators.

"Okay." Warner peered at the doctor, who had finished closing the man's incision. "You're cuttin' him open, removing his organs, but he ain't gonna die. How does that work, Doc?"

The man stepped away from the table as his helper taped a gauze bandage over the incision. "We were only going to take one kidney, and after allowing him three days for recovery, we'd return him to his street. With a thousand dollars in his pocket, by the way."

Detective Beck pulled his arms behind him and applied handcuffs.

"Is this necessary?" He grimaced. "When we explained this to him—the money he'd earn—he agreed to the surgery."

"After you *kidnapped* him," Special Agent Askin said. "That's a federal felony."

"We are just trying—"

"Shut up, Mark," the taller doctor growled. "Anything you say is just going to make things worse." He glared at Warner. "We want our attorneys, and no one else has anything to say."

"Okay with me." Warner gestured to Jack Harris, who had joined them in the OR, along with the rest of Assault Team B. "Get the Hawk and a CSU team up here. And we're gonna need ambulances and a doc or a medic to check out the two patients."

He glanced around the room. "Where the hell is Olvida?"

"In here, Boss." Olvida's voice echoed from a door at one side of the OR. "You guys gotta see this."

Warner and BAU agents Dalwin, Yeager, and Askin tramped across the chilly room and into a much colder area. A quick appraisal showed it was a semi-refrigerated vault, apparently constructed from what was another office. Thick fiberglass-bat insulation covered the walls. A soft, electronic buzz filled the air.

"What the fuck . . . ?" His eyes swept the room, his brow furrowed.

"My reaction, too, Boss." Olvida gave a wry chuckle. "Never seen anything like this before. How about you, Agents?" He glanced at the three Fibbies who had followed Warner into the room.

"Never before at a crime scene. Looks like a morgue." Dalwin walked to one of three tables, each supporting a nude body, one a woman, the other two, men. "These two are on life-support machines."

"And this guy is already missing a few parts." Harris leaned over, studying the corpse's face. "Hey, Boss, isn't this the sniper's last vic, McClure?"

"He was supposedly cremated." Warner joined his detective by the body. "Yeah, that's him, alright."

"You think that slimy Russian sold him for parts, instead of cooking him?" Olvida asked, joining them.

"Either that, or he's part of this cabal . . . maybe even the ringleader." Warner turned away, moving to another gurney. "He had plenty of access to organs in his business. Mourners wouldn't know if their loved ones were just hollow shells. The bastards!"

"These two are definitely on life-support." Agent Ina Yeager gestured at the other two bodies. "Fresh body parts, just waiting for a buyer." She leaned down to read a toe-tag. "This guy's O-Positive, and . . ." She glanced at the other vic. "And she's B-Negative. Together, I think they're a match for almost every blood type." She glanced from Dalwin to Warner. "We'd better get some more ambulances up here, ones that can handle the life-support, and get these people to a hospital. They've got to have family somewhere."

"Yeah. And where the hell did they come from?" Agent Ashkin snapped photos and texted them to the Miami office. "We'll run facial rec and fingerprint scans to see if we can come up with IDs. Somebody must be looking for them."

"Okay," Warner said, studying the two potential donors, "but I'm more interested in the 'how.' Were they kidnapped and made brain dead? I saw that two years ago. Any way you look at it, it's probably gonna be Murder One." He turned at the sound of metal rattling.

Jack Harris was digging through a file cabinet along the wall. "Looks like they kept good records, Boss. I got two drawers full of files with names on them." He withdrew one, flipped it open, and scanned the contents. "Here's a guy who got a new kidney about five months ago."

Warner reached in and plucked out a folder. "Here's one for two new lungs. Jesus, there must be hundreds of them." He turned to Olvida, who had just joined them. "Get these cabinets to the office. We need to start callin' these recipients to warn 'em to be on the lookout for their new organs failin'." He returned the file and started to turn away, then paused. Reaching back, he flicked the tab on a red divider, then a blue one.

"What're these?" He crouched, scanning the extended tab. "Looks like address numbers, but no street name."

"Yeah." Harris' hand skimmed the top of the second drawer. "Same here. Purple and green, with numbers."

"Smacks of more surgery sites." Dalwin joined them, peering at the drawers. "I think you cracked a huge operation . . . again, Al." He patted Warner on the back. "Just eight months since you shattered that nationwide fentanyl ring, and now this. Good job."

Warner grabbed Harris by the arm. "Get whoever you think's in charge over here to give you the rest of these addresses. We gotta move on those places before they know about this bust."

"On it, Boss." He hurried after the group of perps, all handcuffed, filing from the room in the custody of SWAT members.

"Where's Beck?" Warner's gaze swept the area.

"Back here, Boss. Agent Yeager and I found something else." The detective and the Amazonian blond federal agent stood by a huge stainless-steel door, in the far corner of the room.

Warner strode to meet them, his hand stroking his chin. "Looks like the door to a cold-storage meat-locker."

"That's what I thought," Yeager said. "Padlocked."

"Beck, get a bolt cutter from one of the SWAT guys, and let's see what's in there."

Beck hurried after the departing squad.

"You know what we're going to find, Detective." Yeager stood, hands on her hips.

"Yeah, and it ain't gonna be pretty. I can hardly wait." His face twisted into an angry grimace.

~ 57 ~

Seagrave rapped on the doorframe of the bedroom Kim used as an office when she slept over, which was almost every night. With no answer, he peeked in and found it empty.

He hesitated for a moment, conflicted and uneasy over prying into her personal secrets. If she wanted to keep her storage area from him, she must have a reason . . . although he couldn't imagine what it might be. The Harley-Davidson CVO motorcycle came to mind.

Shit, it's my house. No reason I can't go in here. Steeling his resolve, Seagrave slipped into the room. The house's door entry alarm would tinkle if she returned, giving him time to get out. He chuckled softly. *It's not like I'm a thief.*

He scanned the room, looking for . . . what? He had no idea. He ran a hand through his hair and sighed. *What if I do discover she's bought me the Harley? She's sure to feel hurt and disrespected if I try to pay it off for her. So, what am I doing here?*

Despite his reservations, he found himself at her utilitarian red oak desk. Neat and well ordered, which was no surprise. That was Kim, to a tee. He settled in her chair, and noticed his hands seemed to have minds of their own, pulling open drawers he had no intention of searching.

The center drawer had pencils, two pens, paper clips, and the usual desk supplies. One by one, each drawer was opened by those mindless hands, operating on their own. The content of each was scanned by equally disobedient eyes. The file drawer had a few folders with search results for Hunter's liver and not much else.

The top, left drawer had envelopes, scratch pads, and cords for her phone and laptop. His gaze swept the room. She must have taken the computer with her. The top right drawer sported more of the usual desk supplies. Same with the middle drawer, and . . . *What was that?* A metallic rattle, but there was nothing in the drawer to make that sound.

Seagrave opened and closed it and again heard a faint clatter. Running his fingers under the bottom, he discovered some sort of small box. *Hmmm.* After a guilty hesitation, he removed the drawer and raised it above his head.

Yep. A match-box-size container, taped to the bottom. He removed the drawer's contents, stacking everything just as it had been inside, so he could return it the same way. Flipping the drawer over, he slid open the bottom of the little container. Inside nestled two keys with the number "412" stamped on one.

Seagrave hesitated, unsure of what to do. He watched with surprise as those pesky, independent hands closed the box and slipped the keys into his pocket.

He shook his head, glanced at his watch, and sighed. It seemed, against his better judgment, he was going to visit Kim's storage unit without her permission. But not today. She might return at any time, and guilt was already banging at him. He dug the keys from his pocket, deposited them back into the box, and repositioned the drawer.

He would go tomorrow when she had a scheduled shift at the hospital. Seagrave was unsure why he felt compelled to pry into her private space, and he sincerely hoped in doing so, he didn't sabotage his relationship with the most wonderful woman he'd ever known. He hoped she'd understand.

He replaced everything in the drawer exactly as it had been, straightened her desk, and left.

He'd pick up Hunter after lunch tomorrow, while Kim was at work. They'd have a little illicit adventure together and see what his girlfriend was keeping secret. It would do the boy good to get out of the house.

He chuckled softly as he returned to his office. Using Hunter to help mollify his guilt was pretty shameful. *Oh, well.*

Meanwhile, they still needed to locate a liver for him. . . and soon!

~ 58 ~

Warner glanced up from several reports he was perusing about that morning's raid, as Ed Dalwin and all of his BAU team filtered into the conference room. The Special Agent in Charge settled in a chair across from the detective and dropped a small stack of papers on the table. An urn of strong-smelling coffee and the box of inevitable donuts at on the polished oak surface.

"Any news from your field office, Ed?" Warner eased back in his chair, sipped Java from his personal mug, and watched Dalwin flip open a report.

"Already got IDs on the two comatose patients . . . both ex-military and currently listed as homeless." He glanced at his notes. "He's Staff Sergeant Jose Juarez, Army Ranger with a medical discharge last year. Serious PTSD. She's Specialist Anne Bowden, Army Quartermaster."

He glanced at his notes. "Bowden's a ten-year vet who

didn't re-up. Came home to Miami to try to save the family hardware business." Dalwin filled a paper cup with the strong, black brew, leaned back and sighed. "Apparently, Lowes drove them out of business and they lost everything." He took a sip and wrinkled his nose. "Mother died of a heart attack over Christmas, and the father offed himself the next day. Neither of the vics appear to have any family."

"So the net results of all that," Warner sat up and pawed through the papers in front of him, "is they probably were both livin' on the street." He separated sheets with photos and descriptions of the two victims. "I'll send Detective Beck to Overtown to see if anyone recognizes 'em."

"You figure that was the perps' hunting grounds, Al?"

"Yeah. There, Little Havana, and North Miami have the largest homeless concentrations. People these bastards figured no one would miss."

"They claim they were going to pay Orillio Jefferson a grand for his kidney, and put him back on the street." Agent Whitehead perched on a chair next to his boss. "He confirmed that when he came out of the anesthesia." He inspected a chocolate donut, then took a bite.

"You believe that, Agent?" Warner's eyebrows arched. "You're the profiler. They gonna put a dude back on the street who's sure to flash the dough and run at the mouth?"

"No, I think they told him that just to keep him compliant." He laid the snack on a paper napkin and flipped screens on his Android. "According to their appointment book, a second kidney transplant was scheduled for the next day. Jefferson's O-Positive made him a match for both. Doesn't look like they bothered with doing tissue-type matches."

"Well, he ain't goin' anywhere with zero kidneys, that's for sure." Warner shuffled the papers into a stack and plopped them on the table.

"The three bodies—four, if you include Jefferson—are just

part of what we found, Detective." Agent Solto rose from her chair.

"The cold storage room?" Warner tapped his pen on the table.

"Yes." She slid a small stack of photos across the table. "A trove of body parts: skin, corneas, bone—anything and everything that didn't need oxygenated blood circulation." She glanced at her tablet. "There was so much material, it would have swamped your lab. Mr. Gold got approval for us to send all of it up to Quantico. They'll pull DNA from all the tissue and run a search. See if we can tie anything to outstanding cases for missing persons."

"Sounds good." Warner pushed away from the table and gathered up his files. "What about the other surgery centers? The colored folders? We gotta move on those *now*."

"I just got one of the nurses we nabbed to give up the addresses," Agent Yeager said. She ran fingers through her long, honey-blonde tresses. "They're all local Dade County jurisdictions, Detective. How do you want to proceed?" She handed Warner a printout detailing the four locations.

He scanned the list. "We got Miami Gardens, Hialeah, Sweetwater, and South Miami." He turned to Jack Harris. "Contact the sheriff and ask him to coordinate with the local PDs to raid these sites. Get it done now."

"On it, Boss."

"There's federal jurisdiction here, too, Al," Dalwin said. "The Miami field office is organizing four three-man teams. Your local PDs can take the lead and get credit for the busts. We'll be there to assist and file any federal charges."

"Thanks, Ed." He turned to Detective Olvida. "Ask your ADA contact to get warrants for all four. We gotta shut 'em down now, before they learn what happened in Miami Springs."

"On it, Boss." Phone in hand, he punched speed dial as he

strode to a quiet corner of the room.

"I'll assign one of my people to join each of those raids. We should be in on the finish of what we started." Agent Dalwin stood with his five special agents. "What about you and your team, Al? You guys made this all possible."

"Hate ta miss it, but I gotta pass. We got a great sheriff and very competent local cops. Most have their own SWAT teams, and with your people in on it, there'll be more'n enough hands on deck. They can handle it, and it's doubtful there'll be any violence, just like today. I still got our deadly Shadow to catch."

"Understood. Agent Solto and I will remain here to monitor progress and do any searches you need." Dalwin turned to his people. "Split up, pick a team, and get a move on it. Timing on this is paramount."

The four agents collected their papers and devices and headed for the door.

"And, Ina," Warner called as they reached the exit. "Try not to shoot anyone. I ain't gonna be there this time for you to rescue, like you did last time." The room echoed with a round of chuckles as it emptied.

Warner caught Dalwin by the arm. "I need a favor, Ed. Something your guys can probably do quicker than mine."

"Name it, Detective." Their eyes locked.

"I got a hunch that needs fillin' out."

"Okay. What can we do for you?"

"Can you get me a list of any prospective O-Negative organ requests in, say, the Southeast: Florida, Georgia, Mississippi, and the Carolinas?"

"O-Negative? What's on your mind, Al?"

"I've been hammerin' the files on The Shadow's vics. He's clearly a world-class marksman, but the two men he hit just bad enough to render them barely livin' were both O-Negative blood types." He paused and ran a hand through his hair.

"It's this operation we just busted that gave me the idea.

What if our Shadow is trying to create a possible donor for someone with a rare blood type?"

"An O-Negative donor." The agent laid a hand on Warner's shoulder. "Interesting thought. I'll get right on it."

"Thanks." Warner collected his things and started for his office, while Ed Dalwin settled back at the long table and made a phone call.

~ 59 ~

Warner sprawled back, hands behind his head, feet on the corner of his desk, staring into space, his version of contemplative yoga. He was mentally sorting and rearranging data from The Shadow case, seeking an *aha* moment. It lingered there, somewhere just out of reach. A rap on his door pulled him from his thoughts.

"Ed," seeing the special agent entering. "Got something for me?"

"The results you wanted from the transplant list. Seventeen candidates in the Southeast for O-Negative organs. Only three from South Florida." He handed Warner the thin file and settled on a chair.

The detective dropped his feet and slipped closer to his desk. He flipped open the folder. Two sheets of paper listed names, addresses, and details of each prospective donee. Three highlighted with yellow marker: two in Dade County and one in West Palm Beach. His finger traced the first, and then the second, as he absorbed the data. He paused, then reached for a stack of files on his desk.

"Hunter Fiore." He pawed through the papers. "I think he's in . . . ah, yeah. Here. Hunter Fiore." He flipped through the report, and glanced back at Dalwin's list. "Nineteen, and just moved up to first on the list for an O-Negative liver." He glanced at his doorway.

"Olvida," he yelled.

"Coming, Boss." His detective appeared in the entry.

"The first surviving Shadow vic . . . ?"

"Cesar Perez, Boss. What about him?"

"He was on life-support, right?"

"Still is, as far as I know." Olvida withdrew his Android and started a search. "His mom refused to believe he wouldn't rebound."

"You said someone tried to get her to donate his organ because Perez was a rare blood type?" Warner eased back and steepled his fingers.

"Yeah . . . " He scrolled through his screen. "Here it is. Perez is O-Negative. Some guy was trying to locate an O-Neg liver for his son, who was short on time."

"Got a name?"

Olvida scanned his Android and nodded. "Charles Seagrave, but Mrs. Perez wasn't having any. Want me to contact her?"

"Yeah." Warner rose and collected his Glock and shield. "Do it now, and text me her address. Harris," he called, and looked at Agent Dalwin. "Wanna join us on a field trip, Ed?"

"Absolutely." He turned and started away. "Let me collect my gear. I'll meet you in the parking lot."

"What's up, Boss?" Jack Harris arrived.

"Mount up. We're headin' for Jackson Memorial."

Moments later, they hurried down the stairs.

"We got a new lead on The Shadow, Boss?" Harris pocketed his shield and holstered his Beretta.

"We'll see," Warner said. He looked back as Agent Dalwin joined them. "I'll drive with Harris, Ed. You follow."

The BAU agent nodded, and soon, all three were en route

to Miami's prime trauma hospital.

~ ~ ~

Warner, Harris, and Agent Dalwin exited the elevator on the Ryder Trauma Center's floor. Warner led the way to the nurses' station and flashed his shield.

"How can we help you, Detective?" The head nurse was tall and broad-shouldered, but gentle eyes belied her otherwise severe countenance.

"We're here about Cesar Perez." Warner pocketed his badge, and glanced around. "Is he still here, or has he been moved home?"

"No, he's still in L.T. Care, the poor boy." She sighed and reached for a medical record. "His mother is trying to move him home this week."

The loudspeaker system cut her off, booming with a call for Dr. DelTorro to report to an OR.

"Sorry about that. Busy day." She plopped the papers on the counter. "Anyhow, as I was saying, his mother doesn't—"

"We know," Warner interrupted. "Who was on duty when he came in?"

"I was in charge that day." Her brow wrinkled. "Why?"

"Didn't someone come by, hoping to convince Perez's mother to donate one of his organs."

"Yes, his liver, as I remember." She replaced the record in its holder. "Cesar Perez suffered acute trauma to the brain from which he would never recover." The nurse folded her hands on the counter. "It was some boy's father and a nurse, seeking a donor. It seemed strange . . . ."

"How's that?" Warner glanced at his companions.

"Well, it was so soon."

"What d'ya mean?" The detective planted both hands on the counter, leaning in.

She paused as a nurse handed her a chart, which she scanned and filed. Finished, she turned to Warner. "Where was I? Oh, yes. The victim had only arrived the day before, and they were here, familiar with his injury and that he was O-Negative. We'd barely completed the lab tests to allow for safe blood donation, and these two knew everything."

"You got names?" Warner's notebook and pen were out.

"Not the man's." She tugged at an earlobe. "The woman was Kim Tate, one of our trauma nurses. But she was off duty that day. They seemed to be friends."

"Think." Warner's intense eyes held hers. "Was his name Fiore?"

She paused, then gave a small headshake. "No, that doesn't sound familiar."

"How about Nurse Tate," Harris asked. "Is she on duty today?"

"No. I believe she's taken a week's leave for some sort of personal business."

"Damn." Warner looked at his companions. "I guess we gotta track down the mother." He turned to the nurse. "Got an address for me?" Olvida's text had indicated the mother had moved, new address unknown.

"I don't know, Detective. HIPAA restrictions—"

"This is a serial murder case, and Perez ain't in any shape to complain." Warner tapped his pen on the notebook.

"All right. I guess it can't hurt." She took his pen and notebook and after glancing at the medical file, jotted down an address and phone number.

Warner thanked her and turned to leave.

"I do believe he gave his card to the mother," she added.

"Who? The father?"

"Yes. I guess in case she changed her mind." She scratched her jaw. "I think he offered her a considerable sum if she allowed the liver donation. The boy's as good as dead, but she won't give up hope for a miracle."

"Good to know." He pocketed the notebook and pen. "Thanks again for your help."

"Oh, and one other thing I just remembered."

Warner and his companions stopped and returned to the counter. "What's that?" Dalwin asked.

"The same man . . . actually the man *and* the nurse, Kim Tate . . . were here shortly after the other victim arrived."

"What other victim?" Warner crowded the counter, his hand doing a staccato slap on its surface.

"The other gunshot victim, also on life-support. I think he was—" She flipped through a file in a cabinet drawer. "—yes, here it is. Robert McClure—"

"McClure!" Harris muttered, tugging at Warner's sleeve. "He was the other non-fatal Shadow vic. We found his body being used for parts at the phony transplant site."

Warner nodded, his eyes searching the nurse's. "And those two showed up again?"

"Yes. And McClure was also on life-support. An unusual coincidence."

"What was unusual?" Warner was almost tap-dancing in eagerness to get moving. "Life-support?"

"Well, yes. Two like that, with the same rare blood type."

"They were both O-Negative, weren't they?" Dalwin glanced at Warner, eyebrows arched.

She nodded. "And that man and Kim Tate were still seeking a liver, I think, for his son, who was the same blood type."

"But they didn't get it, did they?" Warner asked. "What happened?"

"The wife had him disconnected almost immediately. Seemed like a vengeful bitch. He had already left for the mortuary by the time Kim and the man arrived."

"Thanks. You've been a great help." Warner patted her

hand. "Let's go, guys."

The three lawmen hurried off, wondering if they were on to something.

~ 60 ~

Diana Fiore opened the door, a pained smile creasing her lips. She stepped aside and allowed her brother to enter.

"Has he eaten lunch?" Seagrave asked.

She nodded, sighed, and pointed toward Hunter's room.

Seagrave drew her into his arms and kissed her on the cheek. "Don't give up yet, Sis. Kim and I are chasing every angle." He stood back, her head between his hands and thumbed away tears trickling across her cheeks.

"I'm worried about him going out." She laid a hand on his shoulder. "He's gotten so weak."

"I know, but do you want him to hunker down, waiting to die? If this *is* it, let him try to enjoy his remaining time." He took her back in his arms, her head on his shoulder, her body shaking as she cried. They hung together for a moment.

She stepped back, sighed, and retrieved a tissue from her apron pocket, dabbing her tears. "You're right, and he *is* looking forward to an outing. He's in his room, dressing."

Seagrave nodded and patted her on the cheek. "No worries, Sis. I'll take good care of him." He started toward Hunter's bedroom.

"Kim's not with you today?" Diana called after him.

"Nope. On duty at Jackson until five. Said she would research another idea on finding a liver while there."

"God willing." Diana sighed and headed for the kitchen.

"You ready to go, sport?" Seagrave peeked through the ajar

door. Hunter perched on a chair, tying his shoes.

"In a sec." He glanced up, a strained grin crossing his jaundice-tinted face. "Things happen a bit slower nowadays."

"Whenever you're ready. No hurry. We're just going to take a little drive up Collins Avenue and take a peek at this mysterious storage locker of Kim's." He slouched against the doorjamb, watching Hunter's third and finally successful effort at tying a bow.

The boy . . . a young man now, at nineteen . . . struggled up and paused, secured his balance, and sighed. "Not used to just walking being a chore." His grin widened. "But I'm sure as hell glad to get out of the house." He wobbled across the room, lips pressed now in a determined grimace. "Let's go."

Seagrave nodded and took him by the elbow. "We're off to see the wonderful Wizard of Oz." He chuckled. "Or something less magical, I suspect."

"Are you going to try to get in her locker?" He glanced at his uncle. "Won't Kim will be angry? She must have had a reason for keeping the place secret."

"Yeah, I'm not sure what I'm going to do yet." He patted his pocket. "I've got what I think are her keys, but I'm really conflicted. We'll decide, once we get there."

He helped Hunter into the car and then settled on the driver seat. "I'll drive and you navigate. Let's go."

The Lexus sedan pulled away from the curb, heading for the 79th Street Causeway, crossing Biscayne Bay to Collins Avenue . . . and an unexpected destiny.

~ 61 ~

Warner and Harris settled back in his Dodge. He fired up the

485hp engine and switched on the a/c. Their visit to Cesar Perez' mom had lasted less than ten minutes. The first five were a tearful harangue over the fate of her son and the fact his shooter hadn't been caught.

Eventually, Dalwin got her talking about the man seeking Cesar's liver. He'd offered fifty-thousand-dollars, but she wasn't ready to concede her son's life was over. She dug in her purse and produced the man's card, and Warner copied the info onto his pad. They left her still crying and wringing her hands, wrought with indecision over what to do.

Harris perched on the Charger's passenger seat, his PC laptop perched on his knees as he fed the name and number into the department's search engine. Less than fifteen seconds fled by when the computer beeped, its screen filling with data.

"Here it is, Boss." The detective began reading aloud. "Charles Seagrave, forty-two, unmarried, sold his tech firm two years ago to some acronym conglomerate for mega-millions."

"So, not Fiore's father, like he claimed?" Warner stroked his chin.

"No, but apparently the kid's uncle. Seagrave's sister is Diana Fiore, with a son, Hunter. Nineteen."

"What's Seagrave's background?" Dalwin's voice came over Harris' phone, which was on SPEAKER. The agent was in a black Chevy SUV parked immediately behind Warner's coupe.

"Joined the Army at eighteen and got into cyber warfare and computer programming." Harris' eyes skimmed the laptop's screen. "Three consecutive hitches, all in cyber electronics." Harris clucked. "Musta been pretty good. He made major in his nine years, and led some pretty sophisticated teams on the cutting edge of cyber warfare." He glanced at Warner. "Not much details, Boss. All probably highly classified."

"Hmm." Warner adjusted the car's thermostat. "Any weapons trainin'?"

Harris skimmed over several pages in the dossier. "Looks like nothing after Basic. Went right into the cyber program."

"Not uncommon," Dalwin said. "Lots of successful tech companies came from guys with military training."

"There's more." Harris fiddled with the images. "Ah, he *did* qualify as an expert marksman during rifle training. There's a note he was urged to go into the Special Forces sniper program, but refused."

"Okay, maybe we found something." Warner pulled away from the curb. "Let's go visit Mister Seagrave. Where's he at?"

"In Sunset Isles, on the Beach." Harris plugged the address into his phone's WAYZ, which began routing them to Charlie Seagrave's home. "Do we need to bring in Miami Beach PD? That's their territory."

"We can operate under federal jurisdiction," Special Agent Dalwin said through the speakerphone as he followed in his SUV. "Bring them in later, if anything develops."

"Right. So, tell me about Nurse Tate." Warner turned east, toward Miami Beach.

Harris tapped and scrolled for a minute before answering. "Not a lot here, Boss. She's thirty-eight. Been a nurse for about fifteen years, mostly up and down the East Coast. Apparently quite skilled and in high demand. Volunteered for trauma duty four years ago." Harris paged through three screens. "Very little about her youth. Looks like she was born in Philly. Parents both murdered during a street heist when she was six. In and out of foster care, but stayed out of trouble and got educated. Took off after she aged out."

Warner braked at a red light and Dalwin's Suburban pulled next to them, awaiting the green.

Harris sighed, sat back, and looked at Warner. "Looks like she floundered around for a few years before she got her nurse's training. After that, it was all work and not much play, it seems."

"What's her connection with Seagrave, Detective?" Dalwin's voice came over the phone speaker.

"According to what I found on social media, they're in a serious relationship."

"Lovers?" Warner glanced at his partner.

"Looks that way."

"Good. Maybe we'll find 'em together."

With nothing more to say, Harris sat back as his boss concentrated on his driving.

~ 62 ~

Seagrave's Lexus cruised eastward across the 79th Street Causeway, bisecting the sprawl of Biscayne Bay. The late afternoon sun fired up the light chop, glittering like beds of tiny diamonds. Hunter sat pensively in the passenger seat, staring blankly out the window as they island hopped across North Bay Village and onto Normandy Island.

"We getting close, Hunter?" Seagrave glanced at his nephew, who shuddered and shook his head as if coming out of a trance.

He hitched around, looked as his uncle, and struggled with a smile. "Yeah. Once we get off Normandy Isle, it'll be on our left." He spotted the last short span, just ahead, that would take them onto Miami Beach. "You really think this is a good idea?"

"What? Invading her personal sanctum without permission?" He chuckled. "Not hardly."

"So, why are you doing it? She finds out, won't she be awfully angry?"

"Maybe." Seagrave sighed. "I hope she'll understand I don't want her saddled with an expense she can't afford."

"I don't know. She might be madder that you think she can't manage her own finances. Kinda looking down on her."

He laughed. "You're pretty clever for a kid. Frankly, I'm still conflicted about this. I'm not quite sure what I'll do when—"

"Well, you're gonna have to decide soon, 'cause thar she blows." He managed a weak chuckle as he gestured at a large sign at the entrance to an extensive group of metal-sided storage buildings. They turned into the lot, past an unmanned security house, and slid to a stop.

They scanned signs displaying numbers for each row, starting for some reason at 200-250. Seagrave idled across the fronts until he found 400-425 . . . a string of one-car-garage-sized storerooms, considerably larger than those in the first four columns. He turned into that aisle, still cursing slowly.

"What was the key number again?"

"Four-twelve." Seagrave watched the numbered doors slip by. "Should be about half-way down." A moment later, he stopped in front of metal dual-doors—an overhead garage-type rollup, and a normal passage door. A plaque with black numerals "412" hung over the access door.

"Here it is." Hunter turned to gaze at his uncle. "Now what?"

"Yeah, now what?" Seagrave studied the door and knuckled his eyes. "Well, we're here, so let's look around." He exited the sedan and circled the rear to lend a hand to his wobbly nephew. He gritted his teeth at the reality of how the young man was deteriorating.

Seagrave slouched against his Lexus, arms folded, and Hunter joined him. Several minutes trundled by as they studied the entrances in silence.

"Well, those doors aren't going to open on their own. And it doesn't look like you're gonna need some magic saying, like 'Open Sesame.' You've got a key with that number on it." He glanced at Seagrave. "The smart thing . . . the *safe* thing . . . would be for us to climb back in your car and get out of here."

"How did you get so wise?" Seagrave chuckled. "But, I've never been a big fan of doing 'the safe thing,' most of my life. Overall, that's mostly worked out for me."

He pushed away from his car. Hunter followed and tugged at his sleeve and repeated his concern. "Won't she be angry and feel . . . betrayed? That you didn't trust her to have her own secrets?"

"Yeah, probably, but I hope when I point out I was just trying to keep her from making a purchase she can't afford . . . Well, I hope I can win her over." He swiped his sleeve across his forehead, fighting moisture more a product of nerves than the dwindling afternoon heat.

"But you don't know for sure she bought that Harley. Maybe she has other secrets—"

"Maybe, but she plied me with a ton of questions about the bike." He paused at the door, looked at his companion, and shrugged. "I'm betting she bought it. Probably financed, and paying a hefty interest rate."

He inserted the key and sighed. "Why else would she need a big storage space?" He turned the key. "She could store a car in here."

The door swung open on squeaky hinges, and they stuck their heads inside.

"Dark," Hunter muttered.

"Hang on a sec." Seagrave activated his cell phone's light, scanning the wall. "There we go." He flipped a wall switch, and neon overhead fixtures flickered alive.

"Oh, wow!" Hunter's eyes flared with surprise.

~ 63 ~

Warner exited the Venetian Causeway onto Alton Road and shifted the car's visor to the side window against the late afternoon sun. Following the WAYZ velvety voice from the phone, he turned onto Sunset Drive. Two-hundred-feet later, he slid to a stop at the security gate that protected this upscale community.

"May I help you?" The guard was young, muscular, and armed with a semi-automatic pistol and what looked like a can of MACE in his gear belt.

"Detectives Warner and Harris, Miami PD." Warner displayed his shield, then jerked a thumb over his shoulder. "The man in the Suburban behind us is Special Agent In Charge, Edward Dalwin."

The mention of the FBI perked the guard's attention. "What's up, Detective?"

"We're here to see Charles Seagrave. Just need to ask him a few questions about an ongoin' investigation." His dark stare held the guards eyes. "No reason to let him know we're comin'. Got it?"

"Yes, sir. I'll clear you through. You need directions?"

"Nope. Got in on my GPS. Don't worry. We don't plan on makin' a fuss."

"Not a problem. Not sure he's home, though." He returned to the guard hut and raised the gate.

Both cars passed through, heading for Seagrave's home on Lucerne Avenue, one of the few in the community not fronting directly on Biscayne Bay. Minutes later, they pulled up in front of the house.

"Kinda modest, compared the ones we just passed, huh?" The beige ranch house nestled on a smallish lot on a short cross avenue between 23rd and 24th Streets.

"Yeah," Harris scanned his laptop. "Some of those directly on the bay run ten to fifteen mil. Says here he owns a boat he keeps in the marina."

"Nobody's private life is safe anymore." Warner grunted. "It's all on the Internet." He parked his Charger and they climbed out, meeting Dalwin on the sidewalk.

Warner led the way up the walkway to the door. "Let's see who's home, and what they gotta say about our two brain-dead vics." He punched the doorbell button, which initiated a melodious chorus.

"Who's there?" A female voice over the intercom.

"Miami-Dade Police, to see Mr. Seagrave."

A short pause, then, "One moment please."

Warner nudged Harris. "Check the back, in case he's a runner."

The detective nodded and scurried off to the right, circling the building. Agent Dalwin slid to their left for a view down that side. After a moment, he glanced at Warner and shook his head.

Dalwin rejoined Warner as the lock clicked on the door and it swung open. A stout, graying-blond, Caucasian woman stood there, wiping her hands on a dishtowel. Odors of garlic and thyme wafted over them.

"Sorry for the delay. I was preparing Mr. Seagrave's dinner and had to get it off the stove."

"Is he home?" Warner displayed his shield.

Her eyes swept over the two men as she folded her arms across her chest—a classic defensive posture. "What's this about?"

"He's a person of interest in a case. Who are you, ma'am?" He didn't think she was the nurse, Kim Tate.

"I'm his assistant. I care for his house and occasionally prepare meals if Ms. Tate is busy. Mr. Seagrave isn't—"

"I'm Special Agent Dalwin, FBI." He flashed his ID. "We

want to ask your boss some questions. This is an urgent matter."

"Ms. Tate, too, if she's here." Warner pocketed his badge.

"Sorry." She sighed and stuffed her hands into the pockets of her apron. "Mr. Seagrave left right after lunch, and I haven't seen Ms. Tate all day."

"Any idea where they went?" Warner had his notebook and pen in hand.

"I believe Ms. Tate is on shift today."

"Jackson Memorial?" Warner asked. Jack Harris came from the back to join them and gave a small headshake.

"Yes. Mr. Seagrave went to his sister's. He said he was taking his nephew for an outing."

"Hunter Fiore?" Dalwin asked.

"Yes." She shook her head and sighed. "Poor boy doesn't have much time left if they don't find him a transplant."

"Seagrave is close to his nephew, ain't he?" Warner jotted a note.

She nodded. "More like a son. He's desperate to locate a liver donor before it's too late. He and Ms. Tate think of nothing else."

"So we've learned. Got an address for the sister?" Warner's pen poised over his notebook.

"Of course." She stepped aside. "Come in and I'll get it for you." She led them into what appeared to be a den. Mounted trophy heads, mostly antlered game, decorated the walls, and two large fish, a sailfish and a dorado. Photos showed a man—surely Seagrave—posing beside an African lion in one and next to a hanging jaguar in another.

"Seagrave's a hunter?" Warner gazed at the displays. "Likes dangerous quarry, it seems."

"Oh, yes. A real outdoorsman. Loves to hunt and fish." She nodded at the photos. "That lion had killed several men at a Zimbabwe mine, and the jaguar was snatching small children at night from a Colombian village. He volunteered to hunt them down. He's got quite a collection of rifles."

Warner and Dalwin exchanged glances.

She flipped through an address book on the desk, paused, and copied an address on a yellow PostIt, which she handed to Warner.

"Can we see 'em? The guns?" His dark eyes held hers.

"Oh, I wouldn't feel comfortable. Besides, they're all locked in his gun safe." She stepped back, hands on her hips. "Anything else, officers?"

"No." Warner stuck the slip onto his note pad. "We'll get outta your hair. Thanks for this." He handed her his card. "If you see or hear from him, tell him we're lookin' to ask a few questions. Same for Ms. Tate, too."

"I will." She led them to the front door. "I hope they're not in any trouble. He's a very nice person. So is Ms. Tate."

"Not to worry." Warner turned to her as the others exited the house. "Just got a few questions they may be able to answer. Maybe shed a little light on an investigation." He joined Harris and Dalwin at the curb.

"Let's go. I got a naggin' hunch somethin's gonna pop."

Both vehicles raced back across the Venetian Causeway, drivers squinting to the lowering sun.

The Fiore house was next. Warner wondered where that would lead them.

To answers, he hoped.

~ 64 ~

"Sonofabitch!" Seagrave stepped in front of Hunter, arms akimbo. "She did it."

They stood just inside the door, staring at a red Harley-Davidson CVO Touring motorcycle, trimmed with black leather seats. Seagrave sidled up to the bike and ran a hand over its body.

"Looks like she got all the bells and whistles, too. An upgraded passenger seat, dual metal saddlebags, and a rear luggage box." He sighed and glanced at Hunter whose face sported a loopy smile.

"This baby had to cost close to fifty Gs." Seagrave stood back, shaking his head. "How the heck does she expect to pay for this with a nurse's salary?"

"She bought it 'cause she loves you, Unc. She's probably saved up, since you pay for everything." He laid a hand on his uncle's shoulder and gave a small squeeze. "Don't you think you're gonna ruin it for her if you try to pay it off."

"You got a point. She's the epitome of an independent woman. Maybe we oughta get out of here so we don't ruin her surprise." He glanced around the storage area as he turned to leave. "I should never have . . . ."

Hunter had wandered over to a large cabinet that looked like a wardrobe locker.

"What are you doing, kid?"

"Just curious." He paused and gestured toward the wall. "Look at all these cabinets. Looks like she stored stuff here, away from the house."

"Yeah, strange." Seagrave joined him. "We've got plenty of vacant closets at my place." He reached out and pulled open the double doors of the apparent closet.

"What the . . ." He shuffled back a step before moving forward and plucking a hanger off a clothes rod. He turned and thrust it toward his nephew.

"What the heck is this?"

"Looks like a Halloween costume."

"Yeah, maybe." A tattered outfit, typical for a homeless

man or hobo, draped from the hanger. "Or a disguise." He pointed to a shelf above the closet rod. "Look at all the wigs."

He began pawing through the outfits, shaking his head. "Men, women, even a fat suit." He glanced at the floor. "Some of those shoes have three-inch lifts."

"Why would she need all this stuff?" Hunter removed a shoulder-length auburn wig from the shelf. "Looks really natural."

"I don't have the slightest idea. It's clearly something she didn't want me to know about."

The boy returned the wig, and Seagrave closed the doors. "It almost seems like maybe she's living some kind of double life. You think that's possible?"

"You got me." Seagrave knuckled suddenly dry eyes. "I thought we were totally open with each other. No secrets, but now—I just don't know."

He pivoted slowly, eyes sweeping over several other tall cabinets, lining both walls.

"I'm getting real nervous about our being here." Hunter leaned against the locker. "Kim seems to have things she didn't want you to know about. She going to be really pissed if she learns we were snooping around."

"You got that right, son." *I sure as hell don't want to mess up my relationship with the only woman I've ever really loved.* He took Hunter by the arm and started for the exit, glanced over his shoulder, and puttered to a stop.

"Damn! I'll probably regret this, but I gotta see what's in those other cabinets."

"I'm really curious too, but that's not a good idea." He pulled at his uncle's arm.

"Probably not, but I'm planning on marrying Kim, and I've just learned she may not be whom I thought she was." He grasped the boy's shoulders with both hands. "You can wait in the car, if this makes you uncomfortable."

"No, I'm just as interested as you are, and I've grown to love her, too. But despite my curiosity, this makes me nervous."

Seagrave sighed, then smiled, and patted the boy's cheek. "Me too, but I'm gonna do it anyhow. Let's see what's in this next cabinet."

They approached a six-foot-tall, double-door metal locker, about five-feet wide. The man looked at his young companion, shrugged, and pulled at the doors.

Locked! He peered at the handles and saw built-in key-locks. He tugged again to no avail.

"Damn. Hey, wait . . ." He dug Kim's keys from his pocket. He'd forgotten there were two smaller ones on the ring. Keys that might fit these locks. Seagrave gave a sidewise peek at his nephew and gave a soft grunt.

"Let's see if these work." The first one went into the lock but wouldn't turn it. The second, however, was successful. Seagrave took a deep breath, glanced again at Hunter, then swung the doors open.

His eyes flared and he gasped as he lurched backwards.

"What the hell . . . ?"

"Jesus!" Hunter echoed, throwing an arm around his uncle's shoulder for support.

~ 65 ~

Warner's Dodge Charger crossed the Venetian Causeway en route to Miami, still tailed by Special Agent Dalwin in his Chevy SUV. They exited north, merging onto NE 6th Avenue, headed toward the Fiore home in North Miami Beach. He adjusted his visor against the glare of late afternoon sun and glanced at Harris, who held up his phone and nodded.

"You there, Ed?" The device's SPEAKER was still engaged.

"Right behind you, Al." A short pause, then, "What are you thinking now, Detective?"

"Something's goin' on with this Seagrave—and maybe the nurse." He braked at a red light, fingers drumming on the steering wheel. "They're Johnny-on-the-spot almost immediately after two Shadow vics, both O-Negative, are rendered brain dead but on life support." The light changed and he took off.

"I agree," came over the phone. "As if they knew what was going to happen before the shooting actually occurred. You think the Tate woman used her hospital creds to check medical records, and found they were O-Negative?"

"Quite possible," Warner said.

"You guys find it interesting that Seagrave qualified as an expert marksman in Basic?" Harris looked at Warner, then turned toward the phone. "Think he could be your elusive Shadow, Agent?"

"It's crossed my mind," Dalwin replied, "and they wanted him for sniper training."

"What's Yeager say? She's your resident sharpshooter."

"I talked to her and Lon Pauletti, who's even better. Top shot in the entire agency."

"And?" Warner looked at the route displayed on the WAYZ app on his phone. Five minute to destination.

"They agree that to make those shots intentionally would require skills beyond their own . . . and, as you can attest, Ina is damned good."

"Saved my bacon last year." Warner chuckled. "So, do they feel what happened to these two vics was unlikely to be an accident? I'm not crazy about convenient coincidences."

"Me either," Dalwin said, "but to be *that* good would take a lot of training—and superb natural ability. Still, I've learned over nearly twenty years of frustration, never sell The Shadow short."

They had turned onto NE 163rd Street and then a side street, lined with modest CBS ranch homes painted in a variety of pastel colors. Warner slid to a stop at the curb in front of the Fiore home, a pale yellow bungalow. The BAU agent parked across the driveway, blocking any possible quick escape, should that scenario occur.

They gathered on the front stoop and Warner rang the bell. A slightly plumb, middle-aged woman peered at them through a glass sidelight.

"Miami Police." Warner displayed his shield. "We'd like to talk to Charles Seagrave, if he's here."

She hesitated, then opened the door. She studied them, brow wrinkled, and ran fingers through her short, ash-blond hair. "He's not here. I'm his sister, but this isn't his house."

"We know." Dalwin showed his ID. "But we were told he was coming here to visit your son, Hunter."

"FBI?" Her eyebrows knit as she turned, waving them in. "What do the police and the FBI want with Charlie?"

"We've got some questions for him, and Nurse Tate." Warner pocketed his ID. "Do you know where they are?"

"Charlie and Kim?" She folded her arms. "I haven't seen her today. Charlie came to take Hunter on an . . . an outing of some sort." Tears began a slow trickle across her cheeks. "My son . . . my son is very ill, and my brother is trying desperately to find him a liver before . . . before it's too late." She brushed away the moisture.

"We know about that, Ma'am," Harris said. "He's a rare blood type, and—"

"That's what we want to talk to your brother about, Mrs. Fiore." Warner's eyes held hers. "I know this is a very difficult time for you." He hated seeing her in such pain. "Do you know where they went?"

"You just missed them. They left about a half-hour ago,

going somewhere in Miami Beach." She sighed. "I think they were visiting some sort of storage unit. You know, one of those complexes full of rental lockers. A guys-only outing."

"You got an address?" Harris withdrew his Android and dialed up a map of Miami Beach.

"No, they didn't say, but somewhere near 79th Street."

"Okay, thanks." Warner turned toward the door. "Can't be more than one or two there. Let's go, guys."

"Is Charlie in some sort of trouble, Detective?"

"We just wanna ask him some questions, Ma'am. He may have information on one of our investigations." The three men filed out, heading for their vehicles.

"I hope that's all," she called after them. "I don't know how I'd get through this with Hunter, if Charlie weren't there. He's my rock."

Warner glanced back and saw her linger on her stoop, watching them speed away, tears again blooming in her eyes.

~ 66 ~

"What the hell . . . ." Seagrave slapped his brow.

"Jesus!" Hunter draped his arm across his uncle's shoulder and leaned in for support. "Can you believe this?"

The two stared into the metal cabinet, unable to accept their eyes.

"This is a serious arsenal." Seagrave edged forward and ran a hand along a row of pistols suspended across a shelf. "A Glock 40, a Beretta 9mm, .357 and .44 magnums . . . Christ, there's even a palm gun."

"What's a palm gun?" Hunter touched a small automatic pistol, attached to some complicated-looking leather straps.

"It's a sneaky weapon, Hunt. It's attached to the forearm, under a loose-fitting shirt." He touched the straps. "There's a way to release it, so it just pops into the hand. Used most likely for an ambush."

"What does she need this stuff for?" Hunter gestured at another shelf. "And look at all those knives."

"Yeah." Seagrave's eyes swept the rack of blades. "K-Bars . . . those are military . . . stilettos, and that looks like the famous Bowie knife." He pivoted to look at the cabinet's right side.

"Four rifles, two shotguns, and a sawed-off twelve-gauge." He picked up one of the long guns. "This is a .375 H & H magnum. That's a heavy-duty hunting rifle. Scoped and everything." He set it back in the rack. "Wow, why the hell does she own all this stuff? It must have cost a fortune."

"What's *that* thing?" Hunter pointed at a weapon hanging on the left side.

"A crossbow, for chrissake." He lifted it off its hooks. "Boy, this thing's got some major draw weights." He pointed to a stack of shafts nestled in the corner. "Those are quarrels . . . special arrows for this beast. It takes a real professional to handle this monster. It's a nearly silent, long-range killer."

"So, is Kim a weapons expert?"

"I didn't think so. She never asked to hunt with me." He rehung the bow on its mounts. "It's hard to make sense of this." He pivoted and saw another narrower cabinet along the back wall. He shrugged and started toward it.

"I wonder what we're gonna find in there?" He glanced back at Hunter, following him across the floor. "At this point, nothing would surprise me." He paused, momentarily struggling with conscience, then grunted, and tried the other key, which turned easily in the lock.

The door opened, and Seagrave shuffled to one side to eliminate a shadow caused from the lights behind him.

"Hmmm." He squatted. "Now, that *is* a surprise."

"I didn't know Kim played the guitar." Hunter bent to look at the instrument case.

"Neither did I." After a short hesitation, Seagrave grabbed the handle of the large guitar case and lifted it from the cabinet. "Pretty heavy. Maybe one of the electric ones." He laid it on the floor, popping the two latches.

Hunter grabbed his shoulder. "We shouldn't be doing this, Uncle Charlie. I'm just as curious as you, but we're invading Kim's privacy. She's gonna be really angry at us."

Seagrave looked back and patted the boy's hand. "You're right, but this thing has become so bizarre, I can't help myself." He returned his attention to the case and flipped open the lid. "I can't understand what Kim's doing with all this . . ." His eyes flared, and he reached in, barely touching the barrel, as if to see if it were real. "Wow! What a beauty." He plopped down on his seat and withdrew the parts.

"What is *that?* A gun?"

"I believe it's a sniper rifle. A McMillan." He cocked his head back, staring at a shelf. "Those cartridges on the shelf. Are they 12.7s?"

Hunter rose, acquired a box, and knelt next to Seagrave, showing it to him. He opened it and picked out one on the four-inch-long rounds.

"Yeah, fifty-caliber. I fired this gun, a McMillan TAC-50, when the army was recruiting me for sniper school. This, and the Barrett-50 were the go-to weapons for over-watch and sniping for the Rangers." He fitted the stock in place and snapped on the Leupold scope. He pushed to his feet, cradling the rifle in the crook of his arm. "The best marksmen have been known to make a kill with this weapon at nearly two miles." He snugged it against his shoulder and peered through the powerful scope. "I can't figure it. This isn't a hunting weapon—"

Hunter tugged at his sleeve. "I just had a scary thought."

"What?" Seagrave lowered the barrel.

"Isn't that the type of gun the sniper—The Shadow, they call him—used to kill all those innocent people? It's been in the papers."

"The Shadow? Yeah, they've been chasing him for twenty years. He's even given us a chance at a liver . . . ." Seagrave sputtered to a stop, eyes popping as his jaw dropped.

"Holy cow! You think *Kim's* The Shadow?" Seagrave spun, striding a few steps away. "I can't believe it. That sweet, loving woman doesn't have a mean bone in her body."

"I know, but how do you explain all this stuff? Aren't these the tools of an assassin? Scoped rifles, crossbows, Bowie knives . . . and that palm gun you showed me."

"Jesus, Hunter, I don't know. It's all too much—"

"Oh my god!" The boy grabbed his uncle's shoulders. "Think about this. She loves you, and you love me. All you guys think about is getting me a liver. It's so special that you both care so much." He held Seagrave's eyes with his. "And hasn't this killer provided us with two possible donors?"

Still cradling the rifle, he massaged his eyes. "You ought to be a lawyer. You make one helluva case." His eyes swept the two cabinets. "I'm having a tough time wrapping my mind around this. Kim, The Shadow!" He shuddered.

"So, what are we gonna do?" Hunter watched his uncle struggle with inner thoughts.

Seagrave glanced around, his lips in a knife-thin grimace. "We're gonna put everything back the way it was and get out of here before—"

"What the hell's going on here?" A new voice rang through the room.

They pivoted toward the entrance. A single figure stood silhouetted in the doorway.

Seagrave groaned.

Caught, red-handed.

~ 67 ~

Warner glanced at Harris as they hurried south toward the 79th St Causeway for a return trip to Miami Beach.

The little detective raised Agent Dalwin on his cell phone, again triggering SPEAKER. "He's on, Boss."

"Ed, you there?"

"Right behind you, Detective."

"Yeah." He looked in his rearview mirror. "I see ya. So, what's your take on all this?"

"We've got nothing substantive to indicate this Seagrave, and maybe his nurse girlfriend, are in anyway complicit in these shootings." He paused.

"But you instincts tell you different, don't they?"

"Yes." A soft sigh. "Too many seemingly unconnected things are nestling together. There's something going on, and . . . ." He trailed off.

"Ya don't wanna jinx it by sayin' it out loud, so I'll do it. We may be on to The Shadow, after all those frustratin' years."

They crossed 125th Street, southbound, still twenty minutes from their objective. The golden disc of the Sun was squatting just above the horizon. Warner pivoted the bill of his ball cap to block the glare.

"I hope your right, Al." Another pause, then. "But if that's true, we're going to need backup. This perp is dangerous and slippery."

"I agree. Call your team, and I'll tee up mine. Everyone's to wait just outside the storage complex until we're organized." He glanced at his watch. "We're still fifteen minutes out. When we go in, I wanna have all the bases covered.

"Copy that," Dalwin responded, and disconnected.

"Get Olvida and Beck movin', Harris. I need everyone on site, pronto. Use sirens and lights until they're a half-mile out. Don't want our friends to know the cavalry's comin' until we're ready."

"You really think this Seagrave is The Shadow, Boss?" Harris hitched around on his seat, then held up a finger as he began relaying instructions to their team. He finished and redialed Dalwin.

"Maybe. My gut tells me there's a lot more goin' on here than we know. We'll see within the hour, I guess."

They settled in silence, and Warner concentrated on his driving during the growing rush hour. He expected they'd be on site well before any of either team arrived. They'd keep tabs on the subjects, if they found them, but they may be forced to make a move if Seagrave and whomever was with him tried to leave.

Warner hoped it wouldn't come to that.

~ 68 ~

"Shit!" Seagrave stared at the figure in the doorway, its hands on hips, backlit by the setting sun.

Hunter grabbed his arm and stage-whispered, "Is it Kim?"

"You're damned right it's Kim," she said, and strode into the room. "What the hell are you two doing, prowling around my private locker?" Her eyes caught the McMillan rifle, still in Seagrave's grasp, and she broke her stride, then continued forward. She voiced a soft groan.

"Found some of my toys, have you, Charlie?" She paused in front of them, arms crossed, her glance sweeping from one to the other. Her face softened, seeing the boy sag against his uncle.

"How're you doing, Hunt?" She stroked his cheek. "You look haggard."

"I'm *feeling* pretty haggard. And I'm confused and scared at all this." His gesture swept the room.

"How'd you find this place?" She fastened on Seagrave's eyes. "And why are you here?"

"I found it," Hunter said. "I was visiting some friends up this way last month and saw you drive by." He hesitated. "I tried to catch up to say 'Hi,' when I saw you pull in here, and thought maybe you didn't want company just then."

"Good guess. So . . ." She took a small step back and sighed. "So, you told your uncle, huh?

"I pried it out of him." He reached over and squeezed Hunter's shoulder. "I guessed you sprung for that bike," gesturing toward the Harley, "and I was upset that you may have made a purchase you couldn't afford." His turn to sigh. "I admired the intent, but thought I might pay it off to ease your burden."

"You shouldn't have. I love you guys," her voice taking on a hard edge, "but this is a serious invasion of my privacy." Her eyes swept the room, her lips pressed narrow as a knife slit.

"Yeah." He glanced around the room. "I can see that. We gotta talk about this."

What's there—?"

"Hang on." He pulled his nephew in for a hug. "You're worn out. Go wait for me in the car while Kim and I sort this out." He handed Hunter his keys. "Start it up and run the a/c. Take a nap, if you can."

"But, can't I—?"

"No." He patted the boy on his back. "This is adult talk, between Kim and me. I don't want you involved."

"Oh, all right." He sighed, gave them both brief hugs, and

started for the door. "I *am* pretty bushed."

They watched his slow departure, then Seagrave turned to Kim and brandished the McMillan.

"What the hell is this, Kim?" His voice hoarse and strained. His swept an arm across the room. "All of this?"

"Nothing you should know about, Charlie. It's got nothing to do with you."

"But, now I *do* know about it, and it scares the hell outta me."

"So, forget about it. Wipe this place from your mind." She grabbed his hands. "You've never been here. This can only bring you trouble."

"No good. I *have* been here. I *have* seen everything. I can't just erase it. I . . ." He took her chin in his fingers, raising her eyes to his. "I can't believe who I think you *really* are."

She brushed off his hand and turned away. "And who is that?" Her voice a choked whisper.

"You're . . . you're The Shadow, aren't you?" He caught her arm, pulling her back, and held up the sniper rifle. "The infamous contract killer the FBI's been hunting for two decades."

"Okay, what if you're right? What are you going to do about it?"

"Jesus, I don't know." Their eyes locked. "Are you gonna kill me too, now that I know." He saw tears bloom, her head giving a small shake. "What in the hell are you doing here, shooting all those innocent people?"

She stepped back and knuckled her eyes. "Putting my secret in jeopardy, that's for sure. I stepped out of character for this."

"But why?"

"To save *Hunter*. To create possible donors for him." She groaned softly and ran a hand through her hair. "Did it perfectly twice, and both fell through. Idiots! Goddammed

Murphy and his fucking law." She jammed her hand in the pockets of her slacks. "That where I was today, casing one more opportunity for tomorrow. One more attempt to give him a living donor."

"I don't understand." He shook his head. "You *know* he's important to me, but this seems a bridge too far, just because we're in love."

"I adore that you love him so much." She took his face between her hands and gave him a soft kiss.

He pulled back and stared at her, moisture welling in his eyes. "I still don't get it. You did all this because I love my nephew?"

"Not entirely. While he may be your nephew . . . he's also *my* son!"

~ **69** ~

Warner and Dalwin parked their vehicles on the shoulder, just across from the entrance to the StoreIt complex. The rows of storage units were strung out parallel to the road, making it impossible to scan the facility for vehicles. They'd await backup and then they'd cruise the lines from both ends, hoping to locate Seacrest's vehicle . . . if he were still there.

"How long before Olvida and Beck show?" An inner voice urged Warner to get moving on their target.

"I just got a text from Beck, Boss. Maybe five minutes." Harris turned to his cell phone, sitting on the dash. "How about your team, Agent?"

"Agents Yeager, Askin, and Pauletti should be here about the same time as your team. Agents Whitehead and Solto are working with your local PDs on cleaning up the organ transplant scam."

"Okay." Warner's hands strangled the steering wheel. "I wanna get hoppin' on this ASAP." He glanced at the cell phone on SPEAKER. "You gotta be itchin' to get in there to see if we're finally onto your Shadow."

"Damned right, Detective. He's the most elusive Unsub I've ever hunted, but I don't want to get expectations too high. Unfortunately, we've been disappointed before."

"Yeah, well . . . okay, here's my guys." Olvida's green Caprice slid to a stop in front of Warner's Dodge. "Let's get vests on and check weapons." He peered down 79Th Street. "As soon as your guys get here, we'll move in."

Dalwin made a call from his cell phone. They avoided radios on an operation like this, in case the perps listened to the police bands. He disconnected and slipped on his Kevlar vest. "One minute out."

"Okay." Warner turned to his detectives, already secured in their vests. "Olvida and Beck load up M4s. If this *is* The Shadow, he's been too deadly to take any unnecessary chances."

"Let's not get our hopes up." Dalwin repeated as a black Chevy Suburban pulled in, disgorging the three BAU Special Agents. "It's hard to believe that careful, slippery bastard has exposed himself like this."

A moment later, Warner's team and the four FBI agents drove their four vehicles onto the storage lot. The Miami detectives peeled off to the left, and the federal agents went right. They'd cover both ends of the rows of storage lockers in a coordinated sweep. Crossing the lane between the third and fourth rows, they spotted two vehicles, about halfway down.

"See 'em, Ed?" Warner said into his phone.

"Yes. A Lexus and what looks like a Honda CRV."

"That should be Seagrave." Warner turned onto the path and stopped. "He drives a Lexus SUV."

Jack Harris, perched on the passenger seat, scrolled through pages on his Android. "Seems to me . . . Yeah, here it is. A tan Honda CRV spotted near two of the shooting sites." He glanced at his boss.

"You get that, Ed?" Warner asked.

"Yes. Maybe reason to hope this isn't another dead end with this bastard. What's your plan, Detective?"

"Without probable cause, we gotta wait for a warrant. How's that comin', Olvida?" He saw Dalwin's Suburban ease into the far entrance to the row of lockers and stop. "Something's definitely goin' on down there. We need that warrant . . . *now.*"

"Got an ADA working on it, Boss. He texted that the judge wants something more than two suspicious vehicles. He . . . hang on a sec."

Warner drummed fingers on the leather-wrapped steering wheel. "What the fuck's his problem? We're sittin' here . . . ."

"Just talked to the ADA, Boss." Olvida stepped out of his car, phone to his ear. "Sez he's got a line on another, friendlier judge." He looked toward Warner and shrugged. "Hope to have the warrant within ten minutes."

"Well, we gotta wait unless something gives us cause." Warner exited his coupe, his phone in hand. "Meanwhile, let's block both ends of this alley with a vehicle." He pointed at Olvida. "Your Chevy across this end, and one of the SUVs at the other."

"Right," from Dalwin. "And we need that warrant. I don't want to give this Unsub any angle to squirm out of a bust because we didn't do it by the book." He positioned his Suburban across the far entrance.

"I agree. Best we can do is being ready to move the second we get the okay." Warner's eyes swept over the rest of the team. "Weapons checked, vests secure, and be alert. From what we know about The Shadow, if in fact this is him, things can happen fast, and with deadly consequences if you're not sharp." He pocketed his phone, rechecked the magazine in his Glock, and patted a pocket, holding two spares, each loaded with fifteen rounds.

"Okay. Let's move into position. Quietly, and keep about thirty feet short of that door. All phones on vibe only and radios on mute." He slid into his Charger and coasted to a quiet stop, fifty feet short of the two parked vehicles. His team followed on foot.

Warner exited his vehicle and pointed toward the lockers. "That passage door's ajar. Something's definitely goin' down in there." He peered across the narrow roadway and saw the BAU team also settled in position.

Now they would wait, and Warner always found that difficult.

All eyes focused on the partially open door.

~ 70 ~

"He's your *son?*" Seagrave lurched back, brushing her hands away. "What the hell are you talking about?"

"It's true. I've followed Hunter's life for years. When I learned of his liver problem and your devotion to him, I sought you out."

"So, we didn't meet by chance?" His brow wrinkled, his lips twisting. "You *seduced* me, just to be close to Hunter?"

"At first." She sighed and grabbed his hand to keep him close. "But I then fell in love with you." A small smile tickled her lips. "Never been there before." She caressed his cheek. "Never had the time or interest in love, 'til I met you."

"I don't understand." His left hand grabbed her shoulder.

"How in the hell is that boy your *son?*"

"It's a long story." She sighed and studied her sneaker-clad feet.

"I'm listening." He leaned against the cabinet, the McMillan still cradled in his arms.

"You know I grew up in foster care after my parents were killed in a car accident?" She studied his eyes.

He nodded. "Not always an easy way to live, but you've seemed to prosper."

"Yeah, but it also makes you feel vulnerable, especially because my sister and I were sent to different families."

"You have a sister? How come—"

"That's a whole story you don't need to know about. We grew up apart and barely had contact for years. But that's got nothing to do with what happened to me."

She ran fingers through her hair and held his eyes with hers. "When I was sixteen, I . . . I was raped by my high school adviser. Right in his fucking office." Her damp eyes glittered, her lips pressed into a narrow slit.

"You got pregnant?" His eyebrows arched.

She nodded and shrugged. "And rather than believe me, the school expelled me to avoid scandal." Kim thumbed away tears. "My foster family said they'd support me if I had the kid. They were Catholics and didn't hold with abortion. Nor did I."

"So, you had Hunter?"

"Yeah. Of course, I didn't name him, of course. We found a good family through an intermediary to adopt him."

"The Fiores. Good choice."

"Yeah, the best." She folded her arms, running her hands over her biceps. "It was supposed to be a blind adoption, but I ferreted it out."

"Then what? You started following him?"

"No. I had other fish to fry."

"Like what?" Seagrave pushed away from the cabinet.

"I started tracking Mr. Zengara."

"The rapist?"

She nodded. "I cataloged his regular activities. He visited a back-alley bookie every Wednesday. College games, I think. It was the perfect spot. I waited nearly a year."

"You killed him, didn't you?" Seagrave's eyes narrowed.

"You bet! I'd got a five-inch switchblade and practiced my move on a clothing manikin I found behind a strip mall. Killed that dummy twenty times until I had it down pat."

"Jesus, weren't you scared to actually kill someone?"

She shrugged. "More nervous than scared, but I was motivated by anger. When the day arrived, I came out from behind a Dumpster and stuck it in his heart." She shrugged. "Never said a word to the bastard, but I loved the surprised look on his face." Her eyes were intense. "Not just because I got revenge on the bastard. It gave me goose bumps. I *loved* it!"

"You loved your first kill?" His eyebrows knit together. "I can't believe—"

"Not the kill, really. Well, maybe him, because it was personal." Her eyes went soft. "What really turned me on was that all my careful planning was so *perfect*. I'd always been kind of a free soul, and this took discipline and exacting execution. Things I'd never done before." Her eyes dropped and studied her shoes.

Seagrave sighed. "No one ever suspected you?"

"Nope." She looked up. "I took his money and credit cards. Shredded the cards but kept the three hundred bucks. It was classified as a mugging."

"But how did that lead to this?" He brandished the rifle.

She gave a wry grin. "Turned out, a contract killer for a Cuban mafia was also a patron of that betting parlor. Despite my best care, he noticed me hiding behind the trash bin, watched me do the deed from a window, and followed me." She shrugged. "I guess he liked my careful preparation and unhesitating move. He kept after me. Took him a couple of visits to convinced me I could be a great assassin." Kim shifted her stance and stuffed her hands in her pockets.

"He had a contract he said a woman would be perfect for." Her eyes took on a distant look. "We trained for a month, but I was still hesitant. Zengara had it coming, but I wasn't keen on killing someone without reason." Her eyes found his. "But once I learned who the mark was, he had it coming, too. My new champion said he'd never seen a 'natural' like me."

"So, you did the job? A contract killing?" He shook his head. "I can't believe this."

"Well, I did it. A piece of cake, smooth as silk. It was the careful planning and execution that was exhilarating. Nothing personal about any of my targets . . . until now." She shivered, bringing her eyes back to his. "Anyhow, when he paid me ten grand, any lingering reluctance evaporated. I as a seventeen-year-old foster kid who'd just made a bundle of cash. I knew this was my calling."

"Jesus!" was all he could squeak out.

"Yeah, I understand, but since we're here, you might as well know it all." She paced in a tight circle. "Tito'd get the contracts, and I'd execute most of them. He gave me weapons training . . . he was ex-army ranger . . . and planned the hits. It was eerie how natural shooting became for me. He was a trained sniper in the military, but said I was the best he'd ever seen." She paused her meandering.

"He took credit for the kills, and no one even knew I existed. I liked it that way, and once I learned all he could teach me, and knew his contacts, I assured no one would ever learn who I was." She faced away, then turned to him.

"You . . . you *killed* him?"

She nodded and stepped closer, grasping his arms. "I had to. It was my only way to stay safe. If he were ever nabbed, he'd give me up in a flash to save his own hide." She released her hands. "I had all the contacts and knew how to reach and be reached by them, and had a ton of cash stowed away. I didn't need or trust him."

"So now what?" he raised his voice to a harsh growl. "Now that *I* know your secret, are you going to kill me, too?"

"Oh, no, darling." Her fingers traced the side of his face. "I *love* you. And, I'm still trying to create a donor for Hunter. I've got one more chance tomorrow—"

"To do what?" he screamed. "Kill more innocent people so Hunter might live?"

"I'm just trying to save my son." She stepped back, tears trickling in tiny rills down her cheeks. "It all I think about."

"You believe that's what he'd want? Then you don't really know Hunter." He groaned.

"Now what am I supposed to do?"

~ 71 ~

Warner, his detectives, and the FBI team fidgeted, hanging in a small circle. All wore Kevlar vests and carried a variety of weapons. With nothing to do, Jack Harris eased over to examine the two vehicles. Looking into the Lexus, his eyes widened. "Oh boy." He turned and scurried to Warner's side.

"What's up?" They spoke in whispers.

"There's a guy stretched out in the Lexus, Boss. Looks like he's asleep."

"Think it's Hunter Fiore?" Warner scratched his chin.

"Could be. He's young but I don't know what the kid looks like. If he wakes up, he might warn whoever's inside that we're here."

"That could be dangerous," Agent Dalwin said. He and his

team had quietly joined them. "If Seagrave *is* The Shadow, this could become a very deadly encounter."

"We gotta get movin'. What the fuck's takin' so long on that warrant?" He looked at Olvida.

"Just got a text from the ADA, Boss. He thinks he's convinced the judge." He glanced at his phone. "Five minutes. Ten at the most."

"The longer they fuck around, the tougher this is gonna get." His fingers sought out the X-shaped scars, hidden above his right ear, two reminders of previous dangerous times.

"Hey." Beck tugged Olvida's sleeve. "You hear that?"

"Yeah." He turned to Warner. "Yelling going on inside that unit, Boss."

"I'm pretty sure I heard 'Kill people,' guys," Agent Yeager's blond hair swirled as she looked back at the group. "Probable cause?" She glanced at Warner.

"Anyone else hear that?" Warner scanned the rest of his group.

"That's what I heard," Agent Askin said. "Definitely something about kill people."

"Me, too," Olvida added. "Clear as day."

"Okay." Warner pushed away from his car. "Probable Cause trumps a warrant, especially with three of you hearin' the threat." He grabbed Detective Beck's arm. "You keep watch on whoever is in that Lexus, and keep him under control if he wakes up." He rechecked his Glock, adjusted his vest, and started toward the entryway.

"Let's mount up and get in there. And be careful." His eyes swept the other six. "I don't want any shot up cops today."

As per protocol, the three Miami detectives led the approach, with the FBI providing backup.

Things might finally be coming to a head.

~ 72 ~

Seagrave glared at her, still cradling the sniper rifle in his arms. "I'm in love with the infamous Shadow? Jesus!"

"I never expected you to learn that." She sighed. "I guess the risks I've taken to save Hunter finally made me vulnerable." She moved closer, one hand caressing his cheek. "And I never expected to fall in love."

"Dammit, you're my first love too, and now this." He brushed away her hand. "What do I do when I discover my sweetheart is at the top of the FBI's Most Wanted list?"

"Forgive me, darling?" Her eyes searched his. "I intended to retire after . . . this. Just disappear and cut off all my criminal contacts." Tears welled again. "I hoped to spend a lovely, quiet life with you."

"We're just supposed to ignore you've killed people for a living? Twelve in the past month, all innocent of any crime." He groaned and shook his head. "How can I forget that?"

"I'm trying to save my son." The waterworks were in full flow from her eyes. "I'd have donated part of my liver if I were a match, but I'm not. His only chance was if I could provide a donor." She backhanded away her tears. "I'd made the perfect shot. If that damned Perez woman hadn't clung to an impossible hope, she'd have saved six victims, Hunter would be on the mend, and none of this," gesturing at the lockers, "would have ever been found."

"Yeah, well things don't always go as planned, do they?"

"Mine *always* do . . . except for now." She gave a tiny shrug. "So now what? You gonna turn me in?"

"I don't know what to do." He shook the McMillan at her.

"If I say 'yes,' you gonna take this away from me and kill—" He stopped, eyes flaring, when the metal door flew open, banging resoundingly against the wall. A stream of heavily armed men poured through the opening.

"Police!" the guy in front yelled. "Drop the weapon, Seagrave. Your days as The Shadow are over."

~ 73 ~

Seven lawmen spilled into the room, fanning out in both directions, weapons at the ready.

"Huh? What the hell . . . ?" Seagrave's jaw dropped.

Kim spun around, then grabbed his shoulder and snaked behind him, one arm wrapped around his waist.

"Put the rifle down, Charlie, or they'll shoot you," she whispered. She pulled him back until she was partly inside the open weapons cabinet.

He craned his neck, looking at her, his eyes as big as quarters.

"Slowly. Hold it by the barrel and lower it to the floor." She molded her body tightly against his and reached back, snagging a Glock .40-cal from the rack. "Don't bend over. Just lay the butt on the ground and let it fall."

"What the hell's goin' on?" The dark-eyed lead cop inched forward.

She recognized the man, who seemed in charge, as Detective Al Warner, the so-called Miami Hero. She switched her focus to Special Agent Ed Dalwin of the FBI. She'd frustrated him for many years. No choice but to set the record straight.

"You got it wrong—again, Agent Dalwin." The McMillan

clattered to the floor. "Charles Seagrave's not your Shadow. *I* am." She gave a mirthless chuckle at the FBI team's stunned expression as they exchanged glances. She slipped the Glock into her waistband and plucked a Beretta 9mm from its mounts, switching it for the Glock.

"We gotta move." She drew him with her as a shield, sideling toward a rear corner of the storage room.

"Give it up, Kim. You don't have a chance," Seagrave muttered. "You're gonna get us both killed."

"They're not going to shoot as long as you shield me." Her arm around his waist plastered his body against hers as she edged slowly into a corner of the room. "They want me alive, but I don't intend to give them that option."

"Jesus! I don't want you dead. I'm going to stay right here and give you cover until we can work out a peaceful surrender." He folded his arms over hers. "From what I've read, they don't actually have proof who killed all those people. It's all circumstantial."

She groaned. "Not after they run ballistics on my weapons. That'll tie me to most of the deaths." She sighed. "I'll either make it out of here or die trying." She paused. "Damn, if I were a match for Hunter, I'd let 'em shoot me so he could have my liver." Tears filled her voice. "All I wanted to do was save my son, and I've *failed*."

"Put down you weapons, Tate." Agent Dalwin pushed forward, leveling his pistol. The other six lawmen stood in classic firing poses. "You're trapped. There's no way out."

"Sure there is, Eddie boy." It was a brittle voice Charlie didn't recognize. "I could kill you all before you get a shot off." She'd switched to the fifteen-shot Glock and fanned it over the seven cops. "The blond Amazon and Pauletti first. Your best shots. The rest go down inside of three seconds."

"You can't get us all," Warner's voice calm, "before one of us nails you. Don't commit suicide by cop."

"I don't intend to die here . . ." She fidgeted with something on the wall behind her ". . . and I don't want to kill any of you, either."

"Then give it up," Warner held his hands up, his pistol swinging from a finger through the trigger guard. "We can do this peacefully, and no one has to get hurt."

"Kim, please." Seagrave squeezed her arm wrapped around his waist. "Don't do this. I don't care what you've done, I don't want you dead. They've got you—"

"Shhh, Baby." She whispered in his ear and slowly withdrew her arm. "Nothing's gonna happen to me. At least not now." She released the last of her grip, totally obscured behind him. "Just stay right there, and try not to move for the next minute." She kissed him softly on the neck. "I *do* love you, more than you'll ever know."

He felt her move, and then sensed a change in the air—almost a soft breeze. He remained frozen in place, watching the officers fidgeting in place.

"Okay, Tate." Warner glanced back at the other six, every gun ready to fire. "You've stalled long enough. It ain't gonna get you anywhere." He motioned with his head, and Harris and Olvida arced away in opposite directions, trying to gain an angle on The Shadow.

"Boss!" Harris looked at Warner, his face screwed into a grimace.

"Don't take the shot, Harris." Warner edged forward.

"No worries. I got nothing to shoot at."

"What?" Warner strode forward, shoving Seagrave aside.

"How the fuck . . .?" He glared at the wall.

"She's gone!"

~ 74 ~

They converged in grim silence, weapons at the ready, on the corner of the room where Kim Tate—the ever elusive Shadow— had seemingly been trapped.

"Where'd she go, Seagrave?" Warner snatched the man's arm.

"I don't have a clue, Detective. I just stood still, trying not to get shot." He couldn't stifle a grin. "Looks like she lived up to her nickname."

"I got it, Boss." Olvida pushed open a small panel on the back wall. "Looks like she created an emergency exit." He poked his head through the opening and scanned the path.

"Clear," he called and slipped through the narrow opening, waving for the others to follow.

"Dammit." Agent Dalwin and his team started for the front entrance. "That slippery bitch is in the wind." He yelled over his shoulder. "We'll go out and check the front, then circle back on both sides, Al. You go that way. She can't be far."

"Harris," Warner growled, "cuff this guy to that post We'll deal with him later." With that, he and the other five cops were gone.

A moment later, Seagrave stood alone in the empty locker, his left arm shackled in place, trying to get a handle on too many disparate things racing through his head.

Kim, The Shadow! Holy shit. I was . . . still am, I guess, in love with a notorious assassin. Hunter's mom? He rubbed his eyes with his untethered hand, unable to suppress a wry chuckle. "Never get between a she-bear and her cub," he muttered.

"You got that right, Charlie."

"Huh? What?" He spun around and nearly stumbled, spying Kim emerging from behind the wall.

"Where the hell did you come from?" His eyes swept from her to the front door, and back. "They're out there, chasing you."

"Chasing their tails, you mean." Her face was hardened into grim lines. She glanced at his shackled hand, and a smile tweaked her lips. "Got you hooked up, huh? Safer for you."

"How the hell . . .?" He took her hand in his.

"With you as a shield, I slipped out my escape hatch and hid in a little niche I created. They ran right by me."

"Your escape hatch? How'd you know you'd need—"

"I *always* have a second way out." She pulled away, scooped up the McMillan rifle, grabbed a box of cartridges from a locker, and strode toward the Harley. "I gotta split." She mounted the big bike, laying the rifle across the handlebars. "They'll be back any minute. Tell 'em the truth and you'll be okay."

"Where are you going?" He gestured at her.

"I got one more shot at saving Hunter, and I plan on taking it. Sorry about borrowing your new bike." She started it up and cleared the kickstand.

"You can't get far. They'll know what you're riding."

"Got a different set of wheels I think I can get to in time." She donned one of the helmets that sat on the rear seat and tossed the other at his feet. "I'll miss you." She threw him a kiss, cranked up the engine, and leaning low, blasted through the doorway. She skidded into a sharp turn and raced down the lane toward the exit.

Warner materialized out of a narrow passage between units. "Tate!" he yelled as she sped toward the 79th Street entrance. He raised his Glock, then paused. Too much traffic on the cross street to risk an errant shot.

"Shit!" He watched the Harley and rider shoot through a small gap between Olvida's Chevy and the curb and flee across the causeway.

He ran into the storage space as Dalwin and the rest of their team burst inside, filing through the narrow, previously hidden doorway.

"What the hell's goin' on?" Warner strode up to Seagrave and Dalwin joined him.

The agent grabbed the detective's arm. "Was that Tate?"

"Yes." Warner sighed. "Looks like she got away."

Warner waived off his detectives as they started toward their cars. "You'll never catch her, riding that bike." He snatched Seagrave's shoulder. "Where the hell did she come from?" Warner withdrew his police band radio.

"I guess she had some kind of hidey-hole, just outside. You guys ran right by her."

Warner barked an APB into the radio, describing the bike and rider, then pivoted again to Seagrave.

"You didn't try to stop her? That could be a serious charge of aidin' and abettin'."

Seagrave shrugged. "No way I'd hassle the most dangerous assassin the FBI's ever chased. I'm not suicidal."

"Okay, I get that. Any idea where she's headed?" Warner and his team surrounded Seagrave.

He shook his head as Harris released his cuff from its anchor. "Only that she was intent on creating a new liver donor for her son." He rubbed his still fettered wrist.

"Her *son?*" Warner's forehead creased.

"Oh, yeah. You don't know. Hunter Fiore is her son."

"Jesus!" Warner glanced at his two detectives, both with mouths agape.

"She's going to shoot another O-Negative victim?" Agent Dalwin grabbed Seagrave, turning him.

"I guess." He shrugged, his face cratered with despair. "It's all as much news to me as it is to you." He stared toward the door, but Harris snatched his arm, yanking him to a halt.

He shook free and looked to Warner. "Can I go break this

to the kid sleeping in my car?" He sighed. "Helluva a thing to learn who your real mother is, at a time like this."

"Shit." Warner clipped his radio to his belt. "Miami PD already found the Harley, but she's nowhere in sight." He stared at Dalwin. "Your fuckin' Shadow is still invisible."

"At least we know who she is," Dalwin said and picked up his radio. "Now all we got to do is figure who's her likely next victim and try to nab her there."

"Yeah, that's all." Warner grunted, sarcasm lacing his voice. His eyes swept the other faces, hands planted on his hips. "Well, it's gonna be someone visibly out in public in the next two days."

He turned to his detectives. "Harris, you escort Mr. Seagrave to his car and stick with him while he talks to the Fiore boy. Hang here until we have people on site to secure the scene and all these weapons. Then bring him to the station until we sort this out."

"On it Boss."

Warner pivoted to Olvida. "You and Beck check the society pages and public outings. We gotta find who's gonna be exposed, and if they're O-Neg."

He looked at the Special Agent in Charge. "If we feed you names, Ed, can your guys dig into medical files to check their blood types? The data's gonna be available somewhere Tate could find it." Warner's eyes drilled into Dalwin's. "You got someone willin' to break into HIPAA confidential records?"

"Without a warrant? Not in the department, Al." He touched Warner's arm before he could turn away. "But I've used an off-book hacker for—sensitive—matters like this. I want The Shadow bad enough, I'm willing to bend a few rules." He paused. "A good defense lawyer might be able to use it to her benefit, though."

"Do it." Warner shrugged. "I'm guessin' this babe's not gonna go quietly."

"Okay, then. Let's go." Dalwin signaled to his team, and a

moment later, the storage locker was empty, the sudden quiet hanging like sodden drapes.

~ 75 ~

Seagrave, sans handcuffs and with Jack Harris lingering outside, slid onto the driver seat of his Lexus 570 and gazed at his nephew, sprawled on the fully reclined passenger seat, still asleep despite all the ruckus. He clenched his jaw, then sighed and reached over to stroke the boy's arm.

"Wake up, Hunt."

He stirred, eyes fluttering open, and tilted his head toward his uncle. "Hi, Unc." He shuddered slightly, then powered the seat upright and glanced around. "Where's Kim?"

"Gone."

"Gone where?" Hunter's eyebrows knitted.

"While we were . . . clearing things up, the cops and the FBI arrived." Seagrave's eyes drifted away. "You were right, Hunter. Kim *is* The Shadow."

"Wow! What happened? Did the feds nab her?"

"No, she escaped." He sighed. "She lived up to her rep."

"Jeez, that's rad." He reached to touch Seagrave's wrist and the corners of his mouth sagged. "Oh, god, I'm sorry. You guys were so perfect for each other, and now . . . ." He trailed off.

"Yeah." Seagrave shrugged. "Looks like there's no future for us, with her a contract killer." He rubbed the back of his neck. "Not sure how I feel. The Kim I know seems nothing like such a deadly woman."

His eyes caught Hunter's. "There's something else you need to know."

"What?" The young man swiveled and faced his uncle.

"It . . . it wasn't an accident that Kim and I met." He took the boy's hands. "She searched me out. Met me for a reason."

"A reason? What reason?" His brow creased. "You mean she didn't really love you? That sucks—"

The older man shook his head. "I don't think she expected it, but she *did* fall in love with me. So she said, anyhow." He swiped away moisture from his eyes.

"So, why did she hit on you? Money?"

"No." A small headshake as he glanced away. "Turns out, Kim probably has plenty of her own, considering her real livelihood."

"Okay." Hunter nodded. "If not money, then why?" He rubbed his bloodshot eyes. His illness sucked away his vigor.

"By being near me . . ." He squeezed Hunter's hand, ". . . she could be near you."

"Me? Why me?" He searched his uncle's face.

"You've learned you were adopted?"

Hunter nodded. "Came out when we discovered I needed a new liver."

"Adopted as a newborn?"

He nodded again, eyebrows arching.

"Kim," Seagrave patted Hunter's hand, their eyes locked, "is your mother."

"My . . . *what?*" He snatched away his fingers, slapping them over his lips. "How—?"

"It's complicated, and I just learned the details thirty minutes ago. Here's the deal . . . ."

~ 76 ~

I made a third pass, weaving through the three-block area

surrounding the Coral Gables courthouse and adjacent park. My scruffy white Ford Focus hatchback didn't attract much attention. I'd stashed the car at my rented duplex in North Miami, one of three safe houses I'd set up throughout Dade County. All leased with well crafted fake IDs and rent paid a year in advance. I'd equipped each with a non-descript vehicle, ten thousand dollars in cash, and a cache of weapons. Precautions if I were ever on the run, as now.

But escaping to safety wasn't on my mind at that moment. Providing Hunter with a new liver, courtesy of Celia VanMartin, dominated my thoughts. I glanced at my Rolex. Forty minutes to go. Plenty of time to set up, provided I didn't see any unusual surveillance. Didn't seem likely that Detective Warner or my long-time FBI adversary, Special Agent Dalwin, had any idea where I'd be today.

Still, I never left any little detail to chance. I'd set up alternate escape routes, in case things went bad. The royal palm lined streets offered cover for watchers, but nothing set off alarm bells in my head. I pulled into the same eight-store strip mall I'd used when I cased the site three days ago. The lunch crowd was long gone, and dinner patrons had not begun to arrive, the perfect mid-afternoon lull.

I'd spent serious time and effort on my new disguise as a Latin salsa musician. The one I'd first planned sat in a locker at my storage unit, no longer available. Instead, tea-colored stain tinted my face, cosmetic putty gave me a large, hooked nose, and cheek inserts rounded my face. A ragged red wig and shaggy, arched eyebrows hid my brown hair. Blue contacts colored my eyes. Baggy linen pants would conceal my walking with flexed knees, reducing my height by two inches. The cops surely had facial rec programs in gear on all the streets and CCTV cams throughout the county, so I hoped my disguise was face-altering enough to foil those apps.

I no longer had my guitar case. The McMillan rifle's barrel

and stock were in a much smaller trombone case. The scope and tripod sat inside a small backpack. I replaced my usual bedroll with a quick-inflatable air mattress, unconcerned over leaving DNA behind. They'd have plenty of that from Charlie's and my homes.

One more sweep of the area with my binoculars, checking the most likely places for something "off," but found nothing to trigger an internal alarm. I exited the Ford and started the short walk toward my chosen sniper site. The building's parking lot would be more convenient for a quick departure, but also more likely to draw attention. A late spring mini-cold front hadn't dropped the temp much, but had dried the air, which made for better shooting conditions.

I made continual surreptitious inspections of my surroundings, seeking danger, but still found nothing alarming. I shrugged. My highly tuned mental radar . . . a sixth sense I'd cultivated . . . had saved my ass four times in the past. It pinged at me now, but with no basis I knew of, so I cast it aside, yet remained vigilant. Nothing would dissuade me from this mission. Hunter needed a liver, and I was going to get it for him. No way could Warner and the feds know my location.

Another glance at my watch showed I still had twenty minutes to set up. Plenty of time, without leaving me exposed too long. Regardless of what happened today, I intended to split in a hurry. I had a corporate jet waiting for me at Opa-locka Airport, with a flight plan filed for Grand Cayman. Once airborne and out of the US Air Defense Zone, I'd convince the pilot, at gunpoint if necessary, to switch off his transponder and drop under ATC radar.

After we establish a southeasterly search direction for the cops, we'd make a low-level turn for a quick trip to Costa Rica, where a private airstrip awaited me. I would spend a half-year or more at a medical spa for extensive plastic surgery revisions. Kim Tate would disappear without a trace.

I ambled across the street and headed for the back of the building. Little vehicle and pedestrian traffic, as expected on a Saturday, and the parking lot was nearly empty. No cars or SUVs that smacked of law enforcement were in sight, but they wouldn't be that obvious if they lay in wait somewhere.

Goose bumps scattered across my spine and my scalp tingled . . . my usual warning signals something was amiss. I paused and again studied my surroundings. Nothing there that should set off my radar, but it continued pinging at my mind.

I sighed and continued on, my thoughts returning to Central America. Unhappily, after we landed, I'd have to kill the flight crew. Too many innocents were dying for this cause, but Hunter's life trumped theirs. I could leave no witnesses to my travels. A Colombian drug lord was ready to buy the plane at a bargain price, and he'd transform it with a new paint job and tail number. Another connection erased.

Careful attention to details should leave no trace of my whereabouts. I'd established a network to monitor Hunter and report to me, through three cutouts, none of whom would know my actual location. After a year or so, I'd return to the States.

I had no illusions of ever being in Hunter's life, should I succeed in saving it, but I was haunted by the idea of somehow getting back together with Charlie, if he'd have me. Thoughts of losing the only love I'd ever had depressed me.

Arriving at the rear of the building, I avoided the CCTV camera and found the rear door still unlocked. I slipped inside and peeked into the lobby. Empty, as expected on a weekend. As I was about to enter, the elevator pinged, and a man and a woman stepped off. They paused to talk, and then came toward me, heading for the parking lot.

With no place to duck into, I turned and retreated out the door. A left turn gave me cover behind a portico pillar, away from their likely path to their vehicles. As expected, they moved off into the lot, never noticing me.

I glanced up and wondered if my evasive move was captured on the CCTV camera. Too late to worry about that. I should be gone well before the authorities were alerted.

I reentered the building and crossed the lobby, hugging the wall to avoid detection, and entered the stairwell. Just six flights to reach the roof, an easy climb.

~~~

Detectives Olvida and Beck slipped out of the utility closet a half-minute after the stairwell door closed behind The Shadow. They had monitored her with a fiber optic camera slipped under the door as she moved through the lobby and entered the doorway to the stairwell.

"She's on the stairs, Boss," Olvida said into his comm, "coming to you. We're about to enter behind her."

"Copy that," Warner said. "Be quiet and *very* careful. I don't want any shot-up cops. We're starting down now."

~~~

As I reached the third floor landing, I paused. A gentle breeze kissed my cheek for ten seconds, then ceased . . . stairwell doors had opened above and below me. My ears twitched, sensing footsteps on the lower stairs. Yes, two people, quietly ascending from below. My super-tuned senses heard things others missed. I turned and hurriedly began to climb. Whoever they were, they weren't here to help me. Cops? How in the hell . . .?

The quiet scuff of more footsteps jerked me to a stop, but these came from above. I hesitated. No reason for anyone to be on these stairs but me. They were designed for emergency exit of the building.

Had I walked into a well-planned ambush? I had to get off these stairs. I drew my Glock and crossed the landing to the exit door. Locked! I slipped out my lock-pick wallet, which I carried with me everywhere, but then noticed the key slot was jammed with something. No exit there.

I dropped to one knee, opened the trombone case, and assembled the McMillan rifle. It was originally designed as an anti-armored vehicle weapon. While I didn't have armor-piercing cartridges, my metal-jacked slugs would probably blow right through the stair casings.

No law enforcement had ever died by my hand, and I didn't want to start now. We'd played nearly twenty years of hide-and-seek, a fun game I'd always won, but my crusade for Hunter required me to take chances I'd avoided in the past. Looked like that was about to catch up to me again.

I sighed, a tear sneaking from the corner of my eye. Hunter wasn't going to get a new donor today. My son was going to die because his mom couldn't provide for him. My teeth ground together, my jaw clamped so tight it began to cramp. These bastards have fucked up everything. Heat rose in my head, flushing my cheeks.

"Whoever's on the steps better stop moving," I shouted, my heart pummeling my ribs. "You don't want to die here today."

A leaden silence hung over the narrow space.

~ 77 ~

Warner eased open the rooftop door and peered in. He glanced at Harris and nodded. They stepped inside and began a cautious descent. He paused after a half-flight, head cocked, picking up some quiet scuffling and the rasp of metal on metal.

Probably The Shadow, who may have been alerted to their presence.

"You, on the steps, stop moving," the voice, rasped by tension, rang out. "You don't want to die here today."

"Give it up, Tate." Warner held up a hand, restraining Harris, who seemed eager to charge into a meat grinder. "We've got you pinned down, and all the exit door locks are jammed. There's no way out this time."

"We'll see about that, Detective." Her voice now steady and conversational. "I've never killed cops. Don't make me change that." Quiet for the moment, punctuated by some metallic scraping and clicking.

"Sounds like she's assembling that .50-cal sniper rifle." Warner glanced at Harris, who shrugged.

"Looks like you've lived up to your rep, Warner." Her voice drifted up from below. "How'd you find me?"

Before he could answer, she shouted, "Hey!" and two shots rang out, accompanied by the twang of ricochets. "You guys down there wanna die?"

Warner whispered into his comm, "Olvida and Beck, stay put. SWAT's en route, and the BAU team's on the way too." He eased down onto a stair. "Let's just keep her pinned until the cavalry arrives. Dalwin wants her alive, if possible."

"Copy that, Boss," Olvida replied. "This dame is scary."

"So, Warner, how *did* you find me? You've killed my son, you know." The voice softer, exuding pain. "By stopping me today. Only a week or two left for a new liver to save him. *Bastards!*" The last word reeked with venom.

"Sorry about Hunter." Warner kept his voice calm. "But killin' innocent people to save him just doesn't work for me." He paused, then continued. "Wasn't that hard to figure this out, but it did take some time. We knew you're lookin' for an O-Negative donor for him. We had a team check all the news media and social feeds for people who might offer you a target." He scooted over to allow Harris to settle beside him.

"Agent Dalwin knew a guy who hacked HIPAA records to see if any were O-Negative. We found VanMartin and one other. The BAU team staked out that one. And here you are. Kismet."

"You're a clever sonofabitch. I'll be sad if I have to kill you."

Two shots boomed, skipping off the stairwell walls. The two detectives dropped to the floor.

~ 78 ~

I fired the Glock twice at the stairwell above me, just to keep everyone in place. They were nearly two floors above, so in no real danger of being hit.

The McMillan could punch through the metal staircase, but I doubted it would reach two levels. The five-shot mag was filled with metal jacketed cartridges, plus one in the breech. It was a formidable weapon if I had to shoot my way out of here. I doubted a Kevlar vest would stop one of those 12.7mm slugs, and even if it did, the impact would break ribs and probably cause internal injuries.

That would be my absolute final resort, and I wasn't sure if I could even do it. *Never shoot a cop.* That was one of my rules, and I'd never broken it. Until this op, all my victims had been criminal-types. I double-checked the magazine in my Glock . . . wad-cutters. Plenty of punch, but less penetration.

I edged over and peered down from the stair railing. A shadow fell on the third landing from light streaming through the door's window. Arching my neck, I could see nothing above but stairs. No one made a move on me. Probably awaiting backup. I was a sitting duck for a coordinated attack from above and below, and I had nowhere to go.

Or do I? Hmm. The door to the fourth floor offered me a way out, and I realized the jimmied lock wasn't the obstacle it first seemed.

"Tate!"

Detective Warner, I guessed, trying to engage me.

"Ya got nowhere to go. You're pinned. We can sit here all day. Give it up, lady. No one has to die here."

"Don't give me a reason to kill you, Detective, and no one *will* die today." I hefted the McMillan. What I planned was going to take some quick action and dexterity. "Come after me," I called, "and that'll change. I've got nothing to lose."

I'd constructed a way to get off the stairs, but the trick would be doing it without the cops knowing I was gone. Playing The Shadow again. I knelt, cradled the rifle in my right arm, and drew my Glock with my left hand and snapped in a new fifteen-round magazine.

Okay. Here we go. "Hey." I fired a round from the Glock down the stairs. "Hold your positions if you want to live." Two discharges up and two more down. The pistol went to the floor and the rifle's stock was against my shoulder before the shots' echoes died. A quiet squeal as the 12.7mm slug blew out the door lock. I'd already recovered the Glock and squeezed off two more rounds, one up and one down.

~~~

Warner and Harris hit the floor as the two rounds the woman fired ricocheted off the stairwell wall half a floor below. The .40-cal slugs bounced off a second concrete wall, showering them with chips, and slammed into the one behind them before dropping to the floor.

"That dame can shoot!" Harris growled.

"Yeah, but why now?" Warner glanced at his partner. "She doesn't do anything haphazardly."

~~~

The cops were too busy ducking to realize what I'd done. "Keep in place, Warner, and no one'll get hurt."

"We got all day, Tate." His voice was calm. "You're the one runnin' outta time."

I barely heard him as I slipped through the now open door and into the fourth floor hallway. I glanced at the elevator and shook my head. They'd hear it and would be waiting below when I tried to exit. I had a better idea. The building had an outside fire escape. I crossed to the window with an exit sign above it, and eased it open.

There it was—classic metal stairs with a drop-down ladder at the bottom. Luckily, this was an old time Coral Gables structure. New construction no longer sported fire escapes. Getting down would be a little tricky carrying the rifle, as it didn't have a sling.

I stepped through onto the steel grate platform and closed the window. So far, nothing to indicate the cops knew what was happening. I hurried down three flights, glancing over my shoulder, looking for trouble. Good. Nothing yet. I grimaced at a rusty squeal as I lowered the ladder. Not unexpected, but very unappreciated. The McMillan went over my back, and I folded the bi-pod legs and inserted them under the back of my collar. I straddled the frame and I slid down the stairs to the ground. Rust scale painfully abraded my palms and fingers.

The awkward placement of the rifle dropped me to my knees, and the retracting ladder brushed my chin and clipped my nose. I shook my head and blinked, trying to clear the "stars" I saw. Blood trickled across my lip, and I brushed it away.

Idiot! A quick shake to clear my vision and I cocked my head, ears straining.

~~~

Warner rolled to a knee, peering down the stairs. "I'm gonna take a peek."

"Careful, Boss. She doesn't miss." Harris heaved to his feet.

"Yeah, I know." Warner edged quietly down the stairs. "But something's goin' on." He approached the platform at the turn in the stairwell. Glock held ready, he slid to a knee and peeked around the wall.

"Shit!" He lurched up. "She's gone. Goddammit, she's done it again," he yelled. "A fuckin' Shadow."

Olvida and Beck clattered up from below, as Harris joined him on the fourth floor landing.

"Where the hell did she go?" Olvida scratched his head.

Warner cast around then stepped to the exit door, yanking it open. "Blew out the lock while we were scramblin' for cover, and got inside." He clicked his comm. "She slipped free," he broadcast to backup, which was just arriving. "Maybe coming down the elevator or . . ." he paused at hearing a metallic squeal.

He jumped to a window, noticing it was unlocked, and threw it open, peering down.

"Fire escape! She came down an outside fire escape." He stepped through the opening onto the metal platform. "Whoever's out there, block off the front and rear of that alley, or she'll vanish again." He scanned below but was on an overhang and couldn't see the wall close to the building.

"I split my team, Al." It was Dalwin's voice in his ear bud. "We got the front and back, hopefully in time."

Warner crawled in through the window and back onto the stairs, waiving his men to follow as he raced down. "On our way to you, Ed," he called. "I know you want this perp, but don't do anything rash. I'd like to keep everyone alive, includin' her, if possible."

~~~

Shit! A scuffle of rushing feet from the sidewalk indicated my noisy descent had compromised my escape. I lumbered to my feet and started toward the rear, but sharp sounds from around the corner told me there'd be no retreat there. I scanned the area for cover. A large trash bin provided my only option. The narrow alleyway between buildings, no more than twelve-feet wide, offered my pursuers restricted access, funneling them into my line of fire.

I slid behind the large metal container, squatted, and sighed. Unfortunately, a shootout with the cops portended only one final outcome—my capture or death, and my mission to save my son left incomplete. With luck, and careful preplanning, I might still get away, but—

"Tate."

Detective Warner's voice. Seemed he'd made it to the front. Gotta admire the guy.

"Clever move, but you're still pinned down." He kept his voice calm, conversational. "Give it up and we can avoid any further bloodshed. You got nowhere to go."

~ 79 ~

"Maybe so," Tate yelled, "but a lot of you *will* die if you try to take me. I've got a lot of fire power here."

The five men and Ina Yeager hunkered close to the wall, listening to the warning echoing from the alleyway.

"No kiddin'," Warner muttered, as he scanned his people. "Everyone in vests?"

"Of course," Dalwin said, "but they won't stop a round

from that McMillan. It's an anti-armored vehicle weapon."

"Yeah. Hopefully, she ain't got any of those armor-piercing shells." Warner checked the breach of his Glock. "We're stalemated unless she makes a move."

"I can't figure this out." Harris edged close to the wall to peek around the corner.

"What d'ya mean, Detective?" Agent Whitehead grabbed his shoulder and drew him back. "Careful there. She's deadly."

"Right." Harris shrugged off the hand. "She was always careful never to leave a trace, and yet here she is, taking reckless chances that are getting her nabbed after nearly twenty years of being a ghost. I don't get it."

"She's tryin' to save her son. Create a liver donor for him, and we've gummed up the works." Warner dropped to his belly and took his own careful glance down the alley.

"She's taken cover behind a dumpster, and . . . whoa!" He jerked his head back as a slug shattered bricks a foot above his head. "*That* was close. She doesn't miss much."

"She doesn't miss *anything*, Al." Ina Yeager squatted next to him. "That was a warning, or we'd be looking for part of your skull.

"She's that good? A snap shot from over fifty feet with a Glock?"

"You've seen the precision." Agent Pauletti took Warner's hand and helped him to his feet. "She created two possible donors from over a thousand meters. A centimeter off, and they'd be dead and useless."

"So," Warner dusted off his pants, "how do we end this? We get in a firefight with her, we'll lose people before we can take her down. Good as you say she is, she'll take head shots, avoiding the Kevlar."

"You called in SWAT," Dalwin said. "They'll storm her from both ends, and they've got shields to provide full cover. Safe for anything except those armor-piercers." He laid a hand on Warner's arm.

"I'd love to take her alive, but I don't think that's her plan."

~ 80 ~

I peeked over the top of the trash bin, trying to ignore the less than fragrant odors of decayed food and the burning pain from my abraded hands. I glanced at my bloody palms, swore softly, and wiped them on my pants. Perspiration misted my forehead, despite the cool shade in the narrow passage.

This sucks. They've got me pinned and are probably waiting for SWAT. I'll have no chance to escape once those special operators arrived. Better get moving. No question I can take a lot of cops with me, but any chance of bulling my way out of here are slim, if any. Backup plans relied on living through this.

I've led a charmed but lonely life for twenty years until I connected with my son and his incredible uncle. But, I've failed to save Hunter. He is going to die, and so, probably, will I. But not without giving myself every chance.

I rechecked the Glock and the Beretta. Full mags and one in the breach. Two spare mags for each were wedged in my belt, easy to reach. The McMillan was too clumsy to come with me, but it'd make for a good opening salvo.

This is it. Wish I could've done more for Hunter. I rose from behind my cover and brought my rifle to bear on the FBI agent in the building facing the far end of the alley, watching me with binoculars. The sound-suppressed weapon emitted a quiet squeal as I squeezed off a round. I didn't wait for what I knew were the results.

~~~

"Looks like she's up and moving." Agent Anita Solto leaned on the lobby windowsill, 9x35 Nikon glasses riveted on the scene across the street. "She's got the rifle, and . . . oh, *shit*."

She jerked back and ducked, dropping the binoculars as a 12.7mm slug slammed into the windowsill just below where she'd been sitting, showering her with splinters and concrete chips. She shuddered. *That was damned close.*

She peeked over the ledge in time to see two shots from the powerful sniper rifle clip off chards of brick from the street-side wall where half the FBI team and Miami detectives hunkered down.

Kim Tate, the infamous Shadow, spun and laid down two more rounds from the McMillan at the other end of the building. She discarded the rifle, and with a pistol in each hand, hugged the wall. In a crouch, she strode quickly toward the rear, her head on a constant swivel.

"She's heading for the parking lot." Solto had recovered her binoculars and was tracking their quarry. "Moving fast. But be careful. She's scary deadly." The FBI agent mopped her brow with a sleeve, her heart still tripping at the closeness of the encounter.

~~~

"Anita says she's broken cover and heading for the parking lot." Dalwin grabbed Warner's arm as they edged around the corner, peering into the passageway.

"We gotta move." Warner waved at the five people clustered behind him. "All together. Spread out and keep low. Hopefully, we'll be too many targets for her."

"She's coming at you, Harry," Dalwin barked in his comm to Agent Askin. "Be ready. I'd like her alive, but not at the expense of any of you dying."

"Olvida." Warner glanced at Dalwin and shook his head. "Keep everyone back." He spotted her, crouched low and moving quickly along the wall, partly shielded by the big Dumpster. "If ya come out, we'll be in each other's line of fire."

Tate's head swiveled and she dropped to one knee, spun, and squeezed off two rounds from her Glock.

"Oooff!" "Uggh." Agents Yeager and Pauletti tumbled down like felled trees. She'd targeted the group's two top marksmen. Her instant recognition and reaction had been uncanny.

Dalwin knelt beside them, but saw no blood. A quick exam revealed they'd both taken .40-caliber slugs left-center on their vests, right over their hearts. The impact had whacked them senseless for the moment, but probably had done nothing worse than knocked their breath away and left bruises and maybe a broken rib.

Warner slid to his right for a better angle. "Give it up, Tate," he yelled. "We don't wanna kill you." He tracked her with his own weapon, feet spread, and his shoulder braced against the far wall.

She never slowed as two shots from her left-handed Beretta peppered the far wall's corner, now only ten feet away. Almost in the same motion, she spun and raised the Glock. Warner fired twice a split second before she did. The Shadow stumbled, then surged forward, as the slug from her gun whizzed past the detective, tugging at the edge of his vest.

Jesus, that was close! Before he could recover, the alley echoed with a barrage of gunfire. He shook his head and cleared his vision. Four of his people had leaped into the opening in front of her, firing as they fanned out. Tate squatted lower, plastered against the wall, firing with both hands.

With his men in the line of fire, Warner could only watch. He gasped as Detective Olvida staggered back and went down. In the same instant, Agent Whitehead stumbled to his knees and collapsed. Bursts of bullets continued in a deadly ballet of kill-or-be-killed.

The Shadow jerked backward, went to her knees, fired once more, and crumpled to the ground. Warner raced toward the melee, with Jack Harris at his heels. Dalwin, on his knees, glanced up from attending to his people.

"Go," Yeager croaked. "We'll join you soon as we catch our wind."

The BAU agent sprinted after Warner. "Careful! Don't assume she's out, just because she's down."

Skidding to a halt, Warner found Agent Harry Askin kneeling beside Kim Tate, sprawled on the pavement, both of her pistols kicked away. The agent pressed a cloth against a wound on her right side that may have broken ribs but looked to have missed the lung. His belt already cinched around her left thigh, stemmed bleeding from a through-and-through from Warner's first shots. Detective Beck squatted beside her and wrapped a gash along her right bicep.

Harris collected her two pistols, and talked into his police band radio.

Warner's eyes swept the activity, and he shook his head. Olvida and Agent Whitehead struggled to sit up, panting for breath. Each took .40-cal slugs from her Glock, left-center on their vests. The Shadow laid still, breathing, but not going anywhere soon.

Warner holstered his weapon and eyed the melee. *Christ, what a mess. None of our people actually shot, though.* "Anyone call a bus for her?"

"Done, Boss," Harris said. "Ambulance is on the way."

Beck rose. "Damned lucky she's the only one needing a medic." He ran a bloodstained hand through his hair.

"Don't think luck had anything to do with it, Beck." Warner crouched beside the woman and felt for a pulse at her throat. Surprisingly steady. This was one tough lady.

"What d'ya mean?" Beck knelt next to him.

Warner pushed to his feet and rolled his neck. "She's the best marksman anyone's ever seen." He waved a hand toward their two comrades just managing to sit up. "They each took one to the vest, right over the heart. Same with those two," nodding at Agents Yeager and Pauletti, just joining them. "The head's a lot bigger target than the heart."

"You think she didn't want to kill them?"

"No question. If The Shadow wanted 'em dead, they'd be dead." He went to Olvida and offered him a hand up.

"Lucky me." The detective's voice a hoarse rasp as he staggered to his feet. He rubbed his chest, then wrested the lead slug from the front of his vest, eyeing it. "Bullet proof, but not batter proof." He chuckled softly.

"Better than last year when you actually got winged." Warner patted him on the shoulder. "The four of you need ta get checked out, though. Could have a cracked rib and/or a bruised heart. That .40-cal delivers a hefty punch."

His eyes swept the small crowd, and he nodded. "You guys did good work today. We all did." He cocked his head at the warble of fast approaching sirens. The EMTs had made record time. They couldn't get Kim Tate to the hospital quick enough, but her wounds didn't appear to be life threatening. Four squad cars and a SWAT van peeled in, their sole task now taping off and containing the crime scene.

"So, you think she was committing suicide by cop, Boss?" Beck gazed down at Tate as the medics tended her.

"No. I think she *was* tryin' to make it outta here but knew the chances were slim." He ran a hand over his stubbled chin and sighed. "I do think she had less incentive to live, knowin' she'd failed to save her son."

Warner took in the bustle of activity. Kim Tate, the deadly Shadow, lay on a stretcher, saline IV hooked up, just loading into an ambulance. One of the newly arrived officers climbed in the back of the ambulance to accompany her to the hospital. Warner glanced at Dalwin, who stood arms akimbo, watching The Shadow's departure in a flurry of pulsing lights and blaring sirens . . . the end of a twenty-year frustration. Warner shook his head.

A fierce she-bear, ultimately failing to protect her cub.

Another once-baffling case closed.

His usual sense of satisfaction was strangely lacking.

~ 81 ~

Warner and his team milled around the recent site of havoc as the sun edged toward the western horizon. Twenty minutes had passed since The Shadow had departed for Jackson Memorial, and they were tying up loose ends with CSU and SWAT. Eventually, the detectives and the BAU agents congregated by the front of the building. All had shed their Kevlar vests, and most sported somewhat subdued grins.

"Well, we all survived, thanks to that deadly babe's personal code, I guess." His eyes swept over the six BAU agents and his three detectives. "You need to get your people to Jackson for a check-up," he said to Agent Dalwin. "You too, Olvida. Vests or not, takin' that .40-cal round can cause some internal damage, especially right over the heart."

The four mumbled quiet, grumbling accents. Ina Yeager rubbed her chest. "I've got a pretty big bruise alright." She gave a small headshake. "I've never seen anything like that woman's accuracy. It's obvious she didn't want to kill any of us, but putting the rounds right over our hearts made a statement."

"Scary's more like it." Olvida was eyeballing his own bruise through his unbuttoned shirt. "Nice of her not wanting to kill cops."

"I gotta say, that woman continued to earn my grudgin' respect. She gave it all up to try to save a son she hadn't even met until this year." Warner glanced up as a red and white ambulance peeled into the street, screeching to a stop at the curb. "Anyone call for another bus?" Answered with unanimous negative headshakes. His eyebrows arched as two EMTs leaped from the rear door and began withdrawing a stretcher.

"Sorry we're so damned late," the black medic said. "Got tied up and boxed in by a bad car wreck. Where's the patient?"

"What the fuck are you talkin' about?" Warner snatched the man's arm, hauling him to a halt. "One of your ambulances picked her up twenty minutes ago." His dark eyes bore into the medic's.

"A female shooting vic?" He glanced at his Android. "No, we're the first responders out of Jackson. We've been spread very thin today—"

"She's not at the hospital?" Warner glared at the man.

"Not as far as I know, Detective. This was our call."

The group clustered around Warner, their agitation palpable.

Warner growled. "Apparently, that wasn't a Jackson EMT that picked her up. Somehow, she musta had people who intercepted the call. I'm bettin' that clever bitch anticipated everything."

"Jesus." Agent Dalwin's eyes were as big as quarters. "She had an ersatz ambulance waiting nearby, in case she ran into trouble. What about the blue who rode with her?"

Warner tracked down the sergeant in charge of the uniformed cops. It wasn't one of his men, nor had he come with SWAT.

Warner returned to his crew. "Looks like she had a phony ambulance and a fake cop teed up in case things went south for her. They musta hacked the hospital's line and intercepted the emergency call." Warner turned to Harris. "Anyone get the number on that bus?"

Headshakes and mumbled negative responses were unsurprising.

"Can't very well put out an APB on an ambulance without some way to identify it." Olvida was working his Android tablet.

"Forget it. At this point, we're not stoppin' every EMT out there. She's in the wind . . . once more." Warner frowned. "Looks like The Shadow's gone invisible again."

"Sonofabitch." The Special Agent in Charge slammed a fist into his hand. "You called it, Detective. Can't help but admire that clever bitch. She was ahead of us at every turn."

"Now what?" Detective Beck's eyes swung from his partner to his boss.

"We put an APB out on her." Warner grabbed Olvida's shoulder. "Contact Seagrave for some photos. He must have some. Get 'em up on facial rec and start the search."

"I'll get officers to the three commercial airports." Harris was tapping his cell phone.

"All the private ones, too," Warner said. "And bus and train stations."

"Car rental services," Agent Whitehead said. "Anything she can use to get out of town."

"Yeah, well we can't cover 'em all." Warner massaged his eyes and groaned. "Besides, she may have just gone to ground. She's gotta have secret warrens to crawl into, like the one where she dropped the Harley, where she can wait 'til the heat dies before makin' a move."

"True, but she's pretty shot up." Yeager worked at her tablet. "I'll get our people on hospitals, clinics, and even veterinarians."

"Hey, I just realized, facial rec probably won't work." Agent

Solto jammed her fists onto her waist. "You guys never saw her face today, but I did when I was doing over-watch. It's totally change, probably with costume makeup."

"You didn't get a photo?" Dalwin asked.

"Just one, and her head was turned. I was otherwise busy trying not to get shot. She knew I was there and put a 12.7 right into the window sill, six inches below my face." She shivered. "Gotta admit, she scared the hell out of me."

"Okay." Warner rubbed the back of his neck. "No facial rec, but she's pretty badly wounded. No way to hide that. Let's get on it."

~~~

Back at HQ, Warner pushed away from his desk and strode into the office bullpen. "Harris. Olvida. Anything?" Two hours had elapsed since what they'd thought had been The Shadow's violent end.

"Nothing good, Boss." Jack Harris rose from his desk. "We got all the major airports covered within forty minutes. Some of the locals like Opa-locka, Homestead and Miami Executive took a little longer."

He glanced at his Android tablet. "Bus and train depots covered within the hour. Airport car rentals are done, but there are so many satellite locations . . . ." He looked at Warner and shrugged.

"Yeah." Warner sighed and shook his head. "She could be anywhere, usin' who-knows-what to sneak away." He stepped toward Olvida, peering over his shoulder. "Any suspect activity?"

"I've been checking the reports." Olvida paged through several screens on his tablet. "No sighting of anyone resembling her condition. Let's see . . . ." He flipped through more screens. "A thirty-eight foot Cigarette Top Gun speed boat blasted out of the Haulover Inlet twenty minutes ago, headed for the Bahamas. No details on where it came from or who is aboard."

"It's got a forward cubby cabin, right?" Warner looked around.

"Yeah," Agent Whitehead leaned in, studying the screen. "Plenty of room for Tate and a stretcher."

"Could be her—"

"Hang on, Boss." Olvida jotted a note on a yellow-lined pad. "There were also two corporate jets that got away before we shut down the airports. One, a Gulfstream IV with four passengers, from the Boca airport, flight planned for Atlanta. The FBI's people will be there to greet them on arrival."

He switched screens. "The other, a Cessna Citation, took off from Miami-Opa-locka Airport after we closed the field."

"What the fuck! They couldn't stop it?" Warner glared at the monitor's screen.

"Guess not." Olvida scrolled down. "They had the two long runways blocked, but the plane got off Nine-Right without tower clearance. Usually considered too short for jets."

"That sounds like her, too." Warner leaned over his detectives shoulder, scanning the screen. "Any destination info?"

"Flight planned for Grand Cayman, no passenger manifest, and . . . oh, shit."

"What?" Warner and Dalwin crowded in on the detective.

"Just cleared the Air Defense Identification Zone over the Atlantic, and their transponder went silent. Then it dropped below radar." He shook his head and groaned. "Gonna be tough to track."

"Any of those could be her, goddammit." Warner rushed to his office. "Harris, get on the horn to the Cayman police. We need coverage on any airport that can handle that jet. If that was her aim, with the head start it's got, she could be on the ground in less than an hour. Once there, she could board a commercial flight to who-knows-where."

He reappeared, pocketing his shield and Glock. "Olvida, you contact the Bahamas and check on that fast boat's passengers. Lots of islands they coulda run to, but she'll need Nassau or Freeport if she wants to fly out."

"The Caymans, Boss?" Harris disconnected from the call. "Doesn't make sense. Extradition's no problem with them."

"I doubt she's plannin' on stayin'. That may not even be her destination, with the plane goin' off radar." Warner bounded down the stairs, taking them two at a time. "Maybe she has hidden assets there or the Bahamas and is gonna jump somewhere else. We'll get ready to go if they snag her."

They hit the ground running for Warner's car and the race to Opa-locka airport and the Department's own Citation jet, which was getting teed up for a quick departure.

By the time they arrived, Warner received the news—the Cessna jet never landed on Grand Cayman Island. It was gone, and no one knew to where. A high probability that was The Shadow's escape, and there was nothing to do about it at that moment. It may also be a red herring, but they'd alert the police of any Central or South American countries, plus all the Caribbean islands. With any luck, they may pick it up where ever it lands. And meanwhile, they'd check out all the other possibilities.

The Cigarette speedboat had docked at Freeport, but only contained two couples out for a joy ride. Some stranger offered them the boat for the day as a good-Samaritan act he was doing for his church.

Warner suspected Tate was behind both, creating diversions. He'd learned The Shadow had mastered the art of deception, always one step ahead.

The Shadow had truly become invisible once more. Time to think outside the box if they were ever to catch her.

~ **82** ~

Charlie Seagrave clambered aboard his sportfisherman, shrugged off his air tank, and slipped out of his buoyancy vest. He needed something to distract him from the news that Kim had been caught, shot, then escaped again yesterday afternoon.

He perched on the fishbox and kicked off his flippers. The weight belt released next, he deposited it, along with the hull scraper, his fins and mask into a storage area under the boats floorboards.

Seagrave slipped on a sweatshirt against the cool morning air and settled in the captain's chair at the helm. He sighed. Sixteen hours since Kim had pulled her vanishing act. Despite the horrendous things she'd done, she'd put her life on the line in an effort to save her son.

A failed effort, unfortunately for Hunter. Kim and the boy used to help him scrape barnacles and scum from the boat's hull, but Kim was gone, and the poor kid could hardly get around anymore. Tears crept into his eyes. Two or three more weeks and the boy would be gone, barring some miracle.

He shook his head, sighed, and gathered his car keys and wallet. At least he was a free man for now. Detective Warner and Agent Dalwin had each made vigorous cases with the DA for his innocence in anything to do with The Shadow, despite being her lover, but he was still officially "a person of interest."

His cell phone, set on mute, vibrated on the dashboard's little storage shelf. He groaned, not eager to talk to anyone right then. It continued to buzz, so we withdrew it and glanced at the screen.

An anonymous caller. He shrugged and answered the phone.

"Hello?"

"Mr. Seagrave?"

"Yes." A woman, her voice muted and strained. "Who is this?"

"Juanita Perez."

"Who?" His brow wrinkled.

"Juanita Perez. Cesar's mother. You remember—"

"Yes. Yes, of course, Mrs. Perez." *Holy Christ!* He lurched upright, strangling the phone. "How is your son?"

"Hopeless." There were tears in her voice. "I finally accept this. Your offer—"

"It's still good for another week, if you've changed your mind." *Please, lady, do it now!*

"I . . . I talked with my priest. Cesar . . . he will never recover. We will give him last rites. If you still need—"

"Yes, desperately. My boy has just weeks to live. The fifty-thousand dollars are yours if you get Cesar to Jackson Memorial immediately and the final tests all prove positive."

He whipped out his address book and found the name of the recommended transplant surgeon. "Be sure you tell the hospital staff it's for a liver transplant for Hunter Fiore."

"Fiore? I thought he was your son."

"My nephew, but loved as if he were my own." He thought of Kim, squirreled away somewhere. "His mother will be overjoyed."

She paused and whimpered. "This is very hard for me. I . . . I . . . ." She paused. "I read article by Miami Herald crime reporter, Señor Roush. My Cesar and another man were shot by this one they call The Shadow, to make the organ donor." Another hesitation. "My Cesar, he is O-Negative. Your nephew, too. Is not Tate, that nurse who was with you, that assassin? The one they call The Shadow?" She paused, but before he could respond, she went on. "Does this mean she killed my son to save your nephew?"

He hesitated. "I have no knowledge of that." *Not at that time, anyhow.* "It was a terrible thing she did to your son, and so many other innocent victims." *I can't admit her son was sacrificed by Hunter's mother.* "But through your grief, can you understand mine? Hunter desperately needs a new liver or he will soon die."

"What if . . . what if this . . . what did you say? This tissue match is no good?"

"Then we will both suffer unbearable losses. Hunter has no other options. If there is no match, I will still give you five-thousand-dollars for making the effort, to help you give Cesar a proper burial. But, our previous tests, which you approved, give me hope for the best."

"Oh, god, my poor Cesar." She sobbed, and he heard her blow her nose. "I learn there are many others who need his . . . his organs. But maybe it is not right for your nephew, if this woman kills my son for him."

"I appreciate your pain," *Don't back out on me now, lady,* "but Hunter had nothing to do with Cesar's shooting. I know it is hard to say goodbye to your son. No parent thinks of outliving their child, but if you can let him go, your son's passing could give life to a remarkable young man, whom you'd be very proud to know." Seagrave held his breath and crossed his fingers.

"I understand." Tears again in her Latin-accented voice. "My son is still at Jackson Memorial. You are right that his death should not be wasted, but maybe not with your nephew."

Oh, Shit! "Please don't allow your anguish to punish this sweet boy for the actions of someone he doesn't know." His eyes brimmed. *Hunter didn't know who she really was.* "You've made what I know is an agonizing decision. Cesar will never recover and you now wish to honor him by saving other." He paused. "Let me bring Hunter to Jackson today to meet you. You'll see how worthy he is. Without a new liver for him in the next week, it will be too late."

"Maybe. I can't think now. I must get ready to say goodbye to *my* son. I go now." She disconnected.

Seagrave made a quick call to his sister, Diana, whose scream, almost popped an eardrum when he explained everything. He told her to get Hunter to Jackson to meet the Perez woman. They had to do the sales job of their lives. Hunter's life depended on it. Finished, he laid the phone on the dashboard, leaned back, and knuckled his still moist eyes.

He wished the Kim he knew . . . not the deadly Shadow, but the warm, kind, intelligent woman he'd come to love . . . was there to share this hopeful news. If he could make the "sale," her unmatched skill as a coldblooded assassin with a sniper rifle may save a son she'd just rediscovered, albeit at a terrible cost to a dozen others.

Jeez, I'd better get over there. I'm the best salesman for this. If they could sway Perez to do the right thing for Hunter, he deserved to know more about his real mother after he was on the mend. Maybe skip that she provided the donor by killing innocents. He may learn that hard to live with fact later, on his own. Pretty difficult to hide anything from Google, but they'd deal with it then. Save him now and explain later. That was the best they could expect.

Seagrave pulled a pair of khaki cargo shorts over his swimsuit, slipped on sandals, and leapt from the boat, racing down the dock. He'd meet his sister and her son at the hospital.

Thanks to Kim, the terrible things she did made this possible. That deadly contract killer wasn't the Kim I knew.

Then he was in his Lexus, speeding away.

With a convincing sales job . . . something he was quite good at . . . Hunter was going to live.

~ 83 ~

"Okay people, let's get at it." Warner stood in the department's small conference room, his eyes roving over the six BAU agents and his three top detectives. He glanced at a barren whiteboard on the wall.

"Tate created several red herring's and got us chasin' our tails while she slipped away. This babe's a master of deception and creatin' false leads. So, where did she go? Was she on that plane, or was it just another ruse to confuse us?" Headshakes and shrugs question greeted that question.

"Right. We got no clue, so let's get some." He began writing on the whiteboard. "A fast boat, racing down a blind alley. A corporate jet, playing hide-and-seek . . . another phony lead? Forget the G IV to Atlanta. That was legit. So, two fast escapes one for sure with perp aboard." He pivoted back to his team. "So, that leaves what options, if she's not on that Cessna jet?"

"A safe house where she can hunker down and recover while waiting for the heat to cool down?" Jack Harris offered.

"Okay. Option one." Warner jotted it on the board. "Tough ta ferret out, especially 'cause she's apparently got helpers, so she doesn't have to show her face." He folded his arms. "Clearly, she's got plenty of dough to do whatever she needs." His eyes swept the group.

"No trains, other planes, or automobiles," Agent Dalwin said. "We've got those well covered, and with obvious bullet wounds to her side and leg, she'd clearly stand out."

"Yeah. She needs somewhere to recover, or an escape vehicle she can use without drawin' attention." Warner turned and wrote BOATS on the white surface." He looked back at bobbing heads. "My gut tells me she could be on a large, long-range yacht . . . something not too big and not fast, so it doesn't draw attention . . . headin' somewhere she can feel safe. With her resources, she could have a doc and whatever medical supplies she needs to treat her wounds. They didn't seem life-threatenin'."

"After four cases with you, Detective," Special Agent Yeager rose, hands on her hips, "I've learned never to doubt your gut. So, what do you have in mind?"

"A full-court press with the Coast Guard and marinas to check departures in the last two days of anything meetin' our criteria."

"That's going to be a lot of boats, Boss," Olvida said, also standing. "South Florida is a major center for ocean-going yachts." He glanced at his tablet. "Could be anything from a forty-foot cabin cruiser to a two-hundred-foot mega yacht."

"I'm gussin' something in the middle, like a trawler or long-range cruiser."

"Going where, Detective?" Agent Solto asked. "There're hundreds of Caribbean islands and all of Mexico and Central America. I think you may be on the right track, but we've got to narrow it down or she'll be gone before we can figure it out."

"I'm bettin' south, along the mainland, somewhere in Central America. Costa Rica'd be my first choice. For that Cessna jet, too."

"Why there, Boss?" Harris began typing on his tablet.

"They got a big expat American population so she won't stand out, and a load of high-end medical clinics where she can get treatment." He paused. "Plastic surgery, too, to change her appearance, now that we know who The Shadow is."

"Makes sense." Agent Dalwin hit auto-dial on his cell phone. "I'll get the Miami Field Office to contact the Coast Guard. See what they can do."

"Good." Warner turned to his detectives. "Harris, divvy up the marinas with Olvida and Beck and start checkin' recent departures. Let's get hoppin'."

"We'll use my guys too, Detective," Dalwin said as everyone

rose to leave. "The more eyes, the better."

Warner tugged on the Special Agent in Charge's sleeve as they exited the conference room.

"They got a C-448 high-speed chase boat at the Miami Beach base?"

"I believe so. There's sure to be cutters in the Florida Straits, too, doing drug interdictions."

"Good. We locate what we think may be her boat, we're gonna want to run it down."

"They've got helicopters and patrol planes for that, Detective."

"Yeah, to pin down their location, but if she's on a yacht, she ain't gonna heave to and quit, is she?"

"No, probably not, knowing her history."

"So, if I'm right about the boat, we're gonna have ta board it, probably in international waters. I'm gonna want ta be there, and I suspect you do, too."

Dalwin nodded. "Hopefully, she's too incapacitated to offer resistance herself, but she'll certainly have helpers. It could turn bloody."

Warner shrugged as he turned to enter his office. "A well-armed Coast Guard cutter oughta be a deterrent. One way or another, I'm plannin' on takin' her down if we find her. We miss her now, we may never see her again. At least not as Kim Tate."

Dalwin nodded and hurried off to aid in the search.

~ 84 ~

Seagrave arrived at Jackson Memorial Hospital a few minutes before Hunter and his mother, Diana. Pallid, yellow-tinged skin gave the haggard boy a haunted image and brought moisture to the man's eyes. They found Juanita Perez slouched in a waiting area chair, red-rimmed eyes wrung dry of tears. A coffee-skinned priest perched beside her, fingering a rosary and mumbling prayers.

Seagrave introduced his nephew to the woman, and when Diana silently took one of Perez' hands in hers, the distraught woman raised her eyes and took in Hunter's deathly countenance.

That was Seagrave's best sales tool, and it clearly impacted the woman. She and the boy began a hesitant dialog, slowly becoming more at ease with each other. Thoughts of life and death were no easy subject when looming so close to home.

While they talked, Seagrave got the hospital staff working on reconfirming the tissue match, but that was only a formality. They'd already run the tests with her consent, after his and Kim's first meeting with the woman, right after the shooting.

They'd been at it, off and on, for nearly four hours when Doctor Nakamura, the transplant surgeon, burst into the room. He knelt in front of Mrs. Perez.

"Bad news, I'm afraid." He took one of her hands, and she rose. "Cesar is failing and may not last the day. If it is your intent to grant this boy a new liver, we must get started." Perez sagged back onto her chair, supported by her priest, her eyes wide and blank.

Seagrave dropped at her side, took her hand, and nodded toward his nephew. "Please, Ma'am. You've met Hunter and see how close he also is to the end. You can make Cesar's passing a glorious ticket to life for another fine young man. Someone both you and your son would be proud to know."

The woman's tear-filled eyes regarded Hunter, and she stroked his cheek, sighed, then nodded. Seagrave whipped out an already prepared consent form, quickly signed by both, and witnessed by the priest.

Hunter was rushed off to prepare for the surgery. Seagrave squeezed the woman's shoulder, drawing her eyes. He plucked a check for fifty-thousand dollars from his wallet and pressed it into her hand. "As promised."

She stared blankly at it, little rills spilling across her cheeks, then tucked it into her purse.

"I know there is no compensation for the loss of a son." He pulled her limp body in for a gentle hug. "At least this will ease your expenses in honoring his life and get you back on your feet." He released her and stepped back.

She nodded, then sagged in her chair, head in her hands, weeping softly.

Everything went without a hitch, but Seagrave remained at the hospital with his sister and her family while the boy recuperated. Hunter had become so weak, the doctors were cautious about him surviving the ordeal. But that sweet kid was a fighter, like his birth mom, and he was now on the road to recovery.

~~~

Seagrave parked his SUV in the drive, and shielding his eyes from the morning eastern glare, pushed through his front door, scattering a pile of accumulated mail across the floor. He frowned, and then remembered he'd given his assistant, Annette, the week off. He gathered the envelopes and some fliers and headed to the kitchen in quest of some coffee and breakfast, after two mostly sleepless nights.

Seagrave dropped his mail on the kitchen table and set about brewing a pot of strong java and pouring a bowl of Cheerios. He settled on a chair as the Mister Coffee did its job, splashed milk and blueberries onto the cereal, and began sorting through the letters as he ate. Mostly advertising, donation pleas, a few bills . . . and a letter from a Denver cousin he hadn't heard from in years.

Curious, he slit that open, and his jaw dropped when he unfolded the note and recognized the neat, tight script.

Charlie, my love. I used some contacts to spoof the origin of this letter in case the Feds are monitoring your mail. I am certain they have bugged your phones, so I won't be calling you any time soon.

I'm sorry for any pains I've cause you. Obviously, I never intended for you to learn about my alter ego. I hope you've discovered all my professional hits were against criminals. The only innocents I've killed were in a quest to save my son, and those deaths will always haunt me. I even spared cops' lives in that final shootout.

I was elated to learn my efforts were not in vain. I have watchers who relay me information, and I love you even more for what you've done for Hunter.

Now, here's a happier task I'm sure you'll handle with decorum.

Seagrave sat back and knuckled his eyes. *Wow!* The note went on to list a secure account at Banque Audi Suisse Geneva in the amount of 2.7 million Euros—over three million dollars—where they also held in escrow an unfunded, irrevocable trust in Hunter's name, with Seagrave as trustee. She asked him to fly to Switzerland, fund the trust, and manage the account's investments until her son's thirty-fifth birthday.

In the interim sixteen years, he was to distribute dividends, and principal if necessary, to Hunter and his parents for the boy's education and well-being, all as Seagrave saw fit.

This must remain a secret. His personal wealth should obscure the fact the he was not spending his own money. She didn't want the Feds trying to grab the funds as the product of illegal enterprises. The letter continued:

I know I can rely on you for this because of your love for Hunter. It's as if he's our son, not just mine. I hope you can still find love for the Kim Tate you knew, and not hate me for the other woman I was.

As for me, I'm safe and should recover and be as good as new in the near future. Maybe we can be together again in some parallel universe. I truly love you more than you'll ever know. I'm out of the world of contract killers. Twenty years was more than enough. I have plenty of other resources to support me, so not to worry.

Love always,

Your personal Shadow.

Seagrave brushed away unexpected tears. He stared blankly at the note in his hand, trying to sort through roiling emotions. He sighed, folded the letter, and slid it into a flap in his memo book. He rose, looked around, and then called his sister. Hunter's well-being trumped any feelings, good or bad, he had for Kim.

"Now that Hunter is on the mend," he told Diana, "something has come up, and I've got to make a short business trip to Europe. Two or three days at the most. You okay if I go?"

"Of course. Hopefully we'll have him home by the time you return."

"Swell. Stay in touch, if you need me. My cell is always on."

He disconnected and settled at his computer, searching travel scenarios in his mind. After a moment's thought, he booked a first-class seat to Holland, a rental car, and two nights at the Amsterdam Hilton, although one was probably enough. Confirmations printed, he headed for his bedroom to pack. He had four hours until flight departure, so no time to waste. Thankfully, the authorities hadn't confiscated his passport.

He called Annette as he drove toward Miami International to give her a head's up on where he'd be for the next several days. Seagrave shrugged, unable to sort conflicting emotions roiling inside his head.

Kim was alive. Somehow, despite whom she was and what she'd done, he savored his love for the terrific and passionate woman he knew—not the heartless assassin she was in some other life.

How was that possible, with so many innocents' deaths on her hands?

~ 85 ~

Warner hunched over his desk, scanning reports from two detectives on a pair of murders: a home invasion, and a domestic squabble gone bad. Concentration was illusive, his mind on their hunt for The Shadow.

He shoved the files aside and was about to check on his detectives' progress when Harris and Olvida hurried in, laptops in hand.

"Got something?" Warner leaned in as the two men set their computers on his desk, huddling over his shoulders.

"Lots of boats of all sizes cruising away in the last two days." Olvida flipped to a second screen. "We've got seven that seem to meet the criteria you set up, Boss: two trawlers, three ocean-going sailboats, and two long-range yachts."

"Scratch the sailboats. Too weather dependent for a long crossing to where ever she's goin'." He studied Olvida's screen. "What about the big yachts?"

"One went to Nassau and has been moored there since yesterday. Looks like a corporate boat with a three man crew." The detective clicked on a link. "Offloaded six passengers, and Bahamian police checked them out. The boat's clean, and the people are busy in the casino." He flipped screens.

"Looks like the other one's headed for Bermuda." Warner glanced at Olvida.

"That's the destination they filed with the Coast Guard. They're monitoring its progress, and the Bermudian bobbies will greet them for us. Dalwin dispatched two agents from their Washington field office to join the welcoming party."

"Okay." Warner turned to Harris' computer. "What about the trawlers? They'd be my first pick."

"Both fit the bill, Boss. There's a Bering 80, with a seven-thousand-mile range, cruising southeast into the Caribbean. Could be headed for any island, Venezuela, Colombia, or even Brazil. Or maybe the southern route to Europe. No destination or passenger manifest filed with the Coast Guard, but those are optional. It's a big boat with plenty of roomy cabins."

"Okay, that's a possible, but I sense it's not likely." He eased back in his chair. "Our closest jurisdiction would be the Virgin Islands. See if we got Coast Guard there to intercept it." He gestured at Harris' computer. "What about the other one?"

"A Choy Lee 65 Long Range Motor Yacht." Harris glanced at his notes. "Basically a trawler with a five-thousand mile range, headed south along the mainland. Sailed through Haulover Inlet fifty-two hours ago cruising south, so that should put it about halfway to the Yucatan Peninsula, if it maintained that heading."

"That'd be my pick." He squinted at the computer's screen. "If that's her, I doubt she's stoppin' anywhere in Mexico." Warner stroked his chin. "I'm still puttin' my money's on Costa Rica, or maybe Panama. A lot of Americans in both, but Costa Rica's got more Americans and premiere medical facilities." He rose as his two detectives gathered up their laptops.

"Where's Agent Dalwin?" Warner exited his office, trailed by Harris and Olvida.

"His team's set up in the conference room," Olvida answered. "They're working the phones with the Coast Guard and the Naval Air Station in Key West, seeking help with surveillance."

"Good. Those are just the guys we need if we're gonna chase down those boats. C'mon." He strode cross the bullpen toward where the FBI agents were working.

If they were to catch The Shadow before she disappeared for good, they had to pick a course of action and move on it immediately. The clever woman had set up multiple options to confuse them. Warner's usually reliable gut said this was the best choice if she hadn't already disappeared on that Cessna jet.

He hoped he was right.

~ 86 ~

Warner, Harris, and Agent Yeager were settled in Agent Dalwin's Chevy Suburban, racing south in the waning hours of the afternoon. The Homestead Air Reserve Base, near the southern tip of the state, was their target.

The Special Agent in Charge, at Warner's urging, had wheedled the services of two government Gulfstream jets, one from the FBI and the other from DEA. They were to sprint south, searching for *Wayfarer,* the Choy Lee trawler Warner's instincts said was transporting Kim Tate.

A helicopter, sent by the *Williamson,* a 227-foot Coast Guard fast intercept cutter, awaited their arrival at the air base.

It would shuttle them to meet the ship, which had been patrolling the Florida Straits on drug interdiction sweeps. With a top cruising speed of twenty-five knots, the cutter was three times faster than their quarry.

They would race southwest on an estimated intercept course, based on the *Wayfarer's* speed, and hope for actual contact from one of the jets. If Tate wasn't aboard the trawler, they were out of options. She would disappear, possibly forever.

Warner had received a text from Olvida that Tate's son, Hunter, had just received a new liver, donated by Perez, one of Tate's victims. He wondered if she knew.

He blinked, shaking away his thoughts as they slid to a stop at the Air Base's security gate. Quickly cleared, they sped onto the tarmac and headed for a small group of Coastguardsmen, standing under the idling rotor of an M-60 Jayhawk helicopter. A chief petty officer stepped away from the 'copter and directed them where to park.

Warner, Dalwin, and their two officers piled out of the Suburban and hurried to meet the gathering next to the Jawhawk. Lt. Commander Niles, greeted them and made quick introductions. They shouted to be heard over the *thump, thump, thump* of the slowly turning rotors.

"We just received a contact report from one of the Gulfstreams," the commander told Dalwin. "They've spotted what appears to be your boat off the coast of Mexico, cruising south at approximately eight knots." He escorted them toward the chopper. "We've forwarded the GPS coordinates to *Williamson*, and they've set an intercept course."

Warner and his team began boarding the aircraft, while the commander continued his briefing.

"The ship's expecting your arrival, with instructions to fully cooperate." He stood by the open hatch as the last of the team, Ina Yeager, toting her cased Barrett .50 sniper rifle, climbed in.

"You're using a lot of resources here, Agent. Must be pretty important."

"The end of a twenty-year quest, I hope." Dalwin waved as the copilot edged past him and slid the door shut. He signaled each passenger to don life vests and helmets with headphone for noise canceling and comms. He returned to the copilot's seat, and they lifted off in an arc carrying them south.

"Estimated two-hours-fifty-seven minutes to intercept the *Williamson*," came over the comms. "Sit back and relax. Conditions look good en route, but might be some weather brewing on our arrival."

Warner and Harris exchanged looks, and the smaller detective grimaced. He was never happy on a plane or a boat.

~~~

Three-and-a-quarter-hours later, Warner, Harris, Dalwin, and Yeager stood on the *Williamson's* deck, watching their ride get tied down and serviced.

Warner laid a hand on Harris' shoulder, giving a gentle squeeze. "You look kinda green, Jack." He grinned.

"No fan of bumpy plane rides, Boss." He staggered slightly, catching his balance as the ship split oncoming waves. "Or rocking boats. I'll survive." He shook off Warner's grip.

"Welcome aboard, gentlemen."

They turned to greet a ship's officer, who offered his hand. "I'm Lt. Grace, the ship's XO. Sorry for the rough ride. Passing intermittent squalls, but things should calm down now for a while." He turned toward the bow. "Follow me to the bridge. The captain will give you a briefing on our progress."

They wove across the deck as the ship quartered through eight-foot waves. It was a short climb to the helm, the *Williamson's* command post. They entered, greeted by a chief-petty-officer, announcing, "Visitors on the bridge."

An officer wearing commander's stripes glanced up from the chart table. "Welcome aboard. I'm Commander Lorence, Captain of the *Williamson*."

Agent Dalwin made a quick round of introductions as they crowded around the navigation chart. "How does it look, Commander?"

"That's the *Wayfarer's* current position." He used a pointer to indicate a virtual ship displayed on the electronic chart. "This is us," he tapped a larger image, "and that's our expected intercept course." Blue lines from each icon ventured across the screen to meet at a red "x".

"How long?" Warner glanced from the display to the officer.

"We estimate eighteen hours, provided there are no course changes or deteriorating weather. The latter looks to be settling down."

"Thank god," Harris mumbled.

His three companions chuckled.

Lorence laid aside the pointer and stepped away from the table, folding his arms across his chest. "So, who are we chasing, Agent, that you've got so many government assets at your disposal?"

"One of the FBI's Ten Most Wanted, an assassin I've been hunting for two decades. We call her The Shadow, because she's been invisible . . . until now."

"The sniper I've read about who shot all those people in Miami?"

Dalwin nodded.

"And it's a *woman?*" His eyebrows arched.

"A surprise to us, too," Warner said.

"And the best marksman . . . marks*woman* . . . anyone has ever seen," Ina Yeager added. "And I trained for overwatch at Special Forces Sniper School, so I've seen the best."

Dalwin gripped the commander's arm. "So when we

overtake that boat, extreme caution is required. So far, she's scrupulously avoided killing cops, but—"

"Got it." Lorence patted the agent's shoulder. "I've been instructed to allow you to board the boat and take the subject into custody. We're here to provide backup." He turned to one of his crew. "Ensign Leon will show you to temporary quarters. Get some rest. We won't make contact until tomorrow morning at the earliest."

"How close will you have to be to pick her up on radar?" Warner asked.

"Probably ten miles. A trawler is a small target. I'll send the chopper when we estimate we're about fifty out." The commander walked with them to the gangway. "Get a better fix in case of a course or speed change."

"Good." Warner nodded. "I suggest you keep the bird at max distance, so not to alert her. So far, this woman's been ahead of us at every turn."

"Roger that. Ensign Leon will fetch you when it's time for evening mess. Meanwhile, try to get some rest." Lorence turned back toward the bridge. "Nothing is going to happen until after daylight."

Warner shared a small cabin with Harris, who flopped on a lower bunk and tried to ignore the sounds of the ship as it sliced through diminishing seas.

It was going to be a long night.

~ 87 ~

The Shadow pushed back on the bed and propped herself up on her elbows. She nodded to the slim, pale-skinned man who entered her stateroom and removed his aviator sunglasses.

"Trouble, Edmundo?" She wiggled up into a sitting position with several pillows supporting her back.

"Hard to say." He ran a hand over his neatly plastered, silver hair. "A Gulfstream jet passed overhead twenty-minutes ago, south-bound, at about ten thousand feet, and kept going. Too high to get a tail number, but now another Gulfstream came by, going north at a lower altitude. Don't know if it's the same bird, circling back for a second peek, but we got a number off that one—a DEA jet."

"So, if it's searching for drug smugglers, we'd be of no interest, cruising south." She pressed a hand against her bandaged right side. "Or it could be looking for us. It never slowed or circled?"

He shook his head. "With all the red herrings strewn about, you think Agent Dalwin could guess where we've went?"

"Maybe not him." She sipped water from a bedside canister. "I'd bet on that Miami Detective, Warner, though. The clever bastard figured out the last target when it seemed sure no one could. Thankfully, The Shadow has a paranoid little inner voice and set up a backup escape plan." She groaned. "If not for Warner, we wouldn't be on this boat today. But luckily, Hunter got his liver after all." She slumped back and coughed, a sprinkle of blood staining her tissue.

The man touched her brow. "Still a mild fever. I'll send the doctor. With a compromised lung, he said blood can be expected."

She nodded. "The letter? It got to Charlie?" Her eyes held his.

"Yes. It went as a text from a burner phone to our contact, who turned it into a regular US mail letter. He confirmed delivery two days ago. I believe Seagrave's in Europe this very minute, attending to business."

"Good. The boy's care is paramount." The woman sighed, then touched his hand. "One more thing, Edmundo."

"Whatever you wish, my friend. My life and my brother's belongs to The Shadow, for without her, we and our families would no longer exist."

"A rare contract of compassion, removing that vile threat for you." She paused, catching her breath. "So, if that plane was for us, and we are attacked, whether by sea or air, you and the other men are to stand aside and disavow any connection to me. I hired you and your crew for transportation. This is *my* fight, and I don't want any of you injured."

"But—"

"No argument! You weren't saved to be sacrificed now. I need your sacred pledge." Her eyes bore into his.

He returned her stare, then sighed, his shoulders sagging. "As you wish. So, I fear you intend to go out, as they say, with your boots on?"

"No prison, Edmundo. What we have left in life will be short enough."

"But you've honored a strict, lifelong rule not to kill law enforcement. They are no match for you if only you'll defend yourself."

"I'll figure it out, and besides, we may be worrying over nothing." She eased back on the bed and closed her eyes. "Send the medic, and then I'll rest."

He nodded and left the cabin. About three more days to reach Costa Rica and the chance to reconnect with their tiny team. He hoped their concern over possible surveillance was unfounded. If a challenge came, he would have to deflect as to their destination. And could he really stand aside and not defend her? His family owed The Shadow their lives, but a promise made to her was something you did *not* break.

He sighed and shook his head, hoping it was not a decision he might have to make.

~ 88 ~

Warner emptied the surprisingly good cup of coffee served at the morning mess, along with fried eggs, crispy hash browns, and thick slices of crunchy bacon. He tabled the mug and rose. Agents Dalwin and Yeager shoved aside their plates and joined him.

"Harris still in the throes of *mal de mer*?" Dalwin asked.

"Yeah, queasy and not interested in food right now, but he'll join us." The detective chuckled. "Jack's tough and doesn't want to miss the action."

They exited the mess hall and climbed to the bridge, eager for the latest intel. They entered the command center and found their missing detective talking to Commander Lorence.

"So, what's the word?" Warner looked at the commander. "We heard the chopper lift off while at the mess hall, so we hurried up here."

"I was about to send for you. The Jayhawk just reported sighting the *Wayfarer* thirty-eight miles south-southwest, cruising at about eight knots. Our pilot turned away while still five miles off, but a crewmember glassed someone on its deck, also watching them through binoculars."

"No way we really expected to surprise her, I guess." Warner glanced at his team, then back at the commander. "How long until intercept?"

"Radar has picked up a new line of squalls developing in the area. We'll have to reduce to two-third speed, so probably four hours."

"So, how will this go?" Dalwin's eyes swept the bridge. "We'll have to board the boat, which will make us pretty damn well exposed."

"We have two options. We can launch our twenty-foot

RHIB, and you can board the trawler from that. You'll have four of my crew aboard to supply backup, all well armed. Or, if we can get them to heave-to, our fantail is low enough to allow easy boarding, and we've got two mounted M-2 machine guns to give you cover, if necessary."

"More firepower than I expect we'll need." Warner scratched his neck. "Give us a thirty-minute heads-up, willya, so we can vest up."

"And psych-up," Harris muttered. "I hope to hell this babe keeps to her code of not killing cops."

The group dispersed to a chorus of grunted assents. Dalwin and Harris returned to their cabins, while Warner and Agent Yeager found a place to sit on the aft deck. They stared blankly at the repetitive curtains of spray as the cutter split wave after wave. The air had cooled with the advent of the squalls, and a driving rain was imminent.

Warner glanced at the special agent, the very image of the fabled, blond Amazonian warrior. "I'm thinkin' Ed, Jack, and I will take the boat, Ina. I want you on the roof of the bridge doin' overwatch with your Barrett .50." He craned his neck and studied her prospective perch. "A white sheet from the ship should provide camo cover, along with that radar antenna. I suspect Tate might spot ya otherwise."

Yeager followed his gaze and nodded. "Might be a bit cramped, but I'll manage. Not much more than a hundred-fifty feet. An easy shot from there."

"Yeah, but from a rockin' boat. We'll be mostly exposed while we're in the process of boardin'. We may need the cover." He lifted his arms overhead and stretched. "If this is her, I'm mostly worried about her henchmen gettin' trigger-happy."

"Okay, and I agree. For a coldhearted assassin, she seems to have a strong moral code about whom she's willing to will kill. The only hooker is, this is going to be a no-win situation for her. There'll be no escape this time."

"Yeah, well she'll still have *one* way out, won't she?"

Yeager glanced at Warner and nodded. "Yes, I guess so."

They lapsed into a nervous silence, conflicted with eager anticipation and nagging anxiety.

One way or another, it would all be resolved in four hours.

~~~

Edmundo Segura entered her stateroom, his lips pressed thin, his brow wrinkled.

"Problems?" She wiggled into a sitting position.

"Possibly. A large Coast Guard cutter is bearing down on us from the northeast. It could be just a drug interdiction patrol."

"Seems unlikely, with us heading away from the USA." She sighed. "Play it as planned. This is a medical transport for a patient too ill to fly."

He sat on a stool and took her hand. "And if it is the FBI or this Detective Warner you worry about?"

"You will honor your oath to me, and do not resist them. Make that plain to your men. The cops must believe you didn't know who I was. You were just performing a medical transport."

He sighed, his brow wrinkled. "As you wish, but it will be difficult to—"

"I know, but I insist. None of you are to die today. Now, bring me my two Glocks and four extra mags. If it's them, they'll regret trying to come through that door."

"And Kevlar?" His eyebrows rose.

"No. No vest. It'll just hamper me. This will be all or nothing. And you must remain free to join the others in Costa Rica."

"I understand. As always, it has been an honor to serve you." He moved to a wall cabinet and retrieved the two pistols and several fully-loaded magazines. He handed them to her, then leaned over and kissed both her cheeks.

"*Bueña forte, Corózon.*"

His hazel eyes were wet pools as he exited the cabin.

~ 89 ~

"*Wayfarer,* this is the United States Coast Guard cutter, *Williamson.*" The boom of the loudspeaker echoed across a still-choppy sea. "Heave to and prepare to be boarded."

Warner, Dalwin, and Harris, clad in Kevlar vests and pistols in hand, crowded the starboard gunnel as the boats bobbed, fifty feet apart. Four seamen stood with them, two armed with M-4 automatic weapons, and two with long-handled boat hooks. Agent Yeager lay atop the cutter's bridge, one-hundred-fifty feet away, only her eyes and the muzzle of her .50-cal sniper rifle showing from under a jury-rigged white sheet.

The Choy Lee slowed, lost headway, and came about, rocking to the march of a four-foot sea. The helmsman on the cutter maneuvered his ship so their rear deck matched the smaller yacht's, as they faced in opposite directions. That positioning, at Warner's request, to provide Agent Yeager a clean line of sight, in case she needed to make a shot.

Crossing from one boat to the other would not be a simple task, especially with the trawler's small open aft deck bobbing erratically, four-feet lower than their platform on the cutter.

A slim, silver-haired man exited the main cabin, stepping onto the rear deck. He peered at the men on the cutter, towering above his yacht.

"I am Captain Edmundo Segura. Why do you stop us?" he

called. "We are on a medical transport mission headed for Panama and are no threat to the United States."

"We'll see." The XO, Lt. Grace, had joined them. "Have your documents ready and prepare to be boarded."

He shrugged. "As you wish." He stepped back and waved his man away from the gunnel.

"Your passenger?" Warner called. "A woman?"

"Yes, but—"

"Stand aside. We're comin' aboard." The two sailors snagged the trawlers side rails with their boathooks, snugging the tossing crafts together, as the seas continued to roll by.

Warner mounted the cutter's gunnel, secured his Glock in its shoulder holster, gritted his teeth, and leaped across to the small aft deck of the sixty-five-foot boat. The yacht dropped into a trough as he landed, throwing off his timing, and he stumbled across the deck. A quick hand by Captain Segura caught his shoulder, avoiding a tumble.

"Thanks." Their eyes locked, and then the detective spun and signaled Agent Dalwin, who quickly followed. Warner fielded him with a supporting grab as he landed. The agent steadied himself and drew his weapon, eyeing the boat's crew.

"You comin', Harris?" Warner looked up at his partner who was clearly not eager to make the jump. After a bit of hesitation, Harris took the leap, barely clearing the gunnel. He stumbled upon landing, grunting out a small squeak of pain. Warner snatched his arm, rescuing him from a spill.

"You okay, Jack?"

"Tweaked my ankle. I'll live." He took a few limping steps and settled in a deck chair, his Beretta drawn.

Warner turned to the captain. "Where's your passenger?"

"The owner's stateroom on the lower deck."

"Which one?" Dalwin joined Warner, facing the captain.

"All the way in front, straight on as you descend the stairs, but she may be asleep. I will show you."

"No, you stay here. We're not likely to get lost." Warner started for the main cabin's door and looked back over his shoulder. "What's her name?" He turned as another man, a blond beanpole, sporting a medic's white frock, appeared from the inside.

"What's this about?" His eyes swept over the three intruders. "I've got a seriously ill patient on board."

"Her name?" Dalwin echoed Warner's question.

"Caroline Dubois. We're headed for Panama, for treatment." He glanced at the main cabin's door. "She shouldn't be disturbed."

"Why Panama?" Harris asked. "Plenty of good docs in Miami."

"Of course." The man fingered a stethoscope draped around his neck. "But she has a serious injury that, once healed, will require reconstructive surgery and bed rest. Insurance won't cover much of it, and—"

"Enough blather." Warner shoved past the medic and stood in the doorway to the salon interior. "We're gonna take a peek at your patient, and if she's not who we think she is, you'll have our apologies, and we'll leave."

The man tugged at Warner's arm. "You've no right—"

The detective shook off the hand and nodded at Dalwin to follow him as he slipped into the salon and descended the stairs. A corridor divided two cabins on either side of the boat and ended at the one in the bow, which stretched from beam to beam. Harris remained on the rear deck, pistol in hand, watching the crew, and Agent Yeager surely had everyone on the open deck under her distant gun.

Warner paused at the door, he on its right and Dalwin sidling up on its left. The detective glanced at the agent, then gave a sharp rap.

"Kim Tate, we know you're in there. You've got no way out this time." He grasped the doorknob and jiggled it. "Give it up, and no one will get hurt."

Silence.

He turned the knob, but jerked back, showered by splinters as a slug tore through the door and embedded in the stairway to the salon.

"Detective Warner, I presume." The voice was strained and throaty. "You're as hard to shake as a bad case of the flu." She made a wet-sounding cough. "My old nemesis, Eddie Dalwin, with you, Detective?"

"I'm here, Tate. After twenty years, I'm glad we finally have a chance to meet." Dalwin held up a hand to Warner and signaled him to hang back a bit. "Don't take any unnecessary chances," he whispered. "She's got nowhere to go this time."

"So, what's it gonna be?" Warner called out.

"Stalemate, it seems. I'm not coming out, and you're not coming in without getting perforated." She coughed again. "Don't count on me not killing any of you this time. You know what they say about a cornered animal."

"Look, ya can't outwait us. We got your doctor under guard and can keep him from carin' for you." Warner glanced up the stairs toward the open cockpit. "We can man this boat with a couple of sailors from our ship and sail it back to Miami. You could die en route if ya don't let anyone in."

"Helicopter," Dalwin whispered to him.

Warner nodded. "We got a chopper on the cutter that could fly ya back to Miami in a couple of hours. Get you treatment." He hesitated. "We can even arrange for ya to see your son. He got a new liver, in case ya didn't know."

A whimper and a cough came from the cabin. "I heard. You're a tough bastard, Warner, and the smartest cop I've ever run across." She chuckled. "Don't take offense, Eddie, but *you* never came close to nabbing me."

"But here we are now, Tate," Dalwin said. "You can't win this one. It can only go badly for you. Surrender, and save a bunch of lives."

"The doc and the ship's two crew are just people I hired." A rustling and a small gasp came from the cabin. "They had no idea who I was."

"We'll sort that out when we get you back to the States," Dalwin said. "Same thing with Seagrave—"

"I told you, I'm not going back," her voice suddenly loud, "and I'm *not* going to prison." The cabin door flew open, and she materialized in the doorway, jamming the muzzle of her Glock under Warner's jaw before he could move. Her other arm interlocked with his, her fingers wrapped around his weapon. The move anchored him against her as she made a half-turn and slid left, putting Warner between her and Dalwin.

Their eyes locked, hers clear, glittering with intensity. Nothing to indicate she might be slowed by painkillers.

"Give it. I don't want to kill you, but I will if you force me." She faced him, tight against his body, making it impossible for Warner to make an aggressive move. Surprised at her strength, he hesitated, then released his pistol to her. She managed to tuck into her waistband without uncoupling his arm.

"Thought I was too incapacitated to make a move, huh?" Her voice was hoarse and reflected controlled pain.

"Yeah, I'm afraid we underestimated you again, but you're still stymied."

"Maybe, but now I've got hostages." She panted, catching her breath, then peeked around Warner's shoulder at Dalwin. "Gun on the deck, Eddie. You too, on the aft deck," she called, and gave a small cough. "I'm pretty desperate here, and I've got a twitchy trigger finger."

Dalwin looked at her, then glanced up at Jack Harris, peering down from the head of the stairs. Both carefully laid the weapons at their feet.

"Kick yours to me, Eddie. You on deck, shove yours toward the transom. I don't want any of the crew thinking about being heroes." She nodded toward Dalwin. "Get up top." Her foot slid Dalwin's Glock farther across the hallway.

She followed the ascending agent, easing Warner, who shuffled backward across the gangway, to the stairs. Her grip on his right arm was an iron vise, and the pistol's muzzle pressed tight and unwavering under his jaw, offering him no opportunity to make a move.

She paused at the foot of the stairs, her eyes locked on his. "You wearing an ankle gun?"

He shook his head. She leaned them against a bulkhead, ran a foot over both his shins, and her lips ticked up. "Can't be too careful with a smart cop like you."

Tate turned them slightly and nodded at the open door, above. "Up. We go together, one step at a time. A slip or stumble, and I'll blow your head off and kill everyone on deck." She leaned even tighter against him. "Look me in the eyes." They glittered bright with intensity. "You *know* I can and will do it."

Warner held her eyes for a moment, then gave a small nod. "Yeah. Like you said, a cornered animal . . . ."

"Smart guy. Now, we climb together, slow and steady. It's going to be a tight fit, so don't try anything stupid." They paused twice during the ascent, her face screwed in a tight grimace, but the pistol and her grip never wavered. Once at the top, they sidestepped to just inside the door of the salon cabin and she glanced over Warner's shoulder at the deck of the *Williamson*.

"You sailor boys, lower those M-4s or there's going to a lot of dead people here."

"Do as she says." Dalwin waved at the two men. "She can kill us all in a matter of seconds."

A moment later, their weapons clattered to the deck of the cutter, and Tate eased Warner just through the doorway, their bodies still interlocked, the muzzle of her pistol thrust under his chin. He stumbled, one foot inching between hers. Her grip on his arm hardened, her body wound tight as a spring.

"Easy, Detective," she whispered. "I know all the tricks. You'll be dead before you finish making whatever move you're planning."

Warner studied her, amazed at her continued strength and agility, despite her serious wound. He relaxed, realizing he had no immediate option.

~ 90 ~

The Shadow's eyes swept over Harris, Dalwin, and her three crewmates. She nodded toward the starboard transom. "All of you in that corner where I can keep an eye on you." She scanned the cutter's deck from stern to bow, searching for trouble.

"You got Yeager stashed in a sniper's nest somewhere, Eddie?"

"She's on another assignment, Tate, and didn't come. I wish I *had* brought her."

"Yeah? Lucky me. Okay, it's time to say goodbye." She glanced at the cutter's crewmen. "Release those boat hooks and we're going to get underway." She glared at the XO, hovering at the gunnel railing. "Just back off and let us go. You follow us, and I start killing hostages. I've got nothing to lose here."

Staying close, she drew her captive just onto the deck, her back against the cabin wall, Warner in front, obscuring her, facing the sailors on the *Williamson*. She growled, "Cast off." In that instant, the yacht lurched erratically to the passing of a rogue wave, causing Tate and Warner to tap-dance for balance.

Warner felt a breeze and a bare tug at his sleeve a

nanosecond before hearing Tate grunt.

"Uhhh!" Her gun hand wavered but never left its perch under his chin. Warner saw blood welling from a bullet crease on the corner of her right shoulder. Yeager had taken the shot when it presented itself, but the bobbing boat reduced it to a minor flesh wound.

"Sonofabitch!" Tate snarled. "You lied to me, Eddie!" In a lightning move, Tate lowered her weapon, squeezed off a single shot, and Agent Dalwin collapsed, blood spewing from his neck. Momentarily free, Warner's left hand punched at her wound, bringing a gasp. He then snatched her in a bear hug, as his right arm forced her left behind her. Pinned against him, she couldn't move.

"Quit it, Tate." Their eyes locked. "You've got nowhere to go."

"Bastard!" Pain cracked her voice. "I told you, I'm *not* going to prison." She brought her right heel down hard on top of his left arch, and as he winced, she managed to deliver a knee to his groin.

Warner staggered, and she wriggled partly free. The crew on the *Williamson* scrambled for their M-4s, and though Warner retained a grip on her left arm, she managed two shots, hitting one seaman in the shoulder, and Lt. Grace, who'd drawn his sidearm, in the center of his chest.

A hole appeared in the cabin wall, an inch from her head—another shot from Yeager gone wide due to the pitching of the boats. It was a tight target window to avoid hitting Warner.

Tate moved in on him and pirouetted in a three-sixty, levering her other arm free. He knocked away her gun hand and snatched for his Glock, still in her belt, freeing it as she spun loose. She leaped through the salon's doorway, again barely avoiding another 12.7 round from Yeager.

Warner dropped to one knee, tight against the cabin's bulkhead, out of her line of fire, but she popped off another round through the open door, and Harris, who'd just recovered his Beretta, staggered and slumped to the deck.

"Jack!" Warner's eyes misted, his lips pressed knife-thin, but Harris lay crumpled and unmoving.

"Sonofabitch!" Warner shouted. "I thought you didn't shoot cops."

"Rules change when your life's on the line, Detective. That was Yeager, I presume, taking pot shots from the ship's bridge. I looked, but missed her. Good camo job."

"Now what, lady?" *Gotta stay calm.* "Ya got no more options." He glanced back at Harris and Dalwin, both sprawled on the aft deck, and brushed moisture from his eyes. Tate's doctor hovered over them, checking for a pulse. Blood ran everywhere. Warner groaned, hoping that because they were both wearing vests, it wasn't as bad as it looked. Jack Harris had been his partner from when he became a Detective first class. He shook his head, trying to clear his mind.

A quick look at the cutter showed their wounded being hustled to sickbay, and four more sailors crowded the side railing, two holding M-4s. Warner waived them off. No sense in giving The Shadow more targets right then.

"You're trapped in there, Tate. No place to go, and no leverage. Give it up."

"You're wrong. I've still got you, your two shot buddies, and the crew. Get Captain Segura up here to drive this boat, and I'll let my doctor try to save Dalwin and your partner. With this pitching boat throwing off my aim, I don't think their dead… yet."

Warner stared back at the medic, still hunkered over Dalwin, giving CPR. He rocked back on his heels, glanced at the detective, and shook his head. Warner sighed and gritted his teeth.

"Dalwin's dead, Tate, and the only place your goin' is to prison—or the morgue. No one's drivin' this boat anywhere but back to Miami."

"Well, then I guess you're forcing me to kill you and anyone else who stands in my way. I'm not spending ten years in some dank cell, awaiting a needle in my arm."

Warner heard her move, and instinctively dropped flat on the deck. Two slugs from the distinctive-sounding Glock tore through the bulkhead wall, right where he'd been kneeling, showering him with splinters. Warner let out a loud grunt and thumped the deck with his arm. He shuddered at how close she came to killing him.

"Warner?"

He gasped, mimicking the dying noise of a shooting victim, a sound he knew well.

"Warner?" she called again. He remained motionless and silent.

"Segura!" Her voice had lost some strength. "Get up here and get this boat underway."

Warner caught the captain's eye, shook his head, and held a finger to his lips.

"We cannot, Ms. Dubois." Tears filled his eyes. "The sailors have guns on us, and the doctor is treating the detective. I don't believe they will let us leave."

"Okay. I'm coming to fix that." A scuffling sound came from within as she maneuvered near the door. "I'm going to eliminate those guys with the M-4s and make their sniper duck for cover. Get ready to move."

Segura stared at the doorway. "Is more killing really—?"

"I don't like it, Captain, but it's the only chance I've got to get away."

Warner edged closer to the opening, the gun in his hand, and again lay still, hoping she'd think he was dead.

"But with all their people killed, they have no reason to hold back. They might even sink this boat. Please—"

"Not with three innocent crew members still aboard.

Anyway, it's all I got."

As Warner watched through barely slitted eyes, the muzzle of her pistol appeared, and four quick shots peppered Yeager's sniper nest. The Shadow's arm and head slid out, bringing her Glock to bear on the sailors crowding the cutters railing.

Warner snaked out a hand, snatching her wrist and yanking back, hoping to break, or at least dislocate her arm. Again surprised at the strength of this wounded animal, she slithered partly into the opening and yanked him toward her, discharging her weapon. The slug ricocheted off the back of his Kevlar vest, and they were face-to-face, locked in their mutual grasp, struggling to bring their pistols to bear. Their interlocked proximity gave Yeager no viable target.

"Bastard," she grunted. "You're the only cop I'm going to be happy to kill."

"You're not the first to try," he panted, "and I'm still here."

Tate reared back, hauling him toward her, so he drew in his legs and charged into her. She fell back and used his momentum to yank him over her, her pistol discharging right beside his head. The concussion sent his head spinning as the slug blew harmlessly through the salon's roof.

Their balance lost, they teetered at the top of the staircase, then tumbled and bounced down. Warner lost his gun when his elbow was pinned under Tate's body and slammed against the corner of a stair. Both took a beating, banging heads and limbs, spilling apart at the bottom.

Warner shook his head and tried to clear his vision as he managed to sit up, his back against a corner of the hall. Tate hunkered five feet away, pushing back on her knees. Before Warner could gather himself, she snatched up one of their Glocks, both of which had bounced down the stairs and lay next to her.

Warner struggled for breath and realized his weapon was out of reach. She grimaced and aimed her pistol in his direction, her arm wobbly.

"Give it up, Tate. You ain't gonna make of out of here alive if ya don't quit now." There was something under his right hip, and he trailed a hand there, looking for anything to defend himself.

"And if I let you take me?" Her eyes held his. "Then what?" Her voice lost some of its timbre. "I told you, I'm not going to prison."

Warner saw The Shadow's eyes grow narrow and hard. "You don't have ta do this, Tate—" His fingers curled around the object under his thigh . . . Dalwin's pistol, dropped there when she first emerged from the cabin and took control.

She shook her head. "Hunter's got his liver, so one way or the other, I'm done here. I repeat, I'm *not* going to prison." She waggled her pistol. "Despite what I said earlier, I'm going to regret killing you, Detective." She sighed and raised the still unsteady weapon.

Warner whipped up Dalwin's Glock and fired twice, a fraction of a second before she did. She jerked back, her eyes going wide as two dark holes appeared in the center of her breast, blooming a fountain of blood. He crashed onto his back, taking her .40-cal slug high and in the center of his vest. The Shadow slumped down, her head lolling to one side, eyes instantly vacant.

"Ayiii!" The silver haired man, poised in the upper doorway, took a staggered step, a hand clamped over his mouth, tears filling his eyes.

Warner pushed onto his knees, gasping for breath, and glanced at Segura, then back at The Shadow. A strong reaction for someone just providing transportation, but it *was* a brutal death. He took three tries to lumber erect, groaning at the throbbing in his chest. "That was pretty fuckin' intense," he mumbled.

He shuddered and shook his head. His eyes swept back to

Kim Tate, the elusive Shadow, sprawled across the floor, her pistol still in her hand. He reached down and pried it from her fingers.

"Well, she was right. She's not goin' to prison. The Shadow's final disappearing act." He sighed, then turned and staggered up to the deck He spotted Agent Yeager as she leaped onto the yacht and sprinted to where her chief lay. Her feral moan pierced Warner's head, sending shudders cascading through him. They'd all lost a superb colleague and a good friend when Tate's slug pierced his neck, rupturing his carotid artery. He gritted his teeth, his body a symphony and aches, and shuffled to where Jack Harris lay.

The medic had peeled off Harris' protective vest, which hadn't done its job that day. Tate's bullet had found an opening in the side. The doctor had stemmed the bleeding, but the bullet was lodged in his chest, probably his left lung. They need to get him back to Miami ASAP.

"Miss Dubois?" The medic asked.

"Gone ta meet her maker, if he'll have her." He looked up as several of the cutter's crewmen boarded, carrying two stretchers. He grabbed one man's arm. "Lt. Grace?"

The sailor looked up, his eyes damp. "Dead, sir. That bitch was deadly." He pulled away, and helped lay Jack Harris on the stretcher for transfer back to the cutter.

Commander Lorence assigned two sailors from the *Williamson* to sail the trawler with the boat's crew and the doctor back to Miami where their alibis would be vetted. Were they abetting The Shadow or just innocent pawns? Ina Yeager would accompany them, since the Jawhawk chopper would be at capacity carrying Warner, Harris, and the bodies of Agent Dalwin, Lt. Grace, and the once-deadly Shadow back to the Homestead Air Base.

And Warner still had some loose ends to tie up.

~ 91 ~

Warner slumped at his desk, glad to be back after the morning's deadly dance with death. He glanced up and spied Special Agent Lon Pauletti, standing in his doorway.

"Got a minute, Detective?" The BAU agent asked.

"Sure. Grab a seat."

The special agent settled across from Warner, who leaned back, hands folded across his belly.

"How's Detective Harris doing? Looked to be nip-and-tuck by the time you got him to the hospital."

"Yeah. Four hours in surgery, and he lost a lung, but he's a tough guy. An ex-Army Ranger in Afghanistan. Might be tied to a desk when he gets back, though, and that'll really piss him off." Warner gave a mirthless chuckle.

"Well, I'm glad it's 'when,' and not 'if.' Hate to have lost another one to this mess." Pauletti edged forward his fingers interlocked, resting on the scarred oak surface. "I've been assigned as temporary head of the unit, with Ed's death. The Shadow is finally a closed case." He gave a small headshake. "A terrible way for it to end, with so many unnecessary deaths, but it was apparently what she wanted. We've never dealt with anyone so elusive . . . or so deadly."

"Clever woman. She was determined to escape or die trying. No middle ground." Warner sighed. "She planned for every possible scenario."

"Except dealing with Al Warner." The agent tilted back in his chair and ran a hand through his hair. "I wish I could get you to come work for us." Tears wet his cheeks. "We're one man short now."

"Thanks, but Agent Dalwin is irreplaceable. Besides, I like

it here." Warner leaned over his desk and patted his arm. "Anything else you got goin'?"

"We're still monitoring Seagrave as a person of interest." The agent rose. "He flew to Amsterdam two nights ago, and we had people there to tail him."

"The DA didn't take his passport?" Warner's brow wrinkled.

"A minor oversight." The agent managed a wry chuckle. "He's due back tomorrow, though."

"Well, it cost a heavy loss, but The Shadow's gone, and we took down a huge illegal transplant caper. The World is a lot safer with the help of your team." Warner stood behind his desk.

"Yeah." Pauletti sighed and turned to leave. "Tate gave up everything to save her son, and until this operation, she'd never hit anyone other than a baddie."

Warner nodded. "Even went out of her way not to kill a single cop until she was cornered on that boat. Up 'til then, we were lucky the woman apparently had her own code."

"Yes. Otherwise, at least five more of us would probably have been killed in Coral Gables." The agent exited the office and Warner joined him for the walk out. "Unfortunately, that all went out the window with the mayhem she caused at sea."

"Yeah. A damned waste." He tugged at the agent's arm.

"You gonna hang around for Seagrave's return from Europe?" Warner rested a hand on the agent's shoulder. "We can grill him together. See if there's anything there."

"Planning on it, Detective. He returns tomorrow. I'll text you his flight info."

They shook hands, and the special agent hurried down the stairs. His team, minus Yeager, who was still aboard the returning trawler, awaited him in the parking lot.

~ 92 ~

Seagrave stepped off the KLM flight and started up the gangway, trailing his carryon bag. He reviewed his activities of the past two days.

He had arrived in Amsterdam in the morning, picked up his rental Toyota, and drove to Geneva. A bank VP was typically Swiss—stiff, unsmiling, but very efficient. Three hours later, his tasks completed, he'd returned to overnight in Amsterdam, taking the morning flight home the next day.

He sighed, conflicted by the news Kim had died trying to escape by sea. He still couldn't wrap his mind around the Kim he hadn't known, the deadly Shadow. She'd been efficient though, and had everything in perfect order in Geneva. Now her son was the recipient of 3.1 million dollars, for which Seagrave was the trustee.

As he exited the walkway into the terminal, his stride broke at the sight of Detective Warner and Special Agent Pauletti, standing in the waiting area, obviously there for him. After a momentary pause, he strode toward them, forcing a smile. No way to avoid this. He hoped there was no trouble over him leaving the country while still under investigation.

"Hey, Seagrave." Warner waved. "Welcome home. Got a few minutes for a chat?"

"Do I have a choice, Detective?"

The flight's other passengers bustling by jostled them. They sidled aside to clear the way.

"We can either do this here, amicably," Pauletti interjected, "or formally at the station. Your choice."

"I'm not in a hurry." Seagrave gestured toward an empty departure gate across the main aisle. "We can sit there, out of everyone's way."

A moment later, they settled on seats, and Warner placed a restraining hand on the special agent's arm. He wanted to begin the conversation, and it *was* his jurisdiction.

"You know you're still a person of interest for complicity in The Shadow affair." The detective's eyes held Seagraves. "Be honest here, and things won't get any worse for you."

"I've got nothing to hide." He settled back and crossed his arms.

"Did your trip have anything to do with Tate?" Pauletti held up his phone, indicating it was recording.

Seagrave nodded acceptance and shrugged. "No." Keep answers simple when talking to cops.

"Why the sudden trip?"

"Family business." He glanced at Warner, who had asked the question.

"Look." The detective leaned forward. "The FBI had people on you. We know you drove to Geneva. We know what bank you visited, and we suspect we know why." He paused and glanced at Pauletti who gave a small nod and turned off the recorder. "I believe you're a good guy, Seagrave—"

"My friends call me Charlie, Detective." A smile tweaked his lips. "I got a hunch I may be adding you to that list."

"Okay, Charlie, and I'm Al." He gestured at the non-recording phone. "The agent and I have agreed to do this off the record for now, as long as you're truthful. So spill it."

"I was there to establish an irrevocable trust for my nephew."

"In Switzerland?" Warner and Pauletti exchanged looks. "So it was Tate's money? How much?"

"Why her's? I'm a rich guy. I can fund a trust like that anytime I wanted. The amount is irrelevant."

"In Switzerland? You can do that right here. This was Tate's gift to her son, wasn't it?" Warner studied his eyes.

"That's why I did it offshore." He sighed and rubbed the

heels of his hands across his eyes. Best to shut this down right now. "The Feds would think it *was* Kim's money, and might try to snap it up. Now that Hunter's on the mend, he and his parents need that trust for him to have a decent life. It the least I can do for my family."

Warner shrugged. "Look. We feel for the kid, and frankly, both Agent Pauletti and I had gained a grudgin' respect for your girlfriend until she killed two of our people." He paused as a pair of electric passenger shuttle carts rumbled by, horns beeping.

"She didn't kill cops when she coulda, until we cornered her at sea," the detective continued, "and up 'til now, her contracts have always been bad guys on bad guys." He hitched forward on his seat.

"But she killed twelve innocent people, an FBI special agent, and a Coastguard officer." Warner glanced at Pauletti again, who nodded. "If that trust fund really came from you, no one else needs to know about it. It could spawn lots of lawsuits. Tate's case closed with her death. Anything else pertinent before we put it to bed?"

"No, nothing more." He leaned back, his eyes brimming. "I had no inkling of Kim's other persona. As far as I knew, she was a warm, loving woman, and this whole thing has been a real shock to me."

"Okay. I tend to believe that." They all rose. "The agent and I may be breakin' some rules here, but we'll keep the trust info between us, for now." Warner glanced at Pauletti, who shrugged, then nodded. "A mom blew up her carefully protected career," the detective continued, "and eventually her life, to save her son, in a deadly way to be sure. Nothin' to be gained by addin' this to the mix."

"In trade for that," Pauletti said, "if you learn anything we should know, we expect to hear from you?"

"I promise."

"Ya may not be outta the woods with the DA, though." Warner shook his hand. "I'll do what I can for you, Charlie. I do suggest you stay in town for now. Maybe hire a good attorney."

The men said goodbye, and went their own way.

~ 93 ~

Warner leaned against the Corian bar top in his townhouse, savoring a Dewar's Scotch on the rocks. Eva Guttenberg perched on a nearby stool, a goblet of merlot in hand. She gave her fiancé a winsome smile. "Two big cases closed this week." She brushed his lips with hers. "A busy time, lover."

"Yeah. Busy. Successful." He sipped his whisky. "Cases closed, but one perp took a terrible toll and nearly slipped our noose." He stared into the amber contents of his glass.

"Wow!" Eva chuckled. "Any minute, you'll break into song." She laid a hand on his arm. "Are you glum because of Agent Dalwin's death and Jack getting shot, or is it something else, Al?"

He leaned back, took her hand, and sighed. "I don't know. There's a lot to celebrate, despite our losses. We took out that organ transplant ring, and the DA's goin' after Murder One for the bosses, which the bastards richly deserve. But for the other one. . . ." He trailed off, the corners of his lips sagging.

"Mixed feelings about The Shadow, huh?" She kissed his fingers.

He nodded. "Hard ta figure. She was a stone-cold killer. Baffled the fibbies for two decades. Killed one of their top men, came within inches of snuffing Harris, and almost ended me." His fingers found the crossed scars under his thick hair. "But she exposed who she was. Literally gave herself up trying to save her son . . . ."

"A mama, a she-bear you called her, protecting her cub." Eva caught Warner's chin, turning it toward her. "She sacrificed everything to save a son she barely knew." Their eyes locked.

He nodded again and shrugged.

"The maternal instinct to defend your child," Eva continued, "that *your* mother never displayed for you."

"Maybe." Warner brushed her hand away and pushed out of his chair. "But Mom could never stand against—"

"That's irrelevant." Eva rose and slid against his back, wrapping her arms around his chest. "Your father was a sadistic brute, but that didn't change your desire—your *need*— to feel cared for. Your mom couldn't do that for you." Her lips brushed the back of his neck, her head then rested against his shoulders.

"She never stood up for you, whereas Kim Tate risked everything, her very life, for a son she barely knew." Eva released her grip but maintained body contact. "I suspect you find it hard to hate someone like that, no matter how deadly she was."

"Geez." He turned, pulling her to him. "How did I get so lucky to be in love with my own personal shrink?" His soft chuckle rocked them. They parted, retrieved their drinks from the bar, and settled on the loveseat in the den.

"Well," he sipped his Scotch, "despite being pretty shot up, she still orchestrated a vanishing act . . . and almost got away with it. And it looks like young Hunter is the recipient of all her ill-gotten gains."

"A new liver?" Eva snuggled against his rock-hard body.

"Yeah. The transplant Tate made possible went off without a hitch. The Perez woman struggled with the idea of Hunter being the reason her son was shot, but finally accepted that what was done, was done. She realized Seagrave and his nephew had no inklin' of what Tate was doin'." He draped an arm around her, drawing her closer. "I talked to Seagrave to see how the kid's makin' out." He sighed. "Then there's the money."

"Money? What money?" She glanced at him.

"Oh. I didn't tell ya?" He chuckled again. "We don't know the amount, but Seagrave went to Europe to fund a trust for the kid. We think it's from money Tate probably stashed in Switzerland, but Seagrave says it's his. I'm bettin' it's in the millions."

"Millions! Wow. Where would she get all that cash?"

"A high-priced assassin must get big fees. I suspect she's been accumulatin' it for twenty years. Apparently lived modestly off her earnings as a nurse."

Eva sat up and pivoted toward him. "If that fund is Tate's, it's the definition of ill-gotten gains. The feds will try to snatch it."

"If they know about it. Besides," He hugged her, "it's off-shore, and we can't prove it's hers, so what the feds don't know—"

"You didn't tell the FBI? They're bound to find out—"

"Agent Pauletti already knows, but we've talked. He hates her for killin' his boss and long-time friend, but unless we can trace those funds to her, nobody else needs to know about the dough. The Swiss sure ain't gonna tell us."

"But that's a lot of money." Eva laid her wine glass on a coaster on the coffee table. "Won't it seem suspicious—?"

"Seagrave's got control, and he's a wealthy guy. He coulda easily done it on his own." He rose, pulling her up. "With what Hunter and the Fiore's have gone through, they deserve to enjoy a better life. If Tate provided it for 'em, it's pretty rotten others died to make it happen. But I suspect we'll never know, so leave it at that."

"And Seagrave's in the clear?" They started for the entry to the garage.

"Looks that way. Still a person of interest, but nothin's gonna come of that. He was as shocked about who she was as we were. He's a really good guy, just doin' what he could for his nephew."

"Looks like you found a new friend."

"Uh huh. Even invited me to a hunt at his big game ranch next month."

"Sounds like something you might enjoy."

"Probably." He drew her close and they kissed. "Now I'm gonna buy you a great Italian dinner at Carlo's Bistro, and then we'll come home for some very special dessert."

"Now, that sounds like something *I'll* enjoy. *Especially* the dessert."

His cell phone buzzed as they started toward his car in the garage. He dug it from his pocket. Caller ID said "Olvida."

"Warner." Eva's arm tucked under his as they walked..

"Boss."

"Olvida. What's up?" He paused.

"Boss, you better sit down. I got bad news."

"What? Something about Harris?" He pulled Eva back into the den.

"No, that tough bird is recovering okay. It's The Shadow."

"What? She dead. Case closed." He perched on the edge of his sofa.

"Maybe not."

"What the fuck are ya talkin' about? I killed her on that boat."

"You killed someone, Boss, but it couldn't have been Tate, unless she's got some magic healing power."

"Huh? I put two in her chest, and—"

"Yeah, but there were no earlier wounds."

"What d'ya mean?" Warner scratched his head. "She was bandaged, and I saw her spittin' up blood."

"Right, but there were no wounds under those bandages, and the ME says the blood was 'cause she was dying of stage four lung cancer."

"I don't get it." Warner glanced at Eva. "I *know* who I shot, and unless she's got a twin—"

"That's what the ME said, Boss. The DNA matches Tate, but it's *not* her. She must have been a twin."

"Jesus Christ." Warner leaped to his feet, startling Eva, who grabbed one of his hands. "The fuckin' bitch was a master of deception, but this . . . ? She had a twin sister?"

"Looks that way, and—"

"The twin led us on a wild goose chase while her sister slipped away." His fist shook the air. "Probably on that Cessna jet that disappeared." He started to pace. "And the sister was dying anyway, so she had nothin' ta loose." He continued prowling the room, dinner no longer on his mind.

"Ya better contact Agent Pauletti and inform him that The Shadow is still out there. Gonna make his day." He sank back on the sofa. "It's outta our jurisdiction now, and back in their lap." He sighed. "See ya in the morning, Ralph. I'm gonna need the night to reload after this one."

"Copy that, Boss. See you tomorrow."

Eva settled next to him, putting her arm around his shoulders. "Wow! Tate had a twin? Incredible."

"Yeah, and I just had a scary revelation." He dropped his head into his hands, elbows propped on his knees. "The Shadow I fought on that trawler was the deadly woman we'd come ta know. Tough, strong, and an incredible marksman, and she was just half of a pair. What if they worked together as assassins?"

"Wow, again!" She took his hands as he slouched back. "They'd always have the perfect alibi if they were ever suspected. One would be in plain sight while the other was committing murder."

"My thoughts exactly." He rose and she followed. "I wonder what's she's gonna do now, if she recovers from her earlier wounds? The FBI's got her DNA and knows what she looks like, and there's no twin left to confuse the facts."

He took her arm and headed for the garage. "C'mon. We still gotta eat."

~ 94 ~

She lay in bed in the sterile, white-tiled room, sitting almost upright, reading an article under the glare of too-bright neon fixtures. A whiff of anesthetics tickled her nose, and lingering aches low on her right breast and upper thigh brought moisture to her eyes.

She glanced up as two doctors and a nurse entered. The taller, an ex-pat American draped in clinical whites, was the reason she was at this facility, secluded in a forested glade outside San Jose, Costa Rica.

The physician gathered up her arm and checked her pulse and blood pressure.

"So, Miss Dubois." He stepped back and folded his arms. "You're recovering well. There was only minor damage to your right lung. I understand you have a lot of other work planned for us. Ready to talk about it?"

"Yes. Once recovered from these wounds, I'll want a complete physical remake. Not just my face. Everything." She hitched her body around and laid the papers she was reading on the bed stand. "Total change of my face and body shape. Not even my mother should recognize me." She paused and caught his eyes. "This may sound strange, but I don't want to be beautiful." Her face tightened at a stab of pain as she shifted position. "Not ugly, but plain-Jane like."

She winced and caught her breath, gathering herself. "I was reading about some new trials." She nodded at the papers on the table. "Altering DNA strands."

"Yes." He nodded. "There's been some success at actually curing some genetic diseases, like sickle cell, by correcting the letter codes on faulty DNA strands." He rubbed his chin. "I was unaware you suffered from anything like that."

"I don't, but I'm curious. Would that alter one's DNA enough so there'd be no match from previous samples?" She studied his face, his eyebrows arching.

"I suppose, especially if more than one strand were changed. We would have to alter molecular structure of some nucleotides which would change the DNA sequencing."

"Can you do that here?"

"Possibly. We have a state-of-the art lab and have done some experimenting on this, but for health reasons. Not to change one's DNA identity." The doctor stroked his chin, glancing down, then looked up, his eyes holding hers. "Yes, I believe we can. It would be an exciting development. There *would* still exhibit a familial connection, but not a direct match."

She ran fingers through her hair. "So, we could select three or four strands that would change my DNA signature without really causing any change in who I really am? Maybe even alter eye and hair color?"

"Possibly." He settled in a chair next to her bed. "It's all still very experimental, and it could take up to a year for everything to propagate, if it works at all." He paused, searching her face. "We would use Herpes virus cells, with the infection edited out, to insert the DNA changes into your cells. It's the most efficient vehicle for that task." He pushed out of the chair and edged close to her bed.

She handed him a sheet of paper. "Here are the specifics of

what I'm looking for, both via surgery and DNA modifications."

"Umm." He skimmed the list. "All may be doable, but some will be quite painful. You'll have to remain here for at least a year, Miss Dubois . . . maybe even eighteen months. Are you sure you want to put yourself through this?"

Dubois nodded. "I've got nowhere to go until this is completed." She smiled, and then sighed. "Work up a cost, and I'll approve it for you."

"Very well. It will be our pleasure to serve you, and you have our full assurance of your anonymity here."

"That's why you got my business." She forced a grin.

He nodded, gathered his papers, and started for the door.

"Please send in my man, who is waiting outside."

A moment later a slim, almond-skinned guy slipped quietly inside, his ash blond hair plastered to his head. A sly grin tweaked at his moustache-lined lips. "Looking much better today, *Corózon*."

"Feeling stronger, Gaspar." She studied his smiling face. "So, what's the news on the boat?"

"Unfortunately, it was interdicted and your sister was killed."

"Shit!" She grimaced and clenched her jaw. "We knew it might end this way, but she insisted on being bait. There was no downside for her . . . caught, killed, or dead of cancer within a half-year." She paused, tiny rills of tears trickling across her cheeks. "It was that Detective Warner and my old nemesis, Eddie Dalwin, I suppose."

"Yes." He sighed. "She killed Dalwin and a Coast Guard officer during the battle before succumbing."

"Damn, I hate that." She swiped away the tears. "And your brother, Edmundo?"

He sighed. "In custody in Miami as a person of interest. My contact believes he will likely be released without charges, however."

"Good." Renewed tears trickled across her cheeks. "With Carrie gone to what I hope was a less painful death, I'm free to use her carefully protected identity." She sighed and gathered his hands in hers. "So, my friend, tell me about the plane and the crew."

He edged closer and spoke softly. "All goes well, Kim."

She shook her head. "Caroline. Caroline Dubois, here and forever on. Carrie, for short. Don't get sloppy."

"My apologies." He laid his hand on her forearm and continued, his debonair, Latin accent one that most women found so enchanting. "The jet is sold to a Colombian, as you suggested."

"For . . . ?" Her eyebrows arched.

"Eighteen million, cash. Already deposited in your numbered account, less my five-percent commission. Acceptable?"

"Excellent. More than I hoped." She patted his hand.

"A new one sells for over twenty-five mil, and they're in short supply. He was a happy buyer."

"Good. Take another five per cent for Edmundo. And the crew?"

"Overjoyed to be alive." He chuckled. "When they suspected who you were, and what was happening, they expected to be terminated."

"That was my original plan to protect my location, but I couldn't stomach any more innocents dying, especially after I learned my efforts for Hunter were, after all, a success."

He nodded. "I've found work for them at a resort on the Pacific to keep the occupied. Told them they're on a two-year paid vacation. The co-pilot and the attendant actually seemed eager to enjoy the time off. The pilot not so much, but he accepts his fate."

"Fine. So, all is in place. Inform them that if they remain quiet and enjoy the sun, there's a half-million bonus for each when this is finished." Her eyes bore into his. "Be sure they understand that if just one of them is indiscreet, they all die."

He nodded. "And after you leave Costa Rica?"

"They are free to do whatever they wish. I'll be gone, and they don't know where I've been and what I will look like. Maybe they can write a book." Her chuckle brought a wince.

She closed her eyes and eased back on the bed. "Now I'll rest and grieve for my sister." Tears misted her eyes. "Then I must prepare myself for what will *not* be a pleasant year-long vacation." She sighed and folded her hand across her stomach.

"Again, my condolences. She was the mirror of you in every way. And I don't envy your coming ordeal, *Corózon*." He brushed his lips across her forehead. "You're the strongest person I've had the pleasure of working with, and I and my family owe you our lives. I pity anyone who gets in your way."

The new Caroline Dubois mumbled an assent as the man whose family she had rescued twelve years before from the grasp of a Venezuelan monster, quietly exited the room.

That was the only, until now, not-for-profit assassination she'd ever done.

~ Epilogue ~

Two Years Later

Seagrave's sport fishing boat slid against cushioned bumpers along its berth at the wharf. He cut the twin outboards and switched on the bilge pump to expel whatever wave spray got below floorboards during their high-speed race from the sky-blackening T-storms.

"We had a pretty good day, Hunt, until those storms blew

up with no warning." He shed his yellow slicker, grabbed the dock, and positioned the boat as Hunter snatched a bowline, preparing to jump off and secure it to a mooring cleat. Wavelets lapped musically against the hull.

"Toss me that line, boy, and I'll tie it off for you." He looked up and saw a fortyish woman in natty ocean blue blouse and Bermuda shorts, crouching on the pier.

"Thanks." Hunter made the throw, which she deftly snatched from the air and quickly snugged around the wharf's cleat. She sprang up and hurried toward the boat's stern in time to take that rope from Seagrave and finish the mooring.

"Nice fishin' boat." She stood, hands on hips, surveying *Valkyrie*. "Looks fast."

"This baby can fly," Hunter said as he stuffed his rain gear into a locker and jumped onto the dock. "We raced some T-storms that blew up outta nowhere."

Seagrave stepped off his boat and offered the woman his hand. "Thanks for the help. I'm Charlie Seagrave, and this is my nephew, Hunter."

"Nice ta meet you." She shook their hands.

"I'm Caroline Du-bwah." Her voice carried a lovely southern lilt.

Seagrave glanced at the mooring cleats and noted that they were proper figure-eight wraps. "Sounds French. You new here, Ms. Dubois?"

"Yes. And I'm Cajun. Just brought ma boat over from Naw'lens." How the natives said New Orleans. "And friends call me Carrie. Been wanderin' around, meetin' ma new neighbors."

"Nice to have some real southern blood down here." Seagrave chuckled. "And *my* friends call me Charlie." Seagrave appraised her: about five-foot-eight, sea-green eyes, and shoulder length auburn hair, peeking from beneath a pert sailor's cap. He found something about her voice and the soft drawl very pleasant.

Hunter's eyes swept the moorings. "What are you sailing, Carrie?"

"A Hatteras forty-two fly-bridge. Totally remodeled, with a pair of Cummins four-fifty diesels. Got her fitted for both sportfishin' and cruisin'. Pretty fast, too, for a big girl. Wanna see her?"

"Love to," Seagrave said. "Gotta wash down and clean up my boat first. Maybe ten minutes?" Hunter was already back aboard, clearing away the rods.

Seagrave dropped onto the deck of his open-fisherman and glanced back at her.

She stepped to the edge of the planking. "May I help? I love workin' on a boat."

"Sure." Seagrave offered her his hand, and she sprang nimbly onto the deck. "Welcome aboard."

They got busy, and it was quickly clear Carrie Dubois knew her way around boats. Seagrave glimpsed her from the corner of his eyes as they worked. Pleasant looking, but certainly no beauty. Probably late thirties or early forties. Still, he found some strange attraction, more a feeling of comfort than anything sexual.

He noticed old scarring on her legs, beneath the hem of her shorts. "You gonna be in South Florida for a while, Carrie?"

She paused from wringing a mop, their deck swabbing completed. "Permanently, I believe. I was two years in Costa Rica, recoverin' from a bad auto accident. Broke both ma legs clean through."

"I couldn't help but notice the scarring." He took the mop from her and stowed it and some sponges in a deck hatch. "Must have been pretty bad."

"Yeah, but they got great, cuttin' edge clinics down there. Looks a little funky, but they're ready ta dance." She did a pirouette and a couple of quick steps.

Seagrave chuckled. "Well, we're all done here." Hunter was

ashore with their duffle bags and cooler, which contained three dolphin-fish the lad had filleted on the way in. "Let's go look at your yacht. Don't see many of those classic, wood-hull beauties anymore."

"It's up thisaway." She took his arm as they strolled down the wharf. "Afterwards, how 'bout I buy you and this handsome young man a drink." She smiled, patting Hunter's shoulder. "I got a feelin' I found maself two new friends."

"Me too." Seagrave glanced at her from the corner of his eye and sighed. "I haven't had one of those for about two years."

Carrie grinned at him and winked.

Tiny mouse feet scattered down Seagrave's spine. He hadn't felt a stirring for a woman since Kim had vanished. He sensed this one was something special, despite her easy-going, folksy manner.

~~~

Carrie Dubois grinned to herself. *What will Charlie think, when we finally make it to bed and he notices my butterfly tattoo in that romantic little spot? Something no one but he knows exists. I left it there, just for him.*

Can't rush things, but I can hardly wait.

Together again with the only man I've ever loved . . . and my son. I believe I can trust Charlie with the truth, but what about Hunter? Time will tell.

They had finished their tour of Carrie's lovely mahogany and teak Hatteras fly-bridge cruiser and were about to step onto the T-dock when she noticed two men standing on the main pier.

"Caroline Dubois?" the shorter one asked.

"Agent Pauletti and Detective Warner." Seagrave stepped past Carrie. "What can I do for you gentlemen?"

Warner ignored his offered hand. "We're here for Ms. Dubois, Seagrave." Warner edged past him, ignoring their blooming friendship. "You're Caroline Dubois?" His dark eyes held hers.

"Yes, that's me. What can I do for you?" She laid a hand on Seagrave's shoulder.

"You'll have to come with us." The Detective produced a pair of handcuffs. "You're under arrest for multiple first degree murders when you operated as Kim Tate."

"Are you nuts, Warner?" Seagrave shoved his arm out, restraining Carrie. "This woman has no resemblance to Kim. She's not even the same build or height."

"Maybe so," Pauletti said, "but we have evidence she spent two years at a Costa Rican rehab and cosmetic surgery center."

"There must be some mistake." *Gotta be the fucking pilot. I knew I should have killed him.* "You must have me confused with ma li'l sister, Kimmie."

"Your *sister*?" Warner's brow wrinkled. "Kimberly Tate is your sister?"

"Yes, suh. Same mother, different father."

"Interestin'. But I killed Tate's twin sister, Carrie Dubois, two years ago. How is it there's two of you?"

"Well, I declare. I never knew momma had *twins* with Mistah Tate. Kimmie and I were as alike as a cat is to a mouse. Don't know why she never mentioned her twin or that her sister took up ma name." She swung her purse from her shoulder and opened it.

"*Hands!*" Warner's weapon was instantly trained on her.

"Oh, sorry." She looked up and smiled. "I was just goin' for ma passport."

She offered her bag to the detective. The passport was real, acquired via mail, using an excellently forged birth certificate.

"Nothin' dangerous in there, Detective." *I hope the hundred grand I spent on propagating thirty-five years of detailed personal history is gonna stand up.*

"So, why were you in that Costa Rican clinic?"

"Look," Seagrave gripped Carrie's arm. "I don't know where you got your information, Warner, but—"

"It's okay, Charlie." Carrie patted his hand. "Just a misunderstandin'. We'll get it sorted out." She pulled free of his grip, stepped forward, and offered her wrists.

"Are cuffs really necessary?" Seagrave's eyebrows arched.

"Yeah, it's procedure." He fastened the manacles on Carrie's wrists. "And if we're right about her, The Shadow is too deadly to be careless with." He pivoted to lead his captive away, reciting her Miranda rights..

"Hang on." Seagrave caught her arm, turning her. "Kim never mentioned anything about a sister, Carrie."

"We barely knew each other. Ma daddy died when I was still in the oven. Momma needed a man, so she found Kim's daddy pretty quick after I arrived. They were movin' East, and he had no truck with another man's kid, so she left me with ma spinster Aunt Charlotte in Naw-lens. She adopted me and gave me her name, Dubwah, and Momma didn't care. She had Kimmie and apparently, her twin. I never heard Momma and her man died in an accident until two years afterwards. My auntie passed five years ago and left me a pile of cash." *That carefully built and propagated story should stand up.*

"Okay, let's go." Warner took her by the elbow. "We'll sort this out with a DNA match. Meantime, we got sworn testimony from the pilot you kidnapped. He followed your man, Segura, and discovered the clinic you were at. Took four months to trace you here." Warner edged behind her, hand on his Glock. "You're comin' with us."

"Whatever you need, Detective. I got plenty of time, and nowhere I need to be right now." She glanced back at Seagrave and winked. "Take care of ma boat, Charlie, will you? The ignition keys are in the helm's glove box." She pursed her lips and blew him a kiss. "Hope to see you and young Mr. Hunter again very soon."

Seagrave's eyes flared, his mouth forming a silent "oh." That was the exact air-kiss Kim often sent him when they were together. *What the hell's going on?*

Eventual DNA comparisons would show Carrie Dubois had a familial match to Kim Tate, consistent with sisters. However, Costa Rican authorities cooperating with the FBI, had served warrants on the San Jose clinic. Records showed they had accepted a female patient with bullet wounds to the right chest and thigh, and after healing her, proceeded with extensive plastic surgeries, and even the shortening of her femur bones to reduce her height by two-inches.

The contradictory DNA evidence, which might create enough doubt for a conviction, was trumped by one simple item The Shadow hadn't considered.

One that would seal her fate.

The clinic had kept Olvida's bullet, extracted from her lung, with all its unique ballistic markings intact.

~The End~

If you enjoyed this, the 5th Detective Al Warner novel, the author would appreciate you leaving an honest review at Amazon, Goodreads, or any other readers' blog sites.

And if you haven't read the first four 5-Star rated novel in the series: ***Death's Angel, Born to Die, The Prom Dress Killer, & White Death,*** you will want to learn how Detective Al Warner's previous adventures got him to this place, and how he became *The Hero of Miami*.

Become a Detective Al Warner fan.

Here are brief synopses of each novel. We suggest you start at the beginning with:

Death's Angel
The 1st Detective Al Warner Suspense
Available in print, Kindle, and Audio

The second serial killer in less than a year is prowling the streets of Miami, systematically snuffing out some of South Florida's most beautiful young women. Detective Al Warner is just back on The Job, fully recovered from a bullet wound that cracked his skull during a deadly chance encounter with another madman.

Warner is in the best physical shape of his life, but his days are laced with headaches and his sleep fraught with terrifying dreams. Lack of rest clouds his usually laser-sharp mind but doesn't slow his single-minded hunt for this new killer.

Warner and the FBI's BAU become more frustrated as each new death provides plenty of evidence it's the same Unsub, but no new clues to his identity. They learn the killers name, Angie

Dedios, and eventually realizes it's really "Angel de Dios" . . . the Angel of God . . . but they are helpless as more beauties dies with no new leads as to this deadly "angel's" real identity. Then Warner's love, Sharon Clark, becomes a target for this madman, and Warner must stop him before she becomes his 8th victim. Only chance brings them all together in one final deadly dance of terror.

Born to Die
The 2nd Detective Al Warner Suspense
Available in print, Kindle, and coming soon in audio

Too many infant boys of Palm Beach gentry are dying of Sudden Infant Death Syndrome (SIDS). Only obstetrics nurse, Casey Jansson, is suspicious.

Al Warner, crack Miami Homicide detective, is inactive, languishing on medical leave after a deadly shootout with a serial killer, "The Angel of Death." He's again in superb physical condition, but is struggling to convince the department's shrink he is not suffering from PTSD.

Warner meets Casey at a local pub. Learning of the SIDS deaths from her, Warner concedes it sounds more than coincidental, but can find no obvious motive or opportunity for dying infants. However, with time on his hands, he agrees to help investigate, hoping romance develops later.

Casey ropes Danny O'Brien, a resident doctor and her best friend, into researching the deaths and he comes to a stunning conclusion. Using that information, Casey's obsession eventually tangles her in mortal danger. Only Warner can save her, if he can figure out where she went, and get there in time.

The Prom Dress Killer
The 3rd Detective Al Warner Suspense
Available in Print and Kindle

A psychopathic killer lurks in Miami's shadows, snatching and murdering young auburn-haired women. Strangely, they are killed without trauma and left clad in frilly prom-style dresses.

Miami's crack homicide detective, Al Warner, is on the case, but the killer has left few clues. Why were these girls taken and then executed? Was he intent on killing redheads, or was there some other connection? And why were their bodies so carefully arranged in peaceful repose, wearing prom dresses?

Warner's hunt for this clever psycho is stymied by a lack of clues as he desperately searches for the latest victim. The suspense ramps up when the murderer finally makes one tiny error.

As Warner and the FBI doggedly zero in on their fleeing prey and his newest captive, the action escalates. Unlikely players are drawn into a tense, deadly game. As the stunning climax plays out, Warner is trapped in a classic Catch-22. In order to snare this lethal psycho, he must make a decision that may haunt him forever.

White Death
The 4th Detective Al Warner Suspense
Available in Print and Kindle

Detective Al Warner is back at work, recovered from his deadly final encounter that ended the hunt for *The Prom Dress Killer*.

Ashton Kerry is determined to have his own stash so he

can ditch his family and be with his mistress. He enlists the Cuban mafia to ship cocaine via his company, packaged as printed brochures. Kerry gets a nice percentage of the drugs' value, but in setting this up, the Cubans drown five of his employees in a fake auto accident. Kerry's ties to the Cubans become more complicated–and dangerous–than he ever expected.

Warner's gut tells him the drowning are highly suspicious, and his "gut" is seldom wrong. Another case vexing him is an exploding rash of deadly ODs from fentanyl-laced heroin— White Death. The drug is so lethal, Warner suspects the fatalities may be intentional. Soon everything erupts into a series of stunning revelations and deadly confrontations, with Warner once again thrust into mortal danger.

Find George A Bernstein's works at:
http://amazon.com/author/georgeabernstein